PRAISE FOR
BEN KANE

'Richard the Lionheart's name echoes down the centuries as one of history's greatest warriors, and **this book will immortalise him** even more. **A rip-roaring epic**, filled with arrows and spattered with blood. **Gird yourself with mail when you start**'

Paul Finch, author of *Strangers*

'Ben's **deeply authoritative depiction of the time** is delivered in a **deft manner**. I was **immersed in the detail of Rufus's life**, with its heat and cold, its odours, foods, clothing, beats, politics and all the other minutiae of the age'

Simon Scarrow, author of the Eagles of the Empire series

'Kane's virtues as a writer of historical adventures – **lively prose, thorough research, colourful action** – are again apparent'

Nick Rennison, *The Sunday Times*

'*Lionheart* has plenty of **betrayal, bloodshed and rich historical detail**'

Martin Chilton, *Independent*

'Plenty of **action, blood, scheming, hatred, stealth and politics** here, if that's what you want in your read – **and you know it is!**'

Sunday Sport

'To read one of Ben Kane's **astonishingly well-researched**, bestselling novels is to know that you are, historically speaking, in safe hands'

Elizabeth Buchan, *Daily Mail*

'This is a **stunningly visual and powerful** read: Kane's power of description is **second to none** . . . Perfect for anyone who is suffering from *Game of Thrones* withdrawal symptoms'

Helena Gumley-Mason, *The Lady*

'**Fans of battle-heavy historical fiction will, justly, adore *Clash of Empires*.** With its rounded historical characters and **fascinating** historical setting, it deserves a wider audience'

Antonia Senior, *The Times*

'**Grabs you from the start and never lets go.** Thrilling action combines with historical authenticity to summon up a whole world in a sweeping tale of politics and war. **A triumph!**'

Harry Sidebottom, author of the *The Last Hour*

'The word **epic** is overused to describe books, but with *Clash of Empires* it fits like a gladius in its scabbard. What Kane does, with such mastery, is place the big story – Rome vs Greece – in the background, while making this a story about ordinary men caught up in world-defining events. In short, **I haven't enjoyed a book this much for ages. There aren't many writers today who could take on this story and do it well. There might be none who could do it better than Ben Kane**'

Giles Kristian, author of *Lancelot*

'**Exceptional**. Kane's excelled once again in capturing the terror and the glory . . . of the ancient battlefield, and this story is one that's been begging for an expert hand for a long time'

Anthony Riches, author of the Empire series

'**Carried off with panache** and Kane's expansive, engaging, action-packed style. A complex, **fraught, moving and passionate** slice of history **from one of our generation's most ambitious and engaging writers**'

Manda Scott, author of the Boudica series

'It's a broad canvas Kane is painting on, but he does it with **vivid** colours and, like the Romans themselves, he can show great admiration for a Greek enemy and still kick them in the balls'

Robert Low, author of the Oathsworn series

'Ben Kane manages to marry broad narrative invention with detailed historical research . . . in taut, authoritative prose . . . **his passion for the past, and for the craft of story-telling, shines from every page**'

Toby Clements, author of the Kingmaker series

'This **thrilling** series opener delivers every cough, spit, curse and gush of blood to set up the mighty clash of the title. Can't really fault this one'

Jon Wise, *Weekend Sport*

'Ben Kane's new series **explores the bloody final clash between ancient Greece and upstart Rome**, focusing on soldiers and leaders from both worlds and **telling the story of a bloody war with style**'

Charlotte Heathcote, *Sunday Express S Magazine*

'**A thumping good read.** You can feel the earth tremble from the great battle scenes and feel the desperation of those caught up in the conflict. Kane's brilliant research weaves its way lightly throughout'

David Gilman, author of the Master of War series

BEN KANE is one of the most hard-working and successful historical writers in the industry. His third book, *The Road to Rome*, was a *Sunday Times* number four bestseller, and almost every title since has been a top ten bestseller. Born in Kenya, Kane moved to Ireland at the age of seven. After qualifying as a veterinarian, he worked in small animal practice and during the terrible Foot and Mouth Disease outbreak in 2001. Despite his veterinary career, he retained a deep love of history; this led him to begin writing.

His first novel, *The Forgotten Legion*, was published in 2008; since then he has written five series of Roman novels. Kane lives in Somerset with his two children.

Also by Ben Kane

The Forgotten Legion Chronicles
The Forgotten Legion
The Silver Eagle
The Road to Rome

Hannibal
Enemy of Rome
Fields of Blood
Clouds of War

Eagles of Rome
Eagles at War
Hunting the Eagles
Eagles in the Storm

Clash of Empires
Clash of Empires
The Falling Sword

Spartacus
The Gladiator
Rebellion

Lionheart
Lionheart
Crusader

Short Story Collections
Sands of the Arena

KING

Drumcondra Branch

BEN KANE

ORION

First published in Great Britain in 2022 by Orion Fiction,
an imprint of The Orion Publishing Group Ltd,
Carmelite House, 50 Victoria Embankment
London EC4Y 0DZ

An Hachette UK company

1 3 5 7 9 10 8 6 4 2

A CIP catalogue record for this book
is available from the British Library.

ISBN (Hardback) 978 1 4091 9784 3
ISBN (Export Trade Paperback) 978 1 4091 9785 0
ISBN (eBook) 978 1 4091 9787 4

Typeset by Input Data Services Ltd, Somerset

Printed and bound in Great Britain by Clays Ltd, Elcograf S.p.A.

MIX
Paper from
responsible sources
FSC® C104740

www.orionbooks.co.uk

For Mama and Dada,
with all my love.

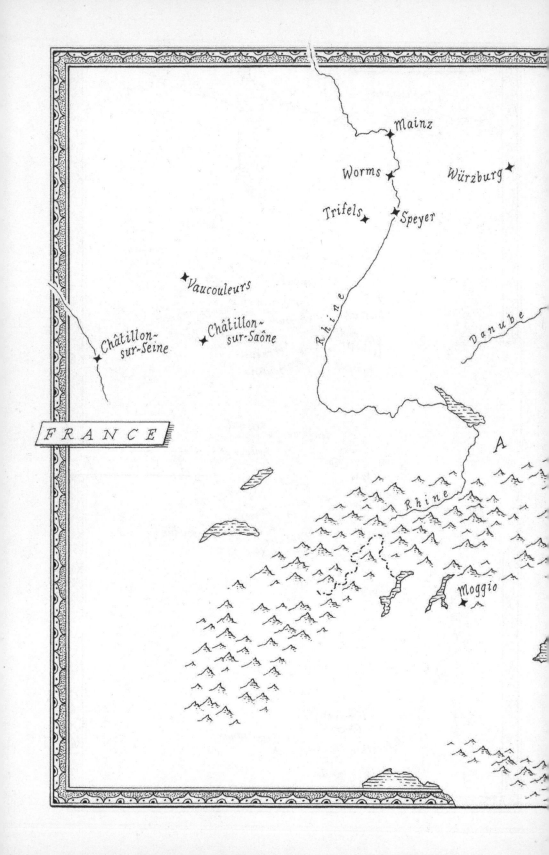

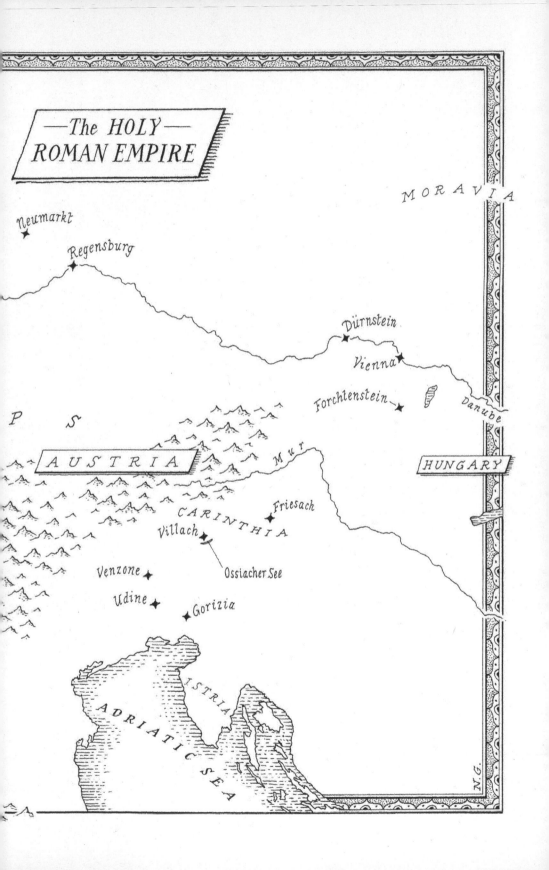

LIST OF CHARACTERS

(Those marked * are recorded in history)

Ferdia Ó Catháin/Rufus O'Kane, an Irish noble from north Leinster
  in Ireland
Rhys, Rufus's Welsh squire
Katharina, Austrian cook
Jean, orphan boy from Rouen
Robert FitzAldelm, knight, and brother to Guy FitzAldelm (deceased)
Henry, man-at-arms in Southampton (deceased)

Royal House of England:
Richard*, King of England, Duke of Aquitaine
Berengaria*, daughter of King Sancho VI* of Navarre, Richard's wife
John*, Count of Mortain, Richard's brother, also known as 'Lackland'
Alienor* (Eleanor) of Aquitaine, Richard's mother and wife of Henry
  FitzEmpress*, King of England, Duke of Normandy, Count of
  Anjou (deceased)
Joanna*, Queen of Sicily, Richard's sister
Mathilda*, Richard's sister (deceased), who was married to Heinrich
  der Löwe*, former Duke of Saxony
Henry* (Hal), eldest son of Henry (deceased)
Geoffrey*, third son of Henry, Duke of Brittany (deceased)
Constance* of Brittany, Geoffrey's widow
Arthur*, Geoffrey's young son
Alienor*, Geoffrey's young daughter

English Royal Court and in England:
André de Chauvigny*, knight and cousin to Richard
Baldwin de Béthune*, knight

xiii

Anselm, the king's chaplain*

William Longchamp*, Bishop of Ely, Richard's chancellor

Hugh de Puiset*, Bishop of Durham

Geoffrey*, bastard son to Henry, Richard's half-brother and Archbishop of York

William Marshal*, one of Richard's justiciars

William Bruyère* and John de Pratelles*, also Richard's justiciars

Church officials: Archbishop Walter de Coutances* of Rouen, Bishop Hubert Walter* of Salisbury, John d'Alençon*, Archdeacon of Lisieux, Abbot John* of Boxley, Abbot Stephen* of Robertsbridge, Bishop Savaric de Bohun* of Bath, Ralph Besace* and Brother Peter, medical clerics

Nobles: Robert*, Earl of Leicester, William des Roches*, Robert de Turnham*, William, John and Peter de Préaux*, Henry Teuton*, William de l'Etang*, knights

Mercadier*, mercenary captain

Robert de Nunat*, brother of the Bishop of Coventry

Richard de Drune, man-at-arms (deceased)

Henry, squire to King Richard

Other characters:

William*, King of Scotland

Philippe II*, King of France

Alys Capet*, Philippe's sister, betrothed to Richard in childhood

Bishop of Beauvais*, cousin to the French king

Drogo de Merlo*, nobleman

Raymond*, Count of Toulouse

Hugh*, Duke of Burgundy, cousin to the French king (deceased)

Baldwin*, Count of Flanders

Austria, Italy, Germany and other locations:

Leopold*, Duke of Austria

Heinrich von Hohenstaufen*, King of Germany and the Holy Roman Emperor

Philip von Hohenstaufen*, his brother, who claimed the throne in 1197 after the death of Heinrich

Konrad von Hohenstaufen*, Count Palatine of the Rhine, and Heinrich's uncle

Agnes von Hohenstaufen*, Konrad's daughter, and his heiress
Engelbert III*, Count of Gorizia, who co-ruled with his brother, Meinhard II*, Count of Gorizia and Advocate of Aquileia
Roger of Argentan*, knight
Abbot Otto of Moggio
Bertolf, novice monk
Friedrich of Pettau*
Wladislaw*, ruler of Moravia
Hadmar of Kuenrig*, castellan of Dürnstein
Albert of Brabant*, bishopric candidate in Liège (deceased)
Pope Celestine III*, head of the Catholic Church from April 1191 to January 1198
Pope Innocent III*, head of the Catholic Church from January 1198 to July 1216
Otto* of Brunswick, son of Heinrich der Löwe and Mathilda, Richard's sister, elected as one of two kings of Germany in 1198
Richenza*, Heinrich* and William*, Otto's siblings
Alienor, lady in Otto's court
Isaac Comnenus*, former emperor of Cyprus (deceased)
Damsel of Cyprus*, Isaac's daughter, taken into Richard's care
Pietro di Capua*, papal legate
Sancho*, Queen Berengaria's brother and heir to the throne of Navarre
William II de Hauteville*, King of Sicily (deceased)
Gilbert de Vascœuil*, castellan of Gisors
Count Adémar Taillefer* of Angoulême
Geoffrey de Rançon*
Aimar*, Viscount of Limoges
Hugues de Corni*
Bernard de Brosse*
Pierre Basile*, man-at-arms
Bertrand de Gurdon, the seneschal of Châlus
Abbot Milo* of Poitiers
Tancred* of Lecce, former ruler of Sicily (deceased)
Guy de Lusignan*, former king of Jerusalem (deceased)
Isabella of Jerusalem*, half-sister to Sibylla, former Queen of Jerusalem*
Humphrey de Toron*, her husband
Conrad of Montferrat*, Italian-born ruler of Tyre, cousin to the French king (deceased)

Boniface of Montferrat*, Conrad's brother
Saladin*, Al-Malik al-Nasir Salah al-Dīn, Abu' al-Muzaffar Yusuf ibn
   Ayyūb, Sultan of Egypt (deceased)

PROLOGUE

I was standing in the courtyard of the great castle at Chinon. Bright sunlight lanced down from a vast expanse of blue sky; birds sang happily in the trees beyond the walls. I could hear the excited cries of a child mixed with the barking of a dog. Rhys was nowhere in sight; I was alone, in fact, which struck me as odd. I could see no pages scurrying by on errands, no men-at-arms patrolling the walkway. There were no washerwomen gossiping with servants. Not even a single groom or a stable lad was visible outside the stables.

As my eyes moved to the keep doorway, the king came striding out. I smiled and my mouth opened in greeting, but, to my consternation, black-haired Robert FitzAldelm was right behind him. Another close companion of Richard's, he was my greatest enemy, and had tried to murder me more than once. My greatest desire was to see FitzAldelm dead, but I had sworn not to kill him.

The king approached, his usually friendly expression absent.

Stay calm, I told myself. You have no reason to worry.

'Good morrow, sire,' I said, bending a knee.

There was no reply, and fear spiked me. I stood, but gave no greeting to FitzAldelm. He smirked. Although my mind swirled with the violence I would like to do to him, I kept my face blank.

'Robert here is making grave accusation against you, Rufus.' Richard's tone was cold.

My heart lurched. There was only one thing it could be, but I was damned if I would admit it. FitzAldelm had no proof – Rhys and I had seen to that. I put on my best questioning expression. 'Indeed, sire?'

'He says that you foully slew his brother Guy in Southampton ten years ago.' Richard's gaze switched to FitzAldelm, who nodded, then came back to me. 'Hours after you and I met.'

When you saved my life, and I yours, I thought, but could not say it.

I

'Well?' demanded the king.

'It is not true, sire.' I acted in self-defence, I wanted to shout.

'He lies!' said FitzAldelm. 'He murdered Guy, sire, for certes.'

'I did no such thing, sire, and Rhys will say the same. He was with me the whole night.'

There was a trace of what I thought was doubt on Richard's face now, but an instant later, my hopes were dashed.

'Robert says he has a witness,' the king grated. 'Someone who saw you in the stews, drinking in the very same inn as his brother.'

'A witness, sire?' I could not help but scoff. The man-at-arms Henry was long dead. I had slain him in cold blood, as I had not FitzAldelm's brother – slit his throat, and with Rhys's help, buried him deep in a midden. The chances of finding another person who remembered me, so many years afterwards, was remote, I told myself. Impossible.

Richard turned to FitzAldelm, as did I.

'Henry!' he called. Loud. Confident.

No, I thought in horror. Surely not.

A man appeared in the gateway. Even at a distance, his beard was evident. Closer he came, and the spade shape of it could not be denied. His face was also familiar.

I began to tremble. You are dead, I wanted to shout. I slew you with my own hands, and buried your corpse. With snaking dread, I watched Henry take a knee six paces from the king, and bend his head.

'Sire.'

'Rise,' Richard ordered. To FitzAldelm, he said, 'This is he?'

'Yes, sire.'

A curt nod, and he glanced at the newcomer. 'Name?'

'Henry, sire. A man-at-arms I am, from Southampton.'

To me, the king said, 'Do you know this man?'

'No, sire,' I lied, somehow keeping a quaver from my voice.

'You did not see him in the inn the night Sir Robert's brother was slain?'

Relieved, I said truthfully, 'No, sire.'

'He saw you, however. Is that not correct?'

'It is, sire,' said Henry, meeting my gaze.

Nausea swept up my throat. Henry was dead, buried, rotted to bone and sinew, yet here he stood, his testimony about to seal my fate with the surety of an enemy's blade.

'Look well,' Richard urged. 'It was many years ago. Men change.'

'I am certain, sire,' Henry answered. 'His mop of red hair is unmistakable, and his raw-boned face. This is the same man, and I will swear so on a reliquary.' There was no more sacred oath he could offer to take.

FitzAldelm's eyes glittered with triumphant malice.

'Tell us what you saw,' said the king.

'He took great interest in a pair of men who had been swiving a whore, sire. When they left, he slipped out after them. One of them, sire, was Sir Robert's brother.'

'How do you know?' said the king sharply.

Henry glanced at FitzAldelm. 'They are – were – as like as two peas in a pod, sire.'

'They were ever so, it is true.' Richard's gaze bore down on me. 'Well? What have you to say?'

Uncertain, panicking, I began, 'Sire, I –'

'Were you in the tavern?'

I looked at Henry, at FitzAldelm, at the king. I felt like a rat in a trap. Stupidly, I said, 'I . . . I was, sire.'

'I knew it!' crowed FitzAldelm.

Richard's mien was thunderous now. 'And you followed Guy and his squire?'

I considered lying, but my face – already flushing bright red – was betraying me. I did not wish to condemn myself further. 'I did, sire, but that does not make me a murderer! How could I do such a thing, one man against two?' I hated my tone, which was as shrill as a fishwife's.

'Because your lowlife squire was waiting outside to help you!' cried FitzAldelm. 'Sire, I have another witness who saw Rhys leave the royal lodgings not long after Rufus.'

A black, bottomless chasm opened at my feet. In its depths, I glimpsed a reddish-orange glare. Hellfire, I thought, waiting to swallow me. Consume me, because of what I had done.

I stood, numb with shock, as a bristle-headed groom was summoned, a man I did not remember but who was known to the king. His account was damning. He had seen Rhys steal after me and, the following morning, heard us talking about my injured arm.

'Well?' Richard roared. 'What say you now?'

I had nothing to lose. 'I did kill Guy FitzAldelm, sire, but it was in self-defence.'

'You stole after him into the alley, and then he attacked *you*?' Scorn warred with the disbelief in the king's face.

'Yes, sire,' I protested.

Richard paid no heed. He was calling for his guards. Burly men-at-arms in royal livery, they appeared with the speed of those who had been waiting to be summoned.

I was dragged away, still proclaiming my innocence. Deep in the bowels of the keep, I was hurled into a windowless, fetid, stone-flagged cell. The door slammed shut with an air of finality. I hammered my fists on the timbers. 'Let me out!'

An uncaring laugh was my reply. It was Robert FitzAldelm – he had followed the men-at-arms.

I pounded on the door again. 'I am no murderer!'

'Tell that to the executioner.'

'The king will never issue such an order!'

An amused snort. 'You know him less well than you think, then. The date has already been set.'

More than once in my life I had seen men punched in the midriff just below the ribcage, the sweet spot that when struck expelled all the air from their lungs, and sent them floorward, slack-jawed and half unconscious. FitzAldelm's words hit me with the same force. My legs gave way, and I slumped to the stone flags. I leaned my head against the thick-timbered door, dimly hearing through it FitzAldelm's foot-steps as he walked away.

It was more than my strength could bear to hold me upright. Pla-cing a hand behind me so I did not fall and strike my head, I lay down. Wanting the blackness to take me. Wanting never to wake up and face the cruellest of fates, ordered by my liege lord, whom I loved like a brother.

I closed my eyes.

A hand gripped my shoulder, sending stabs of terror through me.

I woke, sweating, frantic. Instead of cold stone beneath me, I felt plank-ing. Heard the creak of timbers and the gentle slap of water off the hull. My senses returned. The blackness around me that of night-time, not a windowless cell. I was at sea, returning from Outremer, and Rhys had woken me.

He was crouched by my side, his face twisted with worry. 'Shhhh,' he hissed. 'Someone will hear.'

But to my great relief, nobody had. The confrontation with Richard and FitzAldelm had been a vivid nightmare. My dark secret was safe.

For the moment.

PART ONE

PART ONE

CHAPTER I

The Istrian shore of the Adriatic Sea, December 1192

Cold seawater squelched in my boots. My tunic and hose, also soaking wet, clung to me. Shivering, I tugged my sodden cloak tight around myself, and turned my back on the south, wishing in vain that that would stop the icy wind from licking every part of my goosebump-covered flesh. Of the king's score of companions, I was the only unfortunate who had fallen into the sea as we disembarked from our beached ship. Richard stood a dozen paces away, haranguing the pirate captain who had delivered us to this benighted spot, a featureless stretch of coastline with no villages or settlements in sight. Marsh grass and salt pools extended as far as the eye could see, suggesting a long walk inland.

'Change your clothes now, while you have the opportunity.'

My sour-faced attention returned to Rhys, who had laughed at my immersion as hard as the rest. In truth I could not blame him, nor anyone else. The water had not been deep; I had come to no harm, other than a soaking. And after the travails of the previous few weeks, God knows we needed a moment of levity. Nonetheless, my pride was stinging. I gave him a non-committal grunt.

'You will catch cold ere we find a place to spend the night.' Now Rhys's tone was reproachful. He had already contrived to go through my wooden chest, and was proffering a bundle of dry clothing. 'Take it – go on.'

Teeth chattering, I studied the group. Few men were paying any attention, busy as they were with selecting whatever gear they could carry. We were all soldiers, I thought. We had suffered and sweated and bled in Outremer together, had seen countless comrades fall to Saracen arrows, or die of thirst and sunstroke. We had cradled our friends' heads in our laps as they left this life, choking on blood and asking for their mothers.

In the face of that, baring my arse did not matter.

Stripping off my boots and clothes, I gratefully tugged on the new garments, ignoring the comments of Baldwin de Béthune, who noticed what I was at. He was a close friend and, like me, one of the king's most trusted men. I thought with a pang of de Drune, another friend who would not have missed this chance to jibe. But the tough man-at-arms would poke fun no more. He had been swept overboard during the first of the storms that had battered us since our departure from the Holy Land almost two months before. I hoped his end had been swift.

'Two hundred marks, and *this* is where they brought us to land?' Richard's volcanic temper showed no sign of abating. He threw a mur-derous look at the pirate captain, who had wisely retreated to his vessel. When the tide came in, as it would that evening, he and his crew would do their best to push the long, low shape into deeper water. We were not waiting to help.

The pirate was a rogue, I thought, and the price he had charged for our passage was extortionate, but he was not to blame for the beach where we stood. 'He could do little about the storm, sire.'

Richard glared at me, but I had spoken the truth.

Ferocious autumn gales had battered our large buss all the way from Outremer; we had been fortunate not to drown. At Sicily, the king had decided the open seas were too dangerous, so we aimed our prow for Corfu. Our plan had been to voyage up the more sheltered Adriatic, but further bad weather and an encounter with the pirates had seen Richard drive a bargain with the corsair captain. His two galleys were more seaworthy than the fat-bellied buss which had carried us away from the Holy Land. Or so we thought.

High winds – the bora – had struck soon after our departure from Corfu, and driven us, helpless, up the Adriatic. Three days, or had it been four? My memory could not be relied upon, so exhausted and sleep-deprived was I. Ceaselessly thrown up and down for hour upon hour, from side to side, forward and back, I had vomited until it seemed my stomach itself would come up my red-raw throat. There had been snatched, uncomfortable periods of rest, but never enough. I had forgotten the last time food had passed my lips. When the ship had run aground in the shallows, I had felt nothing but relief. Eager for dry land beneath my feet, paying not enough attention as I prepared to disembark, I had fallen into the sea.

'Aye, well, there's nothing to be done about where we are now,' said the king. 'And standing around will not get us to Saxony any sooner. Let us go.'

He was not now the godlike figure he had so often been in Outremer. There was no bright sun to wink off his mail, no high-prancing stallion to set him high above us. Even in plain tunic and hose, Richard remained an imposing and charismatic figure. Several inches taller than six feet and broad-shouldered with it, his handsome face framed by windblown red-gold hair, he *looked* like a king. He acted like one too: fierce-tempered, regal and fearless.

When he led the way, we twenty willingly followed.

I was unsurprised that Rhys was the first with a question. In an undertone, he asked, 'How far is it to Saxony?'

'I do not know. Hundreds of miles. Many hundreds.'

I had told him this before, but Rhys's expression darkened anyway.

'It will not all be on foot. We will buy horses.'

He rolled his eyes. 'I would we had left earlier. We might have sailed all the way.'

'That was never a possibility.' I explained again to him how the winds and currents that had helped us east across the Greek Sea were too powerful to permit westward travel through the narrow straits that separated Spain from Africa.

Rhys fell silent and, downcast myself by the long journey before us, I began to brood. Landing on the French or Spanish coast might have been an option, but it was precluded by Richard's long-running enmity with the Count of Toulouse, who, with his Spanish allies, controlled the region. We could not travel up through Italy either, because most of its rulers were in league with the Holy Roman Emperor. Heinrich VI, one of the most powerful monarchs in Europe, historically held no love for Richard because of *his* support for another Heinrich, der Löwe, the former Duke of Saxony. Recently, the divide between Richard and the emperor had deepened. The French king Philippe Capet had met with Heinrich VI on his way back from the Holy Land, winning him over and forging a new alliance.

Thoughts of Heinrich der Löwe made me remember, wistfully, Alienor, the blonde beauty who had served Matilda, his late wife and Richard's sister. It had been years since I had seen Alienor, but the mere thought of her quickened my blood. There was even a chance we might meet. Once our roundabout route had taken us through Hungary, we would travel to Saxony, ruled by Richard's nephew, and further northeast to the lands of Heinrich der Löwe. I prayed that Alienor was alive, and in Heinrich's service. Then, guilt-ridden for thinking of her while still in love with Joanna, the king's sister, I put her from my mind.

It was as well that I had elected not to wear my second pair of boots. For an hour or more we trudged through a sandy marshland, its only inhabitants the seabirds that lifted, screeching, at our approach. We waded through saltwater pools; it was my turn to laugh at de Béthune and the rest as they sank to their knees, cursing their own soaking boots. Reaching the shore finally, we came upon a collection of rundown hovels that would struggle to be called a hamlet.

While Richard hung back – a man of his size and stature would stick in anyone's memory – de Béthune and I went with the royal standard bearer, Henry Teuton, to find out where we were, and to buy any horseflesh that might be on offer. Thanks to the soldiers we had met in Outremer, de Béthune and I had some Italian, and Henry Teuton was fluent in his father's language. Between us we managed; the silver coins I proffered also loosened tongues. The area we found ourselves in was the county of Gorizia. I thought nothing of the name, but I caught de Béthune's expression as its ruler, Meinhard II, was mentioned.

Telling his apprentice to fetch out the horses he had, the smith explained that Meinhard co-ruled with his brother, Engelbert III, the lord of the nearest town, also called Gorizia. It lay some miles away, at the foot of the mountains.

As we haggled over the nags, de Béthune risked much by asking about Meinhard's and Engelbert's relationship with emperor Heinrich VI. The smith twined a forefinger and middle finger, indicating they were close allies, and my concerns rose.

But the king laughed when de Béthune told him what we had heard. 'We are in enemy territory from the outset,' he declared. 'As it was in Outremer, when Saladin's men threatened us at every turn.'

Our confidence bolstered by his, we grinned at one another.

William de l'Etang, another of the king's close companions, frowned. 'I remember the name Meinhard, sire.'

'Speak on,' urged the king.

'I am sure he is related to Conrad of Montferrat, sire – his nephew, I think.'

De Béthune and I gave each other a look; Richard's expression tightened.

Conrad had been an ambitious Italian nobleman who rose high in Outremer society. Crowned King of Jerusalem the previous spring, he had been murdered within the week. Everyone in the Holy Land at the time knew that the Assassins – a mysterious Muslim sect – were behind Conrad's slaying, but malicious gossip spread by Philippe Capet and his followers since had been remarkably effective. Conrad's family were not alone in believing that Richard was responsible.

'Better that we should *not* pretend to be Templars,' Richard declared. This had been his initial plan. 'We would draw unwanted attention; our heads must be further below the parapet. Pilgrims, we shall be, then, returning from the Holy Land. Hugo of Normandy will be my name. There is no need for you to have a false identity, Baldwin. You shall act as the military leader of the party.'

This seemed a better ploy, I thought. My relief was momentary, for with his next breath the king ordered Henry Teuton to take one of the four new horses and ride ahead to Gorizia. There he was to ask the authorities for safe passage, a guide and treatment according to the Truce of God, a Church ruling that protected those who had taken the cross from physical violence. Pulling off a magnificent ruby ring, Richard handed it to Henry with the declaration that this should be a mark of his good faith.

Their thoughts on roaring fires and hot meals, few of the group took notice.

I could not believe the risk-taking, however. 'This is his idea of travelling in secret?' I whispered to de Béthune.

'I agree with you, Rufus, but he is our lord.' He saw my face, and said, 'Cross him at your peril. He is in a fey mood.'

I saw that de Béthune was right. The king's bonhomie on the ship had been genuine enough, but the beaching of the vessel in the middle of nowhere, our long trudge to an armpit of a village, the swaybacked, spavined horses – all that had been on offer – and Meinhard being Conrad's nephew had hit Richard hard. If he could not be a proud Templar, the next best thing was a rich and influential pilgrim. And by his haughty expression, his mind would not be changed. I decided on another course of action.

'Sire, let me go also.' Adding that I wanted to improve my German and that Henry was a good teacher was enough. Richard even gave me one of the three remaining nags, a ribby chestnut.

We set off at once. The interrogation began before we had ridden a hundred paces.

'You vant to learn Tcherman?' Henry had a thick, hard-to-understand accent.

'Yes.' I was not about to admit my main purpose. Henry was a no-nonsense, direct type I could see marching into the castle at Gorizia, loudly asking for all of Richard's requests. I hoped for a more discreet approach and, if possible, that the ruby ring should stay hidden.

I could tell Henry none of this – dutiful and rigid, he would fulfil the king's orders to the letter – and so my punishment was to endure a prolonged, finger-wagging lesson in basic German that lasted for the entire ride to Gorizia. I sound ungrateful; Henry was in fact a half-decent teacher, and I learned more in those miles than I had during the entire voyage from Outremer.

Gorizia stood at the foot of a hill upon which perched the castle, Engelbert's stronghold. The town had its own wall; there were guards at the main gate, but to my relief we passed through unchallenged.

'Do not look around so much,' Henry said in an undertone.

I checked my enthusiasm. After the guts of two months at sea, with the only interlude being at Ragusa, even an inconsequential place like Gorizia had me gazing about like a wide-eyed child. Although Henry was right to bring me back to our mission, I thought, we were not in so much of a hurry that I could not visit a nearby bakery. Tired of mouldy bread and salted pork, the smells emanating from it were too much to resist. Hurling my reins at a protesting Henry, I strode inside, emerging soon after, triumphant, four honeyed pastries in my grasp.

'Two for you and the same for me,' I said, prepared for his outburst. 'We can eat and walk towards the castle at the same time.'

Won over, Henry ceased grumbling, and set to with a will.

The guards at the castle entrance were a slovenly crew, their mail covered in brown rust spots; they paid us as little attention as their counterparts at the town gate. Their lack of interest was explained by the crowds in the courtyard beyond, where we discovered – happily – that Count Engelbert was holding court in the great hall.

We left our horses in the charge of a stick-thin, sharp-featured boy of perhaps twelve years. Eyes fixed on the two silver pennies Henry brandished as his reward afterwards, the lad swore that he would guard the horses with his life.

'See that you do,' Henry warned him quietly, 'or we will hunt you down and open you from balls to chin – as we did with many a Saracen.'

Pale-faced, the lad nodded.

We joined the queue of petitioners, locals come to plead their cause with Engelbert, who sat with his feet up on a table, playing idly with a dagger. He was the picture of boredom. The line advanced at a snail's pace, but eager not to draw attention, we dared not jump it. If we talked, it was in low tones; the fewer people who heard either French or my bad German, the better. Time dragged by. I listened in to the conversations around me, trying to understand. To my frustration, I recognised only words here and there rather than the full meaning of what was being said. There would be plenty of time for further lessons from Henry on our long journey, I told myself.

Two cases had been dealt with when I heard church bells in the town tolling one. My hopes began to fall. There was no obligation on Engelbert to hear the case of everyone in the queue. He could call a halt whenever his patience ran thin. To our good fortune, however, he flew into a rage with a hand-wringing peasant. According to Henry's amused translation, the wretch was lamenting the theft of his hens – by a neighbour, or so he claimed. Unconvinced by the claim, Engelbert ordered the unfortunate peasant from his sight. He refused to hear the petition of the next man as well – a merchant whose stammer annoyed him – and reached a decision about the next case the instant it had been explained to him. Moved up the queue three places, we drew near enough to watch Engelbert.

Perhaps thirty-five, he had thinning brown hair and a prominent forehead. Although he had lost his temper with the peasant, his face was amiable, and he was laughing now at whatever the latest plaintiff had said. This was no reason to let down our guard, however, I thought. Engelbert was an enemy.

Our turn came at last. Bored, cold from standing around – for like all great halls, the room was as draughty as a barn – I marshalled a humble but enthusiastic expression onto my face as, urged by a steward, we advanced towards Engelbert's table. Both of us bowed deeply, as we had agreed. Flattery could only help.

His initial glance was disinterested. Then, taking in our muddy, travel-stained clothing and our daggers, which marked us out from the other supplicants, his expression sharpened. Not only were we strangers, but armed ones. An eyebrow rose, and he said something in German.

Henry replied, and I heard the words for 'Holy Land', taught to me on our ride to Gorizia. He was telling Engelbert we were returning pilgrims.

The count's face came alive. He asked a question, and then another and another. I heard mention of Jerusalem, Saladin, Leopold and Richard.

Henry's answers, calm and measured, took some time. I stood by his side, wishing I understood more of what he was saying. The less he gave away, I had told Henry as we waited, the better. Plead our case simply, I said, and do not mention de Béthune and the merchant Hugo unless you have to. Henry had not liked that, but conceded it might be awkward if Engelbert, interested, demanded to meet these pilgrims. The ring, I warned, would also attract too much attention. On this Henry had balked, stubbornly saying that the king had ordered it be offered to Engelbert. Anxious, I had managed to persuade him not to offer the priceless gift unless he felt it absolutely necessary.

The count asked another question, and Henry replied. This time, I heard 'Acre' and 'Joppa'. My mind filled with memories of our brutal march from the first to the second, and the titanic battle against Saladin outside Arsuf. I cast a look at Henry, whose face had grown animated. He too had been there. I began to worry that he might inadvertently reveal something about Richard. Keep it simple, I thought.

A messenger approached Engelbert, affording me an opportunity to speak with Henry. 'Have you asked for safe passage?' I said. 'Has he granted it?'

'I did at the start, yes, but he began asking questions at once. He is fascinated by the campaign against Saladin. What can I do but tell him?'

I had no answer. Refuse to answer Engelbert, and we risked his denying us safe passage and a guide. Offer too much detail, and he might glean that our master was not de Béthune but someone far more important. We had put into enough ports on our voyage for word of the king to have spread this far.

His business with the messenger concluded, Engelbert returned his attention to Henry. Now there was mention, several times, of '*Herr*', the German for master or lord. Henry replied; he said 'de Béthune' and 'Hugo'. He asked for safe passage again, I could understand that, and after a heartfelt '*bitte*', or 'please'.

Alarmed that he sounded too desperate, I casually turned my head towards Henry. He did not see me. I slid my boot sideways and, touching his, kicked him.

He glanced at me, and I mouthed, *Do not give him the ring.*

His brow wrinkled. His lips framed a 'What?'

Christ, I thought.

A question from Engelbert; he was frowning.

Henry did not immediately reply.

I threw caution to the wind. 'What is he saying?'

'He says he can offer safe passage and the Truce of God, but guides with knowledge of the mountains are hard to find. He wants money, I think.'

A grim look passed between us. We had only the silver coins in our purses; enough to buy food, but nowhere near the sum required to win the favour of a man like Count Engelbert.

Henry was like me, ever a man of action. The muscles of his jaw bunched, and then he was reaching into his purse. Out came the ring.

Engelbert could not conceal his avarice. The ruby at the ring's heart was deep red, the size of a large pea. It was worth a fortune by anyone's standards. He held out a hand. There was silence as he examined it and, after a tense few moments, a broad smile.

Henry and I glanced at each other in relief.

The count thanked Henry, and then said something else. The only words I understood, and they were enough, were '*König*' and '*Löwen-herz*'. My blood ran cold. King. Lionheart.

'He says that no nobleman, still less a merchant, would offer so rich a gift,' muttered Henry.

'He is right,' I hissed, wishing that I had stood up to the king, and asked for a purse of gold bezants instead of his magnificent, far-too-obvious gift. 'But you must persuade him otherwise! Tell him the ring was taken from a dead Turkish noble on the battlefield.'

Henry did his best, his tone eloquent and persuading.

He was still mid-flow when Engelbert placed the ring on the table with an empathic, metallic clunk. '*Nein*,' he said. '*Nein. Ihren Herr ist ein König. König* Richard.'

Henry fell silent. My eyes shot to the guards lounging behind the count. I fully expected them to be ordered to arrest us. We had no chance of fighting free, unarmoured and with daggers as our only weapons. I cared nothing for us, but the king *had* to be warned.

Rather than issue a command, Engelbert smiled. It was an open smile, with no hint of malice. He spoke fast then, earnestly. I heard the words '*Kaiser*' and Heinrich. Breathing fast, sick with tension, I waited until he had finished, and Henry could translate.

Henry grinned at me. 'He insists that our master is Richard, and he holds the king in great admiration for what he did in Outremer and has no wish to do him any harm. The same cannot be said for his brother Meinhard, or the emperor Heinrich.'

'Can Engelbert supply us with a guide?'

Henry shook his head. 'There is no time to find one. We must leave Gorizia today.'

'Are things that bad?' I asked, my hopes of a comfortable bed in a warm inn dwindling.

'So he says. Meinhard would pay a huge sum to anyone delivering the Lionheart into his hands. No one in the town can be trusted.'

We thanked Engelbert and took our leave. At the door, I looked back. The count had not called forward the next petitioner but was talking intently to his steward. Then, as if he discerned my stare, he turned his head. Our gaze locked for a heartbeat. Engelbert smiled, but his eyes were as cold and calculating as a falcon's.

I told Henry what I had seen. It was likely, we decided, that Engelbert would send word to Meinhard about the king's whereabouts.

'*Tadhg an dá thaobh*, he would be called in Ireland,' I said.

'*Tie-gh on daw . . .?*' Henry mangled the words. 'I do not understand.'

Chuckling, I explained, 'Timothy of the two sides. He has a foot in both camps.'

Henry looked downcast. 'You were right. I should not have offered the ring to him.

'Look on it as a blessing,' I said. 'If you had not, we would have sought accommodation here in Gorizia and, like as not, had our presence reported. But for Engelbert's warning, we might have been taken while here.'

This realisation was scant solace as we set out southwards to find our companions. The wind was sharp as a knife. Yellow-grey clouds threatened snow; even as I lifted my gaze upwards, little skirls came falling from the sky.

Only God knew if we would find shelter that night.

CHAPTER II

The road to Udine, Friuli

A day later, we found ourselves some distance north-west of Gorizia. The road, if the rutted, uneven surface we rode upon could be called that, was largely empty. The harsh weather meant few travellers were abroad; those we met avoided eye contact, grateful to pass by a large group of armed men unharmed. Our hands never strayed far from our weapons, while our gaze constantly flicked over the rolling landscape for signs of movement.

Henry Teuton and I had found the king not long before nightfall the day before. Richard had been angered to hear of Engelbert's duplicity, but thankful also for his warning. Rather than continue our journey through the falling snow, we had searched out shelter. The owner of a smallholding set away from the road was persuaded by a handful of silver to let our group bed down in his hay barn. Hunched in our blankets, eating the loaves I had thought to buy ere we left Gorizia, we had held a council of war.

The king's decision-making process had been short and sweet. With Meinhard II alerted to his presence, and men probably already hunting us, it was far too risky to continue on the meandering route Richard had first decided upon. Rather than travel to Hungary, we would take a shorter route north-east, entering Austria via the Alps. From there we would cross the Danube into Moravia, whose ruler Wladislaw was no friend of the emperor's, and continue our journey to Saxony and beyond. Richard also decided that we would again claim to be Templars. Our group's size and unmistakable military bearing lent itself far better to this deception than that of merchants.

Setting out long before dawn, we had skirted Gorizia while its inhabitants were still wrapped in their blankets. We were all hungry; the farmer's parting offering, a pan of thin, tasteless pottage, had given each of us only a couple of mouthfuls. We were cold too. The snowfall had been relatively light, but the wind had not let up. It howled down from the mountains with a fierce, unrelenting glee. My face had long since gone numb, and every gust that tugged at my cloak knifed straight through to my flesh.

'This reminds me of the ride to Gorre.'

Startled, for in my reverie, I had not noticed the king come alongside, I repeated, 'Gorre?'

'Have you forgotten it?'

My stiffened cheeks somehow allowed a smile. 'How could I, sire? That was the most brutal experience of my life.'

'Aye. It was worse than this,' said Richard, sounding as if he needed to convince himself.

Unsettled, because it was so rare for him to express any doubt, I said heartily, 'Far worse, sire. Rhys?' I glanced down at him, trudging along beside me. Although Henry Teuton and I had contrived to buy three more horses in Gorizia, there were still not enough horses for all the knights, let alone those of lesser rank.

'I was warmer then, thanks to my two cloaks, sir.' He used the title only because Richard was present. 'I had more food then also – bread and ham.'

I groaned. 'Do not remind me.'

'Good at procuring supplies, are you?' Richard asked. There was a knowing look on his face. Often soldiers had to fend for themselves.

'I have some success in that regard, sire.' One of Rhys's hands moved about under his cloak; he hurried around the back of our horses, coming up on the king's right side. He proffered a wedge of cheese. 'Would you like this?'

Richard chuckled. 'Is the smallholder cursing you even now?'

'That is possible, sire,' said Rhys, his lips twitching.

Richard broke off a piece, and insisted Rhys take back the cheese. When he protested, the king told him it was his – to share with everyone at the next halt.

Rhys gave me a rueful look but, as he admitted afterwards, it was a reasonable enough command. We were in this hell together.

We reached Udine as dusk was falling. The guards at the gate were suspicious, and barred our way. Twenty armed men were a potential

threat to law and order. They accepted Henry Teuton's explanation
– all delivered in the most pious manner – that we were Templars
returning from Outremer.

They waved us through, nodding their thanks as Henry called down
God's blessings on them. 'Try The Sheaf of Wheat, straight down
the street,' one called out. Henry translated the rest, that it was the
largest tavern in town and the only one likely to have enough rooms
for us.

Richard had already agreed to the proposal that de Béthune and
I had made, that our large group would attract too much attention.
Twenty men were not sufficient against the numbers that would be
sent against us, so having only ten mattered not a whit. The cold figures
drove home the starkness of our situation. Mad moments during battles
aside, never had I had to consider being unable to protect Richard.
Now any success would come from stealth and subterfuge, not courage
or martial prowess. It felt shameful, and not the way a king, my liege
lord, should have to travel. There was nothing to be done about it, so I
gritted my teeth, asked God for His protection, and rode on.

Not far from the town square, a half-decent premises called The
Moon and Stars had one very large room. The king's party, aided by
Henry Teuton, and including me, Rhys, William de l'Etang, Robert
de Turnham, the king's chaplain, Anselm, and four others, would stay
here. De Béthune took charge of the rest, and went in search of another
tavern.

Unhappy – I had not been separated from de Béthune for two years
and more – I followed Richard into The Moon and Stars' stable yard.
Leaving our horses in the care of a scrawny ostler, we made for the
main, two-storey building. Like many of the buildings in Udine, it was
timber-framed and roofed with thatch.

Anticipating the interest our arrival might cause, I suggested to
the king that Henry Teuton and I go first, and that he, stooping a
little to conceal his great height, came close to last. Judging by our
companions' expressions, none would have dared say this to the king,
but Richard acquiesced. He was quiet, even subdued, which pained
me.

The place was similar to taverns throughout France and England.
Scattered rushes covered the floor; judging by the smell of stale beer
and grease, they had not been changed in some time. Men sat at

rough-hewn benches and stools, drinking and talking. Someone was singing, out of tune. Two dogs tussled over a bone while beside them, oblivious, a facedown drunk snored. The sharp-eyed proprietor cuffed a serving boy around the head for spilling beer, then hurried with an obsequious smile to a merchant at the counter.

All eyes were on us as we found seats in the furthest corner from the door. Keeping our voices low, we made sure to leave our cloaks over our swords. The king grew impatient that we had not been immediately attended to. His temper, ever quick, burst into flame when a serving wench did not see his beckoning gesture. He roared for a jug of the best wine, to be brought this instant. Heads aplenty turned at his outburst, and I groaned inwardly. It was not as if I could even hope that Richard would not be noticed amongst us. Massive in frame, with his characteristic mane of red-gold hair, he stood out like a sore thumb.

More customers entered, and gradually the focus of attention drifted away from us. With our numb feet and hands regaining feeling, our minds turned to food and drink. The serving wench brought wine for the king as well as jugs of the local beer, which to my surprise was quite good. After that came well-received bowls of pottage and platters of bread and cheese. When my belly was full, I took a second seemingly casual look around the room. To my relief, no one seemed to be watching us.

Our hunger sated, we did not linger in the taproom. As I said to the king, the less people saw of us, the better. Our room was on the first floor, four beds and a storage chest its only furniture. The king took the best bed. Anselm the cleric got one too. William de l'Etang, Robert de Turnham and I tossed a coin for the remaining two, and I lost. There would not be much sleep had tonight, I thought. The men on the floor would be packed tight as salted herring in a barrel, and the inevitable visits to the chamber pot would involve standing on and waking everyone else. The king lay down at once, declaring himself weary. There was a sheen of sweat on his forehead; I prayed that the cursed quartan fever, which had so plagued him, was not about to come back. While Rhys sat on guard by the door, the others settled down, quietly arranging damp boots close to the small fire or oiling and sharpening their blades.

I had no desire to retire yet; nor was I in the mood for conversation. Sitting on the floor, half listening to the others talk, I fell to brooding. I silently cursed our ill luck, the enemies at every turn, the storms that had driven us off course. I cursed the foul weather and the length of the journey before us; I cursed Engelbert, Meinhard, Duke Leopold and the emperor Heinrich. I cursed the mouldy-walled bedchamber we were cooped up in, and the fleas that would feed on us as we slumbered.

Before long, I decided there would be no sleep for me that night unless I cleared my head. I glanced at the king. His eyes were closed, his breathing even. Satisfied, I picked up my cloak and threaded a path to the door.

'Where are you going?' asked Rhys.

'We need more horses. If the ostler here has none for sale, he will know someone who does.'

He was already on his feet. 'I will come as well.'

'No need. I will not be long.'

'It is unwise to go out alone. If not me, take Henry Teuton.'

I refused, knowing my only reason was my bad mood.

Rhys gave me a 'do not say I did not tell you so' look.

I paid no heed, slipping out into the corridor and down the creaking stairs to the warm, sweaty fug of the taproom. Resisting a sudden urge to drink myself into oblivion, thereby forgetting my worries, I went outside.

My notion of speaking with the scrawny ostler paid off. Some hard bargaining saw me purchase, for a high but not extortionate price, five horses which looked as if they might actually carry us through the mountains. The same could not be said of the wretched beasts we had bought at the coast. Pleased, but still wide awake, I decided to find the inn where de Béthune and the rest were; I knew its location because two of the men-at-arms with him had come while we ate. My friend might have found more horses, I thought. At the least, we could share a jug of wine and reminisce about happier times.

The wind had died down, and a fat moon hung silver in the sky. By its light, I made good progress through the empty lanes and streets, my boots crunching through the frost. I walked fast and confident, my hand on my sword hilt, checking behind me every so often. Not finding the inn 'a left, over a junction and two rights' from my accommodation, I realised I had gone astray.

Turning on my heel, I spied a shadow dart into an alley past which I had walked not a dozen heartbeats prior. Furious not to have noticed that I was being followed and, if I admit it, eager for a confrontation, I picked up a stone and raced towards the narrow opening. Halting just before it, I hurled it around the corner. As the stone clattered off a wall, I trusted it as enough distraction and barrelled into the alley, dagger at the ready.

A figure stood within, slight, clad in dark garments. It whirled towards me — my throw had done its work — and I saw a mouth open in shock. Moonlight glinted off a blade. I dodged sideways, and the thrust that would have gutted me sliced the air instead.

'*Wer bist du?*' I snarled. 'Who are you?'

There was no answer, just another arcing swipe of the blade.

I hesitated no longer, charging forward as my opponent's arm reached the limit of its swing. My left arm grappled for his right, the one holding his knife, hoping I caught it before he had time to react. We closed, chest to chest, and I smashed my head against his, feeling a satisfying crunch as his nose broke. He let out a yelp of pain, and reeled back. Perhaps I could have disarmed him, but I had no wish to. My right arm came up, and I lunged with my dagger. Iron grated off bone, and then the blade slid home, deep into his chest. He gasped, a little surprised sound, and I stabbed him again, twice, in the angle between neck and torso.

He was dead before he hit the ground. Blood gouted from my second and third cuts, rapidly staining the frost covering my boots. I cast about, heart pounding, my eyes raking the shadows for a second enemy. There was none.

I bent to check the corpse. Half of me expected him to be an agent of Meinhard's, sent to track down the king, but the ragged clothing and bare feet told me otherwise. This was a common criminal, a cutpurse. I dragged him into the moonlight, the better to see his features. Cold shock bathed me. A blank-eyed, beardless face looked up at the star-filled sky. I had slain a youth, no older than thirteen or fourteen.

In that guilt-ridden moment, I would not have been surprised if Henry, the man-at-arms who had featured in my recent nightmare, had next appeared before me. I would not have had the strength to defend myself.

Footfalls came from the street and I rushed to the corner, wondering if I had another fight on my hands, but it was Rhys. I was a little amused – he had a habit of disobeying orders, and appearing at just the right moment.

'I heard struggling,' he said. 'Are you hurt?'

'No.'

He peered around me. 'Is he dead?'

'Aye,' I said bitterly. 'A boy. I killed a boy.'

'He attacked you?' Rhys walked past, and stood over the corpse.

I told him what had happened.

Rhys stooped, then brandished a viciously thin blade. 'He would have stabbed you in the back, like as not.'

'I suppose.'

'And in the darkness, you had no way of knowing he was a boy.'

'True.'

'If you had not slain him, it might be you lying there.'

He was right, and I knew it. What troubled me was the delight I had taken from the short but savage fight. Consumed by my dark mood, I had shown no mercy, been utterly ruthless, just as I had with Henry all those years before.

'Kill or be killed.'

I started. 'What?'

'It is as simple as that: his life or yours. Accept it.'

'Aye,' I said, but I felt like the worst kind of murderer.

We found de Béthune's inn soon after that, and together shared a jug of wine. He had also purchased another two horses, meaning we now had a mount for more than half our number. Pleased by this, cheered by the wine and good company, I dragged Rhys away to retrace our steps to The Moon and Stars.

The yard there was quiet; no one issued a challenge as I walked past the stables, intent on showing Rhys our new horses. I should have realised he would be less than impressed: he would still have to walk. Disgruntled, he headed towards the tavern while I sought out the best of the new mounts, a dark grey. He had stuck his head over the half-door and, as I drew close, pressed his velvety nose into my palm, his lips nibbling.

'I have no apple to give you,' I whispered, stroking him. Reminded of Pommers, my faithful destrier, I felt a pang of heartache. We had been parted since Corfu. There had been barely enough room on the pirate ship for twenty extra men; Richard had paid a fortune for the group's mounts to be cared for and transported to Normandy the following spring.

Pommers would be all right, I decided. No one was hunting for him, as they were for Richard.

Suspicious that Rhys might have sneaked into the taproom for a last drink, I poked my head around the door, and spied him at the counter, sweet-talking one of the serving wenches. Managing to catch his eye, I indicated with a curt jerk of my chin he was to leave. Planting a kiss on the wench's lips – she made no objection – he swaggered over.

I pulled him into the corridor and out into the stable yard where no one could eavesdrop. 'What are you playing at? This is no time for cozening!'

'Maria, her name is. Pretty little thing.' He mimed curves with his hands. 'She has flesh in the all the right places too.'

'Someone could have heard your accent,' I said, hiding my amusement at his irrepressibility. 'That was a stupid risk to take.'

'It would have been, if ploughing her had been the only thing on my mind.' Rhys grinned at my confusion. 'There was a man at the counter talking to the innkeeper. I was keeping an eye on him.'

'What was he doing?'

'Asking questions.'

'About the king?'

'Aye.'

I forgot all about the serving wench. 'Did you hear what the innkeeper said? Did he mention our party?'

A reproachful look. 'I might have learned more if you –'

'The fact that he was poking his nose where it is not wanted is enough,' I said, cutting him off. 'Upstairs. We have to warn the king.'

As I laid a hand to the latch, I heard, from down the corridor, the door to the taproom opening. Cautious, I stood back, and mimed to Rhys that someone was coming. We stepped back into the shadows, the better to see who might emerge. No one came outside. I placed an ear against the door and listened, and heard the unmistakable sound of light footsteps on the stairs.

'He is going up, not wanting to be heard,' I whispered.

'A mark of silver it is the man who was at the counter.'

I pulled out my dagger for the second time that night.

With a questioning look, Rhys ran a hand across his throat.

In my mind's eye, the bled-out youth stared blankly up at me. I could not countenance another killing so soon. 'No! We need to interrogate, not murder him.'

'As you wish.' Rhys shrugged.

Not for the first time I decided that Rhys's ability to be so emotionless would make him a good assassin. Pulling the door towards me an inch at a time, wary for the slightest creak, I managed silently to open it enough for us both to slip inside. Up the stairs we went, quiet as possible, but we were two big men, and the stairs were shoddy, in a cheap inn.

First a step beneath me creaked, then one under Rhys. The element of surprise lost, I charged up the stairs with Rhys hot on my heels. The unlit corridor at the top was short; the figure of our quarry was visible as a shape darker than the surrounding gloom. I checked my instinct, which was to charge headlong. I had no wish to be gutted on a swift-drawn knife.

'Drop any blades you may have,' I ordered.

A snort. 'For all I know, you are footpads come to rob and murder me. Only a fool disarms without knowing who issued the command.'

There was something in his fist – I could see it – but there was also stirring within our room. Content, I waited.

The door opened, spilling light along the wooden floor. William de l'Etang came out, sword raised, *behind* the man.

'Who's there?' William demanded in bad German.

In French, I said, 'William, I am here with Rhys. We followed this rogue upstairs.' I advanced several steps, gesticulating with my dagger. 'Drop your weapon!'

Something fell with a clatter. The man held up his empty hands. 'My name is Roger of Argentan. I mean you and your master no harm.'

Argentan was a town in Normandy – I had been in it more than once. Suspicion prickling, I drew closer.

He met my stare, and made no threatening move. Stocky, better dressed than a cutpurse, he had short, dark hair and a close-cut beard.

I kicked away the sword he had dropped, and searched him for more weapons. Finding none, I shoved him towards William. 'Into our chamber,' I said brusquely.

With William in front of him and me at his back, my dagger ready, he obeyed.

Awakened by the noise, Richard was sitting up in bed, the coverlet over his legs. There was a pallor to his complexion I did not like, but his gaze was sharp as ever.

The stranger's eyes went straight to him.

'My apologies for waking you –' I said, only just managing to check the word 'sire'.

Richard waved a hand. 'It is late for visitors, but I was sleeping poorly anyway. Roger of Argentan, did I hear? We are a long way from Normandy.'

To my astonishment, Roger went down on one knee. 'I have lived in Italy for many years, sire.'

Unsure how to react – and my reaction was mirrored by every face I saw – I stood there, speechless.

Richard's reaction was rapid. 'Have you lost your wits?' he cried. 'Stand up – I am no king.'

Roger did not budge. 'But I know you, sire. I saw you in Caen once when I was a boy.'

'Saw who?' the king scoffed.

'The Duke of Aquitaine, sire. Nowadays, you are Richard, King of England.'

A taut silence filled the room. Uneasy stares were exchanged. At my side, Rhys's knuckles were white on his dagger hilt. I touched my own blade, and wondered uneasily how it would feel to open Roger's throat. That was what the king would order with his next breath because this man, surely here at Meinhard's behest, could not go free.

'You are mistaken,' said Richard, his voice thick.

'You have no need to lie, sire!'

Before he could utter another word, I had my blade snugged under his chin. 'Insult my master so again, and it will be the last thing you do,' I said.

Roger's eyes – wide, but unafraid – came up to meet mine. 'The king need not fear me,' he said. 'I am a Norman, first and foremost.

Richard is my liege lord. I would *never* do him any harm, or endanger his life.'

The king gave no order that I should lower my blade. 'Norman you may be, Roger of Argentan,' he said, 'but here in Udine you serve . . .?'

'The Advocate of Aquileia, sire, Count Meinhard, second of his name.'

'Meinhard was nephew to Conrad of Montferrat, whom it is alleged was murdered by King Richard's order. He is also an ally of the Holy Roman Emperor, Heinrich.'

'Even so, sire.'

'Why then should I trust a word that comes out of your mouth?' asked the king. 'I have a good mind to make a quick end of you!'

'Do what you will, sire. I am your servant,' said Roger meekly. 'Does it not strike you as odd, though, that I did not arrive with soldiers? I could have, if I had wanted to, but instead I came alone, to warn you.'

Richard's eyes narrowed. I too had heard the truth in Roger's words. Sneaking up to our chamber alone was not the action of a man who could have surrounded the inn with armed men.

'Rufus, lower your blade. Stand, Roger. Speak your piece,' said the king.

Giving me a wary glance, Roger obeyed. He had been sent by Meinhard to Udine, he explained, as other agents had been sent to towns in the area. Every innkeeper was to be questioned, and details sought for each and every party of travellers. Particular attention was to be paid to large groups, those speaking French and any spending freely.

Richard scowled, and I wondered if he remembered his earlier angry demand for the best wine in the place.

'I have been to every hostelry and tavern in Udine, sire. I was suspicious of your men in the other inn.' Roger saw the king's look and said, 'The stable lads heard them speaking French.'

'God's legs,' said Richard. 'Can we hide nowhere?'

'Not in Udine, sire,' said Roger sadly. 'It was plain when I spoke to the innkeeper that your group included an important personage, and the moment I heard your description, it was clear who you were. If I found you this easily, sire, others can too. You *must* leave in the morning if you are not to be captured.'

Rhys and I exchanged a grim look.

It was hard not to feel as if we were in a trap with the noose slowly tightening on us.

CHAPTER III

We were up long before dawn and the crowing of a cock from a nearby backyard; we dressed and readied our gear in silence. By the look of my companions' faces, none of them had slept well either. More worryingly, Richard looked ill. His face was flushed, and he was sweating. I asked if he was all right, and whether I should send for a surgeon. He snapped that he was not a child in need of a nurse, and that leaving Udine was the only thing that mattered.

He was in such a temper that I did not say his health was also paramount, especially given his history of illness. Instead, I conferred with William de l'Etang, Robert de Turnham and Anselm. We agreed that the king seemed fit to travel, but that if his condition worsened we would have to find a safe place for him to rest. Anselm mentioned a Benedictine monastery at Moggio, some days' ride away. The monks there, he swore, would happily shelter the king who had done so much in Outremer. None of us asked aloud what we would do if he deteriorated sooner than that.

I determined to keep the pleasing prospect of Moggio to the forefront of my mind. Taking our journey a step at a time made the impossibility of it seem more bearable – feasible, even.

I went downstairs with Rhys and Henry Teuton. We had given orders late the previous night that our horses were to be ready by dawn, but to see a job done properly, as the saying went, it is best to do it oneself. It was fortunate that we went outside fully armed. We found more than a dozen locals armed with staves and axes loitering by the door to the inn. They were shocked to see us. For a moment, no one said a word; we simply stared at each other. Beyond them, I spied one of the ostlers peering from the hay barn; he had a black eye and a split lip.

It was easy to imagine what had happened. Full of bravado at the thought of capturing a king, the mob of townspeople had come to the inn, where harsh reality – challenging the king's soldier followers – had sunk in. To bolster their courage, the locals had attacked and beaten the unfortunate ostler. Now they were trying to rally themselves enough to climb the stairs to our chamber. A few words with Rhys and Henry established they were of the same opinion as I was; they also agreed these sewer scrapings needed to be dealt with at once, before any reinforcements arrived.

Drawing our swords and screaming '*Dex aie!*', the English royal war cry, we charged the mob. Three men against fifteen might sound insane, but we were battle-hardened veterans while the men facing us, civilians all, had probably never done more than fight in a drunken tavern brawl. They took to their heels and fled, skidding on the icy cobbles in their haste. Only Rhys, youngest and keenest of the three, got close enough to land a blow, a swingeing sideways cut with the flat of his blade. His quarry was sent tumbling, smacking his head as he landed. Rhys let him get up. The man, paunchy, well built, was so terrified that he made no attempt to run.

'Go!' Rhys pointed his blade at the street.

The man did not move.

Rhys advanced a step. 'Boo!' he shouted, as a child does to frighten another.

The man fled, his wails loud enough to wake the dead.

The three of us laughed until it hurt. I left William, still chortling, with the horses. Rhys set out, guided by one of the ostlers, for the inn where de Béthune was staying, while I went to advise the king of what had happened. Richard was amused, but the danger we were in was plain.

We had to leave without further delay.

De Béthune and one of his party arrived even as we were saddling the last of our horses. They came into the stable yard, hooves clattering, their horses breathing heavily. A second, larger mob had besieged their inn, it transpired, and they had had to fight their way free. Blood had been shed – Christ be thanked, none of it ours – but eight men had been taken prisoner.

Richard was all for charging through the streets to free them. 'I cannot leave them behind!'

'The risk is too great, sire,' I said, with de Béthune loudly echoing my words.

The king was incandescent, irate. He paced up and down, cursing. 'I cannot abandon them – I will not!'

'There are thirteen of us, sire, including you,' I said. 'The mob is how big, Baldwin?'

'A hundred at least.'

'Valiant as you are, sire, and we with you, there is no guarantee we would succeed in freeing our comrades,' I said. 'Far more likely is that you will also be taken captive.'

'That *must* not happen, sire,' said de Béthune.

Richard's stony gaze went from one of us to the other and back again. 'Very well,' he snarled. 'We shall do as you say, although I am a worse man for it. May God forgive me.'

De Béthune looked as relieved as I felt. We saddled up, making ready to leave at once.

'Hark!' said the king.

A bell was tolling from a church some distance off. Prime had not long passed, and it was far too soon for tierce.

'An alarm,' I said.

'Aye.' Richard's expression was grim. 'Let us go, or they will trap us in here for certes.'

There was no sign of the mob when he led us out of the yard; he turned right, aiming for the gate opposite the one we had entered by the previous day. The ten of us on horseback rode in front, with Rhys and two men-at-arms close behind. Tantalising smells came from a bakery; I cast a longing glance at the pastries and loaves on offer as we rode by, but this was no time to act as I had at Gorizia.

We almost made it to the gate. I had begun to believe that Roger's warning had come in time, that de Béthune's group were the unlucky ones, that we would leave Udine without challenge. I was not alone. Richard was talking with de Béthune about crossing the Alps; Henry Teuton was twisted around in the saddle, trying to teach Rhys German.

Around the last corner we came.

'The bastards,' I said.

De Béthune swore also.

The king chuckled. 'They really do not want us to leave.'

A hundred and fifty paces off a wagon lay upended, blocking the street almost entirely. A small gap had been left to one side; it was wide enough to allow someone on foot to squeeze past, but a horse would never fit through. Men were visible behind the just-erected barricade; they were pointing at us and shouting. I could not make out what was being said. A gaggle of the cockiest – youths, of course – stood out in front of the wagon. They too were yelling and gesticulating. I discerned only one word: '*König*'.

'Let us to the other gate, sire,' said de Béthune, the calm head. 'Reach that, and we can ride around the town unhindered.'

'What is to say they have not blockaded it as well?' asked the king.

'I shall send a couple of men to check,' said de Béthune.

'No!' said Richard.

I sensed his purpose then. It was madness, laden with risk, and yet, as always when he leaped into the thick of it and pulled me with him, I exulted.

'The side alleys, then, sire. There must be a way around, another route to the gate.' De Béthune looked to me for support, but I gave him none.

'We stay here!' Richard's eyes were gleaming, and not from fever.

De Béthune was coming alive to our master's intent. 'The danger, sire, is too great.'

'We charge at once, in pairs,' said the king, low and authoritative. 'Our horses, nags though they are, will clear that wagon.'

I was delighted. The dreariness of our voyage and our skulking from town to town had long since palled, and I had no desire to be taken captive as our comrades had. I also wanted to forget how I had knifed a child in an alleyway. My companions' expressions were also excited – we were knights, not merchants. Fighting was our raison d'être.

'Use the flats of your blades,' said the king. 'Harm no one unless you must. You men on foot, chase after the last riders as if every demon in Hell was after you. The mob will have broken by then – you need only to get by the barricade and find us on the other side.' He laughed then, wild and free. 'If by some chance the rabble stands its ground, give us all the aid you can.'

Rhys grinned. This was his style too. The other men-at-arms seemed just as resolute.

35

Worry creased de Béthune's face. He was no coward, though; the king's safety was ever his concern. 'Sire –' he began.

'Do not waste your breath, Baldwin,' said the king. 'If you love me, follow.'

There was no arguing with that. De Béthune sighed, and said, 'Sire.'

The king cocked his head. 'Rufus?'

My heart skipped a beat to be chosen first. 'I am with you, sire.'

We drew our swords.

Our horses, ill-used and lowly, had never galloped at a barricade before. Never charged an enemy. Wiser men would not have demanded they do both at the same time, as the king and I did, but wise men rarely fight battles or make decisions between one beat of the heart and the next. Those horses responded valiantly, each seeming to encourage the other. We went from a standing start to the full gallop in four paces, almost as fast as a trained destrier.

'God is with us, Rufus!' cried the king. '*Dex aie!*'

I echoed his scream, aiming my sword point at the insult-shouting youths.

Shock froze them temporarily to the spot. Given their bravado and insult-throwing, it was hilarious, how every last one of them looked terrified. Then a mad scramble ensued. Some clambered straight over the wagon, while others fought their way into the narrow gap. More than one fell and was trampled by his uncaring friends, but all of them vanished as we thundered closer. A line of blanched, fearful faces regarded us from the other side of the wagon.

They assume we will not do it, that we will rein in at the last moment, I thought with frenzied amusement. They do not know Richard.

Thirty paces remained.

A stone whizzed past my head, and then another.

'*Dex aie!*' the king bellowed.

I leaned forward on my horse's neck. 'Come on, boy!' I urged. 'You can do it!' I do not know if he understood a word of French, but he responded with heart, increasing his pace.

Side by side with the king, I reached the wagon. Side by side, our horses jumped. Down they came on the far side, hooves dashing sparks from the cobbles. Men scattered in all directions, like hens with a fox in the coop. From the corner of my eye, I saw Richard throw back his head and laugh with pure, unadulterated joy. I laughed also, joyful to be with him, confronting our enemies.

We rode down the street with not a man opposing us. Dozens of dread-filled faces regarded us from the alleys and lanes on either side. There were no missiles – yet. At length the king reined in so we could watch our comrades' progress. Over the barricade they leaped in ones and twos, with no resistance. Then Anselm's horse clipped the wagon with a back hoof. He was never a good horseman and, when his mount landed awkwardly, there was an inevitability to the way he toppled off, arms and legs flailing.

There was also a predictability, as a pack of dogs rounds on fallen prey, the way men came swarming out to attack poor, unarmed Anselm.

I saw it. So did the king. But the others riding towards us, faces alight with triumph, did not. Too late, we urged our horses back up the street. Too late, we cried the alarm.

Thank God and all His saints for Rhys and the two men-at-arms, who came at that very moment through the gap between the wagon and the wall. Weapons at the ready, alert for danger, they charged the townspeople threatening Anselm. Three men, armed with sickles and axes, dared to stand their ground. Blades flashed. A crossbow trigger clicked. A trio of corpses decorated the cobbles. The rest of the mob fled, like the yellow-livered curs they were.

'Shall we go after them, sire?' There was a fierce, hungry look in Rhys's eyes.

Richard hesitated; it was clear he also wanted the fight to continue. Then sanity returned. 'No. There is nothing to be gained by it. Help Anselm.'

The chaplain was winded but unhurt otherwise, and his horse was soon retrieved. In tight order, the men-at-arms carrying their crossbows at the ready, we made our way to the gate. It was shut. A score, perhaps, of guards stood in front of it, but they were no soldiers. Most had either seen too many summers or too few. Their weapons were shoddy, mail shirts rusted. Several did not have helmets. Their commander was an officious-looking type with a fur-trimmed cloak and gilt-edged sword scabbard; he paraded up and down, delivering a haranguing speech that was no doubt meant to set a fire in their bellies.

Richard spoke to Henry Teuton, who rode forward, both hands raised in the universal signal of peaceful intent. 'Open the gate,' he cried.

'*Nein*,' said Fur-trimmed Cloak, eyeing first his men and then Richard. 'Surrender, your majesty,' he said in thick-accented French.

The king gave no reaction whatsoever.

'We will win through whether you stand or make way,' said Henry Teuton. 'If we fight, most of your men will be slain. How many have ever used their weapons in anger, I wonder?' He studied the guards behind Fur-trimmed Cloak, and asked, 'Are you ready to die?'

They gave each other unhappy, uncertain looks.

In the same moment, we drew our swords. Our men-at-arms filed past the horses on either side, and aimed their crossbows.

Fear is infectious, and it spreads with frightening speed. The first man had barely sneaked past Fur-trimmed Cloak when another followed. A third whispered something in a comrade's ear, and edged the other way. Just as a few pebbles can start a landslide, their action nudged the rest into action. Fur-trimmed Cloak blustered and threatened in vain, but soon he was the only one left in front of the gate.

Purple-faced, he lambasted his men from on high. They paid him no heed. Safely arrayed to either side of the gate, solemn-faced, they almost seemed an honour guard to the king.

'Stay where you are at your own peril,' Henry Teuton advised Fur-trimmed Cloak. Henry raised a hand and beckoned.

Rhys and the men-at-arms hurried forward.

Fur-trimmed Cloak made no attempt to intervene as they lifted the heavy locking bar up and out of its cradles, and set it on the ground. He said nothing when the gates were hauled open, hinges screaming. The men-at-arms got a baleful glare, but that was the extent of his courage. As the king and I rode forward he shuffled aside, face scarlet with humiliation.

I could not help myself. As I drew parallel, I leaned down from the saddle and shouted, 'Boo!' It amused me to use the same word Rhys had a short time before.

A wail of pure fear ripped free from Fur-trimmed Cloak's mouth; but for the wall behind him, he would have fallen over.

God forgive us, we laughed and laughed.

I am sorry to say that this welcome levity did not last. Clear of the protection of the rampart, we were exposed to the elements once more.

A blasting, icy wind tugged at our cloaks and numbed any exposed flesh. Snowflakes drifted down in twos and threes, a warning of what could come.

With gritted teeth, we set our faces towards the fortified town of Venzone, twenty-odd miles to the north. With our route now along the Via Julia Augusta, a paved road from Aquileia to the Alps, I had hopes of reaching it before nightfall. That was until I glanced at the king. Winning free of Udine had taken a real toll on him. Skin the colour of old wax, gaunt-cheeked, Richard was hunched in the saddle like a man twice his age.

We would be lucky to cover half the distance, I decided. Fresh worry knifed at me. Travelling at a snail's pace meant our pursuers would catch up with us long before we crossed the snow-capped mountains, let alone traversed the territory of hostile nobles such as Duke Leopold of Austria.

I could do nothing about our situation, save pray. I began silently to recite the Our Father, over and over again. I had a strong suspicion that God would revile me as a murderous sinner who only sought out His company at utmost need. Nonetheless, I did not stop.

If nothing else, I thought with black amusement, the exercise served as distraction from the hellish journey.

Perhaps God did listen to my prayers. The king rode all day without complaint. More than once he found the energy to ride back and encourage Rhys and the men-at-arms, trudging through the snow behind us. At Venzone, he overrode my request to seek shelter, insisting that we press on to the monastery at Moggio.

In truth, it was a good decision. Venzone would probably have been as perilous as Udine, with garrison and population both on the lookout for Richard. It was a sad day, I reflected, when lowly townspeople could dream of capturing a king, but it was also a harsh reality that had to be accepted. Better to find sanctuary in a monastery, where fewer questions would be asked and where medical help might be found for the king.

Richard's great strength gave way as we rode in through the gate. But for my arm, he would have fallen from the saddle. 'Steady, sire,' I muttered. 'We are here now.'

He turned his deep-sunk eyes on me. 'Do not let them bleed me.'

'Yes, sire.' I too was not fond of this treatment, beloved of so many surgeons.

It was the last thing he said for days.

The king's illness, another bout of the dreaded quartan fever that had previously afflicted him, proved to be a blessing in disguise. He received the best of care – one of the monks had studied in the world-famous medical school at Salerno – and we had shelter from the brutal weather. These were not the only benefits. My concerns about pursuit proved correct, but when the first armed party of horsemen arrived the day after we had, they were given short shrift. I witnessed the encounter; a narrow slit window in the king's guest dormitory gave onto the courtyard. Fur-trimmed Cloak was one of the riders, although he was not the leader. That fell to a stern little fellow with sharp eyes and a cold, arrogant manner. One of Meinhard's officers, I understood him to say, the words *'ein offizier des König'* and 'Meinhard' carrying up to my vantage point.

Cold and arrogant he might have been, but he was no match for the monk who ran the stables and farm. Under his pious, humble manner lurked a resolve as steely as any knight. There were no large groups of pilgrims returning from the Holy Land here, he declared. Nor were there any merchants, not even wealthy ones by the name of Hugo. No, it would not be possible to search the monastery.

Furious, but unwilling to draw down the wrath of the Church on his head, the sharp-eyed officer pricked his spurs into his horse, making it rear up. Fearing that the monk's brains were about to be dashed out, I watched in amazement as he stood calmly with the hooves flashing by his head. Powerless to do more, the officer left in high dudgeon with his men. The sound of their hooves had not yet died away when the monk glanced up at my window. The trace of a smile passed across his lips, and my regard for him rose even higher. The monks knew or suspected who Richard was, I thought, and had decided to protect him. In this harsh, mountainous land, not everyone was an enemy.

'Who was that?' Richard had woken, and heard the noise from the courtyard.

De Béthune, who was sitting by his pallet, gave me an enquiring look.

I considered lying, but the king had ever been one for truth and directness. Ill or not, he would want to know. 'Meinhard's men from Udine, sire. Do not worry. The monk who spoke with them is stout-hearted and fearless. They left in a most unhappy mood.'

Richard's dry lips cracked into a smile. Drained by this effort, he lay back and fell asleep.

'Can we be sure they are gone?' de Béthune asked, concerned.

I had already given thought to this. 'I will send out Rhys and a couple of the men-at-arms.'

De Béthune nodded, then his gaze returned to Richard. 'They will not stop searching for us. Meinhard might order them to search the monastery.'

'We have to stay here for the moment,' I said.

'That is plain.' He lowered his voice. 'But how long will it be before the king is strong enough to travel?'

I gave him a grim look.

It was the question hanging over all of us, and one we had asked the monk caring for Richard several times. His reply was infuriating, and always the same: 'It is in God's hands.'

I said as much to de Béthune, and went in search of Rhys. With little to do, he would relish the task I was about to set him. I was tempted to go myself, but I did not wish to stray far from the king.

Rhys was in the hay barn that lay beyond the walls, on the edge of the monastery's farmland. The rest of the men-at-arms were there too. Hard-bitten, rough-round-the-edges characters all, they did not enjoy the life of a religious community. Dry and snug, the hay barn provided a place of their own, away from we knights. I envied them; we had only our shared dormitory or the chapel.

The sound of laughter and ribald comments reached me from some distance away. I was pleased. While I and de Béthune were constantly worrying, the men-at-arms' morale seemed to be unaffected.

I found them playing dice on an area of earthen floor that had been cleared of hay. I was amused to see one of the novice monks squatting by Rhys, his face intent on the nearest game. A mop-haired, strapping lad whose main duties were on the farm, I had seen him in the barn more than once. By his youthful face, I guessed he was no more than fourteen or fifteen. The boy I had slain in Udine came to my mind, and a pang of guilt tugged at me.

'A six!' shouted Bald Jean, one of the oldest men-at-arms. He raised his fists in triumph. 'I win!'

'No, you got a five,' said the novice in reasonable French. 'Look, the dice has rolled again.'

Rhys and the others crowed their amusement as Jean protested, 'It was a six – you all saw! The dice only moved because the cursed floor is so uneven.'

'Aye, but as you well know, Jean,' said Rhys, chuckling, 'the score is valid only when the dice has stopped moving. That is what we agreed from the start.'

'Which means *I* win!' The novice's grin covered his whole face.

Rhys clapped him on the back. Jean glowered and muttered as the other men-at-arms derided him for trying to cheat.

I stepped forward as the hilarity died away. 'Are members of the order permitted to gamble?'

The novice turned, his face paling. 'Good sir, do not say anything, I beg you. This was the first time I –'

'Save your lies,' I said, but my tone was gentle. 'I care not if you play at dice.'

'Thank you, sir, thank you!'

I was amused; for all his obsequious gratefulness, he was remarkably swift to scoop up his winnings.

Rhys clambered to his feet and joined me. 'Any news of the king?'

'He is sleeping.' I told Rhys about the visit paid by Meinhard's official and Fur-trimmed Cloak. 'I do not trust them. They might have set men to watch the monastery, or perhaps to interrogate any monks who venture beyond its walls.' Prickling with unease, I let my eyes wander over the nearby fields, and the wooded slopes beyond.

Rhys understood at once. 'Do you want me to have a look?'

'Aye, you and the others. If the monks ask, tell them you are off hunting.'

Rhys nodded. 'Bertolf will help – he claims to know every track and path around here like the back of his hand.'

'Bertolf – is that the novice?' I asked, staring at the youth, already in the midst of another round of dice.

'Yes.'

'How does he speak French?'

'He learned it from an old monk, another Norman. Says he likes languages. If not for the old monk, he would have left the monastery long ago. He has no great love of prayer, and from his questions about the whorehouses we visited in Sicily and Outremer, I suspect he feels the same about chastity.' Rhys was trying not to laugh.

'Could he be persuaded to join us? Having a second native German speaker would be of great help in the towns.'

'He will bite my hand off at the mere suggestion. I shall ask him as we search the woods.'

Pleased, I told Rhys to report to me when he got back, and went to check on the king.

Dusk had not long fallen, darkening the dormitory. Around the king's bed, a dozen tallow candles kept the shadows at bay; a crackling fire in the nearby hearth gave off a warm orange glow. I was perched on a stool by Richard's side, watching him sleep. I had relieved de Béthune upon my return from the hay barn. The king had just wakened, and been pleased by my decision to send Rhys out scouting.

'He is a good man, your squire,' Richard croaked.

'Indeed he is, sire.' Although I knew the king held him in high regard, it was doubly pleasing to hear it said aloud. I wondered wryly if the king's opinion would change if he knew of Rhys's involvement in my killing of Robert FitzAldelm's brother, Guy. If Robert ever succeeded in denouncing me, Rhys would be as damned as I.

Floorboards creaked. I twisted, and saw Rhys hovering in the doorway, unsure whether to approach. 'He is back, sire,' I said.

Richard eased up onto an elbow, his gaunt face alive with interest. 'Bid him come hither. I would know what he saw.'

I beckoned. Rhys came and bent a knee. 'Sire.'

'You are cold,' said the king, noting, as I had, Rhys's pinched cheeks and blanched hands. He ordered a protesting but grateful Rhys to go and thaw out in front of the fire. I was filled with admiration. Despite his illness, Richard had not lost his way with men.

'Look,' said the king. 'He has news for us.'

I was delighted that he had the energy to take such an interest in his surroundings. There had been none of this since our arrival, just brief lucid moments amid a constant, raging fever. I glanced at Rhys, who was jiggling from foot to foot like a small boy in need of the garderobe. 'You are observant, sire.'

'I judge it good too, by his pleased manner.'

The king was right, I thought. Rhys had the self-contented air of a man who has done well. He saw us staring and came over, rubbing his hands.

Again the king refused to let him speak until a cup of warm, mulled wine had been brought. Only when Rhys had had several mouthfuls did Richard give him leave to speak.

'My thanks, sire.' Rhys's tone was heartfelt. 'It is cold enough to freeze a man solid out there.'

'Did you find or see aught?' asked the king.

'We did, sire. Two men were hiding in the woods, in a well-placed spot on a rocky promontory that climbs above the trees. From its top, the monastery's main gate is readily visible.'

'Meinhard's men?' Richard demanded.

'Yes, sire. So they said, after we persuaded them to talk.'

Neither the king nor I had need to ask what this meant.

'If they saw a large party like ours arrive or leave, sire, they were to carry word to Udine with all speed.'

'Did they know if Meinhard plans to insist that the monastery be searched?'

'No, sire.'

'And the rest of the men who came here, are they still hunting on the road north?'

'They thought not, sire, because the officer in charge had been told to go no further than the border with Carinthia, which lies less than a day's ride away.'

Richard looked pleased. 'And the two men?'

'You need have no concerns in that regard, sire,' said Rhys quietly.

'If they do not return, though, their masters will be suspicious,' I said. 'If a search party is sent . . .'

'They will discover one body on a ledge thirty feet from the top of the cliff, and the other at the bottom, with not a mark of a blade on them,' said Rhys, explaining. 'One man fell partway, and in trying to help him, the other slipped and tumbled all the way. Their horses will be found by local huntsmen. Bertolf will see to that.'

I shook my head, impressed by Rhys's duplicitousness.

'Finely done,' said the king, pleased and impressed. 'We may win free of Meinhard yet.'

CHAPTER IV

Three days passed. The weather improved, and the snow on lower ground melted. We had a worrying time of it when the bodies of Meinhard's men were found, and word was sent to Udine. Richard was still too weak to travel, so we had to risk staying put. The arrogant official came again the following afternoon, with greater force, and was met by Abbot Otto himself, a venerable, kindly faced man. Otto agreed to a search of the monastery – by the bullish attitude of Meinhard's official, it would have happened regardless – but had had the wisdom to see us guided to the monks' cells even as the unwelcome visitors arrived.

Even Meinhard's lackey did not have the courage to force his way into the monks' quarters. Nor did he have the wit to order his soldiers to the hay barn, where our horses were stabled. He departed in an even fouler temper than before.

We had had another narrow escape, but there was reason for a little optimism. It seemed likely that Meinhard would now abandon his search for us, thinking we had slipped through his net. We had also, thanks to the abbot, procured more horses. All of us would ride now.

By the twelfth of December, the king had regained enough strength to leave his sickbed for the first time. The monk who had been caring for him advised another sennight of rest. Richard's instant, typical response was that we would leave the following day. De Béthune and I conferred in private with Anselm, William de l'Etang and Robert de Turnham. All of us agreed that the benefit of leaving outweighed the benefit of staying, and as I said, to general laughter, agreeing with the king was far easier than risking his ire.

We clambered from our blankets on the thirteenth as the abbey bells tolled prime. I peered through the frost-rimed window of the dormitory at a clear, starlit sky. To my relief, there was no fresh snow.

We gathered in the darkened courtyard, blowing into our hands and stamping our feet as Abbot Otto gave us his blessing. He had given permission for Bertolf to accompany us, admitting to the king that he had long expected the lad to leave.

Richard was in high spirits as we set out, following the Val Canale, the valley that led east and north into the Alps. We met almost no other travellers, and there was no sign of Meinhard's soldiers. This was no reason to let down our guard, for we had entered the wild, inhospitable terrain of Carinthia, which was famous for its bandits. Nary a one showed his face, however – in the main, I suspect, because of the treacherous going. The further we travelled, the worse the conditions became. We spent that day and another slipping and sliding through slush and snow, at constant risk of our horses breaking their legs. Mercifully, this did not happen. At night, our simple shelters were farmers' barns. Their owners' trust was bought – we hoped – with weighty payments of silver coin.

The brutal travel was taking its toll on Richard. He had a hacking cough, but was adamant that we continue. De Béthune and I did not argue; forbidding and hostile, Carinthia was no place to linger. The third day saw us bypass the town of Villach rather than risk being recognised. We rode along the northern shore of a massive body of water, the Ossiacher See, Bertolf called it. He proved his worth that afternoon, guiding us to another Benedictine monastery close to the lakeshore.

Once again monks gave us food and shelter, and asked no questions.

Weary from travel and worrying over the king, I slept like a dead man that night. There were no nightmares about Henry, or the youth I had slain.

Dusk on the sixteenth saw us, bone-weary from a thirty-mile ride, approaching the walls of Friesach. It was a town grown rich thanks to a nearby silver mine, and not somewhere especially wise to show our faces. Low on supplies, however, and with the king succumbing to another fever, we needed food and medicine, and shelter, possibly for several days. No farmer's barn could provide all of those – even Richard had conceded that.

The fading light could not conceal the size of the walls that ran off to either side of the mighty gate. Friesach was far larger than Gorizia,

Udine or Villach. With luck, I thought, we could lose ourselves amid the crowds, and lie low for a few days. From here a long, hard ride north-east awaited us, to Vienna, deep in Duke Leopold's heartland. A puffed-up bladder of a man, I remembered, whom Richard had chosen to humiliate after the fall of Acre. I hoped the king would not live to regret his actions.

'There you are.' Henry Teuton emerged from the gloom, leading his horse by the reins. He and Bertolf had ridden ahead a while before, to seek out a quiet inn that could accommodate the whole group.

I peered past him. He had been waiting by the roadside, in the shadow of an abandoned wagon with a broken axle. 'Did you find somewhere to stay? Where is Bertolf?'

'Yes, an inn not far from the gate. As for Bertolf, he is off wandering about. Listening in on conversations, looking out for soldiers and so on. No one takes any notice of boys, he said. I hope I have done right?'

'Yes, that seems wise.'

'The king?' Henry's gaze moved to Richard, a short distance behind me. He was swaying gently in the saddle, and his eyes were half closed.

'He is not well,' I said, stating the obvious. 'The sooner we get him to bed, the better.'

Henry put a foot in the stirrup and leaped onto his horse's back. 'Follow me, with just the king. Let the others come after, in ones and twos. That way the guards at the gate will pay little attention. Tell them to look for The Black Swan, a hundred paces from the gate on the left.'

He waited as I rode back to tell de Béthune, then rejoined the king.

'We are almost there, sire,' I said, quiet enough that only he could hear.

Richard mumbled a reply. I was about to take his reins so I could lead his horse, when he lifted his head. Humour sparked in his eyes. 'I am not quite that ill, Rufus.'

Gladder than I had been all day, I nodded.

We rode through the gate after Henry Teuton.

A short while later, we were seated around a long table in the corner furthest from the door to the main taproom. The Black Swan was a decent-sized inn, and it was very busy. This was not to my liking, but our need to find shelter and Richard's condition had taken precedence.

48

We had had to wait for a time in the courtyard until Henry Teuton had secured a space for us. The king, bless him, had fallen asleep on his feet.

I considered taking him to our room, but he needed to eat – none of us had had a decent meal since the previous evening. He sat now on my left side, drowsy but pleased enough to be waiting for pork stew, the dish suggested to us by a full-hipped young serving woman. She had brought jugs of mulled wine, and the men-at-arms were downing it fast. I leaned across to Rhys, and warned him no one was to get drunk.

I got a few sour glances as my command went down the table, but the pace of consumption slowed. I let my gaze wander the room for the dozenth time. No one was paying us particular attention, which was something. There was still no sign of Bertolf, which I liked not at all.

As if he had heard a summons, he appeared in the doorway. His face was closed, nervous. My heart sank, and I nudged de Béthune's foot under the table. Bad news, I mouthed.

Bertolf went to bow as he reached the table, and then remembered. Stiffly, he bent his head to show respect. The king smiled. 'Take a seat, lad.'

Rhys shoved up a little so Bertolf could perch on the end of the bench.

We were all staring at him, aware that our fate was balanced on a knife edge.

'Well?' I demanded, quiet but forceful.

'Give him some mulled wine,' said Richard, courteous as ever.

'My thanks.' Bertolf gulped down a mouthful, then placed the cup on the rough wooden table. 'It is not good out there.'

We listened in grim silence. Friesach was full of soldiers, scores of them, and they were systematically searching every inn and tavern. All the stables in the town were also being visited.

'Who is their master?' I asked.

'Friedrich of Pettau, one of Duke Leopold's leading barons,' said Bertolf.

'Leopold, eh?' The king chuckled sourly. 'He would give much to lay his fat little paws on me.'

'They are hunting for any man who speaks French. And more specifically' – Bertolf lowered his voice – 'for the king of England.

The reward is twenty gold pieces. I heard that in two different places.'
Ashamed by what he had had to tell us, he buried his face in his cup.

Richard snorted. 'I am worth only twenty pieces of gold?'

His attempt to lighten the mood sank like a stone. Scarcely a man in Christendom would pass up a reward of that size.

I glanced at de Béthune, wondering if the same thing was in his head as in mine. A fellow knight, William de Préaux, had given himself into captivity in Outremer so the king might escape.

'You cannot be taken, sire. You *must* not be,' said de Béthune. 'I will not let it happen.'

He *had* come to the same conclusion. Quickly, I said, 'Nor will I, sire. You must go at once, with just a few companions. The rest of us will serve as sacrificial lambs.'

'I like this not at all,' Richard growled. 'Abandoning my men in Udine was bad enough. Now this . . .'

'It is either that, or we are all taken, sire,' urged de Béthune. 'From what Bertolf has said, it will not be long ere soldiers walk through that door yonder. We will not fight our way free again.'

The king said nothing, for the pork stew had arrived and, with it, fresh bread. We attacked the food like dogs that had not eaten for days. Richard wolfed his down. As he muttered between mouthfuls, it would be better to have a full belly on the road than not.

De Béthune frowned at me, and whispered from the side of his mouth, 'You go. I will stay.'

'One of us has to accompany the king. It should be you,' I stubbornly replied. I did not wish to leave the king's side, but the burden of what I had done in Udine hung round my neck like a lead weight. Sacrificing myself would perhaps go some way towards lightening the burden.

Richard wiped his mouth, and stood. 'Bertolf, you will serve as interpreter. Henry Teuton can translate for Baldwin. William,' he said to de l'Etang, 'I wish you to come also.'

Bertolf and William looked pleased. They got to their feet.

My breath caught in my chest. He was not going to leave me behind, surely?

'Baldwin, Rufus, Robert, Anselm,' said the king, his attention moving to Rhys and the others. 'All of you are dear to me. I will never forget this thing you do for me.'

There were tears, suddenly, in more than one man's eyes. I wiped mine away savagely. 'Sire, I –'

'Stay, Ferdia.' The king did not often call me by my given name.

'Yes, sire.' I studied the tabletop, unwilling to meet his gaze. 'May God watch over you.'

There was a muffled sob. It was Anselm, bless him.

My heart beat an unhappy pattern against my ribs. Then, flayed by guilt that I had not seen Richard leave, I looked up. Rhys was staring hard at me. Alarmed by an urgent roll of his eyes to our left, I turned my head slowly, studying the customers.

First, I noticed a fat man, supping greedily from a tankard. Not him. His comrade, as thin as the other was stout, was holding forth about something. Not him. Two men with scarred arms and in leather aprons, smiths or metalworkers, guffawed at something one had said. Not them. My attention lingered on a weasel-faced youth without a drink, but then I saw his arm, covered by a cloak, with only the tips of his fingers showing, moving close to the purse on his unseeing neighbour's belt. A cutpurse, I thought, not caring at all.

A *pssst* from Rhys, and I followed his gaze.

All I caught was a man's back as he went out the door.

'What?' I demanded.

'He was watching the king like a hawk as they went outside,' muttered Rhys. 'He stood there for a few moments, as if unable to make up his mind, and then followed them.'

I was on my feet before he had finished. I swept up my cloak.

De Béthune gave me a questioning look.

'The garderobe calls,' I lied. I bent to Rhys's ear. 'You stay.'

He gave me a mulish glance I knew only too well.

'We cannot all go with the king,' I whispered.

'Then I will follow you, alone.'

'Do not,' I hissed. 'I am ordering you, as your liege lord.'

His response was a black scowl that would have made a baby cry. I gripped his shoulder, to show him how much I cared, and said quietly, 'We will meet again, as God is my witness.'

As I walked to the door, I heard de Béthune talking loudly in French, and Anselm doing the same. They were drawing attention to themselves, to improve the chances of Richard leaving unnoticed. A lump swelled in my throat. There was no way of knowing if I would see any of them again, my comrades and friends, or Rhys, my constant companion these past thirteen years. He was more than that in reality, the younger brother I had never had, and now I was abandoning him.

I pulled the door wide. I used the gust of cold air that hit to sharpen my mind, to put aside my heartache. The king was in danger, and not just from Friedrich's soldiers. Down the corridor I went, light on my feet, and slipped through another door into the darkened courtyard. There was no one close by. From the open door of the stables came a dim yellow light. I spied Richard and William and, a moment later, Bertolf leading a horse. A stable lad was with them, nodding, and handing over a pair of bulging sacks. Barley, I thought. They were about to leave.

My eyes flickered around the courtyard, searching every nook, every shadow. In an angled corner between the inn and the next building, I saw a cloaked figure. He was looking intently at the stables. Unsure whether this was the man Rhys had seen, and if indeed he had realised who Richard was, I vacillated. My slaying of the youth in Udine had been self-defence. This would be as cold-blooded as Henry's murder in Southampton.

The king led his horse outside. William was right behind him. Bertolf came out last, his horse throwing its head up and down in evident unhappiness.

The man tensed, and then he was moving, towards the gate that gave onto the street.

I waited until he was just out of sight, and then I was after him like a sight hound on a hare. Never had I run so fast, so lightly, nor placed my feet with such care.

'Rufus?' I heard the king say.

I paid no heed. Out into the street I went. Praise God, there was no one else in sight, apart from my quarry. I bounded after him. I could not move in complete silence; he spun in alarm as I drew close.

'*Der König?*' I asked, praying that he reacted.

Shock burst across his face. He nodded.

My dagger rose high.

His mouth opened. He stumbled back a step.

In my mind's eye, I saw the pale, smooth cheeks of the youth I had killed in Udine. I saw Henry's eyes, wide with fear, as Rhys held him ready for the slaughter.

'*Nein, bitte,*' pleaded the man.

I punched him in the belly and, as he fell, I smacked him behind the ear with my dagger hilt, hard. He landed on the cobbles and did not move.

I ran back to the entrance.

Richard was emerging onto the street. His horse flicked back its head, alarmed by my rapid arrival out of the darkness. He tightened the reins. 'Rufus?'

'Yes, sire,' I said, panting. 'That man was going to raise the alarm.'

'You stopped him.'

'Aye.' I prayed I had not killed him.

'Faithful heart, thou art.'

'Sire?' I whispered.

'Get your horse, Rufus.'

And so, in the end, there were four of us.

CHAPTER V

My memory of the three-day, almost one hundred and fifty-mile ride that followed soon became hazy and hard to recollect. One thing I knew, though. One thing was clear. The ordeal was certainly equal and perhaps even worse than the ride to Gorre, almost ten years before. In fairness, the weather was not as bad: it snowed only a little. On the way to Gorre we had had to ride through blizzards. The roads were in better repair too. It was the unrelenting hours in the saddle that hit me the hardest. I was used to riding (not like Richard, placed on a horse's back before he could walk) and I had many years of experience. Never, though, had I ridden for three days and nights, not stopping for supplies, and with only brief periods of rest. By the end of it, my rear end was blistered almost as if I had been burnt by fire. William and I bitched to each other throughout, which helped us to cope. Poor Bertolf, no horseman, was in far worse shape, but he bore up well. Youth was on his side.

How the king did it defied belief. I believe it was through sheer force of will that he mastered his illness and his fever-wracked body. The price was the loss of his usual persona. A husk of a man, he rode when it was time without complaint. He ate when I gave him a mouthful of the little food we had, drank when I handed him a costrel, lay down to rest when I did. But he did not speak unless addressed, and only replied with the bare minimum of words. He hunched in the saddle, stoop-shouldered as an ancient, face hidden by the cowl of his cloak, and a death-grip on the reins. He paid no attention to our surroundings. On level ground where the going was easier, he slept as we rode.

Concern for his health, his very life, nipped at me constantly, but we had committed ourselves. To stop, to go back, would make matters worse. We would end up captives, like de Béthune, Rhys and the rest.

We could only go on, praying, hoping that we evaded capture and that the king's constitution could take the punishment.

When the tracks permitted, William and I went on either side of Richard, to catch him if he fell. I watched over him like a mother, helping him to dismount, hand-feeding him, supporting the cup as he drank. I tucked him in his blankets at night as tenderly as I might have done my own child, sitting close by long after he had fallen asleep. When William forcefully insisted that we took turns at playing sentinel, I lay down, but any rest I got was poor and fitful.

Past the castle at Forchenstein we went, and around the town of Neumarkt. North-west, circumnavigating Teufensbach to ford the River Mur, before the energy-sapping effort of having to cross the same waterway, more forceful, opposite a shrine dedicated to Mary Magdalen. I fell in, saving Richard from doing so, and swam the rest of the way holding onto my horse's tail. We stopped to give thanks in the church. Thankfully it was deserted, allowing me, blue-lipped and teeth chattering, to strip and don dry clothing. We entered the Mürz valley, went by Judenberg, the town of the Jews, and then over a broad plain that culminated with a long, sweeping descent. There we reined in, numbed, starving, and if I admit it, close to despair.

God only knew how long we could have kept it up. If I hazarded a guess, a single day more would have seen all of us succumb to complete exhaustion. As I stared, dazed, at the town below, perched on the banks of a broad river, all I wanted to do was lie down on the frosty ground and sleep for a month.

William broke the silence. 'Where are we?' he asked through sore, cracked lips.

I came back to the present, but my mind was fuzzy with tiredness. 'I have no idea.'

Richard made no answer; he was half asleep.

William eyed Bertolf. 'Do you know?'

'By the size of the waterway, sir, it must be the Danube.'

'Which means the town is . . .' I did not dare say it.

'Vienna, sir – I think.'

William grinned at me; I found the energy to do the same back. We were not out of danger by any means, but we had achieved much.

'And the border with Moravia, how far is it?' asked William. Wladislaw, Moravia's ruler, was no friend to Heinrich or Leopold.

'If that is Vienna, sir,' said Bertolf, 'less than fifty miles, or so I have been told.'

'Fifty miles?'

Startled by Richard's voice, William and I glanced at the king. 'Yes, sire,' I said, heartened by his clear eyes. God willing, I thought, his fever had broken.

'We can cover that by tomorrow evening, for certes,' declared the king. He swayed then, and would have fallen had William not kneed his mount forward and reached him with a steadying hand.

Any doubt that I had had about our need to stop for the night vanished. William, supporting the king, knew it too. 'You would wear us out, sire,' I said, my tone light. 'And the horses are very nearly spent. If they are to carry us to the border, they need rest and a good feed of oats.'

Richard did not hear. His energy expended by the short interaction, he had again closed his eyes. A sweat sheen marked his brow and his sunken-in cheeks. He looked like a corpse sitting in the saddle.

My fresh-risen spirits plummeted. 'The border might as well be a thousand miles away,' I said. 'He needs a bed, and medicine and food. Now.'

'Aye,' said William heavily. 'We must brave the lion's den, and pray he does not notice.'

If this was Vienna, we were about to enter Duke Leopold's capital.

'I would prefer to send Bertolf ahead first, scouting' – I lowered my voice to a whisper – 'but the king is fading. If we do not urgently see to his care . . .'

William gave me a grim nod.

'Lead on, Bertolf,' I said.

We urged our horses down the slope.

Bertolf's guess was correct; a shouted question at a peasant chopping wood revealed the nearby town to be Vienna. It proved to be further than it had looked from the slopes above and, with midwinter close upon us, time was not on our side. Shadows were lengthening, and the red-orange ball that was the sun had dipped to the western horizon as we rode into a village some distance from the walls. Ertpurch, it was called.

'I do not want to enter another town in darkness,' I said sidelong to William.

'Nor I.'

'Bertolf, let us find accommodation here, if we can.'

'Of course, sir.' The youth, by now a trusted companion, grinned. Whether it was because of his inexperience – to my mind, he had not the knowledge or wisdom to know quite how much danger we were in – or just his character, he had remained cheerful throughout our ordeal.

He enquired at a forge and came back with the news that a widow woman living in the next alley rented out a room to paying customers. With it being so close to Christmas and Vienna's market in full swing, the smith had said, the room might be taken, but it was worth a try. If she had space, we could use the stable buildings behind the forge for our horses.

Our luck was in.

Beady-eyed though the widow was at first, her manner changed once she had six silver pennies in her grimy hand, and her sympathy came to the fore when she spied the condition of the king. While William took the horses back to the forge, the widow hurried us inside, clucking over us like a mother hen. Bertolf and I carried him through the dirt-floored front room, lit by a few tapers, and into the back. The rough-plastered chamber was not large, and it had only a single pallet, but it was out of the weather, and there was a fireplace. It had no window but, after what we had been through, it felt like a royal palace.

'*Danke schön*,' I said, doing my best to sound with two words like Bertolf or Henry Teuton. The less she knew of us, the better.

She gave me a toothless smile and babbled away in German as she fetched a handful of rush tapers and a few threadbare blankets. I nodded and smiled, pretending I understood. I was undone when she finished with a question. Busying myself with laying the king on the bed, I pretended not to hear. Thankfully, Bertolf heard, and answered. The old woman disappeared and, a moment later, I heard pots clattering.

'She has little food, but will cook some soup,' said Bertolf. 'If we pay extra.'

I snorted. 'Six silver pennies for the night, and she wants more for some watery broth?'

'I will have your soup if you do not want it,' said Bertolf.

'No!' I shot back, relieved to be smiling at last.

It was the kind of remark Rhys would have come out with, and my heart twinged. Maybe I should have told him to come with us, I thought, discounting the idea in the same instant. Four of us, three well-armed and richly dressed, attracted enough attention as it was. A fifth man, obviously a soldier, would have increased the risk even further. Hard though it was to bear, my duty to the king came before my responsibilities towards Rhys. It was not as if I had abandoned him, wounded on the battlefield, I told myself. He was in captivity, it was true, but he was alive.

That made me feel no better.

The old woman's cooking was dire. In truth, no one could make a flavoursome soup out of beets and turnips, but three days with almost nothing to eat meant it and the stale barley bread that it came with were as welcome as a haunch of roasted venison. Even Richard ate a bowlful, and seemed a little improved by the warmth of it in his belly. He fell asleep again the moment he lay back on the bed.

'You must go out for medicine,' I said to Bertolf.

Always more cautious than I, William gave me a dubious look. 'I doubt a hamlet such as this will have an apothecary.'

'Then he must go into Vienna.' My reply, shot through with concern, was sharp.

'The risk —'

'Is worth it,' I hissed. 'The king is ill!'

William's eyes went to Richard, lingered, and came back to mine. 'Aye. You are right.'

'What shall I buy?' asked Bertolf, ever eager to please.

'Oxymel,' I said, remembering the medicines prescribed by the surgeons time and again with the king's illnesses. 'Galingale, black hellebore, if you can find it, and columbine.'

'Wood sorrel is good for fever,' said William.

'Cinquefoil too, according to the monk who ran the infirmary at the monastery,' Bertolf added.

'Buy whichever of them you find, and all, if you can. We need blankets too, enough for the four of us. And food.' Stomach already growling again, I reeled off a long list of my favourites.

Bertolf's expression grew worried.

'Rufus is fooling with you,' said William with a chuckle. 'The medicines and the blankets are the most important things. Bread, cheese, cured meat – simple things like those will quell our hunger well enough.'

Serious-faced, Bertolf repeated back the medicines, word for word. 'Also blankets, bread, cheese, cured meat,' he said, adding almost every delicacy I had mentioned.

'You have an impressive memory,' I said, laughing. 'But I spoke in jest about those things. The foodstuffs William told you will be sufficient.'

He nodded, and I handed him a pouch of gold bezants. 'Find a moneychanger to change those – do not get cheated, mind! The coins will mark you as someone returning from the Holy Land. Make sure you have answers to any questions.'

'I shall be the servant of a merchant returning from Acre,' said Bertolf, who had heard the story of the king's first assumed identity.

'Good,' I said.

'Hugo of Normandy,' said Bertolf.

'Do not give away his name, unless you have to,' I warned.

'One of us should go with him,' said William. Quietly, in rapid French, he said to me, 'One slip of the tongue, one false move, and he could bring Leopold's men down on us.'

'I know,' I said, hating how his words made my stomach churn, 'but neither of us can speak German well enough to pass scrutiny. He has a better chance of going unnoticed on his own.'

William nodded reluctant acceptance.

We gave Bertolf a last warning to be careful. He went off grinning, wrapped in his cloak, with a firm grip on the purse underneath.

I shut the door as firmly as it would allow, wishing it were more robust and could be locked. As it was, a decent kick would take it off its hinges, but there was nothing to be done about it. I told myself no one knew we were here, that we were safe.

William sat on the floor, wrapped in his cloak, and whether he meant to or not, dropped off at once. Richard was also asleep, mercifully. After setting a fire in the hearth, I perched on a rickety stool in front of the weak flames. I was bone-weary, eyelids drooping with exhaustion, and yet determined that one of us should remain awake to protect the king. My valiant efforts worked for a time, but in the end, I could no more stop myself from dozing off than push water up a hill.

The rasping scrape of the door coming open roused me in full alarm. I leaped up, half dragging out my sword before I realised it was Bertolf entering. Over his shoulder, I spied the old woman but, to my relief, no one else. I twisted away from her, sliding my blade back into the scabbard, hoping she had not seen my violent reaction. The king had not even stirred, and William – on his feet, dagger in hand – was out of her line of sight, which was fortunate. I shut the door on her, smiling and nodding my thanks, and aware that she had probably heard us speaking French. More coin was called for, I decided. Abjectly poor as she was, a dozen silver pennies would seal her lips until we were long gone.

The sacks Bertolf was carrying clinked promisingly; a bundle of blankets tied with lengths of twine hung from one shoulder. He was beaming from ear to ear, pleased as an archer who has hit the target's centre from two hundred and fifty paces.

'I got all the medicines you asked for, sir, and more besides,' he said, laying down his sacks and producing bottle after stoppered bottle. 'Oxymel, lots of it. Columbine. Black hellebore – that was even more expensive than the rest – and wood sorrel. Cinquefoil. I bought some aqua vitae too, on the recommendation of the apothecary. One of the best treatments for fever, he said.'

I had not the heart to say that he had seen Bertolf coming from a mile off, but busied myself giving the king several mouthfuls of oxymel and wood sorrel; according to Bertolf, this was what the apothecary had advised to start with.

This done, my attention returned to Bertolf. 'Were you questioned much? By the moneychanger, the apothecary or the shopkeepers?'

He gave me a confident smile. 'Nothing more than you would expect, sir. I told them all the same thing, that my master was a merchant, Hugo.' His expression grew a little embarrassed. 'That name slipped out a couple of times.'

I was disappointed but not overly surprised. Guileless, young, thrilled by the responsibility given him and the weight of gold in his purse, Bertolf would have been walking the streets seven feet tall. 'And Normandy,' I said, hoping he had had enough wit to keep this detail to himself, 'did you mention that?'

A flush crept over his downy cheeks. 'Once, to the apothecary.'

'Bertolf!'

'I am sorry, sir. He did not believe I could afford the things you asked for, you see. I was trying to prove that my master was wealthy and important. It just came out.' He hung his head.

My gaze went to William, who gave me a there-is-nothing-we-can-do-about-it-now shrug. 'Set it from your mind. It is of no matter, likely enough,' I said, hoping I was right. 'What about soldiers?'

'The streets are heavily patrolled.' He flashed an impudent grin. 'I was not stopped even once.'

That was something at least, I thought. 'Are they looking for the king?'

Bertolf's smile weakened. 'Yes, sir. I heard one sergeant ask another if he had heard or seen anything of the Lionheart.'

'How did he answer?'

'That he had not, but it would only be a matter of time. The net is closing, he said. If and when the king reaches Vienna, he will be found.' Bertolf looked unhappy. Then he brightened. 'But we are outside Vienna, sir. God willing, they will not search beyond the town walls.'

'Let us pray they do not.'

William muttered his agreement, and drew closer to the end of the bed, where Bertolf had begun to lay out the food he had bought. Concerns drowned out by my own reawakened hunger, I marvelled at the magnificent array. There were loaves of white bread, a stack of fresh oatcakes wrapped in cloth. Little round cheese tarts, and herbed fish pies. Crystallised fruits and spiced almonds. Honey tarts with almond custard. To wash it all down, he had purchased two costrels of decent Rhenish wine.

'You did well,' I said to Bertolf. 'Very well.'

I did not bother asking the old woman for crockery. Nor did William.

When the king woke a short time later, he was also cheered by the feast and ate enough to keep me happy. He promptly fell asleep again. Bertolf and William retired soon after; I gladly prepared to do the same.

Wrapped in blankets, I lay on the floor with my back against the door, content as I could be. Our food would last a short while, and if we could avoid detection each time Bertolf went out, Richard could recover here for several days. It would tempt fate to stay any longer, William and I had agreed. We had not yet discussed – I suspect because it was too uncomfortable – what we would do if the king's condition did not improve.

Exhausted, I had not the strength to think on it further.

Instead I let sleep take me.

CHAPTER VI

I dreamed of prison. Of a dungeon, in which I found myself incarcerated not with the king, but Rhys. A small, dank chamber, walled and floored with stone, and only a tiny window for light, I remember it reeked of piss and worse. Our gloating gaoler was Henry, the man-at-arms I had murdered; his helper was the beardless youth I had slain in Udine. From time to time, FitzAldelm came to gloat. He spat in my food, or threatened me, or beat Rhys, while I, held back by the drawn sword of one of his henchmen, watched in helpless fury. He laid not a hand on me, because he said the king wanted me whole and unharmed when I went to the executioner's axe.

FitzAldelm delighted in announcing that I was finally going to pay for the killing of his brother. When I protested truthfully that Guy had attacked me first, he laughed in my face, saying that the word of a lying Irish mongrel could never be trusted. Uncaring of my fate, I lunged at him, and was beaten to the floor by his laughing men.

'Curse you, FitzAldelm!' I roared.

'Rufus?'

I came awake in a heartbeat, realised that I was in the widow's backroom, not a cell. The hard floor beneath me was beaten earth, not stone. I leaned up on an elbow. 'Sire?'

'You cried out. Are you well?' He also spoke in a whisper, mindful of William and Bertolf, who slumbered on, oblivious.

'A nightmare, that is all, sire. How do you feel?'

'Weak as a kitten.' Darkness could not conceal his rueful tone, nor the relief in his next words. 'My fever is gone, let us hope for good.'

'God grant it be so, sire,' I said, with much feeling. 'Are you thirsty?'

'As we were at Arsuf,' he answered, coughing.

I scrambled up and gave him a beaker of water. I had set it and a jug by the head of his bed earlier.

He drank it down, and another, then handed the empty beaker back with a murmur of thanks.

I waited, in case he wanted anything else.

'You spoke a name, Rufus. Cried it out.'

My heart raced like that of a hooked trout. 'Did I, sire?'

'I did not hear it well, being mostly asleep, but if I had to guess, you said, "FitzAldelm".'

'I do not remember, sire.' Never had I been gladder to have the gloom conceal my expression. 'It was one of those unsettling dreams that you cannot recall – you know the type.'

He made a little hmmm sound, as a man does when thinking.

I kept my mouth shut, and prayed he said no more about it.

To my considerable relief, he fell asleep soon after.

I was not granted the same mercy. I lay on the floor and brooded, not about the youth in Udine – he had tried to kill me, after all – but Henry, whom I had murdered. Despite all my efforts to forget him, all the feats of arms I had done in God's name in Outremer, still he came to haunt me. I could live with it, I decided, as I had before. Henry was not real, and FitzAldelm was not here to make threats. The risk that I might find myself in a dungeon with William and the king was far more real.

That sour-as-curdled-milk thought kept me awake for a long time.

I had not long been asleep, or so it seemed, when William was shaking my shoulder. I regarded him through eyes gritty with tiredness. 'What is it?'

'The king wishes to use the chamber pot.'

The three of us bundled into the widow's living area, William shutting the door behind us so Richard might have privacy. She gave us a gummy smile, and asked something in German. Bertolf's reply seemed to satisfy her, for she resumed brushing the floor with a twig broom.

'She wanted to know how our master is,' Bertolf explained.

'He seemed a lot better in the night,' I said.

'Aye, and that state continues. He has already eaten well this morning, and wants more,' said William. 'Bertolf is to go out for cheese soon.'

I sighed. 'That is not what we agreed.'

'I did my best,' said William. 'You try and tell him otherwise.' 'Him' meant Richard.

That was a hiding to nothing, I decided, and there could be little risk in Bertolf visiting one shop. I glanced at the window; full daylight was still a way off. 'What time is it?'

'More than an hour after prime, I would guess,' said William.

'Best that Bertolf go now, while few people are about.'

And so it was agreed. Bertolf was gone and back by the time the church bells were tolling tierce. He was even cockier than the day before, declaring that the streets of Vienna were quiet, and that in the falling snow no one had even given him a second glance. He had disobeyed my orders, though, returning with honeyed pastries and almond wafers as well as cheese. Richard's eyes lit up when he saw the sweetmeats, and my scolding of Bertolf was therefore half-hearted.

Happily, the king seemed to be well on the way to recovery. He rose from his bed during the day, and insisted on helping the widow with her chores. Delighted, chattering away to him in German, with Bertolf interpreting, she had him slicing cabbage and onions. It amused me and William greatly.

'I would love to tell her that she has the king of England as her drudge,' I said.

'And I.' William jerked his chin. She was showing Richard that he was not cutting the onion finely enough. 'Do you think she would still chide him so?'

I snorted with amusement. 'She would die of fright, more like.'

'He is enjoying it,' said William.

'Simple tasks and honest labour are good distractions from more weighty concerns.'

'True, although I think the attraction would soon pall. Can you see him doing that every day?'

'No,' I said, smiling. 'And if he continues to improve, I cannot see him staying much longer.'

My hunch was correct. That evening Richard declared he wanted to leave the following day. Only after William and I had begged him did he agree to one more night under the widow's roof.

The next morning was even colder than the previous one. Bertolf was to go out again, for we were short of fresh bread, and I wanted more cinquefoil for the journey. It was the drug that had worked best on reducing the king's fever, and I had decided the risk of visiting the apothecary was less than that of Richard falling ill as we rode for Moravia.

Bertolf bundled himself up in cloak and mantle, and promised again to be careful and not to talk to anyone. Richard was dozing and, judging it safe to leave him in the widow's care, I went across to the forge, where William was seeing to our horses. We worked in stalls alongside each other, currying coats and manes in companionable silence. It was warm in the stable, the air laden with a pleasant fug of hay, horses and dung. A pair of scrawny cats watched us from an overhead beam. Outside, I could hear the ting, ting of a hammer and, by times, a whoosh as red-hot iron was plunged into the cooling trough.

'Do you think we will succeed?' I asked, pitching my voice low. We were alone, but I wanted no one to hear French. The old woman knew, and that was enough.

'In reaching the border with Moravia?'

'Aye.'

'A few days ago, I would have said no.' William regarded me over his horse's back. 'Now I am beginning to think that we just might.'

We grinned at one another. I thought guiltily of Rhys, de Béthune and the rest, and hoped that they would soon be ransomed.

Bertolf had not returned by the time we crossed the alley to the widow's house, which I thought was a little odd. I said as much to William, and we agreed that he had probably gone on another spending spree. So complacent had I become that as I went through my gear, my thoughts were on the type of sweet pastries he might have purchased.

William went out to the tiny back yard; he had promised to chop firewood for the widow. Richard was sitting on the bed with his back against the wall, running a whetstone along his sword.

'I wonder when I will next wield this in battle,' he said wistfully. 'God's legs, but we had a fine time in Outremer, eh?'

I caught his eye, and smiled. 'We did, sire.'

So many things were etched forever in my memory. Landing on the beach at Acre to the tumultuous welcome of the Christians. Rhys's crossbow duel with Grair. Our massacre of thousands of Muslim prisoners. The burning-hot march south, when we were assailed by the Saracens from sunrise to sunset. The dust, the cursed dust that

66

got everywhere. The constant, tongue-swelling thirst. The numbers of dead men and horses we left unburied in our wake. The fighting – at Acre, at Arsuf, at Joppa, in the hinterland near Jerusalem – with Richard leading us throughout, often when the odds were completely, madly, against us.

And Joanna, there would always be golden-haired Joanna. My very core melted even to think of her. I had first been captivated by the king's sister in Sicily, and it was there that I lost my heart to her, and won my first kiss too. In Outremer, our affair had blossomed fully; I had become the lover of a queen. A pang of sorrow, of deep loss, pierced me; I could not help but bodily wince. I would have lived the rest of my life as we had, given everything I owned to keep it so. Even my friendship with the king would not have been too high a price to pay.

It was not to be. Could never have been.

A mere knight cannot wed a queen, still less one who is sister to the king of England. Joanna was gone, and although I might see her again when we returned to Normandy and Aquitaine, she would never be mine again. A woman of her stature, still in the prime of her life, was a valuable pawn. Richard had never spoken of possible matches; it was a dagger to my heart even to imagine her married to a man she did not know, let alone love. I had refused to think about her wedding before. I had told myself that my service to the king was all that mattered. Now, suddenly, I could not put her and her fate from my mind.

'Rufus?'

My gaze came back into focus, on Richard's face. It was a shock to find that part of me hated him in that moment. If our roles were reversed, I thought, I would let you marry her, and damn the consequences.

'Ferdia?'

'Sire?'

'You are sad, as I am. You also wish that we had stayed in Outremer, and finished the task we began.'

No, I wanted to say. I care nothing for Saladin and Jerusalem. I love Joanna. I care only about Joanna.

He took my silence for agreement. 'One day we will return, Rufus, you will see. Once we win free of this quagmire and get back to

England, I will soon set things right. Johnny will come fawning to my side, as he always does, and his supporters will crawl back to their holes. We shall cross the Narrow Sea and deal with Philippe after – he may prove trickier to deal with, but I cannot see us being delayed for more than a year, a year and a half at the most.'

Sick to my belly, I nodded as if convinced. He will see through me, I thought. Even after long practice, I found it hard to assume the inscrutable expression that was second nature to the king.

Luckily for me, Richard's passion for the war in Outremer had taken over. He went off on a long diatribe, waxing lyrical about the massive army he would assemble. There would be none of the mistakes made during our previous sojourn. Jerusalem would fall within a year of our arrival, he declared.

I will stand beside you every step of the way, I thought. As his sworn man, such was my duty. My love for Joanna had to be set aside, agonising though that was. My eyes came back to Richard; he was pacing about the room, talking and gesticulating. My heart rose a little; it was impossible not to love his spirit, his appetite for life.

A heavy, repetitive noise from the alley sliced through my happiness with the swiftness of a falling blade. 'Sire!' I hissed.

He had not heard what I had, the tramp of feet. His expression grew puzzled. 'What is it?'

'There are men outside, sire. A lot of them.' I had a sick feeling in my gut.

His grip on his sword tightened, as it does when a man is about to go into battle. Then, a sad smile, a recognition of reality, and he laid it on the bed. 'Go and see, Rufus.'

'Sire.' I buckled on my belt. Pride would not let me appear unarmed, no matter what odds I faced. I strode from the room and met William entering from the yard, rusted axe in his hand.

His face was grim. 'You heard it too?'

'Aye.'

'What did the king say?'

'To see who it is.'

'I will come too.'

I gave him a proud look. An army might have faced us outside, but by Christ that would not stop us from facing it and, if necessary, dying in defence of the king.

The widow was already at her front door, eye pressed to a knothole. Gently, I tapped her shoulder. '*Soldaten?*' I asked.

Face twisted in terror, she nodded. She made no protest as I motioned her to step aside. My heart thumped as I bent to the knothole. I recoiled as my vision filled with a broad, mail-clad figure advancing on the door.

Bang, bang, bang. The timbers shook; motes of dust spun free, twisting in the air before me.

'*Wer ist da?*' I asked. Who is there?

'*Aufmachen, im Namen von Herzog Leopold!*' The door shivered beneath a fresh barrage of blows.

This was the worst possible news. I glanced at William. He nodded.

I undid the latch, and opened the door.

A blond-bearded knight about my own age stood on the threshold. He was wearing a black-and-white hatched surcoat over his hauberk, and had a sword belt around his waist. At least a score of men-at-arms stood behind him, all armed with crossbows. There was no sign of Bertolf, which was almost more worrying than if he had been present. He was a prisoner, of that I was sure, and had probably been tortured to reveal our location. There was no other explanation for this knight and his soldiers.

He glared at me. '*Wo ist der König?*'

'Do you speak French?' I asked in that tongue.

He frowned. 'A little, *ja.*'

'I speak almost no German.'

A stiff nod. 'Let us use French, then. Where is the king?'

For a heartbeat, I considered pretending that Richard was not within, but to do so would have been futile. 'He is inside,' I said.

'Bring him out.'

I stuck out my chin. 'Why?'

'I am here to arrest him.'

'Arrest?' I scoffed. 'He is the King of England!'

A hint of colour stained his cheeks. 'Nonetheless, I am commanded to arrest him and take him into custody.'

'On what charges?'

'The unlawful abduction of Isaac Comnenus of Cyprus and his daughter, the murder of Conrad of Montferrat and, not least, the insults offered to Duke Leopold at Acre.'

'Those charges are preposterous! On whose authority are they issued?' I demanded, although the answer was as obvious as the nose on the end of my face.

His lips thinned. He knew I was being obstructive just for the sake of it. 'Duke Leopold.'

I longed to punch the knight's teeth down his throat, to draw my sword and storm into the alley, cutting down every man in my path. It would have been a swift death, but a pointless one, so I swallowed my pride.

'Wait here,' I said through gritted teeth, and shut the door in his face. I half expected a booted foot to kick it in, and a tide of men-at-arms to come flooding in after. Nothing of the sort happened. Instead, I heard only a muffled question, from a subordinate perhaps, and an irritated reply from the knight.

'They are scared of the king,' I said, exchanging a proud look with William.

As I stalked past the widow, she whispered, her face awestruck, *'Der König?'*

'Ja,' I said, and she began to weep.

I went into our little chamber. Richard was waiting, his face calm, even serene.

'It is Duke Leopold's men?'

'Yes, sire. Twenty men-at-arms, led by a knight.' A desperate idea flashed into my mind. 'William and I can hold them; you could get away over the roof of the neighbouring house –'

He cut me off. 'It is over, Ferdia.'

My mouth opened.

'I am done with running.'

'Sire,' I said, feeling a horrid, creeping numbness.

'But I will not surrender to a mere knight.' Fire sparked from Richard's eyes. 'Let him fetch Leopold, and I will come out.'

The knight's beard positively bristled when I delivered the king's message. I relished every word, and took even more pleasure from closing the door in his face for a second time. He made no attempt to batter it down, instead ordering most of his men to remain where they were. A moment later, I heard horses moving through the alley.

In the time that followed, Richard combed his beard and donned his cleanest tunic and hose. He slipped the ruby ring we had shown Engelbert onto the middle finger of his left hand, and allowed me to strap on his belt. His boots had been polished by poor Bertolf the previous day. He wore no crown, and deep lines of tiredness marked his thin face, but he was as regal as he had ever been: tall, broad-shouldered and with a presence that even a blind man would notice.

When he emerged from our room, the widow, who had been waiting anxiously, fell to her knees and began kissing his feet. She was crying, and babbling in German. Richard was gentle with her; he bent and raised her up, saying in French that all was well.

'What is she saying?' he asked us.

She was still talking, a stream of words interspersed with sobs and tears.

William and I listened. After a moment, I said, 'I think she is apologising, sire, for making you chop her vegetables. She is asking your forgiveness. She had no idea you are a king.'

Richard smiled, and took one of the widow's little hands in both his massive ones. 'Madam,' he said.

Silenced, she brought her watery eyes up, tremulously, to his own.

'There is nothing to forgive, madam,' he said. 'It was a pleasure to stay in your house, humble as it is. *Danke. Danke.*'

Her chin wobbled; a fat tear ran down each lined cheek, but she nodded in some kind of understanding.

Satisfied, Richard had me peer out of the knothole. 'Well?' he demanded. 'Have they tired of waiting and left us?' He chuckled.

My field of vision was narrow, but I could see three men-at-arms. 'No, sire,' I said heavily.

'Come now, Rufus,' he said, his tone bright. 'Your arse at least must be grateful that we will no longer have to ride day and night. I know mine own is.'

I stared. His lips were twitching. I could not help but burst into laughter.

The king and William joined in, convulsed with mirth.

The poor widow looked on in complete bemusement.

The three of us retired again to our chamber and, at Richard's instruction, played dice on the bed. I had never seen the king gamble before;

he approached it with the same fierce competitiveness that he attacked life. Neither William nor I were surprised as he deprived us of first one, then two, three, six silver pfennigs each. I have no doubt that our losses would have continued had not Leopold arrived. There was no mistaking what was going on; the sound of horses and men, and the noise of a large crowd carried in from the street.

We went into the main room. The terrified widow cast us a look; there were fresh tears in her eyes. I reassured her as best I could, praying that my rudimentary German was sufficient to explain that Richard would insist Leopold did not punish her. I have no idea if she understood, but the weighty little purse I offered caused her eyes to dry at least.

The door reverberated to a pounding fist. '*König* Richard!' cried a voice.

'Open it,' the king said.

I obeyed, and the blond-bearded knight and I regarded each other for a third time. Over his shoulder, I spied Duke Leopold astride a fine charger. He had brought with him a further twenty men-at-arms, and a dozen knights. Beyond them was a large, excited mob; fingers were already pointing. I heard the word '*König*' passing from one person to another. Leopold had had the news announced, I decided. Our departure through Ertpurch would be a victory parade for him.

'Sir.' The blond-bearded knight stiffly inclined his chin.

I gave him the same courtesy. 'Duke Leopold is here, I see.'

He nodded, and said in French, 'Your king –'

I hesitated.

'– is here,' said a voice behind me.

Quickly, I moved aside, allowing Richard to step into the alley. The blond-bearded knight fell back, awe writ large on his face. He bowed deeply. The king paid him no heed, his gaze instead raking the men-at-arms and their levelled crossbows. Pride filled me; the majority bent their heads in respect and, but for the strangled, furious order of a sergeant, I judged most of their weapons would have been lowered towards the ground.

Leopold had dressed for the occasion. His fur-trimmed cloak and matching mantle were magnificent. Gems glittered from his ringed fingers; precious stones encrusted his belt and scabbard too. He was still possessed of a florid face, however, and, being short, had stayed on his horse to remain higher than Richard.

Their gaze met.

The king raised an eyebrow, managing to convey both majesty and contempt. 'We meet again, Duke Leopold.'

'King Richard.' Leopold offered a perfunctory dip of his head. 'It *is* you, albeit dressed like a brigand. I wondered if it could be true at first, but I should not be surprised. Your messenger boy sang like a canary.'

Fury flooded my veins. Although he concealed it well, Richard would be no less affected; he valued loyal service above nearly all else.

'You tortured Bertolf?' the king snapped. 'A child?'

'He is almost a grown man, and I would not say tortured,' said Leopold. 'Persuaded would be nearer the mark.'

'Harm him no more, please,' Richard said. 'I ask also that the widow in this house remains unpunished – she had no idea who I was.'

Leopold waved a hand. 'Granted. I have no use for either.'

'Why are you here?' asked Richard, bold and confident.

'To arrest you. Criminals must not go unpunished.'

Richard snorted. 'What criminal activity am I guilty of, pray tell?'

'You know full well, having imprisoned one kinsman of mine – Isaac Comnenus – and ordered the murder of another, Conrad of Montferrat.'

'Isaac got nothing more than he deserved, the faithless dog. He broke his agreement with me more than once, and his men used poison arrows on mine. Those are reason enough to treat him as I did. As for Conrad, well, any man who was in Outremer will tell you I had nothing to do with his death. The Assassins slew him, not I.'

'My jails are full of men who plead their innocence,' said Leopold. 'I suspect yours are the same.'

He and Richard stared at each other, neither willing to look away.

'Will you come freely?' asked the duke.

The king made no immediate answer, and the tension tightened several notches.

I placed myself at the king's right shoulder. William copied me on his left. It was a pitiful, defiant gesture – we two could not fight thirty, especially when our enemies had crossbows – but that would not stop us from defending our king if he gave the command.

'Peace, Rufus, William.' Richard's voice was pitched low. The tone of resignation in it hurt almost as much as a cut from a blade.

He addressed the duke. 'You are a man of honour?'

'*Ja*, I am.' The reply was assured.

Leopold is a proud man, I thought, taking in his upright posture and his stiff formality. If the king had not humiliated him so at Acre, we might not be here. At the end of the siege, Leopold had naïvely placed his standards on the battlements alongside Richard's and Philippe's. The king's response had been to order them thrown into the ditch. Leopold came storming to the royal pavilion soon after, demanding they be replaced, as well as a share of the booty. He had been granted neither, and all but ejected from Richard's presence. Soon afterwards, he had departed Outremer for home.

'I ask, then, that you offer Bertolf and my men also' – the king indicated me and William – 'the same honour I will be afforded.'

Leopold considered this request, then he nodded. 'So be it. They will be well treated.'

Unsheathing his sword and reversing it, Richard walked towards Leopold. He was not about to do anything stupid – I knew that – but that did not stop several of the duke's men from aiming their crossbows at him. My skin crawled. One slip of a nervous finger, and the king could be choking out his life's blood in this miserable alley.

Thank Christ, they held their nerve.

Richard offered his sword hilt first to Leopold, who accepted it with a nod. He passed it in turn to the blond-bearded knight.

'Guard that blade well,' Richard warned. 'I used it throughout my time in Outremer.'

The knight's bow had a great deal more respect than his master's. 'It will be well looked after, sire.'

William and I handed over our weapons. We were not harmed, but men-at-arms surrounded us. Whatever fantasy I had had of escape vanished, and my spirits dampened further.

Saddled horses were brought forward. The blond-bearded knight asked Richard if he would try to escape.

'For certes,' the king replied. 'Why would I not? You have no right to be my captor!'

'In that case, I have no alternative but to bind your wrists, sire,' the knight said reluctantly.

74

'That is your choice.' Richard held out his hands.

The knight looked to Leopold, who gestured coldly for him to continue.

'Let everyone present bear witness to this treatment of a man, a king who took the cross,' said Richard as his hands were bound. 'I fought in Outremer also, while he who gave the order for my arrest left, making no effort to take Jerusalem.'

Leopold's colour rose. 'I have been to war in the Holy Land twice!'

'I do not think your second visit really qualifies,' said Richard. The duke had departed immediately after his humiliating confrontation with the king, and missed the greater part of our campaign, the march south to Arsuf and Joppa, and our abortive journeys towards Jerusalem.

'Get him on the horse.' Leopold was clearly furious, but did not wish the argument to continue with an audience of several hundred.

There followed a moment of confusion. The king was now unable to mount by himself, something no one had anticipated. Neither William nor I had had our wrists tied yet; I muttered to him, and we stepped forward. Richard gave me a grateful look as I linked the fingers of one hand with the other. William went around the other side of the horse, in case our master fell. It was awkward – he had to lean his tied hands on the horse's neck while placing a foot into my cupped ones, and then leap up – but he managed it.

'If only this were Fauvel,' the king said quietly to me. 'I would take my chances, bound as I am.'

I nodded. His stallion, taken from Isaac Comnenus, was highly trained and could run like the wind.

William and I gave the blond-bearded knight the same answer as the king had, and had our own wrists tied. The knight sympathised with our position, I decided. He helped us to clamber onto our horses, checking after that we were secure in the saddle. This done, each of our steeds, which were fitted with halters and lead ropes rather than bridles and bits, was given into the care of a mounted knight.

There would be little to say about the misery of our ride to Vienna, the sides of the streets and roads thronged with people come to see the king of England, except for an odd thing that happened close to the city gate.

I had fixed my eyes on Richard – he was in front of the knight leading my horse – in order to ignore the curious, sometimes gloating faces to my left and right. Not a hundred paces from the gate, though, my horse took fright at a babe who cried out suddenly. It skittered to the left, and I had a job stopping myself from tumbling from its back. My gaze went skyward, left, right, down, before I regained my balance. Amid the confusion of images, I registered something familiar. My gaze returned to the crowd on my left.

Scarcely a face was turned towards me: they were all looking at the king, as might be expected. One was not, however: a man, cloaked and with a mantle pulled over his head. In its depths, I spied a pair of familiar sharp eyes, framed by equally familiar longish black hair. Rhys – it was Rhys! He gave me a nod; I gave him the slightest dip of my chin in reply, but dared do nothing else for fear of being seen. There was no time for anything more, and I did not turn around after I had ridden past.

A mixture of astonishment, relief and delight filled me. I forgot all about my order that Rhys should not follow me. I could not wait to tell the king.

There was no knowing what Rhys could do, but just knowing he was out there raised my spirits from the depths they had threatened to fall into.

With his help, escape might be possible.

CHAPTER VII

Dürnstein Castle, on the River Danube,
Austria, December 1192

I placed my back against the stone wall, pressing until the cold seeped through my tunic. I strode forward, my eyes now accustomed to the dimness. The small window let in plenty of cold air but little light. Our cell faced west, and the weather since our arrival had been overcast, louring clouds often wreathing the fortress from day's beginning to end. A dozen paces I went, to the far wall. I turned, placed my back against the wall there until I felt the chill again, and walked back whence I had come. Two hundred was the count I had reached in my head, but I felt I should have been at fifty times that already. This was the target I had set myself to complete twice daily. In all my life, I had never repeated such a boring task, so many times. There was nothing else on offer, however, other than sprawling on my straw pallet, as William was on his. The only other furniture was two stools, uncomfortable to sit on, and a bucket for life's necessary functions.

It suited William to doze for hours, but I found such lassitude a sure road to madness.

His silence afforded me yet more time to think. A rueful smile twisted my lips. It was all I did now, apart from sleep and pace the room.

It was early morning on the second day since our arrival, after a fifty-mile ride from Vienna. Immediately separated from the king, we had not seen him since. I had heard his voice echoing down the corridor not long after and, calling out before the guards stopped us, deduced that he was in the next chamber. We soon established that some of the guards were friendlier than others, and would allow us to talk to one another. My offer of coin – I had secreted a purse on a neck thong inside my clothing – helped to grease the wheels of their selective deafness.

The king's facilities were a good deal more luxurious than ours – he had a bed, a table and chairs, a fireplace and even wall tapestries – but, like us, was confined night and day. Our only visitors had been the servants who delivered our food morning and evening, watched over by silent, hard-faced guards, but Richard had received Hadmar of Kuenrig, castellan of Dürnstein and one of the duke's most loyal vassals, as well as Duke Leopold himself. The king had discovered from the former that Bertolf had been left in Vienna and, if Hadmar was to be believed, the lad was to be released after he recovered from his wounds.

The king's second meeting had gone less well. The shouting, from both Leopold and Richard, had had William and me side by side, our ears pressed flat to the door, listening. An arrogant glory hunter who thought himself better than everyone else, Leopold had called the king. Worse, he was an opportunistic thief who thought nothing of stooping to murder. This last was another, less-than-veiled reference to Conrad of Montferrat.

The king's response was volcanic. He lambasted Leopold as a jumped-up popinjay, a little man who sought to piggyback on the success of his betters. Where would he have been at the siege of Acre, Richard had mocked, if not for *his* artillery? Still proclaiming himself lord of a sandcastle, the king had jibed.

The savage truth of this final comment – it had been a common saying about Leopold in the Christian camp – had seen the enraged duke storm out of Richard's chamber and disappear down the corridor, yelling obscenities.

Knowing Richard's temper well, William and I made no immediate attempt to speak to him. After the storm, calm weather returns, and so it was with the king. A sympathetic guard was in place later that day, allowing conversation. Richard it was who broke the silence first. He was rueful, acknowledging that his anger had got the better of him, and that his outburst would win no favours from the duke. It was rare, indeed almost unheard of, for the king to make such a public admission. I hoped it did not mean his spirits were sinking, that his confinement was not already pressing in on him. I knew from previous experience – a week-long incarceration after my arrival at Striguil Castle, years before – how it could.

I had asked Richard if he knew what Leopold intended to do with him.

'No, Rufus,' he said, and only then had his weariness been audible. He had laughed quickly, though, and said more might have been forthcoming had he not driven Leopold into a rage.

We did not speak further of our fate, but one thing was plain. Richard's life was not in danger, because no one in their right mind would countenance regicide.

With Leopold bent on revenge, the king's freedom was not going to be easily won, yet simply incarcerating the king would yield nothing. Ransoming him, on the other hand, would earn the duke an enormous fortune. The king was adamant that William and I would be included in the negotiations, which was something to take heart from, and helped when I thought about the months it would take to raise the monies in England. The hard truth was that we were going to be captives for at least a year.

Against these grim realities, I had only Rhys – if he had managed to follow us to Dürnstein. It would take a miracle to free us from this impregnable stronghold, full of Leopold's soldiers, but with nothing else to hold onto, I pinned my hopes on Rhys, the most loyal of followers.

Christmas came and went, the day itself marked only by the sound of singing from the castle's chapel and, later on, a fine meal delivered to our room. It included, to my delight, a flask of good wine and a platter of still-warm roast goose. The king had been invited to join Leopold for the festivities, but had refused. Instead, we called out toasts to each other, and talked loudly about what we would do upon our return to his kingdom.

I wanted to mention Joanna during this conversation, but of course I could not. The closest thing was to ask the king about Berengaria, his queen, who had left Outremer with Joanna, two weeks before us. Their plan had been to land in southern Italy, and from there travel overland to Rome. The Alpine passes were not safe late in the year, and the territory on the western side of the mountains belonged to the Count of Toulouse, one of Richard's oldest enemies. It was therefore likely, the king said, that they would overwinter in Rome and continue their voyage in the spring. They would aim for Navarre, and from there travel onward to Aquitaine. It was not a journey without risk; even by sea, they would run the risk of capture, sailing along a coastline controlled by Toulouse.

The king seemed unconcerned. 'The chances of Berengaria and I both being taken captive is tiny,' he declared with a robust confidence that I struggled to share.

When our conversation was done, and it was time to retire for the night, bitterness took me. I lay on my pallet in the darkness, William's snores reverberating in my ears, thinking of Joanna. Even if she and Berengaria were taken prisoner, they would be ransomed, like the king. She would return to live in the royal court, like as not with Berengaria, for the two got on well. If I went there with Richard, having been released, the chance of rekindling our love would be slight, and life-threateningly dangerous. Joanna's reputation could not be risked against the value to Richard of a new, powerful husband for her, and ally for him. Never again would she be mine. Despite these hard, painful realisations, I could not put her from my mind, no matter how I tried.

I might as well remain in Dürnstein, I decided, and moulder. It was suitable punishment for what I had done to Henry, and the youthful cutpurse in Udine.

I did not let myself stew in this self-indulgent misery for long. My duty was to the king, as it had been these ten years and more. I had also sworn to Joanna that I would protect him with my very life. Powerless though I was, that duty had not changed, and I would do everything within my power to fulfil it. At the very least, I owed it to Richard to keep my morale high.

Ten days went by, one blurring into another. Night followed day, day followed night. William and I would call out good morning to the king, and smile at each other when his answer came loud and cheerful. Prayer came next; I found this hard, regarding myself damned, but joined in with William anyway, kneeling on the cold stone floor. God would accept my prayers, I told myself, offering up my contrition for the killing of the boy at Udine, and burying my unrepentance for the murder of Henry deeper than deep.

Our food came about the same time each morning, not long before the bells sounded tierce. Strange how a man's world can shrink down, making the arrival of bread and cheese one of the most anticipated moments of his day. William and I reminisced about our time in Outremer. Like all my friends and comrades, he liked to remind me of my near-death encounter with a Saracen warrior as I emptied my bowels outside the defences at Acre. In turn, I poked fun at him about his terrified reaction the time a scorpion had fallen out of a boot just as he went to put it on. We played dice for little lengths of straw plucked from our pallets. If the king wished to talk, we spoke with him. Otherwise I paced the room, back and forth, and as often as not William slept.

I remained on constant alert for the sound of footsteps in the passageway outside. Usually, it was just guards coming to relieve their fellows, but sometimes it was Hadmar, or a priest, or even Leopold, come to talk with the king. Then, God forgive me, I would do my best to eavesdrop on the conversation. William was no better; we had to play dice to see who won the best spot at the door. We never heard much, unless Richard lost his temper. After his argument with Leopold, that only happened once more, on New Year's Day. Hadmar it was who caught the brunt of the king's ire, because of the news he carried. Until this point, William and I had been listening in without success.

'Heinrich has done what?' Richard bellowed.

Hadmar's response was inaudible.

William and I stared at one another, wondering. It was inevitable that Leopold would inform his liege lord that he had captured the King of England. Heinrich's reaction was less predictable.

'The losenger! The paltoner! The caitiff! What did Heinrich say again?'

Hadmar spoke louder. 'We have thought it proper to notify Your Highness, knowing that these tidings will bring you most abundant joy.'

'It will indeed! Philippe will leave no stone unturned, will stop at nothing to keep me in captivity, do you understand? He would beggar himself to see it so!'

'Sweet Jesu,' I whispered. 'When Heinrich found out that Leopold had the king, he sent word to France.'

William grimaced. 'I imagine Philippe is still capering with glee.'

'And what does Leopold say about this, pray tell?' roared the king. 'For all his dislike, he cannot wish me put in a French dungeon and the key thrown away.'

'No, sire.' Hadmar's voice was placatory.

'Will he swear then not to hand me over to Heinrich?'

Hadmar answered more quietly this time.

'Nay, of course not, because the emperor is his liege lord!' thundered the king. 'Honour only ever goes so far with most men, I have found, and Leopold is no different!'

Hadmar's efforts to calm the king failed, and soon Richard insisted that he leave.

After his footsteps had died away I waited a short while, to allow the king's temper to ease, and then I asked him, heavy-hearted, if all was well.

His answering bark of laughter was bitter. 'Worse than I might have expected on the first day of a new year, Rufus. Philippe Capet knows I am here, and has expressed a keen interest in paying my ransom. I do not think it matters what price Leopold and Heinrich set: Philippe's hatred for me is such that he will meet it regardless, or even exceed it.'

'It will not come to that, sire, surely.' I hated the false ring to my words.

'I hope to Christ it does not,' said the king. 'You at least shall not share my fate – I will see to that.'

'No, sire! We will stay with you,' William and I cried, stricken.

'I see little point in three of us rotting in jail.'

'We have not come this far to be sent from your side, sire!' I cried. 'We are here for you, always.'

There was silence for a time, and then Richard began to laugh. 'Ah, Rufus, Rufus, my bull-headed Irishman, and you, William, stubborn to the last.' Voice full of emotion, he added, 'Truly, you are my best men.'

William and I grinned at one another like fools.

Life was strange. We were still captives. The prospect of release was uncertain, and possibly diminishing, thanks to the news about Philippe, but the king's recognition gave us fresh heart, buoyed us up like few other things could have.

The next morning, Richard was taken from his room by Hadmar and several guards. I hammered on the door until my fists were bruised, shouting to be allowed to join him, but to no avail. 'Do not harm him!' I screamed into the keyhole. 'Stay strong, sire!'

There was no answer. I sagged to the floor, hating my helplessness, wishing that I could do something, *anything*, for him.

'Where are they going, do you think?' William was no less miserable than I.

I had had no idea until that point. But then, cold clarity.

'Leopold is taking him to meet Heinrich,' I said. 'What better way of increasing Heinrich's greed than to show him the glittering prize?'

This suspicion proved correct. Two of the guards were gossiping outside our room later that day. William and I had enough German to piece together the gist of their conversation, laced as it was with references to '*König*', '*Löwenherz*' and 'Kaiser Heinrich'. I heard mention of a place too: Regensburg. According to William, it was a city to the north, close to the border with Heinrich's realm.

The information had me on my knees soon after, my prayers more fervent and genuine than they had been for some while. The thought of Richard being handed over to Heinrich and afterwards to Philippe while we languished in Dürnstein, impotent, was unbearable.

A dispirited evening followed. We spoke little, and ate less. I paced endlessly, until William, unable to sleep as he usually did, asked me to stop. I sat on my pallet instead, unable to relax, my mind awhirl. Unaware that I was jigging a foot to and fro on the flagstones until an irritated William cried that it was driving him mad, I snapped that his farting annoyed me, yet I had to live with it. I stood up and began pacing again, uncaring this time of his reaction.

I got little rest that night, too hot for the blankets, then too cold without them, unable to settle. When I did fall asleep, I was plagued by disturbing dreams. I saw Richard, manacled in a tiny, windowless cell, his long, matted beard evidence of long captivity. His jailors differed, sometimes Leopold, Heinrich, FitzAldelm or even Saladin. At times I was the prisoner, and a laughing FitzAldelm my captor. I spied Rhys in the background but, no matter how loud I shouted, he did not come to my aid. Joanna came to my cell, but I could not hear what she said. She left, looking distressed, and, bizarrely, Alienor was with her.

Dawn found me red-eyed and in a filthy mood. William was no better, and we ate our bread and cheese in morose silence. Our irritation with each other did not last long, though. We had been through too much for this to endanger our friendship. He ignored my pacing, and I said nothing about his farts. We joked, and diced, and promised ourselves that the king would return. Several days passed with no news. Then Leopold returned – we worked this out from eavesdropping on guards – but without Richard. My initial panic, that the king had been given over to Heinrich, was short-lived, Christ be thanked. He had been sent to another of Leopold's castles, although it was unclear why. The guards' German was too rapid, too guttural to understand, if they were even talking about why Richard had not been returned to Dürnstein.

I fought despair after that. Not since my incarceration at Striguil as a callow youth had I felt so powerless. I took myself away in my head to happier times, with Joanna mostly, but also scenes from my childhood in Ireland, rough and tumble with my brothers, and learning sword play from my father. I recalled meeting Richard for the first time, how he had saved me from a beating at the hands of Guy FitzAldelm and his cronies. I had saved the king's life a couple of years later, right after he had done the same for me, ambushed by brigands in the woods outside Southampton. There were so many good memories; I took heart. I could live on them, if need be, and my captivity would not last forever – nor would that of the king.

To receive welcome news after that felt like balm for the soul.

Castellan Hadmar came to see us, which was strange in itself. Apart from overseeing our arrival, he had had nothing to do with us. His reason soon became clear. We were to be transferred to a castle closer to Vienna, where we would be reunited with Richard. William and I hugged each other, almost as delighted as if we had been freed.

'Thank you, sir,' I said. 'We want only to be where our lord is.'

Hadmar nodded. Short and slight, with a thoughtful manner, he seemed an earnest type. 'I understand.'

'Why was the king not returned here?' I ventured.

He hesitated, and then said, 'The duke judged it too risky.'

I shot a look at William. 'Because of the emperor?'

Again a hesitation. 'Yes.'

'The meeting did not go well, then?'

'It did not.'

'Leopold feared that Heinrich might take the king from him by force?'

'Sadly, yes.'

'That is human nature,' I said, relieved beyond measure that Leopold had been prudent enough not to lose Richard to his liege lord. 'Why pay for something when you can take it for nothing?'

'Even so.' A rueful smile.

'Are we to stay in this new prison then?' I asked. 'Will Leopold talk to Heinrich again?'

'That is his plan.'

I tried a new tack. 'How does your master justify his base treatment of the King of England?'

'The king has been imprisoned because of the insults he made in Acre. He impugned not just Duke Leopold, but Austria itself.' Hadmar seemed annoyed by the memory.

'That is as maybe,' I countered, skirting around his pride. 'But Richard took the cross, and led an army to Outremer. He defeated Saladin, and won the right for all Christians to visit Jerusalem without hindrance. It is shameful that he should be kept prisoner, and sold off to the highest bidder!'

Hadmar squirmed like a fish on the hook.

I grew bolder. 'The duke risks eternal damnation for what he has done – he must know that. When Pope Celestine finds out . . .' Excommunication was the Church's most severe punishment, a condemnation to burn forever in Hell. The mere thought of it terrified most men, myself included.

Again Hadmar looked most uncomfortable. 'The duke would never wish to insult the Church so.'

'Then why is he keeping the king captive?' I crowed. 'Money – there can be no other reason.'

Rather than answer, Hadmar went to the door.

'You know I am right!' I cried.

'Do not anger him,' William warned me in an undertone. 'We must not jeopardise our chances of being sent to join the king.'

'He would not dare keep us here. Leopold has ordered us moved,' I said, full of confidence. Quietly, I added, 'Only a fool disobeys a direct command from his master.'

So it proved. The next morning we were escorted down to the courtyard, which was full of horses, knights and soldiers. There Hadmar informed us that we were to be taken closer to Vienna. It was a long ride, he explained.

Understanding his meaning, and wanting only to see the king, we promised not to try to escape. Pleased, he let us mount up, our hands unbound.

I was on the alert from the moment we emerged from the main gate. My keenness was rewarded when I spied Rhys, hooded as before, leaning against the wall of an alehouse. No one was paying me any attention, and I grinned at him. He flashed a smile, which broadened as I loudly mentioned our destination to William.

We were not alone.

CHAPTER VIII

On the road from Dürnstein to Vienna, Austria

Rhys could not engineer our escape, but he did manage to get close that day, when we halted to water the horses at a roadside inn. He had followed us, easy enough to do on the relatively busy road, and brought his mount to the trough while I was there with mine. Fortunately, our oath not to escape had been taken at face value, and the nearest soldiers were twenty paces off, and more interested in filling their bellies with the piping-hot sausages brought out by a servant boy.

'By God, it is good to see you,' I said, peering at my squire over my horse's neck. He was gaunt, and unshaven, but he was the same old Rhys. 'Are you well?'

He shrugged. 'Well enough.'

'Where have you been sleeping?'

A lopsided grin. 'In a serving girl's bed, mostly.'

I did not ask further. The main thing was that he had not been captured. I decided wryly that being someone's bed companion had helped him to go unnoticed, like as not.

'What of the king?'

I realised that Rhys had no idea of the politicking that had been going on. In a few sentences, I explained. His face darkened at the mention of Heinrich and Philippe.

'If only we could get the king out,' I said, my frustration boiling over.

'I tried to find a way to break into the castle at Dürnstein,' he said. 'But a man would need wings.'

'I fear it will be the same where we are going,' I said. 'I suggest you find your way into another wench's bed – a wench who works in the castle – and see what can be done from there.' I handed over half the gold coins I had. 'These may be of use, greasing palms, getting information.'

He winked and then, noticing Hadmar approach, he led his horse away without another word.

Hadmar's face was troubled; I asked him why.

The innkeeper had had an important guest the previous night, a papal nuncio, no less. The aged Pope Celestine, third of his name, had been swift to act upon hearing of Richard's incarceration. 'He has excommunicated Duke Leopold,' said Hadmar, his brow furrowed.

I had warned him of just that eventuality the day before, I wanted to crow, but it is best not to kick a man when he is down. Staying on Hadmar's good side would aid me far more than the opposite. 'That is heavy news,' I said, 'if not altogether unexpected. What will your master do?'

'Pray,' said Hadmar, without apparent irony.

He will need to do more than that, I thought, daring to hope that Leopold's fear of his papal-guaranteed fate would lead him to free the king.

I rode with Hadmar for the rest of the journey. We shared a love of falconry and hunting, which afforded a rich vein of conversation. I told him of the sakers I had seen used in Outremer, and listened with genuine interest as he waxed lyrical about the peregrine falcon he was training to the gauntlet, slipping in a little subtle flattery wherever I thought it appropriate. By the day's end, his initial reserve had vanished; he was sharing his flask of wine and proposing that he take me out the next time he flew the falcon. I did not push my luck in this regard, instead mentioning that I longed to see Richard, my master. The last time I had been separated from him this long, I said truthfully, had been more than five years before.

Hadmar was a generous-natured man. After our arrival at the castle, an imposing structure atop a hill some twenty miles from Vienna, he went to report to Leopold, but instructed that William and I were to be brought to the king.

Richard had his back to the door when we entered. I smiled, recognising it as a clear show of contempt for his captors. The room was pleasant with two windows, fresh-smelling rushes on the floor, and a fire crackling in the hearth. Fine-worked tapestries enlivened the walls, and the large bed had a bearskin over the coverlet.

The man-at-arms behind us did not speak immediately.

I seized my opportunity. 'Sire,' I said. 'We are here.'

He spun, face alive with joy. 'Rufus! William!' He crossed the room in three great strides and embraced me. Keeping his hands on my shoulders, he stood back a little, staring into my face. 'I have missed you, Ferdia.'

'And I you, sire,' I said, my voice hoarse.

He embraced William, and said, 'I had not thought to see more of my companions so soon.'

Seeing our confusion, he said, 'Count Meinhard was also at Regensburg; he had de Béthune and the others with him, all of them apart from Rhys, that is.' He gave me an enquiring look.

Acutely aware of the guard standing in the doorway, I winked. Richard took my meaning at once, and gave me the slightest of nods. A chance to tell him would come when it was safer.

Richard bade us take stools by the fire, serving wine with his own hand. Only then did he join us. The king raised a toast, to comrades who had fallen in Outremer. 'To Philip,' he said, catching my eye. His squire had been one of my closest friends. He made no objection when I, thinking also of de Drune, added those lost at sea. We drank deep, and stared into the flames.

Logs crackled. White-gold sparks rose. A baking warmth radiated, a delight to my chilled muscles. I edged my feet closer to the fire, much as a dog does, until he can bear the heat no more.

'So Leopold also judges it unsafe to leave you at Dürnstein. He trusts the emperor not even a little bit.' Richard snorted. 'I am unsurprised. The meeting with Heinrich was brief, yet enough for me to see that he is driven by pure avarice. It was plain to Leopold also; he could not get me out of Regensburg fast enough.'

'Why does the duke not ransom you directly himself, sire?' This had been nagging at me since I had first heard of the proposed meeting with Heinrich.

'Even a man like Leopold does not presume to go that far against his liege lord. Would you attempt to ransom Philippe Capet without consulting me?'

I shook my head.

'Leopold has either to free me, which he is unwilling to do, or to come to an agreement with Heinrich.'

I chewed on the grist of that, and did not like the taste. 'Why is the emperor so greedy, sire? Is he bankrupt?'

'His treasury could be healthy enough, I do not know, but he is plagued by troubles. A king's ransom' – here Richard smiled –'would buy off a lot of his enemies.'

He went on to explain how Heinrich liked to stick his nose into his vassals' affairs, and to get involved in matters that were nothing to do with him. The yields of his meddling were plentiful, if unwelcome. From the Rhineland to the north and east of his realm, there were nobles either in open rebellion or on the verge of being so.

'Hearing of Leopold's excommunication will make little difference to Heinrich, then, sire?'

A snort. 'Indeed, in the main because Pope Celestine will do nothing. To act in that manner, you see, might see more of his bishops murdered. Heinrich has done it before.' He was referring to Albert of Brabant, the candidate for the bishopric of Liège, who was reputed to have been murdered by Heinrich's order. 'That is not to say that pressure should not be applied to the pontiff. I imagine that my lady mother has already set quill to parchment on the matter.'

'And Philippe, sire, what of him?'

'He has written to Leopold and, I would suspect, to Heinrich as well. He asked the duke to hold me until a summit could be arranged between the three of them, the caitiffs, to decide upon my fate.' The king's face lit up with anger. 'Philippe stooped even lower, though, in his letter to me. All bonds between us are severed, he wrote. I was to take his message as a declaration of war. War? What does that coward know of that? He could not leave Outremer fast enough after we took Acre. God's legs, but what I would give to be at the head of an army, in the Vexin! I would sweep all before me, not stopping until the very gates of Paris!'

'Philip would soil himself, sire,' said William, droll as ever.

'He would too!' Richard threw back his head and guffawed, the one that came from his belly, the very core of his being. 'Sweet Jesu, but I would pay good money to see that,' he said, wiping away tears of mirth.

I thought it opportune then to lean close, and tell him about Rhys.

'The rogue followed you to Dürnstein and then here?' Richard whispered, his eyes agleam.

I nodded. 'He will do everything in his power to free you, sire.'

'He has a valiant heart, like his master.' The king clasped my shoulder, murmuring, 'Let us hope to God that he comes up with something.'

The next few days passed without any further developments. There was no sign of any of Heinrich's men. Hadmar, who visited regularly, told me even the emperor would not dare to strike so deep in Leopold's territory. The castellan's good nature was further proven when he agreed to Richard's request to see William and me each day. To my surprise, he did it without asking Leopold. When the duke found out a day or so later, calling on Richard when we were in his room, it was already a fait accompli. Rather than appear the churl by having us removed or preventing future meetings, Leopold pretended it was he who had granted permission. I guessed he had realised that easier treatment of Richard was better for everyone concerned.

Whatever the duke's reason, the renewed contact boosted all our spirits. I also had another reason to be happy; Hadmar continued to promise an excursion with his falcon-in-training. I was thinking of this early one morning when the key grated in the lock.

'Breakfast,' I said to William. 'I hope there is honey with the bread.' We did not get it every day, but the honey here was some of the best we had ever eaten.

The guard was first, a friendly, balding type. After him, bearing a tray, came a plump woman with long, wavy brown hair. I stared. This was the first female servant to enter our room; I recognised her too, from the courtyard in Dürnstein.

'Good morrow, Sir Rufus and Sir William,' she said in heavily accented French.

We goggled; she laughed and placed the laden-down tray on the wooden table. I noticed a long scar running from the palm of her left hand all the way up her arm.

'There is rye bread and cheese – good cheese, from a local farm – and honey,' she said in German this time. 'And water from the well.'

'*Danke*,' I said, and then in French, 'you speak my tongue?'

'I am learning,' she replied, adding quietly, 'thanks to your friend.'

My eyes shot to the guard but, used to the routine, he was half standing in the corridor, talking to his comrade outside Richard's chamber.

'Rhys?' I whispered, incredulous.

'Yes.' She looked coy.

My heart sang. 'He is *my* man!'

A smile. 'So he swears at every opportunity. He said to tell you all is well, and he is doing what you asked.'

I nodded, understanding the vague message. Although she was clearly enamoured with Rhys, he did not quite trust her yet. 'What is your name?'

'Katharina. I am one of the cooks.'

'It is a pleasure to make your acquaintance, milady,' I said, taking her hand and kissing the back of it.

She blushed to the roots of her hair, bless her.

Any further conversation was prevented by the guard re-entering the room.

'I will bring your food later as well,' Katharina promised.

William and I thanked her politely, and she left with the guard being none the wiser.

William arched an eyebrow. 'Rhys was swift to act, eh?'

'He has ever been a smooth talker with women. It is not a skill I have ever mastered,' I said, wondering again how Joanna had fallen for me.

'Nor I,' said William. 'It seems Rhys has already won her heart. Do you think she can spirit us out of here?'

It was hateful to have harsh reality sink in so quickly. I sighed. 'One of us might be possible, but three?'

'If she could get one man out, it would have to be the king.'

'Of course.'

'He and Rhys might make it to Moravia from here,' said William, his eyes filling with hope.

It was an uplifting image, I thought, tearing a lump off the still-warm bread. It did not matter how long William and I languished here if Richard could successfully escape.

Katharina was as good as her word, delivering our evening meal later that day. She made it her business to come at least once a day thereafter.

It was plain that Rhys was working magic on her; before long, she began to talk of helping us to break free. It was not easy; even with the guards being relaxed, we could never talk for long without risking their suspicion. It also became plain that Katharina could pass messages to and fro, but escaping our prison would be a different matter altogether. An attempt to befriend a guard who was fond of her pastries was interpreted as romantic interest. She came in the next day with red weals around her upper arms, the result, she told us furiously, of being shoved into a food cellar where the guard had tried to force himself on her.

'Did he . . .?' My fists were balled; I was ready to throw myself into the corridor and beat the man into bloody pulp.

A wicked laugh. 'Ha! No! I kneed the cur in the stones so hard he almost passed out. I gave him a good kicking on the floor, and went straight to the castellan after. You will not see him again.'

'Did Rhys . . .?' He would put the guard in the mud, quick as quick, I thought.

'No.'

'Who then?' I asked in surprise. Generally, soldiers would not be punished for what was a common occurrence.

'The duke loves my Christmas puddings,' she explained. 'He would look dimly indeed on my being manhandled so. Knowing this, the castellan dealt with it. The guard was flogged, and sent to a frontier post on the Moravian border.'

Katharina was quite formidable, I decided, and quite the match for Rhys.

Understandably, the incident put an end to her trying to cozen any more of the guards. We talked about her trying to steal the castellan's keys, or even secreting rope under her dress and delivering it to us; the former we judged far too risky, and the latter too dangerous. It was a hundred feet at least from our window to the level of the dry moat. Even if she could bring enough rope, the descent down the sheer castle wall would be incredibly perilous, and Richard, although he would not admit it, was scared of heights. Knowing that a single slip would prove fatal, William and I judged the risk too great to mention to the king, who might have ordered us to try it anyway.

January dragged past. Katharina fed us as if we were all kings; her meals were the highlight of every day. Spatchcocked chicken with a wine sauce, roast mutton accompanied by fresh wheaten bread, swan with chaudron sauce, the list was endless. It was not just for her puddings, William and I often said to one another, that the duke held her in high esteem. Meanwhile, outside, snow fell. Gales battered the castle, but we were warm and dry behind its thick walls. The weather was too foul to hunt Hadmar's falcon, to my chagrin. I had hoped after the first time to persuade him to take the king out as well, and thereby engineer a possible way to win his freedom. It was not to be, for the moment at least.

Philippe Capet sent a letter to Heinrich, offering to match and surpass any ransom paid for Richard's freedom. Its contents made clear that he wanted the king to remain in captivity for the rest of his days. Leopold relayed this to the king, but had the grace to be embarrassed. But he was not so ashamed, a furious Richard told us later, as to stop his negotiations with Heinrich.

'They are to meet at Würzburg on Saint Valentine's Day,' the king announced in early February. 'The agreement between them is almost complete.'

'Do you know the details of the contract, sire?' I asked.

A grim shake of the royal head. 'Leopold is far too canny to share that information with me yet.'

Although the duke had no intention of releasing Richard without a massive ransom, his previous hostility had diluted to a stiff reserve. He had accepted the king's private concession that his banners at Acre should have been treated with respect rather than being hurled into the ditch and trampled upon by our soldiers. This newfound civility bore fruit; when Leopold departed for his meeting, he would take not just the king, but us as well.

Having Richard present was still deemed too tempting for Heinrich, so our first destination was not to be Würzburg but the nearby castle at Oschenfurt. Both places were a good distance from our current prison, more than two hundred miles. Katharina came also, her cooking a must for the duke, and Rhys followed behind. With his help, it would perhaps have been a good opportunity to flee our captors, but the king wanted to ride without his wrists being bound, so had sworn not to escape. Chivalry forbade him to break his word. We had to content ourselves with spying Rhys now and again on the road, and knowing he was close by.

The weather had improved and, after our long confinement, I relished being abroad in crisp winter sunshine. Our relative freedom had a remarkable effect on the king; at a meal break on the first day, he challenged Hadmar and Leopold to a snowball fight. When they refused, the former smiling, the latter scowling, he ordered William and me to take him on. To my surprise, it was tremendous fun to act like children and, as I realised, for us to forget our situation, if briefly. Needless to say, the king was a far better shot than either of us. I had bruises for days.

I wished that the high spirits of that first day would continue forever, but it was not to be. The bald truth, that we were prisoners, was driven home by the guards who rode close to us at all times, and who stood watch at our doors each night. Leopold's reserve never went away altogether. Even Hadmar, a decent man, would clearly never go against his master and try to free us. Rhys was dogging our footsteps, it was true, and Katharina would do whatever she could, but they had little real chance of freeing the king. It was in subdued manner that we arrived at Oschenfurt the day before Leopold's meeting with Heinrich.

I slept badly that night. When I saw him, Richard's drawn face told me he had fared no better. There was little conversation between us; the king was in no mood to talk. Looking down on the courtyard, I saw Leopold leave, accompanied by a strong party of soldiers. William and I were on tenterhooks for the whole day, wondering what news he would return with. I tried praying, but felt no better. I played dice with William, and lost ten silver pfennigs. He suggested chess; Hadmar had generously supplied us with a board and pieces. I lost at that too, which did not help my mood.

That evening saw us with the king, and in better humour. The three of us were sitting around the fire, toasting chestnuts as we drank wine and reminisced about the battles in Outremer. The king in particular was enjoying William and I recount the unfolding of the mad battle at Joppa, when he had leaped into the sea and charged ashore with only a few men behind him, uncaring of the thousands of Saracens on the beach. How we had survived unscathed then, not to mention the fighting outside the city a few days later, was nothing short of a miracle.

'How could thirteen of us charge Saladin's entire army and survive?' William shook his head in disbelief; I grinned, my pride thrumming at the memory, my admiration of Richard as great as it had ever been.

'God was watching over us, for certes,' said the king. 'What a day that was. I doubt we will ever see the like of it again.'

'The bards will be singing of it for centuries, sire,' I said, heartfelt.

'I hope so.' The king's eyes were distant with memory and regret.

I knew why, although I did not feel the same way. For all the glory of that charge, and our defeat of Saladin's army, we had not recovered Jerusalem. Now, captives for the foreseeable future, there was no prospect of changing that. It weighed heavily upon Richard. God forgive me, I could think only of Joanna.

The clatter of hooves carried up from the courtyard. Our heads turned; we looked at each other, faces taut.

'Leopold has returned,' said Richard. 'Did he come to agreement with Heinrich, I wonder? Will he come to tell me about it, or leave me in the dark?'

Not long after, a heavy tread on the stairs pronounced the former more likely.

I rose from my stool; William did the same. 'We shall give you privacy, sire,' I said.

'Stay.'

It was more of a request than an order, and I realised that the king was dreading what the duke had to say. We sat down again.

Leopold entered without knocking, a light covering of snow on his cloaked shoulders, his cheeks wind-blown red. He had a real spring to his step, and my heart sank. He bowed, a mocking gesture he had rarely bothered with before. 'King Richard.'

'Duke Leopold.' The king did not rise. 'It is late to come visiting.'

'You are not abed; you are still entertaining, in fact.'

'Aye. These men are my companions, my brothers-in-arms.' Unspoken were the words: *you are neither.*

'Forgive my intrusion. I shall leave.' Leopold turned on his heel.

A muscle twitched in Richard's jaw. The duke had outmanoeuvred him, and to speak would admit that.

I acted, to spare his pride. 'Do not go, sir. We would know of your meeting with the emperor.'

Leopold stared.

I did not know if he remembered me from Acre; he had never given any indication of it, which suited me. I did not wish to give him any more reason for mistreatment than he already had. 'Please, sir,' I said, wanting not to beg but to punch his teeth down his throat.

His lips twitched; he could not keep in his delight. 'Would you care to hear?' he asked Richard.

The king grunted.

On another occasion this thin-veiled contempt might have seen the duke stalk out, but not tonight. He drew in a breath and began. The meeting had gone spectacularly well; both he and Heinrich were in complete accord, so much so that—

The king interrupted. 'The price?'

'What?' said Leopold, discomfited.

'How much money do you want?' Richard's voice was a snarl.

Leopold veiled his anger, and said with a toothy smile, 'One hundred thousand marks, to be divided equally between the emperor and me.'

The sum was vast, unimaginable. It was more than the annual income of Richard's entire kingdom. I could not prevent a little gasp.

The king gave away no such emotion. His face could have been carven from stone. Impassively, he asked, 'Is that all?'

Leopold giggled, a horrible sound. 'No. It is not.'

Richard waited, silent, implacable. He would not ask, although inside, I knew he burned to know.

Of course Leopold could not contain himself. It poured out. Half of the hundred thousand marks was to be paid over at Michaelmas, a dowry for Richard's niece Alienor of Brittany when she wed the duke's son.

'Which son?' Richard demanded.

'I have not decided yet,' said Leopold with a shrug.

The disrespect was staggering. I could not have controlled myself as the king did; he merely nodded.

Smug-faced as a moneylender calculating the interest due him, Leopold continued. The second tranche of fifty thousand marks was due at the beginning of Lent next year, in the year of our Lord 1194. Richard was also to provide Heinrich with one hundred knights and fifty fully equipped war galleys, to help his proposed invasion of Sicily. The humiliation did not end there. The king would have to accompany

97

Heinrich to Sicily, bringing another hundred knights at his own expense. In addition, Isaac Comnenus and his daughter, 'the Damsel of Cyprus', were to be freed.

Leopold seemed to take extra pleasure in this last detail, as if its humane origins could excuse his rapacity.

As surety of his compliance with the terms, Richard would be obliged to supply twenty hostages of the highest calibre.

'When will they be released?' The king's tone was matter-of-fact; he could have been discussing the weather.

'After you have obtained an absolution from Pope Celestine for me.'

The vein that signified Richard's purest rage pulsed in his neck; his face remained unreadable. I was outraged too. So was William, but this was not our fight. It would aid the king not at all for us to attack the duke, much as we longed to.

Leopold waited, surprised and plainly unhappy that the king had not reacted.

The silence dragged on. A log fell out of the fire with a thump. No one paid it any heed.

Leopold gave in, and spoke first. 'Well? Have you nothing to say?'

'Get out,' said Richard.

The duke puffed out his chest like a fighting cock. 'How dare you!'

'Get out, or by all that is holy, I will throw you down the stairs!' Richard had risen from his stool. He towered over the duke, seeming in that moment twice the man the other was.

Leopold retreated, his face a pasty grey. His mouth worked; he seemed about to speak, but thought better of it. He left; the door slammed shut, and the key turned in the lock. A sentry spoke. The duke snapped back. Footsteps echoed in the passageway.

Again silence fell.

'There it is,' said Richard. 'It was always going to come down to silver. A lot of silver. This will wreak a heavy toll on England, and Normandy and Aquitaine.'

William and I flailed for something to say, some reassurance to give, but our words sounded trite, hollow. Richard listened, and then he thanked us and said he wished to retire.

Waiting for the guard to let us out, I glanced back at him.

He was crouched on a stool, gazing into the fire. His entire posture screamed defeat.

I could do nothing to help him. My heart almost broke in two.

CHAPTER IX

Despite Leopold's bravado about the agreement with Heinrich, the fine details had to be hammered out. The hostages that were to be given into the duke's keeping as a guarantee of Heinrich's good faith also had to be summoned and gathered. Nothing would happen fast. Freedom still lay months off, yet the king's spirits had revived, as they always did. He was never one to wallow in self-pity, which helped William and me to pull ourselves from the pit of despair.

February became March, and Easter approached. I went hawking with Hadmar several times; Richard was forbidden to join us. I felt some initial guilt about this, but the king was delighted on my behalf. With his blessing, I went. William did sometimes too. The outings were like balm to the tired soul: fresh air, sunshine on my face, and the stomach-clenching excitement of watching a falcon stoop on its prey. I managed short conversations with Rhys on most occasions; made aware by Katharina that we were to ride out, he would seek me out whenever we watered our horses, pretending to be a beggar or an itinerant pedlar.

He always urged me to make my escape. I think it might have been possible; content with my promise not to flee, Hadmar did not set men to close-watch me. Nonetheless, I always refused. I would not leave without the king, who, kept in his room day and night, had no chance of freedom. And whatever Rhys's chances of helping me, to do the same for Richard would be impossible. We were trapped in a vicious circle. Watch and wait, I told Rhys over and again. The right moment will come, God willing. He would shrug, annoyed, and glower when I ribbed him about that granting him more time in Katharina's bed.

Relative to the days spent in our chamber, the outings with Hadmar were few and far between. Playing dice and chess whiled away hours, but silence often reigned supreme. There was much time for thought and self-contemplation. I relived as best I could my time with Joanna. I imagined laughing at her sharp wit, and enfolding her in my arms and kissing her. There was so much more. Not all my thoughts were of love and pleasure, however. I dreamed of finding proof of FitzAldelm's treachery, and denouncing him to the king. I revelled in his execution. I even went back to Ireland, to my ancestral home of Cairlinn, and there lived as its lord.

These thoughts would see me tell myself that one day I would return there. It was an old, repetitive refrain. I hated to admit it, but the desire to do so was the weakest it had ever been. Fourteen years had gone by since I was taken from Cairlinn. All my family were long dead, and our lands given over to an Englishman. I could not remember the last occasion I had spoken Irish.

I was not English or Welsh. I was not from Normandy, Aquitaine, Brittany, or any of Richard's other continental territories. I was Irish, fiercely so, but I was no longer quite sure what that meant. An even more horrible thought often rattled around my head. To go back to Ireland would see me a stranger in my own land.

It was an unpleasant concept, one I tried to bury each time it appeared. I was a captive, I told myself, with no immediate prospect of freedom. Even when I was freed, my duty lay with the king, who would need me as never before to help restore order to his kingdom. Rumours had reached us. Philippe had gathered an army, and was hovering near the Vexin, that long fought-over area between the two kingdoms.

Towards the end of March, two white-robed Cistercians arrived to see the king. John, the abbot of Boxley, was a short little man whose protuberant eyes gave him a startled, almost comedic appearance. Stephen, the abbot of Robertsbridge, was taller, a serious man who spoke in such a slow, ponderous manner he might have been delivering judgement in a court with every sentence.

Leopold himself had brought the abbots to Richard; he hovered in the doorway for a time but, unable to speak French, he eventually departed in frustration. William and I would have also left, but the king wanted us to hear what had been going on, so we sat on stools by a side table while he and his visitors took their ease by the fire.

'You are welcome, good abbots,' Richard said again. 'I have had no news from England these past three months and more.'

They bowed their heads. 'This is why we have come, sire, fresh from a great council of the realm, held not long since in Oxford,' said John.

'It was called by Archbishop Walter de Coutances,' intoned Stephen.

My ears pricked. Walter had heard my confession in Sicily, had absolved me of Henry's murder, when all the while I had not been truly remorseful. Guilt savaged me. The scab was torn away and, under it, I was still unrepentant. Staring at the king, his face alight – the abbots' arrival had given him a new energy – I knew I would do almost anything to retain his trust. Even murder.

'What has Johnny been up to?' asked Richard, and as the abbots glanced at each other in disbelief, he laughed. 'There is little my brother could do to surprise me, Father Abbots.'

'He crossed to Normandy soon after the news of your capture reached England, sire,' said John.

The news was related turn and turn about by the two abbots. After trying and failing to have the lords of Normandy swear their loyalty to him, Richard's brother John had travelled to Paris, where he met with Philippe Capet.

I thought darkly of FitzAldelm, and wondered what role he was playing in these machinations.

'It is unclear what was agreed, sire,' said Stephen, measured and sonorous. 'But word has reached me from a source close to the French king.'

This would be a scribe, I thought, a monk whose loyalties to Mother Church were greater than those he had sworn to Philippe.

'Let me guess,' said Richard. 'He paid homage to Philippe for all my continental territories.'

'And England and Wales, sire,' said John apologetically.

Despite his previous words, Richard looked surprised and, even though he tried to hide it, hurt.

'He agreed to set aside his wife and wed Philippe's sister, Alys, sire. Gisors Castle and the entire Vexin are also to be ceded to the French crown.'

The king shook his head, now evidently amused. 'Johnny, Johnny, have some faith in yourself. Philippe would have accepted far less as a sign of fealty.'

I had to hold in my surprise at his reaction. It had been a long time since I had seen Richard's capacity to forgive his brother's misbehaviour. It was a trait he shared with his late father, and one that left me cold. If either of my brothers had ever betrayed me in such a fashion, I thought, our relationship would have ended on the spot. I might not have slain them, but forgiveness, there could be none. None. Never. Some actions can never be undone, some words never unsaid. They cut too deep, leave ever-painful scars.

'Count John has returned to England, sire,' said Stephen, his tone even more sombre than before. 'I fear his plans to usurp you will continue apace there.'

The king snorted. 'I have no real fear in that regard. My brother John is not the man to subjugate a country, if there is a person to make the slightest resistance to his attempts. He will come around in the end, you will see.'

The abbots looked a little embarrassed. After his forgiveness of John's actions, this was a stinging, if accurate, slight.

I understood Richard's reaction. It was easy for me to stand in judgement, to think I would cut all contact with John forever. I was not the king, and John was not my only living adult kin. If John were executed, the heir to the throne would be the child of Richard's late brother Geoffrey. Scarcely five years old, Arthur was even less well suited to resist the blandishments and threats of Philippe Capet than John. Loathsome though it was, therefore, Richard's decision made sense.

Talk of the kingdom continued; the abbots passed over letters for Richard from his mother, Archbishop Walter de Coutances and other officials. The king was deeply absorbed, and did not notice when William and I left.

Katharina came to deliver our meal not long after. 'I have news,' she said in French, setting down the tray of bread, cheese and cured meat. 'The king is to be taken to Speyer.'

I gave her a blank look, and she smiled. 'You do not know, of course. The imperial court is at Speyer.'

'He is to be handed over to Heinrich there?' I asked.

She nodded.

'Heinrich wants to flaunt him in front of his nobles,' I said in disgust. 'As if he were no more than a caged beast.' I spied something else in Katharina's face. 'What is it?' I demanded.

'I am not sure,' she whispered. 'But I heard mention of a trial.'

I exchanged an unhappy look with William. 'A trial?'

'The castellan told a clerk so, not an hour since,' said Katharina.

The guard came in, preventing her from divulging any further information.

William and I were left to brood over our meal. I could think of few worse things, to be falsely accused in front of a large, hostile audience, with the outcome – continuing captivity – already a foregone conclusion. Give me a line of enemies to charge instead, I thought. Settle the matter with blood and steel.

That choice was not going to be offered to the king.

We arrived in Speyer on Palm Sunday, the king, William and I, escorted by Leopold, Hadmar and a strong party of knights and men-at-arms. Katharina rode in one of the wagons further down the column; Rhys, I knew, would be following on behind. I had grown used to a certain routine with our transfers from prison to prison, but today was different. Upon our arrival in the town, we were not taken to any accommodation, but instead to the great castle. We clattered into the courtyard, drawing all eyes. A steward came rushing over, managing to look officious and disapproving at the same time.

Heinrich was waiting, Leopold immediately announced, and the king was to be taken to see him.

'Have I the time to brush off the dust of the journey?' Richard asked.

'No.' Leopold was as smug as a petulant child.

I bristled, but the king made no protest, slipping from the saddle. He beckoned me and William with a little inclination of his head. We dismounted and joined him.

'Just you,' Leopold said to the king.

'No,' said Richard, and now there was thunder in his voice. 'You have shown me discourtesy at every turn, Duke Leopold, but I will *not* enter the emperor's presence without my men, the most loyal of my followers, and these good abbots, who have come from England to succour me.' He indicated the Cistercians.

He and Leopold stared at each other with clear dislike, neither prepared to give way.

The steward coughed. 'The emperor is *waiting*.'

'I can stand here all day,' said Richard, taking off his gloves and reaching for the wine skin that hung from his saddle bow. Dust-covered, his face worn with tiredness, he still radiated power.

Leopold's gaze flicked to Hadmar and the guards.

Do your worst, I thought.

Leopold let out an exasperated noise. 'Very well. Bring your minions!'

We were taken straight to the great hall, which was empty apart from a few servants by the entrance. They watched, agog, as the steward led us down the vast room. The last of the afternoon's sunlight carried through the glass windows, illuminating a dais at the far end; on it was a wooden throne, and on that perched Heinrich, the Holy Roman Emperor.

He was not a physically impressive figure: small, bony-faced and with a pallid complexion. Rather than adding to his presence, his fur-trimmed robe and the rings that glittered on his fingers made him look like an over-dressed scarecrow. His eyes, however, could not be ignored. Pale blue and unblinking, they were full of intelligence and malign purpose.

This man, I decided, was not to be underestimated. He looked as trustworthy as a snake that has just been trodden on.

'King Richard.' Heinrich spoke in French.

'Emperor.' Richard's tone was even.

'Men are supposed to kneel in my presence.'

'Men.' Richard stood up straight, emphasising his great height. 'I am a king.'

How proud of him I was in that moment.

Heinrich's tongue wet his lips. 'I could make you kneel.'

'*You?*'

One word, lightly delivered, with a world of scorn in it.

'I have but to give the command, and my guards will force you to pay proper obeisance.'

'I suspect my men would have something to say about that,' said Richard, with a glance at me and William.

I swear I grew two inches.

'There is no need for bloodshed,' said Leopold with a greasy smile. 'We are all friends here.'

Richard cast a look at Heinrich, as if to say, *Your move.*

Heinrich made a little gesture of annoyance. 'Let us not waste time. You know the details of the arrangement that the duke and I have come to, I assume?'

'Leopold told me, yes. The demands are amoral and outrageous. They would make the most bloodsucking moneylender wince.'

Leopold purpled, but Heinrich did not take the bait. 'We think the price is fair. What do you say to the terms?'

You can shove them where the sun does not reach, I wanted to scream.

'I reject them utterly,' said Richard, loud and clear.

A tic worked in Heinrich's cheek. 'You are at my mercy. You have to pay. You have to agree.'

'I would rather die than give you a single mark, and as for accompanying you to Sicily – faugh!'

They glared at each other, all pretence of civility gone.

Heinrich tired of it first. He clicked his fingers at the steward. 'Take the king to his quarters. He will need a good night's rest before his trial in the morning.' He could not quite hide a trace of glee at this last detail.

It was old news, however, thanks to Katharina. I had passed on the information to Richard.

'I look forward to it,' he declared. 'Everyone in your court will hear the truth of the matter.'

Heinrich's triumphant look wavered for a heartbeat, no more. He jerked his head, and his guards closed in on either side, a clear gesture of intimidation.

Richard paid not a blind bit of notice. He strode from the room with the same confidence as if he had been in his own hall at Chinon.

I went with him, briefly feeling that we were free.

A pleasant surprise awaited us in the king's quarters, a well-furnished chamber close to the great hall. One of Richard's most trusted advisers, Bishop Hubert Walter of Salisbury, was waiting there. He had been with us until Corfu; while we had voyaged up the Adriatic, he had travelled to Rome, to meet with the Pope, as well as Berengaria, the king's wife.

'Sire.' He came forward, his plump face alight with pleasure, and bowed deeply.

'This is a happy day,' said Richard, smiling from ear to ear. 'Have you seen Berengaria and my sister?'

'I have, sire.' From his satchel, Hubert produced a bundle of letters.

My heart thumped; I also felt a pang of jealousy that the bishop had recently seen Joanna. I burned to ask about her just as the king had, but could say nothing. Our illicit love affair could never be spoken of. I had to content myself with eavesdropping on Richard's conversation with Hubert. It transpired that Berengaria and Joanna had done as the king had thought, and overwintered in Rome. André de Chauvigny, Richard's cousin, and another of his and my closest friends, was with them.

'André will see them safe to Poitou,' said the king.

He was not as certain as he sounded, I knew. To reach Aquitaine without harm, Berengaria and Joanna would first have to traverse the county of Toulouse.

The thought of Joanna being taken prisoner threatened to send my mood spiralling downward. Savagely, I thrust away all thoughts of her, and told myself to concentrate on the king. Richard did not need me, however. He had already finished talking about Berengaria, and was deep in conversation with Hubert and the two Cistercians, discussing the best approach to take at his trial.

Dejected, worrying again about Joanna, I sought my own quarters and there lost game after game of dice to William. The evening was not improved by Katharina's news; by some magic, she contrived to bring in our evening meal. Rhys had not yet arrived, she told us, her pleasant face furrowed with worry.

'His horse will have gone lame,' I declared. 'He will be here by tomorrow.'

I slept not a wink that night.

CHAPTER X

Rhys arrived safe and sound early the next morning, which lifted my mood somewhat. Nonetheless, I was red-eyed and irritable as William and I accompanied Richard to the imperial court. The trial was to take place in the same great hall we had met Heinrich in the day before. From our rooms, we followed the guards down to the courtyard. Overhead, the sky was blue. It was two hours before midday, and beautiful if chilly.

'It is a day to go hunting,' the king observed wryly, 'not to stand trial.' He indicated his travel-stained clothing. 'These are no garments to meet the great and good.' He saw my look, and chuckled. 'You think I dissemble.'

'Yes, sire, but for good reason.'

He chuckled.

The king had refused the barber and hot water to bathe that had been offered to him, and ignored the richly cut garments delivered to his quarters. His reason, I guessed, was to shock, to ensure that everyone in the court knew of the shameful treatment he had suffered.

'We would have done the same, sire, if we had known,' I said, feeling awkward in the clean tunic and hose that had been brought to our chamber. William muttered his agreement. 'We should not look better dressed than you, sire,' I said.

He clapped me on the shoulder. 'They will not be looking at you two.'

I nodded, gratefully realising that he was right. And, I thought, his ragged appearance took nothing from his regal presence. It added to it.

'Are you ready, sire?' I asked.

'I am.' He was striding out with confidence, and his eyes were dancing. 'I am greatly desirous to explain my position and make plain the great wrongs that have been done to me. If the audience has any men of conscience present, they will not be able to deny the truth in my story.'

My heart was stirred by his fighting words.

I hid my doubts as to whether they would serve to see the king set free.

The great hall was full to bursting point. It seemed every noble and prelate for hundreds of miles had come to feast their eyes on the king of England. They leaned out into the narrow path that had been left free along the room's length, peering, staring, passing comments to their companions. Despite the throng, not everyone was present – under questioning, Hadmar had admitted that the noblemen in open conflict with Heinrich had not been invited. It was a pity, but no surprise.

Richard strode down the hall, ignoring the curious audience, his eyes fixed on the dais where Heinrich awaited us.

I let my gaze wander, trying to gauge the mood. I saw a great deal of curiosity, and heard plenty of mutters of *'König'* and *'Löwenherz'*. There was plenty of hostility also, in particular from a snappily dressed man with a pointed beard. He gave Richard a murderous look, which made me wonder if he was Boniface, Conrad of Montferrat's brother. Malevolent too was the glance of the Bishop of Beauvais, close ally of King Philippe of France, and a man I had not expected to be present. By his side was Drogo de Merlo, a bullnecked noble I had first met with the bishop in Cyprus, which now seemed a lifetime ago. He smirked at me and William; I pretended not to have seen.

'Did you see them?' I whispered.

'Aye. They must be here as part of a French embassy,' William muttered.

Before we reached the dais, I quietly told the king who I had seen. He gave me a grateful nod, and mouthed: *Forewarned is forearmed.*

Heinrich was visibly surprised by Richard's threadbare, unwashed appearance. Into his pale blue eyes crept a little respect. He was no fool, and realised why the king had refused to bathe and change. Leopold, who sat by his side, sneered. The emperor's ministers, of which there were many, simply stared.

There followed a prolonged announcement in German, of which I understood very little. This was followed by a long declaration in Latin, which meant nothing to me either. Not for the first time, I wished

I had not wilfully ignored the old monk charged with my boyhood education. William had been more conscientious with his studies; he was able to interpret for me.

The king *could* understand Latin; he listened with close attention as the charges against him were laid out.

He was, William said sotto voce, accused of betraying the Holy Land by making a treaty with Saladin, of the murder of Conrad of Montferrat and the rape of Cyprus, the imprisonment of Isaac Comnenus and the kidnap of his daughter, and of supporting Tancred in his unlawful appropriation of the throne of Sicily. Delivered last – a deliberate measure, no doubt – was the charge of the grave insults given to Duke Leopold at Acre, insults which had also injured Heinrich.

When the official finished the list of accusations, a pregnant silence fell. Heinrich's eyes went to Richard, but he said nothing.

My mouth was dry; this felt like a chess game, with neither player willing to commit until forced to.

The silence dragged on. I could even hear a sergeant shouting orders in the courtyard.

'Well, my lord king,' said Heinrich in French. 'What say you to these charges?'

'You do not speak Latin?' Richard responded, quick as a flash.

A trace of colour marked Heinrich's pallid cheeks. 'I thought you would prefer French.'

'For something this grave, I prefer the tongue of Mother Church,' said Richard, continuing in Latin. He ended with a question.

'The king wants to know if all the accusations have been laid,' whispered William, grinning. 'He asked if there are any more.'

Heinrich's nostrils were flaring with temper, but he answered Richard coolly. There were no more charges.

Richard dipped his chin, the slightest sign of respect possible, and turned to the audience. He stood tall, broad-shouldered, with a piercing gaze that raked those closest. Despite his ragged clothing, he could not have appeared more regal.

The silence deepened until I could have heard a needle fall to the stone floor. My heart was pounding as it did before going into battle. Lord, I prayed, let the king win them over.

Richard began to speak. His tone, dignified and measured, allowed William to keep apace with his translation. He had been born into a rank, the king said, that recognised no superior but God Almighty. He was responsible to no one but the same God. Turning to Heinrich, he declared that neither the emperor nor his court had any right to try him, nor yet to pass judgement on him.

These words saw the colour on Heinrich's face ripen, but he held his peace.

Richard addressed the audience again. Because he was ashamed of nothing he had done, he said, he was content to give an account of his actions not just to the imperial court, but to the whole world. He would start with the nonsensical allegation that he had betrayed the Holy Land. One only had to look at his battles, and, better, his victories over Saladin, to know it was wholly untrue. He had achieved more against the Saracens than anyone had in decades. If the charge could be levelled at anyone, the king said, it was those who had abandoned the struggle after the siege of Acre, men such as Philippe Capet and Duke Leopold.

Leopold's face worked; his fists clenched in his lap, but he managed not to speak. Heinrich was watching him.

After Acre, he had been left almost singlehanded to continue the war, Richard said. The remaining French, led by the Duke of Burgundy and aided by the Bishop of Beauvais, had been of little help. Indeed, when it had come to a possible siege of Jerusalem, they alone had insisted it proceed, against the advice of the local nobility and the military orders. Far from betraying the Holy Land, the king declared, he had remained in Outremer – even as his own kingdom was threatened from without and within – and seen a truce negotiated with Saladin that allowed Christians the right to visit the Holy City for the next three years. Philippe and Leopold, on the other hand, had hurried home.

His insult hung in the air. The Bishop of Beauvais glowered. Leopold shifted to and fro on his chair, clearly burning to respond. Heinrich sat, silent, patient as a spider watching a fly.

Yes, he had met with Saladin, said Richard, just as any general might meet his enemy. He had found the Turkish warlord to be a man of honour, and had exchanged gifts with him, as Frankish opponents might do with one another. The only settlement he had come to with

Saladin, however, had been the hard-won agreement about the borders of Outremer, and the right of Christians to visit Jerusalem. 'I told him before I left,' said Richard, visibly emotional, 'that I would be back to finish what I had started. Because, God willing, I will return to Outremer!'

The audience liked that. I could see heads nodding in appreciation. I thought I detected a little uncertainty in Heinrich's expression. It was becoming hard to see how he could justify the captivity of a man who had not just taken the cross and fought valiantly in the Holy Land, but had promised to return there at the first opportunity.

'And Conrad of Montferrat, sire?' This was the snappily dressed noble I had noticed. In Italian-accented French, he demanded, 'What have you to say about his murder?'

It was a gross discourtesy to interrupt proceedings like this, not least when a king was speaking, but Richard showed no anger. His attention bore down on Boniface – for it was Conrad's brother who had spoken – making the noble shift a little on his feet.

'I had no hand in his killing, as God is my witness.'

'That is not what the Bishop of Beauvais says!' Boniface shot a look at the bishop, who nodded.

Richard let out a contemptuous laugh. 'That man cares nothing for truth or honour! It was he who conducted your brother's illegal marriage to Isabella of Jerusalem, a woman who was already married!'

Everyone stared at the Bishop of Beauvais, who blustered and muttered.

I pictured poor Humphrey de Toron, who had been ill treated and ignored, because the future of the kingdom of Jerusalem – strengthened by Conrad and Isabella's union – was more important than a man's happiness. My own situation with Joanna was not dissimilar, I thought bitterly.

'I was no great friend to your brother,' Richard said to Boniface, his tone earnest. 'Guy de Lusignan was my vassal, so I supported his claim to the throne upon my arrival in Outremer. But I have never been one to avoid the truth when it is staring me in the face. It became apparent that Conrad was better suited to be king; he was a strong leader, and he had the poulains' support.' The poulains were the Franks who lived in Outremer. 'Conrad had my backing when he took power. His murder was a tragedy; it weakened our position against Saladin. Why would I act in that manner, contrary to everything else I did in the Holy Land?' Richard's chin set. 'Anyone who knows me would tell you also that I meet my enemies face-to-face. I do not pay others to stab them in the street.'

He and Boniface locked eyes for several heartbeats. The Italian nodded, but he was not done. 'Why did the Assassins kill him?'

'They had good reason. Conrad seized a ship off Tyre the year before his death. He took the cargo, which belonged to the Assassins, and drowned their agents who were onboard. This is common knowledge in Outremer; there are men in this room who will bear witness to that.'

Again Boniface met the king's gaze, which was direct and unwavering.

'I had nothing to do with your brother's death. I swear it on the salvation of my immortal soul.'

My mouth was dry. If Boniface called Richard a liar, the audience's opinion – which seemed to be growing favourable – would be nigh-on impossible to win back.

'I believe you,' said Boniface, his voice hoarse.

Spontaneous cheering broke out. Even Heinrich's face bore a suggestion of warmth.

From that point, Richard had the room. He paced to and fro, holding forth with such passion and confidence that he seemed to have forgotten where he was, and the indignity of his circumstances. He could have been addressing his own subjects from his throne at Lincoln or Caen.

Leopold and the Bishop of Beauvais scowled to no avail as the king demolished the accusations made against him about first Isaac Comnenus and then Tancred. He came last to Duke Leopold's claims.

'I am a man of honour, first and foremost.' Richard glanced around the room. 'I hope that has become plain.'

Loud cries of agreement rose. There was more applause.

'Would Duke Leopold hold to be the same?' The king glanced at the duke, who, surprised, spluttered that of course he was honourable.

'Why then did he not avenge the insult done him on the spot? *That* would be the mark of a moral man. Instead, he ran home like a whipped child, harbouring his grudge all the way.'

Leopold's look could have slain Richard on the spot, but no one was paying him any attention. Everyone was listening to the king, who was speaking again of his intention to return to Outremer. He would not rest, he said, until Saladin was defeated once and for all, and Jerusalem was again in Christian hands. This, Richard said in a voice shaking with passion, was his heartfelt wish.

Another silence fell.

His gaze roamed the room. *Let you be my judges*, he seemed to be saying.

Cheering and applause erupted yet again. Nobles and bishops hurried to surround Richard, thanking him.

Heinrich's reserve had been swept away. He joined the rest, his once pallid cheeks flushed, eyes moist with emotion. Noticing his presence, those thronging Richard stepped aside in respect. Heinrich clasped the king's shoulders and gave him the kiss of peace.

He pledged to enter into a treaty of friendship with Richard and, as far as he was able, to arrange a reconciliation with Philippe Capet.

The ovations grew even louder. Men were openly crying, and praising God.

I was also moved; not to be would have made me heartless. But as I watched Heinrich sidelong, I became convinced that it had all been an act, a response tailored for the high-running emotions in the hall.

Words meant nothing unless he was prepared to free Richard.

And if he did that without an enormous ransom, I thought, I would fly to freedom from the ramparts of Speyer Castle.

CHAPTER XI

I t was all friendship and light during Holy week. Heinrich treated Richard like an honoured guest. They went together to church, brothers in Christ, observing the rituals that led day after day to the final, glorious celebration of the Resurrection on Easter Sunday. In the crowds outside the cathedral, I managed to speak with Rhys, who had arrived safely a day after us.

The king summoned me to his room late on the evening of Easter Sunday – the new spirit of amity had seen us allowed to move freely between our quarters. Hearing him pluck on a lute, I paused before entering. I knew that Richard wrote poetry and set it to music, but I had never been close enough to hear it well.

> *'No prisoner can tell his honest thought,*
> *Unless he speaks as one who suffers wrong;*
> *But for his comfort he may make a song.*
> *My friends are many, but their gifts are naught.*
> *Shame will be there, if for my ransom here*
> *I lie another year.'*

It was poignant, and the melody was good, but a jangle of notes came next. It was, I thought, as if the king had tired of the song, or, as seemed more likely, his situation.

Not wanting to embarrass him, I silently retraced my steps and came back down the corridor making plenty of noise. From the moment I crossed the threshold, I knew he had bad news. He had already set down the lute.

His face was stern, solemn. There was even a hint of resignation. 'Ferdia.'

'Sire?' The nearest sentry was at the end of the passageway, but I closed the door anyway.

'Heinrich has been playacting.'

'I am not surprised, sire.'

His mouth tightened. 'Nor I. He may have given me the kiss of peace, but he still wants his hundred thousand marks, and the two hundred knights to take to Sicily. Tomorrow, moreover, I am to be moved under close guard to Trifels Castle, where the imperial jewels are kept. I am told it is a gloomy fastness in the mountains to the west of here.'

The emperor's demands were no surprise, but I groaned inwardly that the king was to be moved to another prison. After Dürnstein and Oschenfurt, I had been enjoying the relative luxuries of Speyer. Fixing an encouraging look on my face, I said, 'William and I will be with you, sire, and Rhys will follow us thither too.'

'William will be sufficient company.'

I stared, not understanding.

'Bishop Hubert and the two Cistercian abbots are to travel back to England. I would have you go with them.'

A feather could have knocked me over. 'Sire?'

'It is time to make your escape, Ferdia, if you can.'

No, I thought, panic battering me. Do not send me away.

'Katharina – is that her name? – she will help you, will she not?'

'Yes, sire, if I ask. But why? I want nothing more than to stay by your side, as I have always done.'

A warm smile. 'If only every man was as stout-hearted and loyal as you pair. The truth of it is that I need eyes and ears throughout my kingdom. Bishop Hubert and my mother, and others like the Marshal and William Longchamp, will see to it that England remains calm, but they cannot be everywhere. I am concerned about Normandy: that is where I want you to go once you have spoken with my lady mother. Take Rhys; you and he should not be parted.'

I could not refuse. Could not disobey. 'Yes, sire,' I whispered.

'Robert FitzAldelm is already in Normandy, and the Earl of Leicester is soon to go there by my order. You must set aside your enmity with Robert, and work together. Philippe Capet has an army poised on the border of my portion of the Vexin; given half a chance, he will invade Normandy as well.'

As it had done so often, my face gave me away.

'Ferdia.' The king's voice was stern. 'I am your liege lord, and Robert's. Your duty to me is greater than any dislike of each other.'

I had shied away from the truth for so many years. Now, about to be torn from the king, with no idea when I would see him again, I made a lifechanging decision. If the truth were ever to come out, it was in this fraught meeting. I had no idea how to go about it, but unwilling to deceive my lord any longer, I blurted, 'You cannot trust FitzAldelm, sire.'

A frown. 'Why do you hate him so?'

'He tried to kill me, sire, twice.' I told him of the incidents at Châteauroux and Chinon. 'Rhys was there, the second time, sire. He could tell you the same as I have.'

Richard did not ask further questions – I hoped that meant he believed me – but instead said, 'There is more to this than meets the eye. Robert is a shrewd type. He would not act so, twice, without good reason. Explain.'

It was here, the moment I had dreaded for so long, that had ravaged my dreams, that had gnawed my guts on countless occasions. 'He thinks I murdered his brother, sire,' I said heavily.

'Guy? The knight who was slain in Southampton many years past?'

'Yes, sire,' I said, surprised by the king's memory.

'Did you? Kill him?' His eyes were pitiless.

I swallowed. 'I did, sire, but it was in self-defence. He attacked me.' Out it came, the whole sorry story. How Robert FitzAldelm, Fists and Boots as I called him, had made my life a misery at Striguil. How the king – Duke of Aquitaine then – had once saved me from his attentions.

Richard's face grew thoughtful. 'I remember that day. Go on.'

'Robert took service with you, sire, and I thought I would never see him again. Some time after, his brother Guy came to Striguil from Ireland. Guy killed my parents, sire. He burned them alive in our house, deliberately, giving them no chance to surrender.'

'He told you this?'

Emotion choking me, I nodded.

'So you followed him to Southampton? You were chasing him, not seeking service in my household?'

Miserable, sure that he was about to denounce me for a faithless liar, I said, 'Yes, sire.'

To my astonishment, he roared with laughter. 'Fortunate it was, then, that I saved your life, and you mine, eh, and you accepted my offer?'

'It was, sire.' I could not look him in the eye. 'I served you loyally from the start, I swear –'

'You of all people do not need to justify your service. Which brings me to something I should have done long ago. You shall be the lord of Cairlinn. I will send a letter to the justiciars to that effect.'

My throat closed. I bent my head, managed to mumble, 'Sire . . .'

'It is nothing, Ferdia.'

'It may be of little significance to you, sire, but it means the world to me.'

'Good.' His tone grew graver. 'Tell me of the killing of Guy FitzAldelm.'

Voice shaking a little, I described my late-night hunt through the stews of Southampton. How I had almost given up, until by unhappy chance FitzAldelm had emerged from a backroom of the seedy inn I was drinking in. I had slipped out after him, but the brutal reality of my intention had seen a sudden change of heart. Turning to go, I had trodden on a piece of crockery and alerted FitzAldelm. Attacked by him and his squire, fighting for my life, I would have died but for the intervention of Rhys. 'He had followed me, sire, against my orders.'

'Robert FitzAldelm would have a different version of the story, I have no doubt.' Richard's tone was icy. 'How convenient that he is not here to give it.'

'I can see how it looks, sire, but it is the truth,' I protested. 'This I swear, by almighty God and all His saints. I swear it on the lives of my mother and father.'

'Why did you not come forward when Guy's death became known?'

'No one would have believed me, sire! I was a nobody, an escaped Irish hostage, and he was a belted knight.'

'You could have spoken out regardless,' thundered Richard. 'Instead you let two innocent men go the scaffold in your stead!'

I had no defence to the truth. I hung my head. 'That is true, sire.'

Silence fell. I dared not look at the king, nor speak. Sure that he was about to denounce me for a coward and a murderer, and at the least dismiss me from his service, I wondered what would have happened if I had confessed to the killing of Guy FitzAldelm at the time. Like as not, I would have swung from the end of a rope, with Rhys alongside. Dread snaked up my spine. Richard might *still* order my execution. My immediate gut reaction to that was surprising. Despite what might befall me, I did not regret my killing of FitzAldelm. Vengeance had been served, and my subsequent time with the king had been an added bonus.

'Let us say I believe your account of what happened outside the inn.'

Scarcely believing my ears, I looked up. 'Sire?'

'I am also willing to set aside the two lowlifes who were hung for Guy's death. They admitted to several other murders.' Richard had overseen the interrogation himself.

'Nonetheless, sire, they did not kill Guy FitzAldelm – I did.'

'And Rhys fought and slew his squire?'

'Yes, sire.' *That* had been murder, plain and simple, but the less said in that regard, the better.

The king did not enquire further. 'When did you encounter Robert FitzAldelm again?'

'Some time after I entered your service, sire. A month or more.'

'Was he suspicious that you had been involved in his brother's death?'

'Not at that time, sire.'

'So your enmity stemmed from his previous treatment of you?'

'Yes, sire.'

'When did he begin to suspect?'

'Not for years, sire.' I did not want to mention the circumstances.

The king was having none of it. 'When?'

'It was before your coronation, sire, when we passed through Southampton on the way to Winchester and London.'

'He talked to someone? Found a witness?'

'So he claimed, sire.'

'Did you admit the killing to Robert then?'

'No, sire. He would not have believed my story. I waited to see if he produced the witness, but it never happened.'

'That is strange.'

'Yes, sire.' Dread filled me. I wondered if I should admit to the murder of Henry, the man-at-arms who had seen me in the inn with Guy FitzAldelm, but in the same heartbeat, gave it up as pure madness. The king might overlook the deaths of two criminals, but he would not let cold-blooded murder go unpunished. That dark deed had to remain between me and Rhys forever.

Richard's stare bore down, penetrating and direct.

I deployed all my skill in meeting his gaze, my expression as open as I could make it. I was on the thinnest ice now. If my face revealed too much, or the king continued to probe hard, or he remembered sending me to Southampton – where I had slain the witness, the man-at-arms Henry – he would be like a terrier on a rat. Merciless. Lethal.

'Robert believed what he had been told, though. Why else would he try to murder you for a second time at Chinon?'

'I suppose so, sire. I do not know what goes on in his head.'

'It is not like you to leave an enemy undealt with, Ferdia. Did you not want to engineer a fight with FitzAldelm?'

'Of course, sire, but you look dimly on such things,' I countered. 'I had no wish to be dismissed from your service, and once we set out for Outremer, the penalties were heavy.' They had included the amputation of a hand for injuring a fellow soldier, and being thrown overboard tied to the corpse of one who had been slain.

'A fair point.' He chuckled. 'You could have been underhand. Killed him on a dark, moonless night.'

'That is not my way, sire,' I lied, my mind alive with Henry's shocked face as I cut his throat. 'I used to pray that disease or the Saracens would kill him.'

To my relief, he seemed to accept that.

After another silence, the king said, 'I understand your hatred of Robert now, but not your accusation that he is untrustworthy. What evidence have you of that?'

Again I was caught on the horns of an unpleasant dilemma. Say that I had none, and Richard might discount my opinion. Tell him what I had seen in Acre, and I risked the full force of his displeasure.

'Speak, Rufus!' Reversion to this name showed his patience was wearing thin.

'I do not have absolute proof, sire, but I saw him enter the tunnel in Acre one night, the one that led to the French quarters. He could have had no reason to be there, except to speak with King Philippe or one of his nobles.'

'So one might presume. How is it that you did not tell me at once?' Richard's expression had blackened. The vein in his neck was pulsing.

Sweet Jesu, I thought, I am for it now. I saw no option, though, other than to continue. My father had always told me to tell the truth; it was advice I tried to follow whenever I could. Except, a little devil in my head jeered, when it comes to FitzAldelm. Except when it comes to Henry. Except when it comes to Joanna.

'Well?' The king's voice was silken with threat.

I could think of no lie to tell. Terrified though I was of the path it was leading me down, I could only answer, 'FitzAldelm was blackmailing me, sire.'

'*Blackmailing* you?'

I closed my eyes, my heart aching, seeing Joanna in all her mesmerising beauty, remembering her tell me we could never be man and wife.

'Why was he doing that?'

Hearing the trace of compassion in Richard's tone, I risked all. In truth, now we were here, I could no longer bear to keep the truth from him. I loved Joanna more than life itself, and if I could not admit that, what kind of man was I?

'He knew about your sister and me, sire, or suspected at least. I was desperate that you should not find out, even though we loved – love – each other.' I brought my eyes up to Richard's, although it was the hardest thing I had ever done, harder than any of my feats in battle.

'You and Joanna . . .?' He left the question unfinished. There was a killing rage in his eyes.

Conquering my fear, I forced the words out. 'Yes, sire.'

The mask slipped into place again. The challenge came. 'Do you love her?'

'With all my heart, sire.'

'And she loves you?'

'Yes, sire, as fiercely as I do her.' With supreme effort, I did not let my gaze drop from his. I could feel a pulse hammering in my throat; I desperately needed to piss.

'When did you become . . . close?'

'Outremer, sire.'

His expression grew thoughtful, his eyes distant.

I was still fearful, but part of me was at peace, glad that Richard knew at last. Whatever his reaction, I had nothing to be ashamed of. Nor did Joanna.

Richard spoke. 'She was happy in the Holy Land, happier than I thought she would be with the heat, and the dust, and the flies, not to mention the discomfort of the campaign.'

I was too, I thought. I had never been happier in my life.

'And now I discover that it was because of you, Ferdia.'

'Sire?' I had no idea what was coming next.

'Angry though I am to discover that you and my sister were in secret relations, I – I am glad that she was happy. I am glad for her. I am even glad for you, you bull-headed Irishman.' I grinned with delight, and quick as a flash, he added, 'You can never wed her. New lord of Cairlinn you might be, but she is too great a prize.'

My smile shrank; my heart twinged. 'I know, sire. She made that abundantly clear.'

He looked pleased. 'Joanna's sense of duty has always been pre-eminent. I can remember her leaving to marry William de Hauteville in Sicily. Just a child she was, but so strong and resolute.'

'She is wondrous, sire,' I said, my heart aching with love and loss.

'Aye.' He smiled at me. 'She is.'

In that moment, I would have given up everything for Joanna: my position in Richard's household, my years of service to him, my friend-ships with men like de Béthune, even my relationship with Rhys. All the longing in the world could not change reality, however. She was gone from my life. Even if we met again, things would not be the same.

'Is there aught else you would tell me?' The king was all business again; there was a hardness to his voice as well, an underlying threat.

There was no question I could tell him about Henry. That memory was to be buried deeper than deep, and so I shook my head.

'And so we come back to Normandy. With FitzAldelm seemingly a traitor, I have even more need of a reliable set of eyes and ears there.'

'What should I do, sire? Do you want me to interrogate him?' God forgive me, but that idea appealed.

'Do not act prematurely. Better, I think, to watch and wait. Have him watched, perhaps. Try to find out what he is up to.'

'Rhys will do that, sire.'

A satisfied nod.

I did not mention that I would again have to order Rhys not to slip a dagger between FitzAldelm's ribs. It sometimes seemed that he hated my enemy more than I did.

'Arrest him whenever you think it correct. Keep him in prison until my return.'

'Sire.' I gave him a wolfish grin.

Richard rummaged among the papers on his table, and handed me a rolled parchment. The royal insignia, the Angevin lion, was prominent on the wax seal. 'Give this to Earl Robert.'

'Yes, sire.' I had always liked the Earl of Leicester, but since Joppa, when he had been part of the charge of thirteen against Saladin's army, I regarded him as a true brother-in-arms. 'He has no idea about FitzAldelm, sire . . .' I glanced at the parchment.

Richard tapped his nose. 'Better not to put information like that to paper. If you were taken prisoner by the French, God forbid, then Philippe would learn that we know about Robert. Tell the earl yourself when you see him.'

'FitzAldelm could deny everything, sire, and if he has won the earl's trust, Earl Robert might not believe me, because it is not in your letter.'

Richard swore and cracked open the seal with a thumbnail. Seizing a quill, he added a couple of lines, before melting another blob of wax and sealing the message again. 'I have told the earl that you carry more information, for his ears only. That will suffice.'

'Thank you, sire.'

Again he was all matter-of-fact. 'Hubert and the Cistercians are to leave tomorrow. They will wait for you in the next town as long as is necessary. How soon do you think you can escape?'

I buried my emotions. 'I shall talk to Katharina, sire. Tomorrow, or perhaps the next day, God willing.'

'Soon then. Good.' Despite his briskness, I caught a note of falsity. His emotions were also running high.

'I will pray for you every day, sire.'

'And I for you, Ferdia.'

We stared at each other, a world of emotion passing between us, and then he seized me in a rough embrace. 'May God watch over you,' he said in my ear.

'And you, sire,' I said, hugging him back.

That was the last time I saw Richard for many months.

PART TWO

PART TWO

CHAPTER XII

Winchester, England, April 1193

We arrived at the royal palace as darkness was falling. I remembered it well, although my last visit had been four years prior. The Cistercians had gone their own ways, but I was still with Bishop Hubert. He was to confer with Queen Alienor, Richard's mother, and I had been charged by the king to speak with her also. After that, Rhys, Katharina – it still surprised me somewhat that she was with us – and I were bound for Normandy. If it had not been for Richard's order to stop at Winchester, I would already have departed. Disturbing news was coming over the Narrow Sea almost daily.

Our journey from Germany to England had taken the best part of a month. Protected by the presence of so many prelates, it was uneventful. We landed on the Kentish coast on the twentieth of April, and immediately made our way towards Winchester. There had been no call for Bishop Hubert and I to spend much time alone in Outremer, but I knew him from the hours he and I had been in the king's company together. Spending so much time with him day after day allowed me to get to know him a lot better; my admiration rose by the day. He was no youth, but had a sturdy disposition, and could spend long hours in the saddle as a knight twenty years his junior might do. Possessed of a sharp intelligence and humble manner, he was as at ease with a peasant farmer as he was with a lord. Fond of ale, and quick to laugh, he was, in short, excellent company.

Hubert's greetings on our first meeting after my escape had been effusive. He had been courteous to Katharina beyond what was needful – she a mere cook and he an important prelate – and had heaped praise on her for engineering our escape with Rhys. It had been simple enough, like all the best plans. She had posed as a roadside seller of hot mulled wine on a day I had been out hunting with Hadmar. She and two female accomplices had played their roles to perfection, batting their eyelashes, and serving double measures of wine to my smitten guards. It had been simple enough to leave my horse and slip away to a clearing in the nearby woods, where Rhys was waiting with spare mounts. Richard had sworn to do everything in his power to see that William was not punished; I had to trust to that. Rhys and I had ridden north at speed, outstripping any pursuit. Katharina had joined us two days later at an agreed location; we had ridden together to meet Bishop Hubert.

He had sought me out many times as we travelled north from Speyer. His first wish, as it soon became clear, was to learn as much as he could of the king's frame of mind. He was worried that Richard might spend many more months in captivity before his ransom had been paid. 'The king is a strong man for certes, and he seems in good spirits,' Hubert said to me, 'but this will be a sore test. A close companion like you knows him better than I.'

I had been reassuring, sure that Richard was determined to bear up to his imprisonment with every fortitude. I reminded myself of this as we dismounted in the courtyard of the royal palace at Winchester and grooms took our horses. Queen Alienor would be worried about her son, I thought. It was important that she took no concern from my account.

A steward guided us through the same corridors I had trodden with the king on the eve of his coronation. It could even have been the same steward – he gave me a friendly nod – although I was not sure.

Alienor was waiting for us. Despite her advanced age – she was now more than seventy – I was as ever impressed by her beauty and regal presence. She was grace itself, bidding us welcome and, with a warm smile, telling us to rise from our knees.

'Bishop Hubert,' she said. 'It is a pleasure to see you.'

'Madam. The pleasure is all mine.' He bowed, adroit as a youth, and handed over a letter from Richard.

She must have been desperate to read it, but first she turned her attention to me. 'Sir Rufus, the years have treated you kindly. Are you well?'

'Yes, madam, although I wish it were your son standing here, not I.' I would gladly have stayed in prison to see my king free.

'That would be my preference also,' she said, smiling to show there was no malice in her words. 'But I fear Emperor Heinrich would not have agreed to the change.'

'You speak true, madam,' I admitted ruefully.

'Sit.' She indicated the stools close to the window seat she had been occupying. A gesture saw servants come forward with cups of wine.

While we supped, Alienor read her son's message with a silent but fierce intensity. No clerk was going to take this experience from her. I watched her keenly, but the only hint of emotion I could determine was a couple of little swallows as she finished it.

I could not help but wonder what she would think of my relationship with her daughter. A devil in me wanted to tell her that Joanna loved me with all her heart, to see if Alienor would grant her blessing to our union. I held my peace. In the unlikely event that she gave her permission, it was not her decision who Joanna would wed next but Richard's, and he had made up his mind. I felt the stirrings of anger deep inside. Joanna had married as she was ordered to once already – it seemed unfair that she should have to do it again.

My attention was drawn back to Alienor. Composed once more, she began to question Hubert. He gave a compelling account of the phoney trial at Speyer, and of Richard's masterful performance. 'Only someone with ice in his veins could have remained unmoved, madam,' said Hubert.

'Or someone with his eyes on one hundred thousand marks,' said Alienor, her tone arch.

'Even so, madam. Heinrich is mercenary in his intent, as became clear the day afterwards.'

'Coin always speaks louder than words, sadly,' said the queen. 'Had Longchamp reached Speyer before you departed?'

'No, madam.' Hubert looked surprised.

This was news to me also. William Longchamp had been Richard's faithful chancellor, but his arrogant manner won him few allies. After our departure for the Holy Land, he had alienated many of the nobles and prelates. When news of this had reached the king in Sicily, he had sent Archbishop Walter back to England with the power to strip Longchamp of his office should it prove necessary – and it had. Longchamp had departed England under a cloud, but now it seemed Richard had not lost faith in him.

'Did you send him to the king, madam?' Hubert asked.

'I did. He no longer has many friends on this side of the Narrow Sea, but he has always been loyal to Richard. Despite his record, he can be skilful at diplomacy.'

'After I left, I did feel concerned that the king would have no one to speak on his behalf in the imperial court, madam. My heart is gladdened to hear that Longchamp will soon be there.'

'Richard's letter mentions the sum demanded by Heinrich,' said Alienor. 'It is twice the annual return from the entire kingdom, if not more.'

'A heavy burden indeed, madam, and truly a ransom fit for a king.' Hubert made a face. 'I assume there is mention of how the monies are to be collected?' He and Richard had spent hours hammering out the details.

'Yes. He has ordered a tax on all income and moveable goods at a rate of twenty-five parts in every hundred, and the same on certain kinds of property. The Cistercian monasteries are to give up their wool crop, and every church has to surrender its silver plate, vessels made of gold, and jewellery. Clerics are also to pay over a tenth of their tithe.' The tithe was the annual tax paid by every farmer to the Church. 'The Jews of England are also to be taxed five thousand marks.'

'Similar commands are to go out to every part of the king's dominions. From Normandy to Aquitaine, from Brittany to Maine, every royal subject will have to contribute. Archbishop Walter de Coutances will oversee all, and the funds are to be stored in the crypt of St Paul's Cathedral. The king feels that these measures will suffice. Are you in agreement, madam?'

Hubert was fully aware of Alienor's mental acuity, I thought.

'I am, but I fear it will be Christmastide before the first half can be gathered. My hope in the meantime is that Heinrich can be persuaded to release Richard for a lower figure, with hostages offered as surety for the rest.'

'Is that Longchamp's mission, madam?'

Alienor's lips twitched. 'You are shrewd, Bishop Hubert. It is no wonder that my son has seen fit to appoint you Archbishop of Canterbury.'

Hubert's mouth opened and shut, and opened again.

Pleased for him, I chuckled. It was rare to see him so discomfited.

Delight began to replace his surprise. 'Madam, I am honoured.'

There was more talk of possible ways to raise money, as well as the hostages that would need to be selected to travel to Germany, and the ships that would have to transport them. When Alienor seemed content, it was Hubert's turn to ask about the kingdom. Count John, Richard's youngest brother, came up at once.

'Has he been, shall we say, quiet, madam?' Despite the mildness of his words – no one could deny that John's actions had been traitorous – Hubert looked a trifle embarrassed.

A snort. 'That boy! You mean after he had finished trying to win over William the Lion of Scotland, and giving homage to Philippe Capet?' She made no further mention of the meeting with the French king, during which John had ceded Gisors and the Vexin. If the stories were to be believed, John had declared his hatred of Richard to be so strong that he would destroy the Angevin empire at need. I was glad that Alienor was paying me no attention, for I could not entirely mask my anger. John might be her own flesh and blood, but he was also a treasonous dog. In my mind, he deserved more than a chiding. A good whipping would be a start, I decided.

'Even so, madam.'

'Johnny managed to win over someone at least: Baldwin, the new Count of Flanders. He sent a raggletaggle force of routiers to land on the east coast some weeks ago. I dispatched soldiers to East Anglia; most of the invaders and the rest were sent home with their tails between their legs. Johnny has been in a fearful sulk since; he has used his Flemish and Welsh mercenaries to seize the castles at Windsor and Wallingford, and is spreading the word that Richard is dead.' She tutted. 'Few will believe him, especially now you have returned, fresh from seeing the king with your own eyes. He will posture and declaim, and do little else.'

'The king was adamant that we need not worry about Count John, madam. I am happy to hear you agree,' said Hubert.

'Of more concern is that snake Philippe Capet, and my own troublesome people in Aquitaine,' said Alienor. 'It is not just Gisors and the Vexin we need to be worried about. I hear that Adémar of Angoulême may be about to rise in rebellion again.' Her gaze moved to me. 'My son's letter says that you are to go to Normandy.'

'Yes, madam. I am to serve the Earl of Leicester there.' I said nothing of FitzAldelm.

Nor did she. 'The sooner you leave, the better. Neither of you will know this yet, but Gisors and the nearby stronghold of Neaufles passed into Philippe's control ten days ago.'

Hubert and I exchanged a glance. This was troubling. The great castle at Gisors was key to the defence of the Vexin, which itself served as the gateway to Normandy.

'Why, madam?' I asked. 'Did Philippe send an army there?'

'He did not have to. The castellan of Gisors, Gilbert de Vascœuil, voluntarily surrendered.'

I remembered Gilbert, who had travelled with us as far as Sicily on our way to the Holy Land. 'I would not have thought him a traitor, madam.'

'Nor I, but there is not a more exposed castle among all my son's fortresses than Gisors. With no immediate prospect of Richard's release, and with Philippe prowling like a night-time wolf around the sheepfold, not to mention Johnny's reckless promise to cede the English-controlled part of the Vexin, Gilbert found himself in the most unenviable of positions. Others will follow his example, or I am no judge. Your task in Normandy will not be easy.'

And that was before a traitor like FitzAldelm was brought into the equation, I thought. The king had decided not to tell his mother about him. 'She has enough to worry about at home,' Richard had said. 'You are more than capable of dealing with the cur.'

I was. I just wished I could kill him and have done, instead of trying to catch him out first.

'Sir Rufus?'

I coloured. 'Your pardon, madam. I was far away.'

'Wondering about Philippe's next move?'

I nodded, and was relieved when she next asked about Richard, and ordered me to tell her stories from our time in Outremer. I willingly did that. Richard had written to his mother but, modest with his family, he tended to underplay his part. Alienor listened, enraptured, as I told her of his heroic charge ashore, half-armoured, at Joppa, and of the incredible battle we had fought against Saladin's army a few days later.

'He charged the Saracen host with *twelve* of you?'

I grinned like a fool. 'Yes, madam. Twice, and not a man of us was injured or slain.'

Her mouth was an 'O'. 'It sounds like a miracle. Were you not scared?'

'No, madam,' I said. 'He was not, so neither was I. I wanted to be nowhere else other than by his side. I would have followed him into the jaws of Hell itself. So would we all.'

Pride radiated from her. There was even a hint of moisture at the corners of her eyes. I continued the tale, explaining how, once we had put the Saracens to flight the second time, Richard had ridden up and down, offering battle. 'There were thousands of Turks there, madam, but not a single one answered his challenge. Not one.' I could see him still, lance end balanced on his stirrup, the Angevin lion on his heater shield spattered with blood.

' "Is there any man who will fight me?" he cried in French, madam, and then attempted it in Arabic. "Fight me!" They just stared and stared at him.'

'And you rode back to your lines unhindered?'

'Not a single arrow was loosed at us, madam.'

'Ah, Richard, my son,' she whispered. Now the tears ran. 'Mon Coeur de Lion.'

The rumours were true, I thought. Of all her children, living and dead, she loves him the most.

I left at dawn the next morning, riding without pause to Southampton. Eager though I was to sail at once, the conditions were against me. I pleaded with the captain of the cog tasked with transporting me over the Narrow Sea, but he jerked a thumb at the sky, a gusting maelstrom of thunderclouds, and told me the only men who set sail that day would end up as food for the fishes.

I argued with him to no avail. In foul humour, I began a search for an inn, aware that my desire to quit Southampton had less to do with the weather and more to do with not wanting to spend a night in the town. Rhys, who sensed part of what was going on, muttered that there was nothing to worry about. 'No one remembers you here,' he said. 'Nor me either.'

I was not worried about that. It was guilt that had me in its clutches. Two and a half years before, I had opened a man's throat for no more reason than to save my own skin. Pacing the very same streets that I had walked the day I killed Henry, I could not keep my shame at bay. I visited first one church and then another, praying and lighting candles to no avail.

It was perhaps inevitable that later that evening, as the sun went down, I slipped away from a rarely drunk Rhys and found myself making for the stews. I do not know what I expected to find, or what I expected to come away with. Step by step, alley by alley, ignoring the curious and predatory looks from the locals, I worked my way towards the lane where the man-at-arms Henry had lived. My sense of direction was good; I found the butcher's yard where I had heard a pig being slaughtered as we lay in wait. I padded past the small, thatched houses, counting, until I came to a stop outside the one where I had committed red-handed murder.

I had no idea if Henry's widow and child lived there still, but sweat was trickling down my face, and my heart was pounding as if I had run a mile in helmet and hauberk. God forgive me, I thought. Why did I do it?

Because you would not risk your position in Richard's household, shouted a mocking voice in my head. *Live with it.*

I have lived with it, I screamed silently. And it haunts me day and night.

The internal voice turned into laughter, a cruel sound that cut me to the quick.

I stood there, lost, dazed, ripped by claws of shame and self-hatred.

A child's voice – piping, a little boy's – came from within.

Hearing it drove home the magnitude of what I had done a hundred-fold. Reeling, I had to place a hand on the wall so as not to fall. The thin planking creaked beneath my touch; in response, a dog barked inside the house. I stepped away, panicked that I would be seen, perhaps even recognised. The child asked who was there, and his mother, terror clear in her voice, said loudly that it was nobody and, anyway, his daddy would be back soon.

Hope flared in my heart. Perhaps she had wed again.

A heartbeat later, the child said, puzzled, that he thought his daddy had died.

I squeezed my eyes shut, my guilt tearing at me, as his mother shushed him, and the dog barked again and again.

I could not – would not – make myself known, but I *had* to do something. I unfastened the purse from my belt. It was weighty; there were even a couple of gold coins in it. I stepped up to the door and hammered a smart *rap, rap*.

'Who's there?' The woman tried to keep the fear from her voice, and almost succeeded.

I covered my mouth with my hand, and spoke through it, deeper than I normally would. 'I bring a gift.'

' 'Tis an odd hour to come calling with a gift.' It was natural that she sounded suspicious.

'Who is outside, Mother?' asked the boy.

'A friend,' I lied, feeling like the worst kind of coward. 'I will leave it on the step.' And so saying, I laid down the purse and retreated to the gap between the next house and the one after that, from where I watched the door.

She did not emerge for some time and, when she did, there was a crossbow in her hands. Her husband's, I thought, pleased by her spine, and glad she did not know who or where I was. There was a clink as she scooped up the purse, and then she was gone back inside. Thunk went the locking bar.

In better mood, I made my way back to the inn where Rhys and Katharina had found us rooms. I could not undo my actions, nor bring Henry back, but I could make his wife and son's lives easier.

It was better than nothing.

CHAPTER XIII

Rouen, Normandy, May 1193

I was standing on the eastern walls of the town with Earl Robert of Leicester. A short, compact figure with close-cropped, monkish hair, he paced about, exuding a pent-up energy. Rhys, ever my shadow, lurked in the background. We had met Robert in England – he had arrived late to Southampton – and crossed the sea together, arriving via a circuitous route that same morning, successfully evading the French, who were swarming through the local countryside. The day had been spent with the town council and the commander of the garrison, a combative old wineskin who had served Richard's father. Now we were come to see for ourselves the enemy encampment.

The setting sun's rays had retreated to the western rampart; the temperature where we were was still pleasant, but before long a man would need a cloak. Below us, the town was enfolded by a great sweeping loop of the River Seine, a natural defence. The waterway was not wide enough to protect it from artillery, sadly, which was why Philippe Capet's catapults were lined up, one, two, three on the other side. Piles of boulders were stacked beside each, clear warning of what we could expect in the coming days. The siege proper had not yet commenced. Wagons continued to roll in; there were even tents still being erected.

'A stronghold could be built yonder.' Robert indicated a low hill to the north of the French positions. 'It would control the far bank; no enemy could threaten the town without storming it first.' He sighed. 'The truth of it is that Henry, and after him Richard, never saw the need. The frontier with France is far enough away, with plenty of fortresses of its own, to make a man think one here would be an unnecessary cost. Now, though . . .'

We both stared at the lines of tents beyond the catapults. Flushed with success, for castles had been surrendering to him with horrible swiftness, Philippe Capet had come in person to take Rouen. It was hard to know how many soldiers he had with him, but it was several thousand at least, and with his six-and-twenty catapults, enough to take the town – in theory.

Robert cast an eye at me. 'How long will it take them to smash the holes for an assault, do you think?'

'A sennight maybe,' I said. 'Longer, if the Frenchies manning the catapults are as bad at shooting as their counterparts at Acre.'

Both of us laughed. I heard Rhys stifle a snort. There had been fierce rivalry between the French and English artillery crews in Outremer; in general, our catapults had been more powerful, and with the hard flint balls we had transported from Sicily, far more effective. 'We could send a messenger down there to offer them work,' I said.

This was what Richard had done after Philippe, in a fit of pique, had sacked most of his artillerymen.

Robert's usual stern expression softened. 'Would we had Cypriot gold to pay them, as the king did, but you know as well as I that every penny has to be saved.'

I nodded. After the taking of Cyprus, the royal treasure chests had been bottomless. Now, with one hundred thousand marks needed to free Richard, belts were being tightened everywhere. Earl Robert would normally have expected to bring to war more than fifty knights, and ten to fifteen times that number of men-at-arms and archers. His sizeable contribution to the king's ransom meant we had with us thirty knights, and a bare five hundred foot soldiers. Even when combined with the garrison, it was not enough to defeat Philippe in open battle, but if the walls held, and our defence was stout, and the French did not cross the Seine and invest the town from the south, it might be enough.

'Send men over the river under the cover of darkness,' I said, 'and those engines could be fired. That would set Philippe's plans nicely awry.'

'We think alike, you and I.' Robert's grin was predatory. 'There are precious few men guarding them too, have you noticed?'

'About a score.'

'That was my count also.' There was respect in Robert's face that I had also noted the enemy numbers. 'Is that task something you would undertake?'

My turn for the wolfish smile. 'It is.'

'We must keep that quiet, in case the Frenchie spy should find out.'

When the earl had asked me what extra information the king had referred to in his letter, I had lied and told him only that we suspected a French agent was in Rouen. I wanted to keep the name FitzAldelm to myself until I had absolute proof.

'Rhys!' I called.

He was by my side in a flash. 'Sir?' he said, because the earl was there.

'Earl Robert and I think those Frenchie artillery pieces need a night-time visit from men armed with buckets of pitch. What think you?'

He gave no immediate reply, but leaned on the top of the wall and studied the far bank. Surprised by his insouciance, Robert looked at me. I shrugged, and said quietly, 'He has been with me these thirteen years and more. Saved my life more than once.'

'The king speaks well of him.'

Pride filled me.

'But I have noticed that he tends to act above his station.' Robert's glance was penetrating. 'Towards you.'

I shrugged again, uncaring of his opinion. After all we had been through, after all Rhys had done for me, he was as dear as a brother. 'We work well together, and he serves to my satisfaction.'

'I would not tolerate such behaviour from a squire.' He said this loud enough for Rhys to hear.

'You and I are different creatures, Earl Robert,' I said, meeting his gaze with a steely one of my own. 'How Rhys addresses me is my business, not yours.'

A stiff nod.

Rhys sauntered over. 'Give me a score of men-at-arms, *sirs*' – the emphasis on the last word was stressed, making it almost disrespectful, but not quite – 'and I could fire at least half those catapults. Forty, and we could torch the lot.'

'Earl Robert?' called a voice. It was FitzAldelm, no less.

The interruption meant I lost my chance of seeing whether Robert had taken exception to Rhys's slyly delivered impertinence. We all turned, Robert with a smile of greeting, Rhys and I with cold expressions.

FitzAldelm's high-cheekboned face was a picture, so shocked was it. Coming from our rear, he had not recognised either me or Rhys. I hoped he had not heard what we were talking about either. He bowed to the earl, and ignored us.

'FitzAldelm. You are still alive and hale.' *Unfortunately*, I added in my head.

'I could say the same about you.' FitzAldelm's eyes went to Rhys, who with a blank expression scraped a bow that was just respectable enough. 'Your Welsh lackey is here too, I see.'

'He helped me to escape prison, with the king's blessing,' I said. 'How goes the finding of supplies?'

The pointed dig made FitzAldelm colour. Here was I, boon companion to the king, until recently by his side night and day, while he was a glorified quartermaster, sent back from Outremer more than half a year before.

'It goes well. The town granaries are close to full.' He glanced at Earl Robert. 'You are most welcome in Rouen, my lord. The king sent you?'

'Even so.'

'How find you the defences, my lord?'

'Sufficient, for the most part. The supplies are plentiful too, thanks to you.'

A wide smile. 'I have been busy in the hinterlands to the south, my lord. Every farmer has made a decent contribution towards the town's defences.'

'Good, good,' said the earl, happy that FitzAldelm had things in order. Robert was like me, more interested in fighting battles than the logistics of supplying an army.

I did not ask if many of the farmers' 'contributions' had been made at swordpoint. Matters like that were outside my control, and as long as FitzAldelm did not practise widespread rape and murder there would be no consequences. I wondered what else he might have been up to. Being outside the town would have provided ample opportunity to meet French agents. It would not be so easy now he was back within the walls, but neither would keeping eyes on him day and night. I had duties with the earl, and while Rhys was doughty and would stand on a street corner for as long as I told him to, he could not do without sleep. I considered bringing the earl into my confidence – if I did, he could supply us with men.

I changed my mind the instant I glanced back at Robert and FitzAldelm, who were smiling and reminiscing about the war in Outremer. They were friends, then. It was just as well that Richard's letter to the earl had made no mention of FitzAldelm, and even better that I had withheld his name. Without hard evidence, however, it might be difficult to convince the earl that he was in league with the French.

Catching Rhys's eye, I jerked my head towards the steps. 'I shall organise what we talked about,' I said to Robert, hoping he would just agree.

'Find my sergeant John, from Bath. He will provide you with the men. As for the boats —'

Too late, hating the flicker of interest in FitzAldelm's eyes, I said, 'I will find them.' Whether I could locate enough before darkness fell, I was unsure, but I wanted to keep conversation to a minimum.

'Very good. We shall talk later.'

'FitzAldelm was listening, curse him,' said Rhys when we were out of earshot. 'Cross that river this evening and we could have a warm bloody welcome from the Frenchies.'

'It is not worth the risk,' I said, thoroughly disheartened.

As it turned out, an attack proved impossible that night. It was not due to my reluctance, nor even a lack of boats, but heavy fog. Earl Robert was annoyed; I was secretly delighted. I was assuming that FitzAldelm could communicate with the French, which meant that an attempt could prove disastrous. Not only would we fail to destroy the catapults, in all likelihood we would suffer heavy casualties while doing so. Over several cups of wine, I persuaded the earl to leave me in charge of the mission. I could launch it whichever night I chose, thereby keeping FitzAldelm in the dark.

This achieved, I sought out Rhys, who was in the kitchens of the merchant's house where we had found accommodation. The air was rich with delicious smells: roasting meat, baking bread, spices. I found him leaning against the wall close to the great cooking fire over which was suspended a whole pig on a spit. Katharina, who had effortlessly managed to join the kitchen staff, was nearby, with a firm hold of the ear of the boy whose task it was to turn the spit. She had him on tiptoe, oohing and owing.

'If you need to leave your station,' she said in her still-heavily accented French, 'get someone to take your place. Otherwise, the crackling burns. And that is the best part of the pig!' She twisted until the boy yelped an apology. Then, with a beatific smile at me, she released him.

He scurried back to his spot by the fire, and began to turn the handle again, casting sulky looks in her direction.

'Sir Rufus,' she said, bowing.

'Katharina,' I said, hiding my mirth.

'Are you hungry?'

'A little.' I had long since given up attempting to refuse her largesse. She did not take no for an answer.

She began to fill a platter, describing each dish. Spiced chicken and saffron stew. A beef pie, steamed mussels, fresh bread, a pat of butter. How I would finish a quarter of it, I had no idea, but I would have to try. Despite her kindliness, she had a beady eye. I would admit it to no one, but I was a little wary of getting on her bad side.

Rhys watched her every move. When Katharina noticed, she beamed. It warmed my heart how much they cared for each other. I had never thought my squire would fall for a woman so, but when the thunderbolt strikes we have no choice in the matter. The first time I had ever seen Alienor, lady-in-waiting to Matilda, the king's sister, would live with me forever. So too would the moment I set eyes on Joanna.

As I discovered, Rhys and Katharina had become inseparable. After my escape, it had been the most natural thing in the world for her to abandon Duke Leopold's employ. She had no reason to stay, she explained to me, all the while staring at a mooning, doe-eyed Rhys. Cooks were needed everywhere, were they not? Disarmed, pleased for Rhys, I had agreed that she should accompany us to England. She could act as my personal cook.

'Here you are, Sir Rufus.' She held out the platter, which could not have held another crumb, or another sliver.

'*Danke*, Katharina,' I said, and received another broad smile. I leaned against the end of the wooden counter, ignoring the bemused looks of the house cooks, and set to.

From the corner of my eye, I saw Katharina and Rhys billing and cooing, like two enamoured doves. I felt a spark of hope; with her thus occupied, I could drop food unnoticed to the pair of scrawny cats winding themselves around my legs.

I picked up a chicken thigh. The cats' interest redoubled. One stood on its hindlegs, front paws on my calf, its gaze fixed appealingly on me.

It was as if Katharina knew. 'How is the food, Sir Rufus?'

'Delicious, thank you,' I said, and brought the thigh up to my mouth. I ripped off a hunk with my teeth. 'Absolutely delicious.'

Satisfied, she returned her attention to Rhys. I waited until they were kissing, and then managed to drop the rest of the chicken down to the cats. A goodly piece of beef pie followed, but two cats could only eat so much, and at a certain speed. Discard any more, and I risked being found out. Telling myself that an overfull belly was better than having to cross the river and fight the French, I continued eating.

'When shall we go for the catapults?' asked Rhys. Katharina had gone off to tend to a pot of something. 'Not tomorrow night, for certes,' he said. 'Thanks to that bastard FitzAldelm.'

'Let us see what the morning brings,' I said, 'and how many men-at-arms are on duty near them. If there are more than today, and they are still there come sunset, we shall know FitzAldelm sent word over the river.'

'Even if there are no more guards, we cannot be sure he did not overhear us,' said Rhys. 'It might only mean he did not succeed in alerting his masters.'

We exchanged a grim look.

'If we do nothing, the Frenchies will pound the walls to dust while we watch,' I said. 'We had best do something – but in a few days.'

'Aye.' Rhys beckoned to Katharina. 'She has something to tell you.'

I managed to drop several mussels on the floor unseen before she returned, nudging them under the counter with the point of my boot. The cats scrambled after them, hissing at one another in their eagerness.

She studied my platter, which was now more than half empty. 'You need more, Sir Rufus?'

'No, thank you, Katharina.' I bestowed my best lady-pleasing smile on her, and prayed it worked. 'I could not fit in another bite, tasty as it is.'

'You need to eat more, sir,' she said. 'Skin and bone you are. It is what I am always telling Rhys.'

I glanced at him for support, and got nothing back but a shrug.

'Rhys tells me you have news,' I said, changing the subject.

She looked at him; he spoke into her ear, and she grinned. 'Ah yes. FitzAldelm.' The last word was whispered. She winked at me. 'You want him watched?'

'I do.' I did not say why; Rhys would have told her.

Her gaze moved to the lad whose ear she had reddened. 'He will do it. So will his friends.'

'Who are they?'

'Half a dozen other starvelings. By-blows, orphans, the usual types you find in towns. They sleep rough, or in the lofts of stables, and survive through begging and petty thievery.'

'How came this one' – I indicated the roast-pig-turner – 'to be working in the kitchen?'

'I caught him trying to steal my purse soon after we arrived in the town. I reddened his arse, and took him under my wing. When the steward here took me on, he also accepted the lad.' Katharina smiled, as if it were standard practice to adopt a street urchin, join a household staff uninvited, and bring in the ragamuffin at the same time. 'Knows every street and alley, he says.'

'I ran an eye over the rest of them,' said Rhys. 'A likely lot, they are, like myself at that age.'

I grinned, picturing the stick thin, sharp-eyed Rhys, and how I had won him over with some fresh bread. This might work, I thought. 'And the price?'

'Full bellies will be enough,' said Katharina. 'I can easily see to that, but a few silver coins would not go astray either.'

'That can be arranged,' I said, smiling. 'You are a woman of many talents, Katharina. Quite the pair of intriguers you make, in fact.'

They could not have looked more pleased.

And so it was settled. Jean, as the boy turning the pig on the spit was called, and his friends began to shadow my enemy's every move. As Jean told me cockily the very next day, FitzAldelm could not visit the jakes but they would know.

While we waited for useful information to come from our spies, Rhys busied himself over the next few days with discreetly finding boats. This he did by asking the garrison commander who among the town's boatmen could be trusted, and then seeking these men out with plentiful amounts of coin to hand. Few things buy loyalty and silence like silver. Meanwhile, I selected two dozen men-at-arms of Earl Robert's, all hardened soldiers. I did not tell them my plan; they did not need to know until we were literally about to embark.

Whether FitzAldelm had managed to send word over the Seine, I was not sure. The number of French guarding the catapults remained the same, but that was not to say it was a ruse, designed to lull us into thinking they did not know our intentions. For all I knew, scores of the enemy came down to the water's edge after nightfall, and kept close watch.

There was only one way to find out if Philippe had been alerted, and that was to cross the river.

CHAPTER XIV

P erhaps an hour after compline Jean came to report to me; the routine had become the daily norm. It was the fourth evening since our arrival in Rouen, and until now, he and his band of cronies had discovered nothing of any use. I knew that FitzAldelm rose early, and trained in the courtyard of the house he was renting (incredibly, one of the urchins had found work delivering bread to the house, thereby gaining brief daily entry). FitzAldelm attended morning Mass in a nearby church, but spoke to no one, unless it was the priest. Hearing this, I deputised one of the urchins to watch over the cleric, in case he was a French agent.

The rest of FitzAldelm's day was spent making the rounds of storehouses and granaries, and meeting with town councillors, merchants and wagoners. Any of these could have been French sympathisers; indeed, many of them might have been, but if my spies were to be believed, he rarely met the same men twice. I made sure to get descriptions of the ones he did, and was able to determine that they were worthies of the town, whose loyalty was in little doubt. At night, FitzAldelm returned to his house, only emerging to visit the likes of Earl Robert and other nobles.

Today disappointment oozed from Jean; his shoulders were slumped, and he gave a dispirited response to my greeting.

'Nothing new to report?' I asked.

'He went to an armourer's, sir.'

My attention pricked. This was different. 'Do you know what for?'

A sly grin. 'Of course, sir.'

'Well?'

Jean held out a filthy paw.

'I will decide if your information is worth silver, not you.' I stared, hard-faced, until he looked away.

Sulkily, he revealed that FitzAldelm had taken delivery of a fancy dagger with ornate silver workings on the scabbard.

This was unremarkable. 'Did he stay long in the shop? Talk much to the armourer, or anyone else there?'

A reluctant shake of the head.

'That is no news at all, you rogue.'

A cheeky grin. 'You cannot blame a man for trying, sir.'

He was a plucky little sod, I thought, amused. 'Go on with you. Keep the watch on him close, d'you hear?'

He nodded.

I turned to leave.

'Where are you for now, sir?'

I glanced back. I was heading to the postern door that opened close to the main gate, and from there I would walk to the riverbank. Rhys would be waiting with two men-at-arms. In perhaps an hour's time, they would row us over the Seine, while he and I sat in the prow with loaded crossbows. Our mission would be fraught with risk, but I was looking forward to it. I had not been in a decent fight since Outremer.

'Never you mind,' I said.

'Down to the river, sir, that is where you are bound.'

I gave him a sharp look. 'Why do you say that?'

'Your man Rhys spends his days there, he does, trying to hire boats.'

'How do you know that?'

'One of the lads has been trailing after him, sir.' Before I could react to that, he said offhandedly, 'If I had to put money on it, I would say you are going spying or some such.'

'Whatever I am about is none of your business, nor anyone else's.' I held up a warning finger. 'You had best not have told anyone about this.'

He tapped his nose, solemn as a judge pronouncing sentence. 'No one outside my gang, and they talks to no one.'

Satisfied, I made to leave again.

'Take me with you, sir.'

'It is far too dangerous,' I said without thinking.

'You *are* crossing the river,' he said, triumphant.

'Maybe I am, maybe I am not,' I replied. 'Mention a word to anyone, and you will end up at the bottom of the Seine. Understand?' I gave him the look I reserved for prisoners I was interrogating.

'I won't tell no one, sir,' he said sullenly. 'I want to come with you. I can help. No one passes no heed of a child, if the Frenchies even spot me, that is.'

He was right, I thought. A skinny little wraith, he would be able to steal ashore unseen with a far greater chance of success than Rhys or me. Yet it was madness to take a boy, scarce eleven or twelve years old, into a situation that could easily turn violent. A brusque refusal rose to my lips, and checked itself. There was something in his face, a naked appeal, that touched my heart. He reminded me of Rhys – I could not deny it – and giving him a chance had been one of the best decisions I had ever made.

'You do exactly as I say,' I growled. 'Step one foot, nay one inch, out of line, and I will leave you there for the Frenchies.'

'I will follow your orders, sir, to the letter.' He capered from foot to foot, any trace of cockiness gone, as happy as a four-year-old with a marchpane fancy.

Oddly, it was Rhys who objected more to Jean's presence, but even he admitted that the boy had a better chance of spying out the catapults. 'He is a child,' Rhys protested to me while Jean prowled up and down, eyeing the far bank and imagining what he would do.

I waited a long time after matins before I judged the risk of crossing was worth it. Thick clouds hung overhead, turning the world as dark as the back end of a wine cellar. These were just the conditions I wanted. If a sentry change had taken place at matins, those men were now cold and bored, and with luck, drowsing. Rhys and I eased the rowboat, a craft big enough for four men, down the mud to the river. Jean pushed too, eager to add his puny strength to our effort. It slipped in without a sound, ripples eddying out on either side. I helped Jean aboard, handed over our two crossbows and bags of quarrels, and then clambered in after him, taking care that the end of my scabbard did not knock off the timbers. Rhys pushed the boat into deeper water and as it gained momentum, joined us. While Jean perched at the prow, Rhys took the oars. We had wrapped their middles in thick canvas; they fitted into the tholes snug and silent.

I lifted a hand, and as the river began to take us downstream, we listened.

I could hear men's voices, and a horse whickering, but the sounds were coming from the French camp. Not a sound was audible from the opposite bank, a bowshot away. I nodded at Rhys.

He turned us around, and slow and gentle, began to work the oars.

We inched across, aiming in a diagonal to counter the effect of the current. It did not matter overmuch where we came ashore: the catapults were arrayed along almost a quarter of a mile. Avoiding French sentries was our main concern. From what I had seen over the previous few days, they did not tend to linger near the water's edge, preferring to position their watchfires close to the artillery.

Nothing was different tonight. We eased in towards the French bank, all three of us watching for the enemy. Not a soul was visible. Perhaps fifty paces distant, a catapult was partly outlined by the light cast from a sentry's fire. Keen to keep my eyes accustomed to the gloom, I did not look directly at the blaze, rather at a slight angle. There were several shapes huddled around it, none stirring. If I pricked my ears, I could hear them murmuring. I tapped Jean's arm, and indicated the Frenchies. He nodded, lips peeling back in an excited grin.

I spoke into his ear, quiet as I could. 'Be careful. If you are caught, act as we agreed. You are a boy from St Denis-la-Chapelle, scavenging for food.' This was a village a mile north of the enemy camp.

Jean lifted the burlap bag we had found beforehand. In it were a couple of not completely stale loaves – the very things a boy might steal from soldiers' tents.

'Avoid all contact, and come back soon –'

He nodded again, cocky as you like, and whispered, 'I know. There is no need to check every catapult, just six or eight.'

'We will be here,' I told him.

'And if you are discovered?'

We had previously agreed that in the dreadful eventuality of this, Rhys and I would come back for him every night an hour after matins. The harsh reality of this possibility – Jean being abandoned on the enemy side of the river, alone – now sank home with the viciousness of a chasing mongrel sinking its teeth into my calf. The thought of him having to run the gauntlet of the Frenchies for a whole day and a night, at the least, changed my mind.

'This is too dangerous,' I whispered. 'You will stay in the boat – I will go.'

Jean made no reply, but stood up in the prow – Rhys had brought us right to the river's edge. I sensed his purpose but, before I had time to react, he leaped onto the bank.

I gestured savagely that he was to come back.

Jean paid no heed. His teeth flashed white in the darkness, and he was gone.

Pursuit was out of the question, and the boy knew it. Cursing silently, I looked back at Rhys.

He was grinning. 'The lad is resourceful, you cannot deny it.'

I shook my head in frustration, and asked God to watch over Jean.

I gently lowered myself over the side and into the shallow water. As I had hoped, I was able to pull the boat aground just enough to keep it from floating away, requiring only a decent shove to set it back into the river. Rhys passed me my crossbow and a bag of quarrels, and readied his own.

I set the end of my weapon against my bellybutton and pulled back the string until it caught. I laid a quarrel in place, and then, forefinger close to the trigger, I crouched down and listened. From the fire I had spotted came murmurs, a man's cough, a demand for the skin of wine, but nothing of concern.

It was nerve-wracking waiting there in the dark. I was sore tempted to creep along the bank, assessing the Frenchies' positions for myself, but that would increase the danger for Jean. Fretful, belly twisting, I did nothing.

An eternity passed during which I grew cold, angry, and even more nervous. What I had done was heartless, I told myself, risking a small boy's life instead of my own. I thought guiltily too of the youth I had slain in Udine. The more I brooded, imagining Jean being attacked by a murderous French sentry, the more I felt the need to act. The chances of finding him were akin to locating a needle in a haystack, but, I reasoned, doing something was better than letting him fall into enemy hands, or worse, being slain.

Mind made up, I beckoned Rhys, who shuffled up to the prow. 'It has been too long,' I whispered. 'I am going to search for him.'

He did not say a word.

Surprised, I pulled back to gauge his reaction.

Rhys was staring over my shoulder with a fixed gaze. 'Look,' he mouthed.

I twisted; peered.

Ambling towards us, with the gait of a bored, half-asleep sentry, was a Frenchie. Perhaps forty paces separated us, open ground with not a speck of shelter.

I hesitated, mind spinning crazily.

He would see us before I could get close enough to silence him forever, and once his cry raised the alarm, Rhys and I would be forced to flee. I considered trying to shoot the Frenchie, but my quarrel would have to take him in the throat. It was an impossible shot, taken in the darkness, at a target perhaps six inches by four. There was nothing for it, I decided, but to walk towards him, nonchalant as a fellow sentry, and hope that I got near enough to stab him.

I turned to tell Rhys my plan, and found myself regarding his cross-bow, aimed not at me but at the Frenchie. Rhys's one eye was closed, and the other was sighting down the length of the quarrel.

'Shhhh,' he whispered, soft as a mother to a babe in the cradle.

My protest died. I looked over my shoulder at the Frenchie.

He was about thirty paces away, his posture still relaxed. His attention seemed to be on the ground to our right, his left, but was slowly coming our way.

Acid surged up my throat.

To be sure of the shot, Rhys needed him closer, yet with every step the Frenchie took towards us, the danger magnified a hundredfold. A quarrel flew almost as fast as sight, but quicker still would be a man's bellow for his comrades.

A few more paces the sentry came.

I stooped and laid down my crossbow, then drew my bollock dagger and held it so the blade laid against my thigh, less obvious. I prepared to sprint forward.

At last he saw us. He stiffened. Took one more step in our direction, as if trying to be sure of what his eyes were telling him.

Click went Rhys's trigger. An innocuous sound, at odds with what it signified.

I was praying – I would offer a Mass every day for the next month – when it hit the Frenchie.

Emitting a quiet, choking sound, he dropped like a stone down a well. His arms and legs twitched once or twice and were still.

My attention went past him, to the fire where his comrades sat. None moved or cried out, and I breathed again. I watched them for the space of twenty frenzied heartbeats, but not a one stirred from his place.

My gaze searched the blackness off to our right, whence Jean had vanished. Where in Christ's name was he?

I glanced at Rhys, who had the cockiness to wink.

I gave him an exasperated glance, and turned my attention back to the Frenchies. It was only a matter of time before they missed their slain friend. Much as I wanted to, going to look for Jean now risked my being stranded as well as him. I stood there, feeling like the court fool. Retrieving my crossbow helped, but only a little.

I do not know how much time passed without any sign of Jean, a hundred heartbeats, maybe twice that. It felt like ten years.

A call issued from the direction of the watchfire. 'Guillaume?'

Rhys and I stared at each other, the same awareness in our eyes. Guillaume was the dead man.

'*Guillaume? Où es-tu, crétin?*' The voice was unconcerned. Grumbling followed as the Frenchie's comrades decided who would look for him.

The lack of concern did not allow my nerves to slacken even a hair's breadth. Unless Jean appeared within the next few moments, we were going to be seen for a second time.

'Guillaume?' This was a different voice, and it was irritated.

A man had stood up by the fire. There was a crossbow in his hands.

Sweat slicked down my back. Our luck was up. This sentry would see us or the boat long before his unfortunate fellow had, and his shout would bring dozens of Frenchies haring to the riverbank.

A flicker of movement off to the right caught my attention. Out of the blackness came a short figure, running lithe and silent. It was small enough only to be Jean.

I could not remember ever having felt so relieved.

'Guillaume!' The voice was angry.

Jean's head turned. He saw the Frenchie with the crossbow, who in turn saw him. There was no question that the boy could be a comrade

— he was far too little. In one smooth movement, the crossbow came up and, *click*, the trigger went.

I swear my heart stopped.

It was too dark to see the flight of the quarrel, but Jean kept running, and as a soft splash carried from the shallows, I knew the Frenchie had missed.

An instant later, our ears filled with his cries of alarm.

Jean came hurtling in, a grin plastered all over his face.

'Get in the boat!' I hissed.

He obeyed, nimbly leaping into the prow.

I took a shot at the Frenchie, and missed. Handing Jean my crossbow, I pushed the boat out into the current. I was not prepared for a sudden drop off in the bank – we must have just missed it on our approach. Down I went, head submerged, legs flailing in vain for a purchase. Up I bobbed, drenched and furious.

'Rufus?' Rhys had stilled the oars. 'Rufus?'

'Row,' I ordered, spluttering. 'Row for your life!'

There was no time for Rhys to argue the point. Feet were pounding towards the river; more and more voices were calling to one another, and the *click*, *click* of crossbow triggers was audible too. He went to it, and the little craft took off across the water.

I swam after, praying that my head was too small a target to hit.

Splash. Spray coated my right ear and the side of my face. The quarrel had landed less than a foot away.

I had a strong urge to empty my bowels. There is no dignity to be found in extreme fear. I took a deep breath and dived. I swam underwater, hoping that I was going in the right direction. Not until my chest felt as if it would explode did I surface again. I surfaced, gasping and coughing like a drowning man, my eyes searching for Rhys, Jean and the far bank.

Swamped by relief – I was nowhere near the boat, which was ahead of me, but I was more than halfway across – I risked a look back whence we had come.

Figures lined the water's edge. Crossbows were clicking, but the Frenchies were shooting blind. Quarrels were landing here, there and everywhere. A younger me would have shouted triumphant insults; instead I busied myself with making it to the other side.

I emerged from the river thirty-odd paces from where Rhys had brought the boat ashore. Dripping, casting wary glances at the Frenchies – an unlucky shot might yet hit me – I made my way towards him.

'There you are.' Relief was writ large on his face.

'Aye. Did any quarrels come close?'

He indicated the stern, from which jutted no less than two bolts. 'Both lucky strikes, just as I reached this side.'

I nodded, thankful. If the quarrels had hit closer to the French bank, they would have punched through the timbers and then, possibly, into Rhys or Jean.

'There are so many sentries,' said Jean.

Thunk. A quarrel drove into the earth perhaps ten paces distant. Another landed in the water close by.

'Hold your tongue until we get behind the walls,' I ordered. 'It would be stupid beyond belief for one of us to be injured or killed now.'

He made a face, and I cuffed him round the ear.

'What was that for?' His voice was indignant.

I cuffed him again. 'Sir.'

'What was that for, sir?'

'Not doing what I told you, wretch!' I shoved him along the path that led to the gate.

He gave me a ferocious scowl over his shoulder. 'You could never have done what I done, sir, and not been seen.'

'Oh yes?'

'I counted all the sentries, sir, and' – he thrust the burlap bag violently at me – 'I filled this!'

Rhys and I shared an incredulous look. He was the first to laugh. I could not but join in.

'What is funny, sir?' Jean demanded.

We reached the gate, and I hammered on the timbers in the agreed pattern, twice, a pause, three more, another pause, then one.

'Well?' He was outraged now. 'Half a ham, I got, sir, and a wheel of cheese!'

A sentry asked who was there and, impatient, I told him Sir Rufus, adding, 'Who else would it be?'

As we waited for the locking bar to be lifted, I regarded Jean. 'How many sentries?'

'More than a hundred, sir. I stopped counting after that.'

'You did well.' I glanced at Rhys; there was no need to say what we both knew. FitzAldelm *had* got word over the river. 'Why did you not come back sooner?' I asked Jean.

He shrugged.

He had wanted to impress me, I decided. 'You went to look for supplies?'

'Yes, sir.'

'You are brave, lad, but foolish.' I held up a hand, forestalling his protest. 'A lump of ham or cheese is not worth being caught by the Frenchies. You would still be screaming at sunrise if they had caught you.'

'But I got away, sir!' He grinned, a rat's teeth grimace. 'I pissed in their bedding too.'

The door was creaking open. I was not sure I had heard him aright. 'Eh?'

Any trace of humility was gone; he was triumphant now. 'I pissed in four sets of blankets, sir, or was it five?'

The nearest gate had been opened a foot and a half, no more. Rhys and I, laughing helplessly, led the way through the narrow gap. Jean dogged our heels, proudly revealing that he would have emptied his bowels into the Frenchies' bedding if he had been able.

This only increased our mirth.

I was barely able to acknowledge the salute of the bemused sentry.

Despite the hilarity, a grim awareness was niggling at me.

Thanks to FitzAldelm, we could not risk an attack on the French catapults.

CHAPTER XV

After a late-night feast on Jean's ham and cheese – both were superb, we told him, increasing his delight – I sent him off to bed. He went, protesting, but stifling massive yawns behind his hand.

Our near escape and Jean's revelations meant I was in no mood for sleep. Nor was Rhys. We perched on stools in my room, supping wine.

'As I see it, we are faced with two main problems,' I said.

'Unless we destroy the Frenchie catapults, they will eventually bring down the walls,' said Rhys.

'That is the first.'

'FitzAldelm, the whoremaster, is the second. You should have let me finish him in Outremer.' Rhys's look was accusatory.

'He is mine to kill, not yours.' There had also been an oath to Joanna that I would not harm him.

Now Rhys glared. 'Nonetheless, if I had slit his throat then, we would not be in this situation.'

'Aye, well, you did not.' I was furious with myself – because he was right – but if Rhys had done my dirty work, Joanna would have winkled it out of me. As I had previously, I decided that her respect was worth more than killing my enemy in underhand fashion.

'So what are we to do?' asked Rhys.

I chewed my lip. We both wanted nothing more than to slip a knife between FitzAldelm's ribs and heave him over the rampart and into the Seine, but Richard wanted proof of his treachery. Infuriatingly, what had happened tonight was not concrete evidence. There could be another explanation for the numbers of Frenchies guarding their artillery – a second agent in Rouen, for example, who might have seen our boat and put two and two together. A strong swimmer could cross to the far bank with ease.

The unpleasant truth was that unless we caught FitzAldelm in the act, or he admitted his guilt – both of which were improbable, to say the least – the situation could drag on, allowing him to continue feeding information to Philippe Capet. Meanwhile, the French catapults would pound the walls and threaten us all.

Much as I wanted to remove FitzAldelm from the equation, Richard would want every how, why and wherefore of my mission. I did not fancy trying to lie through my teeth to the king about a murder, and yet to watch and wait endlessly seemed as bad an option.

I reached a decision. 'In the morning, let us follow him to the church where he attends Mass. We shall take both him and the priest for interrogation.'

'You would interrogate a prelate *and* a belted knight?' It was unusual for Rhys to look shocked.

'Interrogate is too strong a word for what I would do to the priest,' I said, winking. 'They are a soft kind. A mark of silver says that leaning on him will be more than adequate.'

'And FitzAldelm?'

I thought of Earl Robert, so friendly with my enemy, and how he might react, and of the king, whose response, although delayed, might be even more extreme. It was worth the risk, I decided. 'Give me an hour, and I will make him sing like a cagebird. His confession will convince the earl. Then we can execute him like a common criminal.'

Rhys hummed and hawed, but he did not argue.

I worried again about the king, but told myself that by the time he found out, FitzAldelm's bones would be mouldering underground. Richard would be able to do nothing, and would accept my account of what had happened.

The prospect of a permanent solution to the threats posed by my lifelong enemy saw me to bed in fine humour. I dreamed not at all, but rose with a smile of vengeance on my face.

I dressed in plain tunic and hose, wanting to appear like any man in the street. I wore no armour, in case it shinked or knocked off something and gave me away. My sword could lie hidden under my cloak.

Rhys breakfasted on leftover bread scraped over with honey, but the only appetite I had was for seizing FitzAldelm. I paced about, watching, impatient, until he growled that he was ready, and shoved a last hunk into his mouth.

Despite the early hour – it was not long after prime – Jean was waiting in the courtyard, fresh-faced though there were strands of straw in his hair, evidence of his sleeping place. 'What are we for today, sirs?' he asked, his face alive with interest.

'Mass,' I said.

He looked unhappy. This was not something we had ever done. 'Mass?'

I let his not addressing me as 'sir' pass. It was the first step on a slippery slope, as it had been before, I realised, my eyes on Rhys. I did not care.

'Yes, Mass. It is good for the soul.' I elbowed him. 'You know that, surely?'

'Aye.' Jean muttered something else under his breath.

I chuckled.

He whipped around. 'Which church, sir?'

'The one close to FitzAldelm's lodgings.'

A sly grin split his face. 'We are not just going to Mass, then!'

'No,' I said, my tone mild, even as my expectations rose. 'We are not.'

Rhys and I left Jean outside FitzAldelm's house; his compatriot, a runny-nosed brat with a wall eye, was already in place. One would come to tell us when my enemy was on his way, and the other follow after, unseen.

The church, which lay only a short walk away, was small. This forced an immediate choice. Linger outside, and FitzAldelm might spot us, or notice as we entered after him, and become suspicious. To go in beforehand and take up a station near the back seemed the better option.

It was cold inside, like all churches, and the matted straw covering the floor was in dire need of a change. Unlike many of the townspeople already present, Rhys and I did not have cushions or stools. Dirty knees mattered not as long as I captured FitzAldelm, I decided. Eyes roving for a cleanish spot nonetheless, I picked my way between the worshippers to the right-hand back corner of the church.

Five or six people between us and the door was enough, I decided. It was unlikely that FitzAldelm would come near us. According to Jean, he liked to stand near the front, close to the priest, so they could talk after the service.

We kept our heads down. Dressed like anyone else, we got only idle glances. Rhys, never much one for praying, picked at his nails and scuffed his feet like a bored child. Rather than stare constantly at the entrance, to spot FitzAldelm entering, I allowed myself the occasional, casual glance.

My imagination ran riot as I waited. After so many years, my enemy would soon be at my mercy. Oddly, I felt little exultation. I hated him, aye, and wanted him dead, but the fire of my hatred had lost its white-hot heat. Whether my killing of Henry had something to do with it, or the amount of death I had seen in Outremer, or the cutpurse I had killed in Udine – I was unsure. Maybe it was a combination of all three. There would be no torture of FitzAldelm, I decided. He would have an appointment with the executioner soon enough.

Deep in thought, I did not see him arrive. It was Jean who brought the news, appearing at my side, and tugging on my sleeve.

'There he is, sir, see?' Jean whispered, his eyes indicating the direction.

Even from the back, I would have recognised that block head any-where. FitzAldelm was purposefully making his way to the front of the congregation. Jean confirmed he was alone, which was pleasing. Rhys and I would overpower him with ease, and the length of rope around Rhys's waist would secure him tighter than a bundle of faggots. The priest, being terrified, would obey my order not to run.

I had rented a back room in a rundown tavern close by; it was accessible via a side alley. The innkeeper's palm, well-greased, would see us afforded complete privacy. A leather gag would prevent the customers hearing FitzAldelm's cries and the priest's sobbing.

Jean was bobbing about with impatience. 'Shall I go closer, and keep an eye on him?'

'Where is your friend?'

'At the door he is. If our man gets past you somehow, he will follow him.'

Pleased that he had anticipated this eventuality, I nodded. 'Go on, then. Do not let him see you.'

Jean gave me a withering look and slipped away between a fat man who was praying noisily, and a toothless crone perched on a rickety stool.

'Was I that cocky?' Rhys asked.

I snorted with amusement, drawing a reproachful tut from a skinny man with almost no hair. I ignored him, and muttered, 'I cannot remember.'

'Katharina is growing fond of him.'

I knew instantly where this was headed. 'He is *not* coming with us when we leave Rouen.'

'If you say so.' Rhys's tone was airy, confident even.

I swallowed my protest. This was not the time, but I could see already how I would fare, one against two, in the battle over Jean's future. The fact that I was Rhys's master and Katharina's employer, that I was a knight and they ordinary people, would count for naught.

A bell rang, and I set aside thoughts of Jean. A ripple of anticipation passed through the congregation. The crone stirred and, with an effort, stood. The priest, a sallow-faced man about my age, came in with two clerks at his back. A small choir was next, six monks who had seen better days. They were no singers either, murdering a Gregorian chant. Their efforts were not helped by the portative organ played by the last man to enter. A bulky apparatus suspended from his neck and played with one hand while he worked the bellows with the other, it wheezed and parped worse than a patient with a severe case of indigestion.

The procession made its way to the front of the church. I noted FitzAldelm give the tiniest nod – to the priest, I assumed – then he turned back to face the altar.

The Mass began. The priest, like so many of his kind, clearly liked the sound of his own voice. Florid in style, he lingered over his words and paused often for dramatic effect. This was bearable for the dura-tion of the short service, but he launched into his sermon with such gusto that I suspected we would be here for a while.

FitzAldelm was in sight – the back of his head was visible – so I let my gaze wander over those around me. I was not alone in paying scant attention to the priest's moralising. Rhys was dozing on his feet, as only someone who had done countless night-sentry duties could. A nearby youth was entirely focused on excavating the insides of his nostrils with a grimy forefinger. Just past him stood a man who appeared unable to stop scratching his groin. Crabs, I decided.

Finally, the sermon ended. The creed and the offertory came after. I gave Rhys the kiss of peace, managing in the process to dodge the crone with the stool, who was hovering with clear intent. Chagrined, she kissed the fat man instead; he seemed as displeased as I would have been.

I did not go up for Holy Communion; nor did Rhys. This got us a mixture of curious, disapproving looks, but I cared not. My wait was nearly over. FitzAldelm would soon be in my power.

As the last stragglers were given communion and shuffled back to their places, I watched my enemy. It was as if he sensed my gaze. He turned and stared in my direction. Although there were plenty of people between us, there was a straight line of sight. Hastily, I dropped my gaze, hissing at Rhys to do the same.

I dared not do what I most wanted – look at FitzAldelm again.

The priest began to intone the final prayers, for Mother Church, for the king, that he be freed soon, for Earl Robert, and his success in defending the town against the French. The bishop was mentioned also, and other priests. On and on he droned.

'Move,' I whispered to Rhys. 'We need to get closer.'

There were more looks as we wove a curving path through the congregation. I was polite, though, and my smiles, by-your-leaves and thanks saw us meet with little objection. My timing was perfect. I reached a point perhaps ten paces behind FitzAldelm as the final prayers, the Paters and Aves, started. Everyone knelt. As the people in front stooped and bent, I did so more slowly, and spied Jean even closer to my enemy. He saw me, and grinned.

I shot a sidelong glance at Rhys. 'Ready?'

'Aye.'

The priest began to intone the blessing that signalled the end of the Mass.

I folded a section of my cloak behind the hilt of my sword, so that it could be drawn the instant I stood. Easing my hand to my side I found a small boy watching me. His eyes were as wide as plates: he knew what the hilt signified. My heart thump-thumping, I gave him a broad, what I hoped was disarming, smile, and placed a finger to my lips.

The priest finished his blessing.

'Mama,' the boy said loudly.

Her head turned.

'Look down,' I whispered quickly to Rhys. I covered the sword hilt with my forearm, and stared at the floor, and prayed that FitzAldelm had not been alerted.

'Go in peace,' said the priest.

'Sir!' It was Jean's voice. Urgent. Insistent.

I rose, hauling out my sword even as the small boy gave his horrified mother a triumphant 'I told you so' look.

To my dismay, FitzAldelm was hurrying towards the back of the church.

Hoping that he was merely going to the sacristy, there to meet the priest, I chased after him. I went fast, stepping as light as a thief avoiding a guard dog. Rhys was with me, blade held low and ready by his side.

For us it was twenty paces to the doorway. FitzAldelm was a great deal closer. Nonetheless, moving faster than he, we would have caught him right at it – had he not glanced over his shoulder. Our presence here, in his clandestine meeting place, told him everything. Fury blossomed on his face, and then he was running.

'You and your friend watch the priest!' I roared at Jean. 'Do not let him go anywhere.'

FitzAldelm hurtled through the doorway.

I reached it a heartbeat later, barely avoiding a face full of timber as he tried to slam the door. He heaved, desperate to slip across the bolt and shut me out. Sensing his purpose, I put my shoulder against the door and pushed with all my might. Rhys joined me, and together we shoved it open a couple of inches. A brief contest followed, before FitzAldelm gave up. The door swung back violently, and we staggered. Footsteps rang off the flags as he sprinted into the gloom of the sacristy.

We went after him like the hounds of Hell.

Lashing out, FitzAldelm pulled over a massive, ornate, cast-iron candlestick.

Right on his heels, I succeeded in hurdling it. Unable to see what I could, Rhys was not as lucky. It connected with his shins, and he fell, swearing violently.

My jump allowed me to close on FitzAldelm. I grabbed his tunic with one hand. I could have plunged my sword into his back – a devil in my head told me to – but I needed to interrogate him. 'Stop!' I ordered.

He paid no heed, only pulled away violently. His tunic tore. I was left gripping a fragment of ripped fabric, and FitzAldelm took on a new burst of speed.

If you had asked me before that point who of the two would have won a footrace, I would have wagered my entire fortune on myself. I was wrong.

In more than one way.

Without warning, FitzAldelm turned left, into an alcove.

I skidded past it, came to a halt, spun around.

Slam. The sound a shutting door makes is distinctive.

I lunged into the alcove, taking in the low, metal-studded door at its back even as my ears filled with the snick of a bolt ramming home. I threw myself against the door, and was rewarded by the agony of iron studs shoving into my flesh. Uncaring, I did it again, and again. The door did not budge even a little. Panting, I placed an ear against it, and heard the echo of running footsteps.

'Where is he?' Rhys arrived, limping.

I hammered a fist off the timbers. 'On the other side of this.'

'The sly bastard!'

'He is all of that,' I said vehemently.

'Where will the passage lead?'

'My guess is that it leads to a tunnel that takes him outside the walls.'

'We need an axe!' Rhys cast about the sacristy, turning the air blue with oaths.

'Even if you find one, he will be long gone ere you smash the door down. Let us see what the priest has to say about where it comes out.' Grim-faced, I headed back to the church proper.

The picture that greeted me was comedic. Waving a rusty knife, Jean had the priest backed up against the altar, while his wall-eyed friend kept several concerned members of the congregation at bay with a similarly decrepit-looking blade.

I let Rhys deal with the townspeople, and stalked to confront the priest. His face, puce with anger from Jean's threats, turned a winding sheet shade of grey.

'Y-y-you may not harm me,' he said. 'This is the house of God!'

'So it is,' I snarled. 'A fine place to plan treachery against Richard, your sovereign!'

Shocked gasps came from behind me, which was pleasing. I had intended to be heard.

A bead of sweat ran down his face. His lip trembled.

'Where does that passage lead?'

He was stupid as well as false. 'P-passage?'

I brought up my sword, and gentle as a surgeon about to cut, laid its tip just under his left eyeball. 'Do not make me say it twice,' I said.

He trembled. A dark stain appeared at groin level on his woollen robe.

I did not care if he shat himself as well. I pressed with the blade, just a little.

'I-it becomes a tunnel that runs under the walls,' he whispered, 'coming out close to the Seine.'

Bitterness washed over me in a tide. 'And there is a boat.'

'Aye.'

There was one consolation to this mess, I decided. FitzAldelm's flight put his treachery beyond doubt. The next occasion we met, I could kill him without compunction.

And I would, I thought, my gaze moving to the gilded cross on the altar.

As God in Heaven was my witness.

CHAPTER XVI

W e rushed from the church to the postern gate nearest the tunnel's mouth, but of the boat and FitzAldelm there was no sign. By the jaunty waves of the French men-at-arms who saw us ranging up and down the bank, my enemy had crossed the river to his new master Philippe Capet. The pair suited one another, I thought sourly, full of guile as they were. I would spread the word about Fitz-Aldelm. With luck, that would prevent him from wreaking any more harm.

I went next to Earl Robert. He was horrified twice over: at Fitz-Aldelm's treachery, and also because I had not brought him into my confidence earlier.

'I am sorry, sir.' My words were genuine. 'You and he seemed good friends. I could not take the risk that you might inadvertently let him know that I was on to him. It was bad enough that he heard us talking about setting fire to the enemy catapults.'

Robert had the grace to look guilty. 'How did I not see it? Why did I not realise?'

'He is as sly as a fox, sir, and has pulled the wool over everyone's eyes for a long time.'

'Thank Christ none of you were hurt that night.' An unhappy shake of his head. 'You say he has been in league with Philippe since Outremer?'

'Yes, sir.' I told the story of the Templar tunnel at Acre.

The question I dreaded followed. 'What did the king say when he heard?'

It had been difficult enough to tell Richard about FitzAldelm's blackmail. I was not about to let the earl in on my dirty secret too. 'He told me to watch him.'

The next question was also unavoidable. 'Why did he send Fitz-Aldelm back to Normandy? Surely it would have been better to keep him close, rather than allow him to plot and scheme with Philippe?'

'In comparison to his brother John, the king judged FitzAldelm to be of little risk,' I said, hoping this sounded plausible.

To my considerable relief, the earl nodded, swallowing the lie. 'I can understand that.' He thumped my arm. 'In future, you are to tell me about things this important! Not for nothing were we two of those who charged the Saracens at Joppa with the king. FitzAldelm was not there – and even if he had been, Richard would not have picked him.'

It pulsed in the air, almost a physical thing, the unbreakable bond that had been forged between the thirteen of us on that day of days.

'I will.' I met Robert's gaze. 'You have my word.'

Later that day, a French boat crossed the river. Bearing aloft the white staff and standard that signified his status, the herald – a knight – walked to the main gate and asked to be admitted.

The earl and I met him just inside the entrance. The garrison commander was with us. His breath was heavy with wine, but he was sharp-eyed as a falcon.

The herald bowed to the earl, and gave cordial greeting to the garrison commander. He glanced at me without recognition.

I made no attempt to introduce myself.

'The king of France sends you word,' said the herald to the earl.

Robert cocked an eyebrow. 'Indeed?'

'John, Count of Mortain, has done homage to him for England, and has given up Normandy, and all other lands on this side of the sea. The king has come hither to take possession of this city. Allow him to enter peaceably, and he will prove a kind and just master.'

'And the safety of the men of the garrison –'

'– is guaranteed until they reach the nearest stronghold that currently remains under King Richard's control.' The emphasis on the word 'currently' was quite deliberate.

'I see.' Robert rubbed his chin, in the manner of a man in deep thought. He glanced at me – I smiled blandly – and then at the garrison commander, who nodded as if some silent message had passed between them.

There was no question of giving in to outrageous demands such as these. We had talked about it beforehand. Robert was playing with the herald.

He let the silence drag on.

The herald's gaze moved around, trying to gauge what was going on. As the moments dragged by, his patience ran out. 'Do you have an answer for King Philippe?'

'I do,' said Robert. 'Tell him that Rouen's gates are open to him.'

'Open?'

'He can enter any time he likes. No one opposes him.'

Full of suspicion, the herald looked at me and then the garrison commander. We gave him blank stares. 'You are surrendering?' the herald asked Robert.

'Tell him the gates are open. He will receive a warm welcome.' The earl's tone was light, mocking.

The herald understood; his lips thinned. 'By your leave,' he said, and departed.

'I would pay a lot of silver to be there when Philippe hears your message,' I said quietly.

Robert chuckled. 'And I!'

But I would have given everything I owned to have captured Fitz-Aldelm instead. His loss smarted like salt in a wound.

The French king did not take up the earl's invitation, unsurprisingly. Over the next few days, both sides settled into a siege proper. To our good fortune, the enemy catapults were as mediocre as the ones they had used in Outremer; their crews were also ill-trained. The Frenchies knocked off chunks of masonry by the score, and killed our men now and again, but were unable to consistently hit the same spot in order to effect a proper breach. The walls that ran along the Seine were soon pockmarked from top to bottom. For the most part, however, the integrity of the defences remained unaffected, and we rebuilt the worst affected spots faster than the Frenchies could hit them again.

Their efforts were not helped by ours. Four nights after FitzAldelm had escaped, long enough for the enemy sentries to grow complacent, I took a dozen men-at-arms over the river. Landing several hours before dawn, we cut the torsion ropes on no less than seven catapults before the Frenchies realised. We retreated into the darkness immediately, suffering no casualties.

Wary of further attacks, the enemy pulled their artillery right into their camp every evening after that. The Herculean task was made that much harder by a spell of warm, sunny weather. It soon became a daily habit for our men to stand on the ramparts, jeering and hurling insults at the Frenchies sweating and cursing as they pushed the catapults away from the riverbank. Inevitably, the marksmen among the garrison began to hold competitions with war bows and crossbows alike, and Earl Robert, keen to keep morale high, put up prizes.

The distance from the wall to the river and over to the other side was a shade over two hundred paces – right at the limit of even a powerful crossbow's range. Recognising this difficulty, Robert offered a gold coin for every Frenchie killed in this fashion, or six silver pennies for a man injured. The rewards for an enemy hit or slain by an arrow were less attractive, but still good enough to ensure that when it came time each day for the French to drag away their catapults, the walls were thronged with soldiers.

After a week, things changed for the worse. Where their new artillery crewmen came from, we had no idea. Some said they were Italian or German, others Flemish. There were not many of them, thank Christ, or larger sections of the walls would have been brought down, thereby sealing our fate. But there were enough to see that five or six of the catapults hit exactly where the aimers wanted.

They selected a spot to the left of the main gate, and hammered it from dawn to dusk on the first day. The outcome was plain long before the barrage ended. A section of battlements had been smashed away, the broken chunks falling down by the Seine, and a zigzag crack wide enough for a man to slide his hand into ran from there partway to the base of the walls.

Earl Robert and I went to inspect the damage as the light vanished from the ominous, red-orange sky. Despite the late hour, it was damnably hot. I cast an eye at the Seine, tempted to join Rhys and some of the bolder men-at-arms later. They had sworn to take a dip in the river when it was full dark. Needless to add, Jean and his cronies were badgering to go as well.

Robert's voice dragged me back to the present. 'The wall here will collapse, if not tomorrow then the next day.'

'It is hard to see how it will not,' I agreed, leaning out into mid-air to get a better view of the crack. A perverse part of me was pleased. Months and months had passed since I fought in a battle. Joppa had been in August of the year before, and it was almost June now. I missed the sheer bloody thrill of going blade to blade with an enemy. I straightened, and caught the earl's eye. 'The Frenchies will attack the instant it has fallen.'

'They will,' he said grimly. 'We will have a desperate fight from the start.'

'If the French get even a toehold in the breach, their efforts will redouble.'

I did not need to add that Rouen would then fall – or the earl would have to agree its surrender.

'If we throw them back, the artillery barrage will resume,' said Robert. 'They will create an even larger breach.'

On the heels of that would come another full-scale assault, which would be harder to withstand. Even if that were thrown back, I thought, the cycle would be repeated over and again until we capitulated or were overcome.

'We could essay another night attack,' I said. 'Go right into their camp in force, and fire as many of the catapults as possible.'

'They will be expecting that.'

'Maybe so,' I said, my stubbornness taking hold. 'That is not to say it is not worth trying.'

'The casualties could be terrible.'

'And they will not be when the Frenchies storm the walls?'

'Night-time battles are devilish affairs at the best of times, and that is before you add in a river at our backs. Imagine a fighting withdrawal to the Seine, with Philippe's entire force ravening after us.'

It was not a pretty picture. I shook my head in reluctant agreement. 'Maybe you are right.'

'I am. The risk is too great.'

There was silence as we fell to brooding.

It did not sit well with either of us that we should have to wait for the French to attack us, wait for them to batter down the walls, and be powerless to do anything in response. Much as we desired it, no miraculous solution presented itself.

The answer, to surrender Rouen to Philippe, was as plain as the nose on the end of my face, but neither of us wanted to voice it.

We came down from the battlements in sombre mood.

At street level, my eye was caught by a group of archers. Lacking a practice range or an open field, they had set up straw targets against the gate, and were good-humouredly competing against one another.

I could not believe neither of us had thought of it before.

'Earl Robert,' I said. 'I have an idea.'

The damage wrought by his artillery saw the French king in combative mood. Early the next morning, a fresh barrage began. But for the efforts of our archers, who were lying in wait, the day might have turned out disastrously. Standing up en masse as the Frenchies dragged the catapults into their final positions, and aiming at the new artillerymen – stupidly, proudly, they wore tabards with a stand-out pattern – they cut down seven with the first volley. Many others were injured, also removing them from the crews working the catapults.

The losses meant the original aimers had to return to their jobs. Happily for us, and our intent all along, the Frenchies' accuracy went back to something approaching its previous poor levels. Their efforts were hampered too by our archers' shafts, which rained down without pause. The artillery crews could not show an inch of flesh without risk of it being feathered. So heavy was the arrow storm that the shields held by the soldiers protecting the artillerymen often resembled hedgehogs; periodically their owners had to withdraw to safety, there to remove the shafts.

Although I was no bowman, I was also present. Rhys had challenged me to a shooting competition the previous night. To humour him, I had agreed, but I gave up soon enough. Why waste the shafts, I told Rhys, when men like him could utilise them to far greater effect? He laughed, and at once began a wager with a wizen-faced Welsh archer who was old enough to be his grandfather.

I did not go back down below. Like everyone, I was taking great delight in the Frenchies' pathetic shots. Some were not even making it as far as the walls. We hurled insult after insult at the artillerymen. They could not hit a barn door at twenty paces. Were they shooting blindfolded? Had a sightless man been given charge of each catapult?

Whether our verbal barbs had any effect, I do not know. It did not matter. Our men's morale was being boosted. I was also happier. The conversation I had had with Earl Robert the previous evening had been really troubling; it was hugely encouraging now to see the Frenchies' efforts reduced to almost complete ineffectiveness.

When word reached Philippe Capet, he was not pleased. This was evidenced first by a commotion in his camp, trumpets blaring and messengers running to and fro. A short time after, groups of men-at-arms, some still donning their helmets or buckling on swords, began to gather on the edge of their camp.

I sent word to Earl Robert at once, and had the alarm sounded. I nudged Jean, who had taken, limpetlike, to staying by my side all day long, and said not unkindly, 'Time to go.'

A hurt look. 'Why?'

'See, over there. The Frenchies are going to attack, and soon.'

'Then I will fight them too!' From nowhere, his rusty dagger was in his small fist. 'You saw me with the priest! I am not afraid.'

I hid a smile, not wanting to puncture his confidence. He reminded me of a farmyard terrier, ready to take on a dog three times its size. I bent until we were eye to eye. 'Your courage is beyond question, Jean, as is your loyalty.' He nodded, mollified, pleased, and I went on, 'You might not realise it, but there is a world of difference between cornering a soft-handed priest and facing a French man-at-arms coming off a scaling ladder with death in his heart.'

He began to protest, but I cut him off. 'No, Jean. Before long, this will be no place for a child.'

To my surprise, he nodded. There was always more, though, always an attempt to come away with some gain. 'Let me bide a moment or two more. The French will not be ready to attack for a while. They are only bringing their boats down to the river, look!'

'You are bull-headed as I am,' I said. Sensing the tide turn, if only briefly, he grinned. 'You can stay until the first boat enters the water,' I said. 'If you are not gone by then, I will give your arse a good tanning.'

He took that in good spirit, and threw himself into hurling insults at the French.

Philippe's soldiers had been busy, I soon saw. Dozens of craft had been built, or more likely, appropriated from every riverside village for miles. Ladders had been built too, plenty of them. They were crude things, yet sturdy-looking. My belly tightened. There was no decent breach, but we could still have a decent fight on our hands if enough ladders went up against the wall.

I cast about for Rhys. He was overseeing the carrying up to the walkway of buckets of quarrels by Jean's friends. Groups of men-at-arms were assembling at the bottom of the nearest set of steps, and, I could see, at the others as well.

I was worrying overmuch, I decided, remembering how our cross-bowmen had held Saladin's mamluks at bay for an entire day at Joppa. They had only had the protection of our spears to stand behind, and here the soldiers had a twenty-five-foot high wall.

'Let the Frenchies come,' I said quietly.

Jean heard. 'Aye, the flea-bitten dogs,' he cried. 'They will not forget our welcome for many a year, those of them that survive!'

'God grant it be so,' I said. 'Now make yourself useful – help your friends with those quarrels. When that is done, you are to go back down and stay there.' I watched him walk away, grumbling, and smiled. Give him a few years, I judged, and he would be a good squire.

Following my instructions with reluctance, our archers delayed shoot-ing until there were hundreds of Frenchies gathered on the opposite bank. The crossbowmen, with their shorter-range weapons, also waited. When they were packed together like a crowd at a Christmas market, I gave the signal.

The enemy knew what was coming. They had dozens of men with shields to protect those charged with getting the boats in the water, and loading on the ladders. Theirs was an impossible task, however, and our archers made the most of their opportunity. First they shot high arcing flights, one, two, three, four in the space of thirty heartbeats. A dense cloud of shafts went up, black, shimmering, graceful against the blue sky. It came down with an incredible, lethal speed.

Shields were peppered. Open spots of ground suddenly sprouted thickets of arrows. Frenchies began to scream. Frenchies began to drop. Frenchies began to die.

Wounded, or scared, or just reacting to the cries of their comrades, the men with shields wavered. Their shields moved, lowered, shifted, and our archers, who had just been ordered to take aim at individual targets, shot and shot into every little space and gap. Not every arrow killed, but they did not need to. They simply kept coming in vast numbers, punching through shields, sometimes finding homes in flesh, sometimes not. Morale, that elusive, fragile thing, can be shattered by many things, and endless numbers of shafts landing with each panicked heartbeat is one.

I did not see where it started, but one moment the Frenchies were still trying to load their craft and even get them launched, and then they were breaking and fleeing in wild panic. Arrow-riddled shields were discarded, wounded comrades left screaming on the ground. Boats perched half in, half out of the water, some with dead men sprawled inside, or draped over the side, legs in the water. Two craft that had been launched but still needed oarsmen began drifting gently downstream.

The archers cheered and congratulated each other, and kept shooting.

I turned my face away. The Frenchies were enemies, and I would have killed my share in face-to-face combat, but this was slaughter.

Philippe, who suffered from petulance at the best of times, must have been incandescent, because he ordered another attack not an hour after the complete disintegration of the first. This was even more doomed to failure, with the riverbank a carpet of corpses and screaming, wounded men, and our archers ready with replenished quivers.

The Frenchies broke without getting one boat into the water, and suffered casualties as heavy as before.

As I said to Earl Robert, come to witness the clash, Philippe must have been dancing up and down with rage, like a little child deprived of his plaything. This was not my imagination, but something he was known to do if his wishes were thwarted. I was correct. The French king had lost control of himself, and the proof of this was an abortive third assault later in the afternoon. It did better than the second, in the main because there were sergeants and captains literally driving men – with fists and boots – towards the river.

Our archers needed no telling, and arced their first volleys high up, so the arrows fell at the rear of the enemy ranks. Perhaps half the officers went down, kicking and screaming, choking out their last bubbling breaths round poplar shafts tipped with steel. That was enough for the ordinary soldiers to take to their heels. They ran as the surviving officers protested in vain.

Our men's laughter and insults followed the Frenchies all the way back to their camp.

Philippe saw reason then, or perhaps his advisers succeeded in dissuading him from needlessly sacrificing more of his troops. There were no more attacks that day, only a herald-agreed hour's cessation of hostilities for the Frenchies to carry away their wounded, and later, an attempt to drag away their catapults. They succeeded with all but two, but again suffered heavy casualties, thanks to our archers. The pair of artillery pieces left close to the bank were too great a temptation to resist. Before it was even dark, with the Frenchies busily licking their wounds and no doubt drowning their sorrows, I slipped over the river with Rhys and fired them.

We stayed on the ramparts late into the night, drinking wine and watching the flames consume the two catapults.

'All in all,' I said muzzily to Rhys, 'this was a good day.'

''Twould not surprise me if that is the end of the siege,' he opined, taking a long pull from the costrel. 'Losses like that will sap most men's desire for a fight.'

I snorted, remembering the French king's spinelessness in Outremer. 'You could be right. Philippe is no warleader.'

'That he is not,' said Rhys, very slowly and deliberately.

'You are drunk!' This was rare.

He belched. 'I might be. 'Tis a fine night for it.'

I took the costrel from him and raised it in a toast. 'Here's to the Frenchies pissing off whence they came.'

He grinned. 'That is worth drinking to.'

CHAPTER XVII

O ur wishes came true, albeit not straightaway. Unseasonal storms and heavy rain battered the area for several days, turning Philippe's camp into a sea of mud. Confined to their camp, the strings of their catapults dampened, they did not attempt another attack. Still they stayed, though, lingering like the smell from a blocked sewer, for another seven days. Then, in a great show of Philippe's petulance, the Frenchies smashed their barrels of wine, letting it soak away rather than leave it for us. They also managed, using considerable amounts of oil, to fire all of their remaining catapults. The conflagration could be seen for miles.

A herald came on the last morning, delivering the French king's threat that he would visit the townspeople with a rod of iron. They were empty words, sent to try to cover up what was a humiliation of the first order.

Sad to say, the lifting of the siege did not mean our troubles were over. Philippe had taken large numbers of castles in March and April, those promised to him by the craven John. Among them were Dieppe, Arques, Eu, Aumâle, Mortemer, Évreux, Nonancourt and Louviers, and Philippe was hellbent on taking more. Verneuil held out against him, its castellan ignoring John's order to surrender to Philippe, but the French king followed that failed attempt by taking in quick succession the border fortresses of Pacy and Ivry. I was not alone in suspecting that the former, which was of little tactical importance, was targeted because it belonged to Earl Robert. Its capture galled him, but as he said, it mattered little compared to Gisors. The loss of that stronghold, so vital for the defence of Normandy, would be a real thorn in our side.

So we thought, and yet the hammer blows did not come. Puzzled, Robert and I discussed it at length. The initiative was with Philippe.

If Richard had been the French king, for certes he would have kept it that way, continuing his attack on Normandy. He would have used Philippe's effective combination of threats and sieges, which intimidated and nibbled away at the morale of nobles and landowners.

There was no doubt in my mind that if this tactic had been pursued, goodly numbers of other castles would have surrendered, weakening Rouen's position further and increasing the likelihood that all of Normandy would switch its allegiance. As it was, the vigorous defence of Rouen and the shameful manner in which Philippe had departed showed that the Angevin lion still had claws.

One week became two. May ended, and June began, and still the anticipated French assault did not materialise. Of FitzAldelm there was no sign. Tasked by the earl with visiting a long list of castles to gauge their owners' loyalties, I made it my business to enquire after my enemy everywhere I went. Rhys and Jean, who accompanied me, went to work in their own fashion as well, spying and asking questions, eavesdropping and greasing palms with coin. We left Katharina behind, much to her disgust.

From Rouen we first went north-east and then, reaching the border with France, cut back down southward. The land was a curious patchwork of strongholds that had gone over to Philippe and those which had stayed true to Richard. We found neither hide nor hair of Fitz-Aldelm. That meant little. He could have passed within a mile of us and we would not have known. For all I knew, he was doing the same as I, but calling in on the lords who had transferred their loyalties to the French king. He could equally have been in Paris, brown-nosing Philippe: there was simply no way of knowing. As our frustrations rose, Rhys often made it plain that we should have slain FitzAldelm when the chance offered itself, and dealt with the consequences – Richard's reaction foremost among them – afterwards.

I did not argue. Rhys was right. My enemy was gone for good. Never would I have the satisfaction of telling a dying FitzAldelm that I *was* his brother's killer. It was bitter medicine to swallow. I visited church after church, making rich offerings and hoping that God would overlook my hypocrisy and accept my prayer that FitzAldelm would come within my reach one more time.

We were back in Rouen in mid-June when disturbing news came from the French court. Philippe, the master of duplicity, had arranged to meet the Holy Roman Emperor Heinrich on the twenty-fifth of the month, in Vaucouleurs.

Earl Robert was as worried as I had ever seen him. He paced about the great hall in the citadel, reminding me of the caged lion I had seen once. To and fro, fro and to, he went, never ceasing.

'Philippe will pay anything to lay his hands on the king. He would sell his own mother if he had to. Once Richard is in his dungeon, he will throw away the key.'

Robert was right, I thought. Relations between the two kings had been bad since their bitter quarrel in Sicily, when Richard had slurred Alys, Philippe's sister, and had only grown worse in Acre, when Richard had shamed the French monarch in front of his entire retinue. Now Philippe loathed Richard with every fibre of his being. He would stop at nothing to make our lord his prisoner.

'Is there nothing we can do?' I cried.

'Not from here,' said Robert bitterly.

As a young man, I might have punched the wall in my rage, but I knew better now. I thought of Richard who, unlike me, was a tactician as well as a soldier, and took solace. 'The king will not be lying idle,' I declared.

Robert gave me a keen look. 'Do you know something I do not?'

'No. But I remember him telling me how Heinrich liked to poke his nose where it has no right to be.'

'The murdered candidate for the bishopric of Liège.'

'Even so. Because of interfering behaviour like that, Heinrich has enemies throughout his realm. Richard, on the other hand, has cordial relations with some of those nobles, because of previous alliances.'

'He has commercial influence with those men too.' The territories on the Rhine all relied on trade with England.

'I wager he has sent messages to every count and prince, every duke and baron from Speyer to the Narrow Sea, asking for their help,' I said, feeling heartened. Richard's royal status meant he was permitted to write letters to whomsoever he chose.

So it proved. Mere days before the meeting at Vaucouleurs, word reached us that Heinrich had reconciled his differences with the majority of his rebellious nobles from the Rhineland. No public mention was made of Richard's involvement, but his mark was all over the rapprochement. The good news continued. Instead of meeting Philippe, Heinrich agreed to hold a great court at Worms on the twenty-ninth of the month, at which he would swear on the Gospels that he had no hand in the murder of Albert of Brabant, the once bishopric candidate in Liège.

With each passing day, our certainty grew that Philippe's military campaign had drawn to a close. Jaded with assessing border lords' loyalty, frustrated that I had found no sign of FitzAldelm, and with little else to do, I began to feel restless, and useless with it. I spoke to Earl Robert about riding to join Queen Alienor in Aquitaine; she was there to put down a rebellion by the ever-troublesome Adémar of Angoulême. We both agreed, amused, that she needed no help, and that she might not take kindly to my leaving Normandy, where the king had sent me.

'I will go mad if I have to sit on my hands for much longer,' I told the earl one evening as we made a circuit of the walls. It had become our evening ritual.

'How do you think I feel?'

I made a rueful gesture of acknowledgement. As the commander of the king's forces in the area, Robert had to remain where he was for the foreseeable future.

'The hunting is good, you have to admit.'

'A man can chase after deer or boar only so many times before it palls.' I felt instant remorse. 'I apologise. I find doing nothing hard to deal with, that is all.'

'Nothing, is it? Sometimes I forget that you have never had to rule your own lands, Rufus, that you have known only skirmishes and battles, and the glory of our deeds in Outremer.' He chuckled. 'The day-to-day running of towns and cities and land is boring, there is no denying, but it is essential. Dealing with self-important town councillors, authorising funds to repair broken drains, holding court so that farmers and merchants can air their grievances – these are part and parcel of what it is to be a lord.' He made a face. 'And when the Frenchies are not here to fight, those mundane things are our day-to-day bread.'

'I am of no help. You can do this with your eyes closed,' I protested.

He knew where I was going. 'Richard tasked you with coming to Normandy.'

Despite the rebuke, I sensed weakness, and pounced. 'Yes, to aid you in its defence against that caitiff Philippe – who, like FitzAldelm, is nowhere to be seen!' I replied triumphantly.

He rolled his eyes, but I knew I had him.

Ere we had finished our stroll, it had been agreed that I should ride to Worms. Although late for Heinrich's impending court, like as not, I would be able to see the king. Of recent days, his conditions of imprisonment had been relaxed. I would endure Richard's reaction to my unexpected and disobedient arrival, I told a finger-wagging Robert, just for the pleasure of being in his company again. I would also report what had happened in Rouen and Normandy, and bring back his new orders.

My options to reach Germany were the longer but safer northern route through Flanders, or the one that went straight as an arrow through France, Philippe's realm. The risks, we decided, were not so bad that I could be called a fool for choosing the latter. In plain clothes, on unremarkable-looking horses, Rhys and I could pass for routiers, mercenaries. If we avoided large towns, and Paris in particular, the chances of being recognised or captured by any of Philippe's vassals was very small. It was similarly unlikely that we would cross paths with FitzAldelm, but I held onto the hope of that as extra justification for abandoning my appointed task.

Katharina was not pleased to hear of our imminent departure. I did my best not to listen to the argument she had with Rhys when he told her, but her outraged voice would have carried to the depths of a mine. It was amusing how meek he was, I thought, considering his ferocity in battle. I remembered then with some embarrassment how easily Joanna had bettered me on many an occasion.

'What do you mean, Jean is going with you?' Katharina thundered.

Rhys's response was indiscernible.

'I found Jean! I engineered your master's escape! I have more right to come with you than that boy!'

Again Rhys's quiet answer could not be heard.

'Do you not love me anymore? Have you tired of me?' Swift as a knife turning in a wound, the way only women can, she changed direction. 'You are in love with another woman – I know it!'

'I am not,' Rhys protested, in the I-am-damned-no-matter-what-I-say way of men in such situations.

I decided to intervene, before he was overwhelmed. It was a short distance along the corridor from my chamber to theirs. I rapped on the half-open door, and entered without waiting for a response. Two startled faces regarded me. Naked relief blossomed on Rhys's; on Katharina's I read a mixture of anger and hurt.

'Your pardon for interrupting,' I said, smooth as a lawyer making his case before a judge, 'It was impossible not to overhear some of your . . . discussion.'

Katharina managed to soften her scowl, but her bow was cursory to say the least.

I let it pass. 'Earl Robert has asked that you stay, Katharina,' I said, lying through my teeth. The earl was very appreciative of her cooking, and had told her so on more than one occasion. Let her take the bait, I thought.

'He has?' Her tone was a little mollified.

'Yes,' I said firmly. 'He will have it no other way.'

Her eyes shot to Rhys, to see his reaction.

'I am not surprised,' he said with the eagerness of a dying man offered salvation.

'The earl is throwing a banquet for Midsummer's night, you see,' I added. This was true, but Robert had made no mention of Katharina to me. 'You are to be the main cook,' I declared, full of bravado.

She cracked, smiled. 'That would be an honour.'

'Excellent,' I said, hoping that Robert would prove amenable to my just-made promise.

I was in luck. The earl *was* happy to retain Katharina's culinary skills for the feast, which was being held, along with a tourney, as a gesture of Richard's goodwill to his local liegemen.

And so three of us, not four, departed Rouen. Jean, riding the donkey I had purchased for him, was the proudest of all. My heart warmed at the sight of him on his lowly mount, proud as a fresh-belted knight on an expensive destrier. I quickly decided he was even prouder than that. He looked transported, like a man who had been first over the walls of Jerusalem, and seen the city taken.

'The boy is here to stay,' I said to Rhys.

An amused look. 'Have you only just realised?'

'I have been denying it for some time, but now I see the error of my ways,' I said, grinning. 'It is time you started instructing him how to use a blade.' There was no answer, and I glanced at Rhys. 'You have begun already!'

An up-down, of-course-I-have, of his shoulders. 'These past weeks have been tedious. It seemed a good idea to teach him some skills, if he is not to come to grief the first time he comes up against someone other than a flabby-bellied priest.'

My lips quirked. I would long remember that scene. 'When were you going to tell me?'

'I am surprised the boy has not told you himself.' He jerked his chin at Jean, who was talking aloud, and by the sounds of it, issuing a stern challenge to another knight.

I laughed, and the tension that had been eating at me over the previous few weeks began to dissipate. I had escaped the day-to-day drudgery of life in Rouen, and although I was not riding to war, I was on my way back to Richard. There was danger too – much of our ride would be through France – which only added to the spice.

Despite my boldness, being chased through enemy territory would have had but one result, and I had no wish to be imprisoned by one of Philippe's lords. As someone far less important than the king, my incarceration might have proved long indeed, and Rhys and Jean would have fared worse. So we kept our heads down, avoiding other travellers' eyes, and rode hard. Apart from seeking accommodation in quiet inns, and changing horses every couple of days, we interacted with no one. Jean had been upset at having to leave his donkey soon after our departure, but he accepted that if he were to continue with us, he also had to travel fast.

Crossing the frontier into Germany, we reached Worms on the last day of June. The town was still thronged with visitors, nobles, dignitaries and prelates, come from all over Heinrich's realm to attend the court. All the best lodgings were taken; a room in a ramshackle inn close to the stews had to suffice. Gaping chinks in the walls, the none-too-clean bed linen and sagging mattresses went unnoticed by Jean. Wide-eyed as a man discovering Croesus's treasury, he declared it to be a veritable palace. That made it bearable for me – almost – but a bad back and a few flea bites were of small concern beside our real purpose in the town.

Discreet enquiries in the tavern by Rhys – thanks to Katharina now able to get by in German – revealed that Richard was still in Worms.

This came as a great relief. I had been worried that Heinrich, the ostentatious public display of his prisoner over, might again have sent the king to a castle such as Dürnstein.

According to the well-lubricated, opinionated merchant Rhys had talked to, Richard was, within reason, free to come and go from the emperor's palace. He had been seen out and about in the town that very morning, visiting an armourer's. Gossip had it that he was to send to England for his falcons.

'If this is true,' I said to Rhys, my spirits high, 'meeting him will not be difficult.'

'Shall we just go and ask to see him?' Rhys was ever the cynic.

The baldness of his statement checked me. I had no wish to announce myself at the palace gates as a follower of the king's and be promptly slung into a dungeon, a possibility that, despite the certainty of a drunk merchant, could not be ruled out.

'Perhaps you are right,' I said with a sigh. 'Let us wait until the morrow. If he emerges from the palace, well and good. We can greet him then. If he does not, we shall have to get a message to him by other means.'

After breakfast the next morning, ruefully scratching my plentiful bites, I sent Jean to watch over the main entrance to the palace. It was not long before Rhys and I joined him, much to his chagrin.

'I do not need you!' He puffed himself up like a fighting cock. 'This is my job – leave me to it.'

'Peace, little man,' I said, cuffing him gently. 'I will not stay in that bedchamber a moment longer. I swear I can see the fleas jumping on the floor. Even if the taproom were not a stinking midden, I have no wish to drink this early, nor to wander the streets like an itinerant pedlar. We shall all wait.'

Grumbling, with a scowl that would put the fear of God into the timid, Jean stalked off, taking up station on a corner opposite to ours.

'Feisty, eh?' was Rhys's wry comment.

I shrugged. Although Jean had an attitude, he also did what he was told when it mattered. That counted for more than his impudence.

The sun beat down, pleasant warmth that would become hard to bear if we had to wait beyond the middle of the day. Ever the hungry one, Rhys wandered over to a cheesemonger's. A party of Templars tramped by, easily recognisable by the crosses on their surcoats. I lowered my gaze, in case any had been in Outremer. A quartet of washerwomen, baskets balanced on their hips, stopped by the palace gate so that one of their number could harangue a guard – her unfortunate husband, it seemed. Dutybound to stay put, he could do nothing but endure the abuse even as his comrades howled with delight.

When the harridan was done, the entertainment continued in the form of an ox-drawn wagon stacked high with hay which was trying to turn into the narrow street between me and Jean. It got wedged between the buildings. Every shopkeeper and passer-by for a hundred paces in every direction came to stare. Suggestions to remedy the problem came thick and fast; it was startling how many people seemed to be expert at cart driving or stockmanship.

Engrossed in the comedic spectacle – the potbellied wagoner swearing and attempting to force the four oxen backward, and at the same time cursing at the advice-givers and trying to stop Jean-like urchins from tugging out handfuls of hay to throw at one another – I forgot why we were there.

'God's legs, what is going on?'

I had no need of Rhys's sharp jab to the ribs. Only one man used that curse, in that exact tone.

Richard was here.

I had had the entire journey to think about what I would say to the king when we met. All I managed, as he rode around the end of the wagon and saw me, was a pitiful, 'Sire.' I dropped to one knee, Rhys copying me.

'God's legs,' he cried again, this time in surprise. '*Rufus?*'

William de l'Etang was right behind Richard, on another horse. His face was a picture. 'Rufus?' he echoed.

I stood, aware that everyone's attention had transferred from the wagoner and his vehicle to me. 'Yes, sire.' I raised my eyes. To my great relief, the king's face was no longer hollowed out, and the deep rings that had been present under his eyes before I left were gone. He looked tanned, and healthy, and as full of life as I had ever seen him. 'It is wondrous to see you, sire.' I gave William a grin, which he returned.

'I would say the same, were you not supposed to be in Normandy.' Despite his words, he was fighting not to smile. 'You must have good reason to be here.'

'In a manner of speaking, sire.' I flicked my eyes left and right. Few among the scores of people goggling at us would speak French, but some might.

He took my intent. 'Ride with me. We can talk outside the city.' He barked an order, and one of his guards meekly dismounted and handed me his horse's reins.

'Look after Jean,' I said to Rhys. 'And tell William what has happened.'

The king noticed Rhys then, and guffawed. 'Sweet Jesu, did you bring the cook – Katharina? – as well?'

'No, sire.' I swung up into the saddle. 'She was not happy to be left behind!'

'I am not surprised. She is strong-willed,' said Richard, laughing. He urged his mount forward into the crowd, which parted like the sea before Moses. 'Tell me all.'

CHAPTER XVIII

Worms, Germany, July 1193

To my considerable relief, the king accepted my reasons for leaving Normandy and coming to seek his counsel. He was unsurprised by the lack of impetus to Philippe's campaign, and greatly entertained by the accounts of Earl Robert telling the herald that Rouen's gates were open to the French king. He revelled in the account of our archers breaking the attack on the breach. I continued with the story of Fitz-Aldelm's flight. Richard shook his head and declared himself a fool for ever trusting him.

Once we were beyond the walls, the guards, four in number, lagged back a hundred paces. I glanced back, surprised.

'I have given my word not to escape,' the king explained.

'It is good they are treating you better, sire,' I said, heartfelt.

'Aye. Things were not this pleasant after you left, I can tell you. That fat goose the Bishop of Beauvais lingered at the imperial court, and he must have bent Heinrich's ear. One morning, for no apparent reason, the guards loaded me down with chains so heavy that a horse would have struggled to move them.'

'Sire!' I cried in horror.

A grim smile. 'Ten days they left me like that, the curs, giving me food that was barely edible. By the time they took off the chains, I was as pale as a ghost, and weak as a kitten.'

I was furious. 'You are sure Beauvais was behind it, sire?'

'Oh yes. He came to gloat over me. If I ever lay my hands on him, he shall receive the same treatment, be he bishop or no.'

'What was the outcome of Heinrich's court, sire?' I had some idea from eavesdropping in roadside inns as we neared Worms, but I wanted to hear it from the king.

'He has made peace with most of the nobles who were causing the dissent.'

'Thanks to you, sire.'

An inclination of the royal head. 'There were letters going to and fro between me and half a dozen princes and barons for weeks. They came around when Heinrich promised to clear the air by denying his involvement in Albert of Brabant's murder. He was lying through his teeth, of course, but appearance is what counts. The main reason for the Rhineland princes accepting his word is that it serves them to be on good terms with me. As for Heinrich, he is relieved not to have half his realm in open rebellion. *My* reward was that he ended his dealings with Philippe Capet.' A pause, then Richard added, 'For the moment at least.'

'Good news, sire.' I could tell it was not that simple, however. 'So Heinrich will allow you to ransom yourself?'

'He will, for one hundred and fifty thousand marks in pure silver, Cologne weight no less.'

'That is half again what he demanded in the spring!'

'It is, but the puppet master holds the strings, does he not? One hundred thousand is for him, and fifty thousand for Leopold.' Richard pulled a face. 'In truth, I am more than a puppet – here we are, free to ride out of the city – but I am still a prisoner, and powerless before the majority of Heinrich's outrageous demands. The terms offered before you left remain in place, for example: the galleys for the invasion of Sicily, the knights to be provided, the hostages to be sent, and so on. My young niece Alienor of Brittany is to wed Leopold's eldest son.' The king's lips quirked. 'It is not all bad. If I can bring about a lasting reconciliation between the emperor and my kinsman Heinrich der Löwe, the ransom will be reduced to its original figure of one hundred thousand marks.'

'When will the hostages be released, sire?'

'Once two thirds of the monies have been received. I am to set Isaac Comnenus free as well, which matters to me not at all.' The rogue ex-emperor of Cyprus had been incarcerated since we had taken the island in a lightning campaign on the way to Outremer. 'His daughter, "the damsel of Cyprus", is to wed one of Leopold's sons also; the youngest.'

Joanna would be sorry about that arrangement, I thought. She and Berengaria had taken the girl under their wing in Outremer. Their time together had seen a strong bond formed. 'And you, sire, when will you be given your liberty?'

'Archbishop Walter, who is in Worms, tells me that one hundred thousand marks will have been raised by October, three months hence. He envisages the rest being ready early in the New Year. It is my hope that Heinrich will release me then.' He saw my expression, and clapped me on the shoulder. 'Six months, Rufus. Half a year. It is not long.'

'I suppose not, sire.'

'I see your mind! You are not staying with me, never fear.'

Annoyed both that he had seen through me – again – and that I had been selfish enough not to want to re-enter his gilded cage, I said, 'I will if you ask, sire.'

'I know that. You are like me, however, and caging a wild beast for no good reason is pure cruelty. If you were a diplomat, there would be no question of your leaving, but you are not.' He smiled, taking the sting from his words.

'What would you have me do, sire?'

'Another long, hard ride awaits, I am afraid, and you only just arrived.'

My interest pricked. 'To where, sire?'

'Mantes.'

I knew of the town, which lay on the Seine, not far west of Paris. 'I will go, sire. To what purpose?'

'Philippe has already had word of Heinrich's court, and what happened there. Apparently, he sent Johnny a message which included the warning, "Look to yourself, the devil is loose." ' Richard chuckled. 'Can you imagine my little brother's face when he read that? I would not be surprised if he quit England's shores for a time. No, it is Philippe I must be concerned about. God's toes, but it is a pity I am not free now, so I could shortly ride up to his gates with an army.'

'That would be a Heaven-sent day, sire.'

'It would! One day we shall do it, mark my words, but for now we must work with what is in front of us. Philippe knows that his position has been greatly weakened by the agreement I have come to with Heinrich. He is keen to consolidate his gains in Normandy. When he receives the letter I sent, hot on the heels of Heinrich's one, he will agree to the conference I have suggested at Mantes. William Longchamp is to lead my delegation. Sad to say, he will have to agree to greater concessions than I would like, but beggars cannot be choosers.'

'When is it to be held, sire?'

'The ninth of July.'

My rear end would not thank me for this, I thought. Hundreds of miles lay between Worms and Mantes. I grinned, as if he had just ordered me to take a five-mile jaunt, and said, 'I had best leave soon, sire.'

'You can go the moment my secretary has finished penning my letter to Longchamp. You will be given coin to buy replacement horses along the way.'

'Thank you, sire.' A thought came to me. 'FitzAldelm might be there.'

A stern look. 'Bloodshed is to be avoided at peace conferences.'

'Men who disappear do not bleed, sire.'

He weighed up my words, and nodded. 'You know I do not stand for such tactics, but what he has done to you over the years is unconscionable. Do what you must.'

Rhys's face lit up with glee when I told him that Richard had given us tacit permission to kill FitzAldelm.

'Let us not cook the goose before it is caught. We have to find him first,' I said.

'What better place to look for him than at Mantes? He is as likely to be there as anywhere.'

'So I hope.'

'We need a plan, else the first moment he sees us, he will be gone as fast as a rat down a hole.'

'Maybe not. Remember, he is arrogant, and those attending peace negotiations are honour-bound to keep the peace. I would not be surprised if he stays close to his companions, and there preens and struts like a peacock, knowing we cannot harm him.'

'Even a peacock needs to empty itself,' said Rhys with an evil look. 'I have always wondered about killing someone in a jakes.'

'He is mine to kill,' I said, repeating the old refrain.

'Yours can be the first blade.'

'I will give you that.'

We nodded at each other, solemn as men taking the cross.

We arrived in Mantes on the evening of the eighth of July, saddle-sore, sunburnt and irritable. I left Rhys to find us a room; Jean, so weary he could barely talk, went with him. I went meanwhile in search of William Longchamp.

His lodgings were in the grand house belonging to the richest merchant in the town. This was unsurprising, for despite his humble origins – perhaps *because* of them – Longchamp liked to celebrate his own importance. He and I could not have been more different in that regard.

The men-at-arms guarding the front door did not recognise me, but they bowed the instant I told them my name. One hurried inside while the other asked my forgiveness for the delay.

A little to my surprise, William des Roches came back with the man-at-arms. A stalwart supporter of the king's father Henry and a friend of William Marshal's, he had fought against Richard and I at the battle for Le Mans, four years before. I fancied I had even crossed blades with him. Like Marshal, he had switched allegiances after Henry's death. While Richard took this in his stride, it had not sat easily with me. Des Roches had proved his worth and his valour in Outremer, however. Although I did not like him overmuch, finding him bristly and contrary, I respected the man.

'Rufus!' He was surprised to see me.

'Well met, William.' I stuck out my hand, and we shook.

His eyes went up and down me. 'You look as if you have ridden a hundred miles without pause.'

'Almost four hundred, and with only a little rest. I come from the king.'

Surprise rose in his eyes. 'You bear news for William and me, then, I warrant.'

'I do.' I tapped the satchel on my hip.

'Come in. Are you thirsty?'

'As I was that day at Arsuf.'

He roared with laughter. 'I doubt that, but I hear you. While you talk with William and the others, I shall rouse a servant to find the best wine in the cellar.'

In the dining hall, Longchamp made a great show of remembering me, although I doubted he did. We had barely exchanged two words the previous times we had been in the same room. Determined to play the courtier as best I could nonetheless, I bowed deeply, kissed his gold bishop's ring, and handed over Richard's letter. I shook hands with the two others in the deputation, the justiciars William Bruyère and John de Pratelles. Good men both, they were deeply loyal to Richard.

Longchamp's secretary, who had been writing as his master dictated, hurried over, but he got waved away. Standing by one of the iron stands on which sat fat-bellied candles, the better to see, Longchamp cracked the seal with a deft flick of a fingernail, and unrolled the parchment. His lips moved as he read; now and again he frowned.

I waited, interested to see if he disclosed any of the details, the contents of which Richard had shared with me.

Longchamp laid down the letter, watching as it partly rolled itself up again, and then his gaze turned to me. 'The king regards you highly, Sir Rufus. He says so.'

'I am ever his servant, my lord bishop.' I bent my chin, thinking it was no surprise that Longchamp had remained unaware of how far my star had risen since Richard's coronation. 'Has there been any communication with the French?' William des Roches had already told me Philippe's delegation were camped two miles away.

A thin smile. 'In a manner of speaking. We were told that Philippe expects to keep all his recent gains. He also intends that the king should make reparatory payments to him. The exact amounts are yet unclear.'

'They are to act as surety against further attacks on Normandy?'

'Even so.'

'But the king needs every last silver penny for his own ransom!'

The thin smile again. 'I am told that Philippe will kindly agree to defer the payments until after Richard's release.'

'That will not be done out of kindness; there must be a sting in the tail.'

'The herald hinted that castles could be handed over as security until the full amount has been paid.'

'Curse Philippe for a malodourous dog,' I muttered. Then, remembering Longchamp was a man of the cloth, I said, 'Your pardon, my lord bishop.'

'You speak nothing but the truth.' A sigh, a first sign of weariness.

'We are caught between a rock and a hard place,' said de Pratelles.

'What if Philippe's demands go beyond the pale?' I asked. 'What if he demands Normandy?'

'These are also our concerns,' said Bruyère.

'Unpleasant and scheming the French king may be, and greedy too, but he is not stupid,' said Longchamp. 'A shrewder enemy I have not known in many a year. Philippe will suck as much blood as he can from us, just like a tick, but he will not bleed us dry. That would force me to throw his demands back in his face, which would in turn reopen the hostilities. That is not something Philippe wants. The ignominy of Rouen is too fresh in his mind.'

'If only we had had the men to chase after him then. We would have hounded him all the way back to Paris.' I sighed. 'But we did not, and here we are.'

'Here we are.'

'It is good that Richard cannot be present,' I declared. 'It would gall him more than he could bear to have to meet Philippe face-to-face and give him what he wants.'

'Philippe is as unhappy about that as our lord is content to be in Germany. Let us take some satisfaction from it.' A sideways, sharp look. 'Despite your evident interest, the king's letter made no mention of your being here to negotiate, Sir Rufus.'

Bruyère's and de Pratelles' eyes bore down on me as well.

It was there between us, unspoken. There had been no need for me to deliver Richard's orders. Anyone could have done it: a low-level courtier or knight, even a scribe.

'I am to return to Normandy after the meeting, on the king's business. Mantes was not far out of my way,' I said breezily. I had no intention of letting Longchamp or the others in on my secret hope, that FitzAldelm might be here.

Bruyère and de Pratelles seemed content, but not Longchamp.

'I see.' He managed to convey disbelief and irritation in the two words, but there was nothing he could do.

We stared at each other.

Into the silence, William des Roches arrived. He had taken it upon himself to go to the cellar for the wine. 'Rufus, your pardon that I took so long.' He was brandishing a large earthenware jug. 'This will slake your thirst.'

'You will want to reacquaint yourself with your comrade, and after, have a bath and rest.' Sounding genuine even if he was not, Longchamp made his excuses and left. Bruyère and de Pratelles stayed for a short while, but then they also retired.

I did not linger myself. William and I were brothers-in-arms from Outremer, it was true, but I had little to say to him. I made polite conversation about the king and drank off a second cup, to be courteous, and then, not needing to feign weariness, declared myself ready for a wash and a good sleep.

I dreamed all night of FitzAldelm, various horrible scenarios. In one, I chased after him on horseback, only for him to escape somehow. In another, he evaded my grasp entirely, riding away from the meeting safe in the company of the Frenchies he now called friends. A third, in which he killed Rhys during a struggle, brought me awake, gasping and drenched in sweat. Not once did I capture my old enemy, still less end his miserable life.

Dragged back to the present by the strident crowing of a cock, after what seemed like no sleep at all, I found Rhys already up and about. He was as bright-eyed as I had ever seen him. I gave him a sour look. 'Sleep well?'

'Like a babe. You did not, I am guessing.'

I grunted, aware of Jean listening to every word, and not wishing to divulge the detail of my nightmares for fear it might cause any one of them to become real.

The location for the two sides to meet was in a field, as was usual in such situations. The local landowner had had the long grass cut and raked away. The green sward exposed by this was square in shape, and its sides two hundred paces in length. In the centre stood a fine pavilion, its sides tied up so that the fresh air and sunshine might enter. It was a glorious summer's day, the trees' foliage a deep, rich green, and the huge arc of the sky a magnificent, luminous blue. Larks sang overhead, a gentle breeze ruffled the uncut grass at the field's edge. It was the type of day, I decided, that a man is glad to be alive. Temperatures would soar as the day wound on, but now, a little after tierce, it was deeply pleasant.

We had been waiting a while, having arrived early. That had been Longchamp's idea; the other two Williams, de Pratelles and I had agreed with him. This was not a battle, when he who chooses the ground to fight on often wins, but the principle was the same. We had taken the spot for our horses that would stay in the shade for most of the day, and selected the best place in the pavilion to catch the westerly breeze.

Longchamp had gone off to pray; de Pratelles was deep in conversation with William Bruyère, and William des Roches was busy instructing the men-at-arms who served as our protection where to stand. I caught Rhys's eye. 'Where is Jean?'

A shrug. 'He disappeared soon after we got here. Probably gone to the village we came through, to see what he can steal.'

'Not today.' This caught Rhys's attention, and I said, 'Five silver pennies says he has gone to the French camp.'

Rhys whistled. 'Of course he has, the little beggar!'

It was as if Jean knew we were talking about him. He came slipping into the pavilion, and made a beeline for us. His wide grin made it evident long before he reached us that he had something to report.

'Been spying?' I asked.

He was surprised, but recovered fast. 'Aye, sir, on the Frenchies. They will be here very soon.'

'Anything else?'

'FitzAldelm is with them, sir. I saw him with my own eyes.'

'Did he see you?' I asked Jean.

A withering look. 'Course not, sir. I kept well back, but there was no need. The likes of him does not notice the likes of me anyways.'

'It still pays to be cautious.' I gripped his shoulder. 'Good work.'

'I saw his tent too, sir.'

Rhys and I exchanged an incredulous glance. I turned back to Jean. 'You went into the French camp?'

An insolent grin. '*No one* pays me no heed, sir.'

'How many times do I have to tell you? Acting like that is dangerous.'

He glowered at me, the stubborn imp. 'No Frenchie is going to catch me, sir.'

'You must not do it again, unless Rhys or I give you permission, d'you hear?'

No response.

I had to take the bull by the horns, I decided, or I would live to regret it, while he would end up taken or slain by the French. 'I am serious, Jean. Do something like this again, and I will cast you out. Do you want to be a homeless orphan again?'

'No, sir.' There was a trace of a wobble in his voice: a crack in his mien.

'Come to me before you do these crazy things,' I said. 'I will not always say no.'

His chin firmed. 'Yes, sir.'

'Now, FitzAldelm's tent. Is it close to the perimeter?'

A triumphant smile. 'Yes, sir, right on the edge of the camp it is.'

My heart leaped. Rhys smacked a fist into a palm.

Hoofbeats interrupted. Loud voices carried into the pavilion.

The French had arrived.

They were led by the Bishop of Beauvais. Portly, round-faced, and as duplicitous a creature as was ever born, he was kinsman and ally to Philippe Capet. He it was who had performed the illegal marriage between Conrad of Montferrat and Isabella, wife of Humphrey de Toron. In Sicily, he had laid over-friendly eyes on Rhys, and of recent days, he had become Richard's tormentor. I had to use all my self-control to slip on an expressionless mask as the introductions were made, and the bishop's languid gaze moved to me.

It was as well I did, because I saw FitzAldelm next, at the back of the French deputation. Deep in conversation with a knight in a sea-blue tunic, he had not spied me yet. I had thought to feel enraged at the sight of him, but instead felt amusement and a deep calm. After all the years of not trusting him, here he was, in the bosom of our enemies, the French. It was his natural home, the traitor. Relief bathed me. There was no more need for subterfuge, or hiding my words behind my hand. Everyone knew whose side he was on, and it was not ours.

FitzAldelm came up beside the Bishop of Beauvais, intent on saying something. Perhaps he sensed my gaze on him, the way men do. His eyes lifted to mine, and he recognised me. The paltoner could not stop his mouth from opening a little in shock. It shut like a trap, and his face changed, going hard as stone.

I gave him a mocking little bow. 'FitzAldelm, it is good to see you.'

My words meant, 'I am here to kill you', and he knew it.

CHAPTER XIX

Confined by the social niceties of the situation, FitzAldelm could not give the reply he would have liked. He muttered something inaudible.

'I wondered if you had made it across the Seine,' I said cheerily, adding, 'after you fled through the tunnel from the church.'

The Bishop of Beauvais gave him a sharp look, which pleased me. I had intuited that FitzAldelm, prouder than proud, would not have revealed the humiliating truth about his flight from Rouen. He visibly squirmed, like a fish on a hook.

'The priest sang like a cagebird,' I went on. 'We know all the details you fed him, which were in turn passed on to your new master, Philippe. The king was most unhappy – not to say angry – to be told of your treachery.'

FitzAldelm's mouth worked, but he could not speak. I knew why. No answer he gave could take away the truth. He was a traitor. I did not allow myself to gloat. Until my enemy was dead and in the ground he was a potential threat.

The bishop intervened, calling out a fulsome greeting to Longchamp, fresh come from his prayers. I winked at FitzAldelm, to goad him, and he responded with a look of naked vitriol.

After many earnest requests for God's blessings on the negotiations, the Bishop of Beauvais and Longchamp began their discussion. I say discussion, but it was more of a list of ultimatums from Philippe to Richard.

The French king was to keep Gisors and all the lands he had seized in the spring. No leeway was offered; if Longchamp refused to accept, there was a clear intimation that the Frenchies would re-invade Normandy. Philippe's canniness showed in his next demand also. Richard's brother John was to have his lands on both sides of the Narrow Sea returned to him in perpetuity.

It went on, the Bishop of Beauvais declaiming, and Longchamp able only to nod or just listen. Adémar of Angoulême and the nobles who had joined his recent rebellion were all to be pardoned and have any lands lost restored to them. The lands confiscated by Richard from the Count of Perche would be given back. The Count of Mellent, another *Tadhg an dá thaobh* – a man with feet in both camps – if ever there was one, was to receive similar treatment.

The Bishop of Beauvais held back the costliest blow until the end. Twenty thousand marks of silver, Troy weight rather than Cologne, were to be paid to Philippe. Starting six months from the date of Richard's release, five thousand marks were to be handed over twice yearly. As surety against this vast sum, the castles of Loches and Châtillon-sur-Saone would immediately pass into French ownership. So too would the strongholds of Drincourt and Arques. The indignity was added to by the caveat that Richard should also pay yearly for the garrisons of each of the four castles. This was no small sum: in the case of Loches, that meant paying for eleven knights and one hundred-and-forty men-at-arms.

At last the Bishop of Beauvais' diatribe came to an end. He mopped his brow with a folded square of cloth, and then his red cheeks. Our selection of where to stand had been perfect. Longchamp, William and I were cool in the shade, while the French were fully in the sunlight that lanced in through the open side of the pavilion.

'Well?' enquired the Bishop of Beauvais. 'Have you anything to say?'

'Are you finished?' asked Longchamp, his tone polite.

It was hard to imagine that the bishop's wine-red complexion could darken, but it did. 'I am!'

'I thank you on behalf of King Richard for your terms. I shall have to consider them with my colleagues.' Longchamp indicated the two Williams and John de Pratelles.

'Consider? What is there to consider?' blustered the bishop.

'Whether or not I will accept your demands.' Butter would not have melted in Longchamp's mouth.

The bishop looked as if he were about suffer a seizure. 'Accept? You have no choice!'

'Ah, my lord bishop, that is where you are wrong,' said Longchamp. He bowed. 'By your leave.'

Calm and assured, he and his three colleagues walked away from the French deputation. I followed, but not until I had winked again at FitzAldelm.

He affected not to notice, but I saw the gleam of fury in his eyes as he turned away.

We took counsel together at the back of the tent. Away from the French, everyone's expressions had changed. I saw concern, anger, helplessness and even a little fear, which mirrored my own emotions. The French delegation might be led by a fat bishop, but we were being threatened with a mailed fist.

'That was all an act, as you probably realise,' said Longchamp.

'You were convincing, though,' I said, getting a small smile in reply.

'God's toes! Philippe has us in a corner,' said des Roches, 'and the bishop knows it.'

'The terms are incredibly harsh, but not unexpected,' said Bruyère.

'We can do little but agree to them – in their entirety,' added de Pratelles sorrowfully. 'What say you, my lord bishop?'

Longchamp sucked in his cheeks, thinking. Then he nodded. 'We must accept.'

'I agree. The consequences of refusing are too grave.' This was Bruyère.

'So say I also,' said des Roches. To my surprise, he glanced at me. 'And you, Sir Rufus?'

I saw the annoyance in Longchamp's eyes, swiftly masked, but along with des Roches, Bruyère and de Pratelles were waiting for me to speak. It was a proud moment, this recognition of my standing with the king.

'Sad though I am to admit it, there is little option but to give in to the Frenchies' demands,' I said. 'The king's opinion is that it will be six months before he is freed, at the earliest. Philippe could wreak untold havoc in Normandy in that time, and *that* would be worse than the extortionate terms being demanded of us here. Let no one tell the Bishop of Beauvais, but we could give away more than Philippe wants and still regard ourselves as having come out with the better end of the deal.'

That startled them, but after a moment, Longchamp murmured in agreement. 'Two more castles, or even six, it could have been, Sir Rufus. Or another ten thousand marks. It is true that any of those – all of those – would be cheaper to Richard than the loss of Normandy.'

We stared unhappily at one another.

Despite our lauding Philippe's retreat from Rouen as a victory, it had been a setback to our enemies, nothing more. Two good months of campaigning remained – three, if the weather held. If Philippe were to march his army back to Normandy right now and bypass Rouen, he could easily cut a swathe of destruction deep into the hinterland, burning crops and threatening towns and villages. Our forces in the area were far less numerous than his, and if Queen Alienor brought soldiers from Aquitaine, the trouble there could reignite. It would take weeks, even months to ship troops from England, and while we waited, there was every likelihood that noblemen across Normandy would open their gates to the French, and swear allegiance to Philippe. By the time reinforcements crossed the Narrow Sea, it could be too late.

Longchamp composed himself, smoothing down his habit. 'We shall let the bishop stew for a little while,' he said. 'But then I will tell him yes. God grant that the king is correct about when he will be freed. Let it take much longer, and he will return to find crows picking the bones of his kingdom.'

'The monies *will* be raised in time, my lord bishop,' I said, sounding more confident than I felt. 'Heinrich will release the king come the New Year.'

'And if Philippe gets involved again?' asked Bruyère. 'Making peace with us here will not stop him from trying to have Heinrich renege on the ransom deal.'

'He is not the only one who might try that approach,' said Longchamp.

'You mean John?' I said without thinking. I felt the others' gaze heavy on me, and was glad they were loyal to Richard. In other company, it would pay to be more discreet.

Longchamp looked at us one by one, the gesture showing he trusted us. 'I do. If he and Philippe offered more than the price the king is to pay, Heinrich might well listen.'

'We should not worry about that now,' I said, determined not to let the mood fall further. 'Let us take Philippe's blackguardly offer, and be grateful.'

Longchamp's chin set. Des Roches smiled. De Pratelles and Bruyère nodded.

Our fortitude made the sourness of the treaty bearable. Just.

I stared up at the clear sky, the blackness of which was leavened by countless winking stars. The moon was at its smallest, a mere sliver, which suited our purpose well. I knew the Plough, and the Great Bear, and a few other stars, but the rest were a mystery to me. I could not help thinking that the same sky was above Joanna, somewhere to the south. My heart ached. Was she sleeping, I wondered, or looking up at the glory of the heavens and thinking of me?

'Ready?' Rhys's lips were close to my ear.

I turned my head. Like me, he had blackened his face and hands with mud. Clad in dark tunic and hose, he was as close to invisible as a man could make himself. I nodded.

The hour was late, nearer to lauds than matins. We had marked the latter by the clanging bells of the churches in Mantes, a mile distant, and then waited. Our camp was quiet; everyone was asleep, apart from the sentries, I hoped. The same peace and tranquillity would reign in the Frenchies' encampment, not least because our meeting the previous day had seen the successful negotiation of a peace treaty. There was no reason for anyone from either side to creep into the other's camp intent on murder.

Unless you were me and Rhys, with a bitter feud to finish.

'Jean?' I whispered. Rhys had exited our tent after me; it had been his task to check the boy was not awake.

'Asleep.'

'You are sure?'

'As I can be.'

'Let us move, then.' Instinct took over; I checked the long end of my belt was looped out of the way, and that my fresh-oiled dagger slipped in and out of its sheath without a sound. Beside me, Rhys was doing the same. Done, we glanced at each other, and then I led the way through the tents, padding cat-soft so I did not disturb any of our companions. It was easy to avoid the sentries; there were only four of them, and they had passed by a short time before. They would not be back for a good while.

It was a straightforward walk to the French camp, and I saw no need to take a circuitous route. Across the meeting place we went, the warm, rich scent of cut grass filling our nostrils, and into the meadow beyond. Our eyes accustomed to the gloom: with the starlight to guide us we made swift progress. The unearthly screech of an owl carried from deep in the wood off to our right. Although it was not aimed at us, I shivered to hear it.

Rhys had been delighted by my plan to creep into FitzAldelm's tent and slit his throat. No one in the French camp knew much – if anything – of my feud with him. With any luck, it would be assumed that FitzAldelm had been murdered by one of his own. Rhys had whetted his knife until it could slice the hairs on his forearm flush with the skin, and grinned evilly at me as he did so. I had done the same with my own blade, but silently, and deep in thought. I had suggested we kill FitzAldelm out of old habit, because I had so often said how I longed to do it.

In reality, though, the burning hot hatred, my fuel for so many years, had burned low. I had felt its lack in Rouen, even if I had not admitted it. I had stoked its flame before seeing my enemy in the great pavilion; if we had come to blows there, I would happily have fought him. Now, though, intent on plain, cold-blooded murder, I felt my purpose waver.

Remembering his beatings, and the times he had tried to murder me, I hardened my heart. It was not as if anyone would miss him either, I told myself. He was not married. There was his terrier, P'tit, if it was still alive, but a dog could not come between me and my revenge.

I felt a hand on my shoulder – Rhys. I stopped, turned, mouthed, *What?*

He tapped his ear, indicating he had heard something, and pointed a finger over his shoulder, whence we had come.

I stabbed two fingers at my eyes and then swept them from left to right, encompassing all the ground to our rear: we were to look for signs of anyone on our trail.

Both of us stood watching, shoulder to shoulder, the only sound our breathing.

At a hundred count, I had seen neither hide nor hair of a soul. Rhys was suffering from nerves, I told myself. I touched his arm, and mouthed, *Spot anything?*

He shook his head, and his lips framed the word, *Sorry.*

No matter, my lips silently replied. *Onwards.*

We heard nothing else to raise our concerns before the French camp loomed out of the darkness, two hundred and fifty paces away. We sank down into the grass. After a long wait, we decided that there were no sentries walking the perimeter. Nonetheless, we covered this last distance on our bellies. Uncomfortable – the grass was long, and dew-laden – and unable to see without stopping to get up on my knees, it took an age to get close.

Finally, however, we had come within twenty paces of the French camp. We rose and squatted on our haunches, to get a sense of direction. I thanked God for Jean's keen eyes. He had noted that FitzAldelm's tent, which stood between two larger ones, had a panel that had been repaired with fabric darker than the rest of the structure. It was almost straight in front of us.

See? I mouthed to Rhys, and pointed.

He nodded.

There was no need to talk about our plan, which was simple. Listen outside the tent, to try to ensure no one within was awake. Slit the canvas quietly and enter. Find FitzAldelm, kill him, and leave. With luck, none of the squires or servants who might also be in the tent would hear. If they did, we would run rather than fight. It was perhaps riskier than cutting more throats, but neither of us had any wish to slay innocent men.

My gaze moved from side to side, and between the tents. No sentries. Not a sound, apart from the cursed owl in the wood. Someone had told me once that the Romans regarded its call as a bad omen; I shoved that thought away.

I covered the last distance on the balls of my feet, grateful that it was grass beneath me, not wooden floorboards. Rhys was beside me, silent as a shadow. By walking the length of the tent's side and glancing along the other sides, I determined that the entrance faced into the camp. That meant FitzAldelm was quite possibly sleeping in the very section we had first reached.

We went back to it, and stopped to listen. There was someone right on the other side of the canvas – I could hear deep, regular breathing, and once, a slight clearing of the throat. I knelt, and placed an ear against the canvas. The man stirred, and six inches from my nose, the fabric moved. I jerked back, swallowing a cry, and then realised his arm had flopped off his mattress, or similar, and touched the canvas.

I gave Rhys a sheepish look. He was grinning.

I pointed into the tent.

FitzAldelm? Rhys mouthed. His dagger was already in his hand. He mimed stabbing through the fabric.

I shook my head. We had to be sure who it was. I did not want another life on my conscience forevermore. That of the youthful cutpurse in Udine was burden enough.

We moved ten paces away, far enough for there to be a side compartment, or at least enough distance from the sleeper. No sounds were audible from the other side of the canvas, so I eased my dagger tip through at ground level, and slowly brought it upwards. My handiwork with the whetstone paid off; the fabric fell open. In the blink of an eye, I had cut a hole large enough to enter.

Again I paused. All I heard was the breathing of the man whose arm had startled me. I glanced at Rhys, who gave me a fierce, encouraging nod. Pulse racing – I was momentarily defenceless – I pushed my head through the rent.

No one shouted an alarm. No one challenged me. It was much darker in the tent than outside. I had to let my eyes adjust, at length making out a stand upon which hung a hauberk. Atop it was a helmet; at its foot was a sword in a scabbard, and a pair of boots. This was a knight's tent at least, I thought, and not a cleric's.

There was a wooden chest closer to me, but no shapes of people, asleep or otherwise. I twisted my head to the left, and made out the man I had heard. His head was towards me, not six steps distant, and it was block-shaped. My spirits rose. It was FitzAldelm – it had to be. Few men in Christendom had a head so characteristic.

I eased back out into the night air, and mouthed to Rhys, *It is him.*

His grin of reply was merciless.

I turned, ready to enter the tent. Rhys would follow. I could have done it alone, but it was his heartfelt wish to bury his blade in Fitz-Aldelm. I could not deny that to him.

I climbed in, dagger in my mouth, and crouched down on my haunches as I had outside. No one stirred, and I reached through the cut in the canvas and beckoned.

Rhys clambered through nimbly, and squatted beside me. His gaze went to FitzAldelm, and returned to mine. Despite the darkness, the triumph in his eyes shone out. He gestured with his dagger, courteous as a lord offering a lady to enter a house first. On edge, yet amused, I would have laughed had not our need to be silent been so imperative.

I crawled on hands and knees towards FitzAldelm, slow and deliberate, vigilant for any change in his posture or breathing. He did not stir, not even when I reached his side and crouched over him.

It was hard to take in. After so long, so many prayers to God for His help, the moment was here. I hesitated, dry-mouthed, but then I remembered how FitzAldelm had tried to kill me, twice. Hatred for him filled me. I reversed my grip on my dagger, so it pointed downward out of my bunched fist, and raised my arm high. I could sense Rhys beside me, quivering like a hawk about to have its jesses undone.

Again I hesitated. Instead of a sleeping FitzAldelm, I saw Henry, whose throat I had opened to protect my reputation, and the youth I had viciously slain in Udine, just because I had felt like it.

Rhys poked me, hard. He did not dare speak, but he did not need to.

I nodded without looking at him, and steeled my resolve. I tensed, preparing to strike – and from nowhere, with timing so perfect I would not have believed it possible, an enormous sneeze erupted from me.

Moisture showered FitzAldelm, who came awake with the rapidity of a striking snake. He shoved me in the chest with the heel of his hand, an instinctive reaction. There was enough power in it to send me backwards into Rhys, which hampered his reactive dagger lunge at FitzAldelm. Rhys fell onto his rear end, with me flailing on top. I tried to get up, desperate, frantic even, to finish what I had not started.

FitzAldelm roared for help, a shout loud enough to wake the dead, and scrambled, half crawling, away from us and towards the hole through which we had entered. With us between him and the entrance to the tent, he had nowhere else to go.

I went after him, but Rhys was even faster. As FitzAldelm reached the cut in the fabric, Rhys's dagger rose and fell, and my enemy screamed. He did not fall, however, and with the next thump of my heart, he threw himself outside like a man diving off a rock into deep water. There was a brief cry, which was echoed and exceeded by one behind me – a loud, 'Are you all right, sir?' in French – a squire, surely, or a man-at-arms who had been on guard outside.

I whirled. A shape had come inside; there was a sword in his right hand. I turned to warn Rhys.

There was another cry from just the other side of the canvas – a child's voice? – and a savage curse from FitzAldelm. 'Give me that!'

Rhys shouted then, a loud, inarticulate sound full of rage.

My guts twisting I knew not why, disregarding the man aiming for me, I shoved my way outside. I halted, trying to make sense of what was going on.

Rhys was a step in front of me, crouched, with his dagger held out before him. I peered past him, and terror seized me tighter than a vice.

FitzAldelm had an arm around Jean's throat, and in his other hand, a blade tucked in under the terrified boy's chin. He leered at me.

'Go left,' I hissed at Rhys. 'I will go right.'

'It is too dangerous!'

Behind us, I heard someone exiting the hole in the tent. Shouts and cries rose from beyond, in the camp. With them was the sound of men, running.

'It will be too late for all of us soon,' I said. 'He will not kill a child.'

'Release the boy, FitzAldelm,' said Rhys, his tone pleading. He took several steps to the left, and I did the same to the right.

FitzAldelm's eyes flickered to and fro, watching us. Jean struggled, but his little arms had no more chance of wrestling him free than I did of pulling the sun from the sky.

'Let him go? Had I not taken his blade, the wretch was going to kill me!'

Too late I realised. Too late I threw myself into the space between us, my hands stretched out not to stab FitzAldelm, but to stop him. Too late. I was too late.

In slow motion, I saw his dagger fall away from Jean's throat, down, to his belly and there slide in, just the once. Jean screamed, a high-pitched keen that set my teeth on edge, and then he was tumbling towards me, shoved forward by FitzAldelm.

Who turned and ran as if all the demons in Hell were after him.

Neither I nor Rhys gave pursuit, as he had known we would not, the murderous cur.

I reached Jean before Rhys. I scooped him up and cradled his little, stick-thin shape in my arms. He was limp as a rag doll, and moaning pitifully. 'I have you, boy,' I said, aware that tears were streaming down my face, that Rhys was dragging me away from the camp, that there were Frenchies close, very close.

We ran. Ran into the darkness, fast as we could, heedless that our speed put us at risk of breaking our ankles. Rhys took the lead and I followed, my pain and grief giving me energy. We ran until my left side burned with a stitch, but I would not stop, not even when Rhys offered to take Jean. We ran until the sounds of pursuit died away, and even then I would not halt. Not until Rhys caught my arm, and growled in my face, 'Stop. The Frenchies have let us go. Stop.'

Some sanity returned, and I obeyed. Chest heaving, I relaxed my grip on Jean a little, and stared down at him. His eyes were closed, and I had to look closely to see that he was still breathing. I dared not look at his belly, not that I would have been able to determine anything. It was too dark, and he had worn a dark tunic like us, bless his heart.

'Let me carry him,' Rhys whispered. 'You must be exhausted.'

'No.' I packed all my anger, all the futility I felt, into that word. 'I can do it. Let us go. Quickly.'

Rhys did not argue, but led the way towards our camp again, only a little slower than before.

The sentries' challenge had never been more welcome. Rhys called out our names, and the password for the night, and they put up their spears. Vaguely aware of their shocked gaze at my burden, I let Rhys guide me to the tent in which Brother Hugo slept. A scribe to Longchamp, he also had some expertise in medicine. We barged in, Rhys simultaneously calling for light and apologising to a startled Hugo, who sat up, blinking.

It was all done for appearance's sake of course. FitzAldelm had known where to put the blade. He had sliced Jean's guts, a miserable, cowardly, killing blow if ever there was one. I had known it from the start, and so had Rhys, but that had not stopped us fleeing with Jean rather than chasing FitzAldelm, nor running like madmen to our camp. It did not stop us begging Hugo to save the boy, praying loudly to God and all His saints, promising the earth, moon, and stars if only he lived.

I watched, trembling, as Hugo cut Jean's tunic from hem to neck with a pair of shears. The boy was barely conscious, and did not react. A sob escaped me to see the narrow, wet-lipped wound in the pit of his belly. It looked so insignificant. It did not look as if it could kill, and yet I knew it would.

'A soup wound.' Rhys's voice was dry and cracked.

I turned to him, dazed, not understanding.

'Give soup to a man with an injury like that. An hour or two later, if you can smell it from the wound, you know the harm the blade did.'

The meaning returned to me, and I nodded.

'He is right.' Hugo's voice was gentle. Kind. 'If the blood loss does not kill the boy tonight, the sepsis will.'

'Do you take me for a lackwit? I have been fighting battles since I was a lad.' Hugo looked shocked, and I realised how harsh I had been. 'Your pardon, brother. My emotions are running high. The boy, he . . . he is dear to me. He should not have been there. He –' I could say no more, and hung my head.

'Hold his hand. Sit by the table, and hold his hand. It will comfort him.'

I stared at Hugo, then dumbly did as he said. Jean's hand was so little in mine, and so cold. I bent over it, and cried the silent, bitter tears of a man who wishes he could turn back time. Who would give his own life to undo the events of the previous hour.

Jean opened his eyes a while later, and recognised me and Rhys, who was there too. He gave us a weak, tremulous smile, and whispered, 'I only wanted to help.'

'And you did,' I lied. 'You did.'

Hope rose in his sunken eyes. 'FitzAldelm?'

'He is dead,' I said, squeezing his hand. It was another lie. Rhys was sure he had only stabbed FitzAldelm in the calf, but I was not about to tell Jean that. I murmured, 'Thanks to you.'

Jean smiled again, the smile of a boy who knows he has done well, and closed his eyes.

They did not open again.

He died as the sun was rising. He slipped away even as golden light came creeping along the floor of the tent, the sign of another glorious day. I sat there, uncaring, numb, looking at his unmoving chest, the grey sheen of his face.

'It is my fault.'

'No, it is not.' Rhys's voice was hard. Certain.

Startled, for I had not realised I had spoken aloud, I said, 'I hesitated. Over FitzAldelm in the tent. If I had stabbed him immediately . . .'

A dismissive snort. 'You *would* have done it, or *I* would. Instead, you sneezed, and what happened, happened. Jean should not have been there. You thought he was asleep when we left. So did I.' Grief reverberated in Rhys's voice. 'We were not to know he followed us.'

'We should have tied him up, then, so he could not come after us!' My voice choked.

'That would not have been enough. He would have needed a gag as well.' A heartbeat's delay, and then Rhys said, 'Can you imagine how angry he would have been with us afterwards?'

Madly, I found myself laughing. Rhys joined in.

They say that laughter is the best medicine, and perhaps it is true. We sat there by Jean's corpse, tears running down our faces, and chuckling as we reminisced over his all-too-short time with us.

After that, we swore an oath of vengeance together.

Neither of us would rest until FitzAldelm was dead.

I added a silent codicil.

The next time, there would be no vacillation.

CHAPTER XX

On the road to Speyer, Germany, January 1194

The storm was still building. Rain was hammering off the roof tiles, and the wind's howl reminded me of a wild beast. The shutters rattled constantly, and cold currents of air kept crossing the room to tickle the back of my neck. I lifted the collar of my tunic and, grateful to be indoors, eased my stool a little closer to the fire.

Rhys knocked and came in. 'If that storm does not let up, we shall be here for more than one night.'

I frowned. 'Let us hope that does not happen.'

Christmastide had been and gone, and January was a week old. It was the year of our Lord 1194, and we were bound for the German city of Speyer, there to meet with Richard. Longchamp had left several days before us.

'You want to reach the king as soon as possible,' said Rhys. 'As do I.'

'It has been too long.' So much had happened since I had last seen my lord. A pang of grief hit me, not because of Richard, but because of Jean. Almost six months had passed since his needless death. Six months since that fateful meeting with FitzAldelm – who had again disappeared without trace. I glanced at Rhys. 'Jean would have loved to meet the king. Can you imagine him?'

'Aye.' Rhys's mouth crooked. 'I can see him begging to be a royal page as well.'

I chuckled. 'I would not have put it past him. He had no shame.'

'And what is more, Richard might have been amused enough to take him on.'

'I would have asked him not to,' I said instantly. 'Jean was mine to ask.'

'Aye.' Sadness flitted across Rhys's face. 'Katharina would have been pleased if you had done that.'

'How is she?' Katharina was in Rhys's room – she had refused to be left behind this time – and I had not seen her since our arrival a couple of hours before. Things between us since Jean's death had been strained.

'Well enough.' A shrug that said otherwise. Jean's death had affected her even more than Rhys and me; at times it seemed as if she had lost her own child. Rhys glanced at me. 'I wonder if I should just marry her?'

'And get her with child?' I asked, not totally surprised.

A nod.

'You could,' I said, 'but it would put an end to her travelling about with us. It is one thing for a woman to be in the company, and quite another for a newborn babe.' He gave no answer, and reading his mind, I said, 'You would not want to leave her.'

'No.'

Relieved, for I would not want Rhys fretting while we went to war with Richard – that was our probable course in the spring – I said, 'Maybe she can find another waif to take under her wing.'

At last, a grin. 'I think that would help. Not to replace Jean, but –'

'I know. It is no harm having an impudent pup to keep us on our toes.'

We smiled at one another, not needing to say what was in our hearts.

Hampered by bad weather and worse roads, we did not reach Speyer until mid-January. Night was falling, and I was in no mood for another flea-ridden bed like the one in Worms. We enquired at the town gate for the best inns, and made for the first one named, which was right on the main square. When the proprietor, an obsequious type with a long flap of hair combed over his bald pate, told me he had no vacancies, I simply tipped my purse onto the counter. Gold winked up at him, and his eyes widened. There was enough to pay for every room in his inn for a week.

'I need two chambers,' I said.

His pause was so brief it was plainly done for effect. Then, 'It will be my pleasure, sir. I will need a little time, if that is acceptable?'

This was to eject the rooms' current residents, I knew. It mattered not. I gave him a broad smile. 'More than acceptable. We shall take a meal until the chambers are ready.'

An expansive smile. 'Excellent, sir. I can recommend the roast pork. My servant will guide you to a private dining booth.' He gestured, and a sheepish-faced lad came forward.

I turned to Katharina – Rhys was in the yard, seeing that the horses were comfortably stabled – and said, 'Shall we, my lady?'

'Thank you.' She smiled, and looked as if she partly meant it at least.

The serving lad led the way. I followed Katharina, hoping that the ice between us would thaw sooner rather than later. In the months since Jean's killing, I had told her a dozen times, and so had Rhys. Jean had been asleep when we left; he had followed us without our permission. That did not stop her holding us both accountable for his death. I knew by Rhys's harried expression that he had it harder than I did, so I stitched my lip and weathered her coldness. I also held my peace because part of me thought I deserved it. Not a day went by when I did not blame myself for what had happened.

The inn's main room was large, and busy. Old habit made me glance around, to see if there was anyone to be concerned about. The customers were a cut above those who had frequented the taverns we had stayed in en route, however. I saw a dozen merchants, fat-bellied or self-important, all with deep purses, and plenty of examples of a better class of townsman. None of them seemed remotely interested in me or Katharina. Satisfied, I slid into the booth opposite her.

The serving lad hovered. 'Wine, sir?'

'Yes, a flask of good Rhenish, but not too expensive.'

He bobbed his head and retreated.

Katharina and I stared at each other. Uncomfortable, I was first to look away.

She broke the ice. 'You must be pleased to have arrived, sir, to be so close to the king again.'

'I am right glad.'

'And he is to be set free within the next few days too.'

'God willing,' I said fervently. News had reached us on the road. Heinrich had received so much of the ransom money that he had set a date – the seventeenth of the month – for Richard's release.

'He will travel to England then, sir?'

'That would be my guess. Much needs to be set aright in Normandy, but order needs to be restored in England before he deals with Philippe

Capet.' I lowered my voice. 'His brother John is chief among those who need to be brought to heel.'

'Why is he like that, sir?' she whispered. 'Blood should cleave to blood.'

'I think so also, but John is cut from different cloth. He always seems to feel hard done by, even though he is the heir to the throne. With the king in captivity, I do not think he could stop himself from feathering his own nest.'

And yet John's behaviour beggared belief. He had crossed to Normandy shortly after Mantes, and attempted to claim the castles promised to him in the treaty. But he was so despised and mistrusted by the castellans that they refused to relinquish charge of the fortresses, even when, I had been told, John had brandished writs in Richard's own hand. He had stormed off in pique to Philippe, and been rewarded with Drincourt and Arques, which by the treaty were supposed to have been given to the Archbishop of Reims.

The wine arrived; the serving lad poured out two cups. I saluted Katharina with mine. 'To the king's freedom!'

We drank. I gave the serving lad a nod. 'It is tasty.'

Another bob of his head. 'And food, sir, would you care to –'

He was interrupted by Rhys, who came hurtling through the door. 'Sir!'

I reached for my dagger in instinct, but then saw his grin. Carefully, so Katharina did not notice, I let my hand fall away. 'What is it, Rhys?'

'You will never guess who I found in the stable!'

This I had not expected. 'Who?'

He turned, and beckoned to the figure standing in the doorway. 'Come on, then!'

I stared. I knew that mop-hair, that strapping shape, but I could not quite believe it was possible. 'Bertolf?'

The former novice hurried over, a grin splitting his plain, honest face. 'Yes, sir, it is I.' He knelt, ignoring my protests, and managed to clasp my outstretched hand at the same time. 'I am so happy to see you, sir,' he said, his voice cracking with emotion.

I had a lump in my own throat. I bade him rise and take a seat beside me. I remembered to introduce him to Katharina, who eyed him curiously.

'Sweet Jesu,' I said, 'but this is an unasked-for blessing. Are you well, Bertolf – recovered from what Leopold's men did to you?'

His expression clouded for a moment, but then he regained his smile. 'Yes, sir, I am fine.'

'How came you here?'

The three of us listened, agog, as it all came out. How he had been freed from prison in Vienna, beaten black and blue and with only a thin blanket for protection against the wintry conditions. In danger of freezing to death, he was fortunate to be taken in the same evening by a kindly shopkeeper and his wife. The childless pair had nursed him back to health, and when he would not stay, supplied him with a horse, money and food. Desperate to return to the king's service, Bertolf had tracked Richard first to Dürnstein, then Speyer, Trifels and Worms.

'Everywhere I went,' he said in his still-accented French, 'I tried to see the king. But no one will admit a peasant boy to the royal presence, still less believe that he is one of his company.' A resigned shrug. 'So I follow to each city and town where the king goes, and pray daily that my fortunes improve.'

'Christ on the cross, your luck changed today!' I exclaimed, exchanging a look with Rhys, who was every bit as pleased as me. 'Who saw the other first?'

'I spotted him, sir,' said Rhys with a chuckle. 'Cleaning out the stable next over, he was. Never noticed me. I went up and tapped him on the shoulder. Jumped a foot in the air when he realised who I was.'

Bertolf grinned self-consciously. 'I thought you were a ghost, or a spirit. I would never have expected to see you here in Speyer.'

'We have come for the king's release,' I said. 'You know he is to be freed?'

Bertolf beamed. 'It is the talk of the town, sir.'

'And so it should be.' I filled cups for Rhys and Bertolf. First we toasted the king's freedom, second our unexpected reunion. Then it was Richard's freedom again, and next our reunion. We laughed, and joked, and drank more wine. All was well with the world. After the long months of grief over Jean's death, and Richard's continued incarceration, it felt as if we had truly turned a corner.

It was a long night.

*

I woke dry-mouthed and sweating, with no idea what time it was. Aware I had important business to deal with, I threw back the fur coverlet at once, and padded slowly to the window. I opened the shutters, letting in light and a blast of cold air. The latter woke me up, which was my intent. I stared down into the yard, two floors below, and my head, already pounding, spun. On unsteady legs, I retreated to the bed, and sat down with a relieved sigh.

I had no one to blame for my poorly state but myself. Hazy memories spun through my mind, of Katharina nagging at Rhys to come to bed as Bertolf and I whooped and crowed and pressed another brimming cup into his hand. She had rolled her eyes and muttered something about boneheaded men, and stormed off to their chamber. I decided that she was probably best avoided for a time.

I could not clear my head further, so I tramped downstairs, relieved that no one emerged from Rhys's room, and out into the inn's yard. I hauled a bucket up from the well, and before I could hesitate, emptied the ice cold water over myself. A bellow of shock erupted from my mouth, but I was awake. Teeth chattering, my woollen tunic and hose sodden, I stood there like a lackwit, wishing I had thought to bring a blanket.

'That is one way to treat a hangover, for certes.' Rhys sounded most amused.

I twisted around. He was standing in a stable doorway, pitchfork in hand, and curse him, looked as fresh as a daisy. Still fuddle-witted, I grunted.

'Sore head?' he enquired.

'Perhaps,' I said, wishing he were in a similar state to me.

'My master cannot hold his drink,' declared Rhys. Bertolf had emerged from another stable; he too seemed unaffected by our carousing.

It was his youth, I thought, as I glowered at them both.

Bertolf lost his grin; Rhys just laughed.

I threw my own dart. 'Is all well with Katharina this morning?'

Rhys gave me a sour glance.

'Bend your ear about staying up late, did she?' I jibed.

Naïve, Bertolf sniggered, but when Rhys rounded on him with a snarl, he darted back into his stable.

'I am going back upstairs before I catch a chill,' I said. 'Have you breakfasted?'

'Hours ago. I could eat more, though.'

'Of course you could.' That Rhys could put away his own body-weight in food was a frequent refrain. 'I will join you shortly. After that, we shall seek out Longchamp and find out if he has seen the king.'

I hoped that by then I would feel more human.

Three of us went. After Bertolf's devoted pursuit of Richard, I felt obliged to let him accompany us. Katharina had asked to come as well; I had had to refuse. She was unimpressed with my truthful avowal that Rhys and Bertolf were unlikely to be given admittance with me. She threw a baleful look in my direction as we left. I soon shoved her from my mind. Between my thumping headache and the fact that Long-champ would comment on my appearance, I had enough to deal with. My best efforts with my wardrobe could not conceal what I had seen in the reflection of one of the inn's few glass windows – sunken-eyed and dishevelled-looking, I was clearly hungover.

We knew where to go. Longchamp was staying with the local bishop, as might have been expected. His palatial residence was just off the main square, so we had but a short walk. Kicking the snow from my boots, I let Rhys lift the great iron knocker on the front door. It struck the timbers with a deep, sonorous sound, and a short time later, the postern gate opened.

A cleric stuck his head out, and regarded us with a supercilious expression. 'Yes?' He spoke in German.

Rhys answered in the same tongue. I understood the words, 'Long-champ' and '*König*', and heard my own name.

The cleric looked me up and down, and sniffed.

My patience, already thin, wore through. 'Tell him that if he does not let us in this instant, I shall tan his hide redder than a deflowered nun's face.'

Bertolf's eyes opened wide with shock; chortling, Rhys obeyed with great enthusiasm.

The cleric looked mortified and furious, but he knew better than to object. With a curt wave, he bade us enter.

He led us in silence to Longchamp's large guest chamber. To my surprise, there were men-at-arms with royal surcoats outside. They stiffened at our approach, but one, a skinny Kentishman, recognised me. He grinned and saluted.

'Is Queen Alienor here?' I asked.

'Yes, sir. She has come to see her son set free.'

What a formidable woman, I thought, not for the first time. 'I am seeking an audience with Longchamp,' I said, 'but you had best ask the queen for her permission before I enter.'

I was admitted forthwith; Rhys and Bertolf waited outside with the men-at-arms. To my surprise, Archbishop Walter de Coutances was also within. He gave me a friendly nod. Longchamp frowned in disapproval – I assumed because of my dishevelled appearance – but Alienor let out a little cry of delight.

'Sir Rufus!'

'Madam, it is a joy to see you.' I came to within six paces of her and knelt.

'It is a pleasure to see you also, Sir Rufus. Rise, please.'

'Madam.' I stood. 'How was your journey from England?'

'Long. Cold.' A bright smile. 'We spent the Epiphany at Cologne; that was pleasant, but Archbishop Walter and I are glad to be here now.'

'Have you seen the king, madam?'

An unhappy shake of her head. 'The emperor will not permit it. He has also changed the date of Richard's release, to the second of February.'

I stared at her in disbelief. 'But, madam, why?'

'It seems that the tale of freeing my son is not quite told.' She glanced at Archbishop Walter.

'There are two reasons, we think,' he said. 'The first is the recent clandestine marriage of Agnes, heiress of Heinrich's uncle, Konrad von Hohenstaufen, Count Palatine of the Rhine.'

This union had not stayed secret for long; I had been pleased to hear about it, because it strengthened Richard's position among the German nobility.

'Agnes's new husband is the son of your daughter Matilda and Heinrich der Löwe, is he not, madam?' Der Löwe, 'the Lion', was a former Duke of Saxony and Bavaria.

A sad nod, for Matilda had died only a year or two prior. 'Yes. Their son is yet another Heinrich – like us, the Germans are unimaginative when it comes to names. He and Agnes were betrothed since birth, but the arrangement lapsed when his father and hers fell out. It is fortunate that the quarrel did not stop them being besotted with each other.'

'How did the marriage come to pass, madam, if their fathers were enemies?'

'Agnes's mother arranged it. Love *can* sometimes conquer.'

I thought with a real pang of Joanna, and how Richard had forbidden any such union. 'That cannot have been her only reason, madam, surely. Philippe Capet's machinations must have had something to do with it also?'

She gave me an appraising look. 'You begin to see the webs of intrigue, Sir Rufus. Yes, indeed. A man who can discard his first wife for another and then seek to throw her aside in favour of yet a third bride is not to be trusted. Agnes's mother is a shrewd woman.' Philippe had contrived to marry Ingeborg of Denmark just a few months before. Unhappy with her, he was currently attempting to set up yet another union, this time with Agnes.

'What does the emperor think of the marriage?' I asked.

Longchamp answered. 'It is reasonable to think he is unhappy, even to believe that he blames the king for it. That would explain his changing the date of Richard's release and his summoning of the Imperial Diet to Würzburg. There is little Heinrich can do about it, however. Agnes's mother will win over her husband Konrad, and his word carries a lot of weight in the Diet. It will be difficult for Heinrich to go against both Konrad's wishes as well as those of a sizeable number of his nobles.'

'I would that that was all,' said Alienor, glancing at Longchamp.

He addressed me. 'Rumour has it that Philippe Capet and the king's brother John have made another offer to Heinrich.'

'Is he actually considering it?' I cried. 'He swore on his immortal soul in Worms to honour the ransom agreed with the king!'

'Vows mean nothing to a man like Heinrich. His duplicity is endless.' There was a cold anger in Queen Alienor's voice.

'Do you know the details of this supposed counteroffer, madam?' I asked.

For a moment, the queen looked very old. She rallied, though, and nodded. 'If the emperor will keep Richard prisoner until the autumn, Philippe and John will each pay him fifty thousand marks.'

The timing was quite deliberate. If the king was freed at the end of the campaigning season, he would be able to take no military action until the following spring. I controlled my fury as the queen went on.

'If Heinrich prefers, they will give him a thousand pounds of silver for every month Richard remains in captivity. Their third offer is one hundred and fifty thousand marks.'

In that instant, my anger reached new heights. I could have struck both John and the French king dead and not even blinked. 'What do they want for that incredible sum, madam?'

'That Heinrich should surrender Richard to Philippe, or to swear to keep him imprisoned for another full year.'

'If Philippe lays his hands on the king, madam, he will never see the light of day again!' I saw the tears in her eyes, and realised, too late, the agony it must cause her to have one son attempting to see another thrown into a French jail and forgotten. 'Your pardon, madam,' I said quickly. 'I did not mean to cause you pain.'

'It is not you who wounds me, Sir Rufus.' There was a sad smile, and then the reserve that Richard was also masterful at slipped back into place.

I marvelled, and yet Alienor had had a lifetime of guarding her emotions. Not only had she been queen for more than three decades, with all that went with it, but her own husband had kept her isolated and captive for sixteen of those years. She was used to suffering.

My eyes moved to the two other men. 'Can they raise those sums of money?'

'It is doubtful,' said Longchamp. 'But Heinrich might not care. It tickles his fancy and swells his head that the French king and Richard's heir will petition for his favour.'

I had always hated politics, and politicking, and this was on another level again. Richard's freedom hung by a thread, dependent on the whim of Heinrich, a man so capricious and ruthless he could have competed against the Devil himself. My instinct was to wade in with sword and shield, in the imperial court if necessary, but by that way lay a stupid and futile death. Not for the first time, I wished I was more devious.

I took a deep breath. 'What are we to do, madam?'

'We shall travel to Mainz, and not rest until we see Richard. He will be working day and night to win over the German nobility; if we can help him with this task, we will. Place enough pressure on Heinrich thereby, and he will not in conscience be able to renege on the agreement made with Richard.' She nodded, as if that uncertain outcome were already determined, and added, 'God is on our side.'

Longchamp and Archbishop Walter offered earnest agreement.

I joined in, but I continued to have grave doubts.

Until the king set foot in his own realm, whether that be Normandy or England, no one could safely say he was free.

CHAPTER XXI

Mainz, Germany, February 1194

By the end of January, we had decamped to Mainz, a pretty town on the Rhine. My decision to send Rhys and Bertolf ahead to secure accommodation proved to be wise. I had taken the latter under my wing. The town was bursting at the seams with nobles and dignitaries from the length and breadth of Germany, as well as a large contingent of Richard's supporters. Notable among the latter was Savaric de Bohun, the Bishop of Bath. A less welcome arrival was Robert de Nunat, brother of the Bishop of Coventry, who was an ally of John. The hostages whom Richard would have to hand over were coming in as well: two younger sons of Heinrich der Löwe, and a son of the King of Navarre.

Queen Alienor, Longchamp and Archbishop Walter spent their time closeted together; Savaric, a heavy-jawed, serious type, joined them daily.

The king had been moved to the town under heavy guard, reaching it on the first of February, the very eve of the conference called by Heinrich to discuss the final terms of Richard's release.

Alienor went to see him the instant she heard of his arrival; by her order, I went also, with Longchamp and Archbishop Walter accompanying us. It seemed plain by his guards' reaction that the king was still to be refused visitors, but Alienor was in no mood to be denied. Magnificent in a deep-blue dress, jewels winking at her neck and wrists, with a gold net encasing her white hair, she was the picture of majesty. Announcing herself, she waved the guards aside in the most peremptory fashion, and like children scolded by a tutor, they mutely obeyed. She gave the yet-closed doors a pointed stare and then moved her frosty gaze to the nearest guard, a man-at-arms older than me. He babbled an apology, and somehow managed to bow and heave open the door.

Alienor stalked past without acknowledgement, but I nodded my thanks at him. When the emperor heard, he and his comrades might well pay for what they had done.

'Mama!' Richard's bellow could have been heard in Paris. He ran to her, and knelt.

She wrapped her hands in his mane of hair and pulled him close. 'Ah, Richard, *mon coeur*.' Even she could not prevent her voice from wobbling.

The outpouring of emotion was so great, so private, that I felt an intruder. My discomfort was mirrored in Longchamp's and Walter's faces. We hung back, not wishing to impose any further.

Richard rose, and kissed his mother tenderly. 'This is a happy day, Mama. I had not thought to see you before tomorrow, at the conference.'

Alienor had regained her composure, and her humour. 'It takes more than a few men-at-arms to stop me seeing my son.'

'I heard. I swear there is not a living man in Christendom who could have denied you, Mama.' A proud smile, and then his eyes moved on to us. 'Longchamp, Archbishop Walter, Ferdia, you are most welcome.'

Settling his mother on a cushion in the window seat, he bade us take a stool each. He himself remained standing in front of the fireplace, the dominant position in the large, well-lit room. The king's rude good health continued, I am glad to say. Bright-eyed and energetic, he resembled the man who had led us in Outremer.

'Have you seen Heinrich of recent days?' Alienor asked Richard. 'What do you know of his mind?'

'I saw him just a few days since, Mama. He had the gall to accuse me of arranging Agnes's wedding.' A snort. 'I soon put him right. Had his memory failed him, to forget how smitten she and the boy Heinrich have always been? The emperor took that in bad grace at first, but then conceded that they are quite the lovebirds.'

'Good,' said Alienor. 'If he said as much to you, he can hardly object to the marriage before the Diet.'

'Heinrich will hem and haw, just to be awkward,' said Richard, 'but he will allow the union. Of far greater importance is the latest shameful offer from Philippe and Johnny. Have you heard the details, Mama?'

She nodded, her expression sorrowful. 'That boy. When I see him next, he shall not hear the end of it.'

'He is not happy unless he is plotting and scheming,' said Richard with a sardonic chuckle.

That boy, I thought darkly, was twenty-seven years old, and moreover, the king's brother. It was one thing for Philippe Capet to act in a loathsome manner, but that the king's own flesh and blood should also do so was incomprehensible to me. Truly, a mother's love was blinding, I decided. Alienor seemed to find John's treasonous behaviour worthy only of admonishment. The king's reaction was also mystifying, for all that he had no adult heir save his brother. And yet it was not for me sit in judgement over John, much as I might have enjoyed that, and so I buried my distrust and listened to Richard.

'Heinrich showed me the letters from Philippe and Johnny as soon as he had them,' said the king to Alienor. 'He sat there smirking as I read. The losenger knew how hard it would hit me, with the date of my freedom just around the corner. Sweet Jesu, one hundred and fifty thousand marks *and* to be handed over into Philippe's keeping! I was very much disturbed and confused, Mama; it was hard not to truly despair of my liberation.'

For an instant, I saw the same emotion – naked fear – in Alienor's eyes. 'Did Heinrich see that?'

'He must have suspected my emotional turmoil, Mama, but I gave him nothing.'

'And how are you now, Richard?' Again she was calm and measured.

He laughed, a short, angry bark. 'I have moments, i' faith, but for the most part, Mama, I remain confident. The princes of the empire will not stand for Heinrich breaking his word, and as for the bishops, well, they will frown on his shameful behaviour even more. He risks excommunication.' At this, Longchamp and Walter nodded. Richard continued, 'Not that that would stop him! Any man might forget his immortal soul for a time with a fortune like that in his treasury. What will keep Heinrich to the straight and narrow, I think, is the loss of face should he go back on our agreement.'

Let him be right, I prayed. The thought of Richard remaining captive, or being surrendered to Philippe, was hard even to contemplate.

'From what you say about him, the emperor will not just roll over and agree to keep the current terms,' said Alienor. 'He will want his pound of flesh.'

'He will, for certes.' This time, the king's laugh was bitter. 'More hostages will be one condition, I imagine. Longchamp, Archbishop Walter, what say you?'

Startled, for this I had not anticipated, I watched as both men quickly declared their preparedness to enter into captivity for the king. Like the rest, they would be held only until the balance of the ransom was paid. Honour bound, although my soul shrank at the prospect of another period of imprisonment, I said, 'I will also act as a hostage, sire.'

'No, Ferdia. You will be needed elsewhere. That is not to say I do not need you both also' – here Richard threw an apologetic glance in Longchamp's and Walter's direction – 'but neither of you have Sir Rufus's martial skills, and those I will require. The taking back of Normandy could prove troublesome.'

Washed by relief, I nonetheless felt obliged to protest. 'If you are sure, sire –'

'Do not pretend you are unhappy, you rogue!' He punched my arm, hard, but he was laughing.

I grinned back. 'I do not know how you have endured it, sire.'

'Truth be told, I am unsure myself. I saw not as much of William de l'Etang as I would have liked. There were many dark days and nights.' He reached out a reassuring hand to Alienor. 'Knowing that you and so many others were fighting my cause was of great solace, Mama. Giving up would have dishonoured your trust.'

'Ah, Richard, my son,' murmured Alienor. 'Until you are free, I can never truly rest.'

He took her hand and kissed it. 'God willing, Mama, and in spite of Philippe and Johnny, that day is nigh.'

'I think it is also,' said Alienor, 'but even with new, high-ranking hostages, I worry that Heinrich will not be appeased.'

'Will it be more silver?' asked Richard, glowering. 'An extra fifty thousand marks to match the other offer?'

'I think it is more than avarice which motivates the emperor. He seems prideful, by all accounts, and overweeningly arrogant.' Alienor cast an enquiring look at the king.

'He is mighty proud, it is true, perhaps even as much as Leopold.'

That takes some doing, I thought, amused.

'Do not be surprised, therefore, if he demands you become his vassal.'

Alienor's words introduced an instant tension. There was only one, quite shocking way this could become reality. I studied her sidelong, wondering if she knew more than she was letting on. It would be unsurprising, I thought, if she had spies in the emperor's court.

'You are suggesting that I do homage to Heinrich for England?' Richard's voice was calm, but the vein in his neck that signalled his purest rage was throbbing.

'I am.'

'Is that what he will demand?'

She made no answer. Their gaze met, and she did not look away. My hunch had been correct.

The king saw it too. 'God's legs! I will never swear allegiance to Heinrich!' He stamped up and down like an angry bull in a pen. 'The king of England is no vassal of the Holy Roman Emperor!'

Longchamp and Walter watched, reluctant to speak while he was in such a rage. I held my peace also. If anyone could calm him, it was Alienor.

She waited until his pacing had slowed. 'Yours would be an empty promise, Richard, as worthless as the parchment it is written on.'

'I can confirm that, sire,' said Walter, breaking his silence for the first time. 'An oath taken under duress is regarded by the Church as invalid. There would be no legal consequences. Any payments expected by Heinrich in fulfilment of your homage would also not be payable.'

'Christ on the cross, I would still have to speak the words!'

'That is true, if Heinrich expects this of you,' said his mother.

'I tell you I will not do it!' A torrent of oaths followed, unusual, and a mark of his outrage.

'Should Heinrich require this as a condition of your release, the choice will be yours, Richard. Become his vassal and gain your freedom, and deal with Philippe Capet forthwith, or languish in one of the emperor's castles until God knows when.'

He scowled at her, as petulant as a rebuked child, and despite the gravity of the situation, I had to bite the inside of my cheek not to laugh.

'Will you risk everything for pride?' asked Alienor.

He gave her a look. 'It is not pride which drives me, Mama, but honour.'

It is both, I thought, although you will not say so.

'There is no dishonour in taking a vow which is invalid because of the circumstances in which you took it,' said Alienor. 'No dishonour in taking a vow which will see you set free to safeguard your kingdom against the ravages of Philippe Capet.'

And your wretch of a brother, John, I added silently.

'What will my men think of me?' He was pacing to and fro, waving his arms.

'They do not care if you become Heinrich's liegeman!' There was a note of irritation in Alienor's voice. 'Do you think men who stormed Acre for you, who fought Saladin's mamluks in the heat and dust, give a fig for an empty promise made to a weasel like Heinrich?'

Richard blinked, brought back to himself, I hoped, by the force of her delivery. He stared at me. 'Rufus?'

'Sire?' I was not sure what he was asking.

'Would you regard me poorly if I took this oath?'

'No, sire,' I said. 'I would understand why you had done it, and think your decision prudent.'

'And the men – Rhys, for example?'

'Sire, he and everyone else would follow you into the jaws of Hell! An empty promise made to Heinrich will mean nothing to them – nothing.'

His eyes held mine, probing, for the space of perhaps five heartbeats. Then he turned away and resumed his pacing. It was unsettling, like being in the cage of a restless lion.

'In any case, your men, and your subjects, do not need to know, sire. The oath does not have to be made public,' said Longchamp. 'Everyone who bears witness to the meeting with Heinrich can be sworn to secrecy.'

Richard nodded, pleased, but he had yet to agree to his mother's suggestion and, in my mind, he looked far from convinced.

Alienor was not finished. 'Your deepest desire is to return to the Holy Land and finish what you started, is it not?'

Silence fell.

Oh, she was a wise one, I thought. She had held this heart's wish of her son's until last. I was Richard's man until my last breath, and I would follow him back to Outremer if he went, but for myself, I cared not if I ever set foot in that dust- and fly-ridden furnace-like land again. It was different for the king, however. Having to abandon his campaign there with Saladin undefeated and Jerusalem untaken had been a grievous wound.

I remembered how insistent Richard had been after the final negotiations in sending a face-saving message to Saladin. The peace agreed was not permanent, the king declared. He would be back with a fresh army, to bring the matter to its conclusion. Saladin's response had been characteristically gracious, and also humorous. He held Richard in such esteem for his honour, magnanimity, and excellence, the emir wrote, that there was no king he would rather lose his dominions to – if he should lose them at all.

My attention moved to Richard, and for once, I saw his mind as clearly as he so often read mine. If he were freed within the next few days, his first priority was to neutralise the threat from John in England, and then retake the castles and land surrendered to Philippe Capet. Only then was there any chance of travelling to the Holy Land for a second time. Even if his troubles with the French king were resolved this summer, which was being optimistic, it would be next spring before he could contemplate taking an army to Outremer, and close to eighteen months or two years before an attempt on Jerusalem was feasible.

That was the better of his two options. Refuse to become Heinrich's vassal and in all likelihood Richard faced a further prolonged period of imprisonment, leaving Philippe free to do his worst against what remained of Normandy. Anjou might be in danger too, perhaps even Aquitaine. In the face of these grim possibilities, the chance of returning to fight Saladin seemed faint indeed. Alienor knew it.

The king knew it.

She had checkmated her son. She would not shame him, though, and so the silence dragged on.

At last Richard shook his head in defeat. 'Very well, Mama. I will take Heinrich's cursed oath, if he demands it.'

Alienor's smile lit up the room. 'I am glad,' was all she said.

While Longchamp congratulated Richard, I exchanged a relieved look with Archbishop Walter.

The next day, events unfolded as we hoped. In a hall packed with his princes and bishops, with Alienor, Richard and his followers, Heinrich first made much of Agnes's marriage, and how it had been conducted without his approval. When the groom's father Konrad spoke in favour of the union, however, and waxed lyrical about the couple – long promised to each other – loud approval came from those watching. He then spoke of Philippe Capet, 'the discarder of wives', and of his foul designs on Agnes. The audience hissed its disapproval. Konrad finished with an impassioned plea to the emperor for his blessing. It was all a display, of course – the emperor had agreed to the marriage just before the proceedings began.

Heinrich pretended to give the matter some consideration, before giving his assent. His next move was to reveal the details of Philippe's and John's offer, and the eyewatering amount of silver they proposed as payment for keeping Richard prisoner or handing him over to the French king. Each announcement was met with cries of protest. Notable were the voices of the bishops of Mainz and Cologne.

Heinrich cocked his head and listened, as if he were a reasonable man and not the rapacious creature he really was. I could not have been alone in noticing how his eyes kept wandering to the dozens of stacked, iron-bound chests by the side of the dais. In them was the staggering sum of one hundred thousand marks of silver, two-thirds of Richard's ransom. When the emperor had finished looking, he again pretended to give the bishops' opinions consideration, before announcing that he could never renege on the agreement made with the English king, his *friend*. Once given, Heinrich lied blithely, his word was unbreakable. Appeased, the bishops quietened.

He would free Richard, the emperor went on, it would be his pleasure to do so. There was but one small condition.

Here it was, I thought. Alienor *did* have a source inside the imperial court.

Prepared by his mother the day before, Richard gave no angry reaction to Heinrich's outrageous demand that he should do him homage for his own kingdom. Instead, he immediately agreed. The emperor could not quite hide his disappointment.

It did not shock me that there was a final sting in the tail. In addition to becoming his vassal, Heinrich continued, Richard had to promise a yearly payment of five thousand pounds sterling. The king did not bat an eyelid, again concurring without protest. He was so nearly there, I thought, it was counterproductive to object. Two, or even three times the amount would not have stopped Richard by this stage. Heinrich had missed a trick, and by the sour purse of his lips, had realised it.

A short time later, the ceremony was over. Witnessed by the bishops, Richard had knelt, and placed his hands between Heinrich's, and sworn the necessary oaths. He had given the emperor a leather cap, a symbol of his vassalage, and had it handed back. Heinrich's expression throughout was gloating. This was his moment of supremacy – he would have had it last all day no doubt. Richard, on the other hand, was the embodiment of tranquillity and acceptance.

He did not even react when the emperor tried one last time to goad him into a reaction. The ransom, Heinrich declared, would have to be counted before Richard could be released. The intimation that the king might try to short-change him was grossly disrespectful; I bridled to hear it. Richard, however, smiled as he had expected it all along.

'The morning of the day after tomorrow, then?' he asked. 'I cannot imagine it could take any longer, unless your clerks are poor with their figures.' Again he smiled, and, this time, it was a lion's smile, fierce and pitiless.

'Aye, that will be time enough.' Heinrich's face was as sour as that of a man sucking on a lemon.

Richard caught my eye and winked.

I gave him a fierce grin.

Another day and a half would make no difference.

Just after the bells had rung tierce on the fourth day of February, Richard emerged into the courtyard of the emperor's palace. Two guards, their part done, watched from the doorway as he walked to his waiting mother. Watery sunlight bathed the scene, as if God Himself was giving his blessing to their reunion.

Neither Richard nor Alienor spoke as they embraced, but the intensity of their emotions was plain to all. There was a lump in my own throat, just witnessing it. Even Bertolf, who had never seen the king's mother before, was visibly emotional.

At length, Alienor pulled back to look her son in the face. 'You are free, *mon coeur*,' she said. 'Free!'

'Thanks in the main to you, Mama. I will never forget.' He raised her hands in turn and planted gentle kisses on them. 'Truly, you are the queen of my heart.'

Alienor smiled, but I thought it was well that Berengaria did not hear those words. Richard held his wife in some affection, but in Outremer, he had not sought out her company as much as might have been expected of a new husband. In the times since, during our voyage on the Greek Sea, and then overland towards Vienna, he had rarely mentioned her. It was not for a king to discuss his wife with his companions, it was true, and yet those of us who were married had made wistful comments about seeing their women again. I wondered if all was well in his marriage; never during these conversations had Richard seemed remotely sad or regretful, while my heart had ached with thoughts of Joanna. To my knowledge, he had not written to Berengaria during his captivity either, although he had sent numerous letters to his mother.

Whatever his feelings for his wife, I decided, the king needed to get her with child, or he would be reliant on John to the end of his days.

'One year, six weeks and three days, Mama. That is how long I was Leopold's and Heinrich's prisoner.' Richard's gaze moved from his mother to me and, at my side, a delighted Rhys. 'Never again.'

CHAPTER XXII

Barfleur, Normandy, May 1194

Sail down, propelled by the last of its momentum, our ship came to rest against the dock. Gulls screeched overhead. The waiting crowd, hundreds strong, cheered. The throng was so dense that an apple thrown in the air would have landed on someone's head. Richard waved; his mother Alienor did too. I let out a sigh of relief. Never a keen sailor, I was always glad to see the end of a sea voyage. A short distance along the deck, Rhys was explaining to Bertolf what would happen next.

Ten days in total it had taken us to cross the Narrow Sea, forced back to Portsmouth on the second of the month by a storm, and stranded there for more than a sennight. We were here now, though, on this twelfth day of May, and the sun was shining bright and strong, as if to convey God's pleasure at seeing the king return at last to Normandy.

The crowd, townspeople and soldiers of the garrison, who had been expecting Richard since the end of April, went wild as he leaped onto the dock. They began to sing and dance.

I picked out the chorus: 'God has come again in His strength. It is time for the French king to go.'

It was hard not to grin at that.

Richard clouted me on the shoulder. 'Glad to be back, Rufus?'

'Yes, sire. At last we can deal with Philippe.' And with luck, come up against FitzAldelm, I thought. I might see Joanna too, although what good that would do me I did not know, given that we could never be together, still less wed.

'You have been chafing as much as I,' he said, smiling.

I nodded, relieved that a month of meetings and conferences, ceremonies and dealing with paperwork was over.

'To have come any sooner would have left matters in disarray, Richard,' reproved Alienor.

228

'I know, Mama,' he said patiently.

It had begun with the state council in Nottingham, a few days after the castle's fall. The siege there had been brief, thanks to the king's fierce assault, and the realisation by the garrison that Richard was not in fact dead – this a vicious rumour put about by John. Very much alive, the king had met with William Longchamp, Hugh de Puiset, Archbishop Hubert Walter and his half-brother Geoffrey. A host of other bishops as well as David, the brother of King William of Scotland, had also attended. For four days the great and good had wrestled with the kingdom's finances and other matters. Aware of how men in high station loved their status, Richard had used the opportunity to auction off the most lucrative ecclesiastical and secular offices of state, some for the second time. Longchamp and the king's half-brother Geoffrey had not been alone in having to bid to retain their long-held positions.

They had also debated the merits of confiscating John's English possessions. Won over by Alienor's argument that to do so would drive him further into the willing arms of Philippe Capet, the council had instead ordered John to present himself to Richard's court by the tenth of May, or face banishment.

I had been bored to tears by the whole procedure.

It was as if the king also remembered. 'While I wrestled with affairs of state, you, Rufus, had the chance to go hunting in Sherwood Forest as often as you wanted.' He had visited it twice, and had been entranced.

'The hunting *was* good, sire.' I did not say that more than once I had imagined aiming my bow at John or FitzAldelm, rather than a stag.

'I could have stayed there for a month after the council had ended,' said Richard.

Instead he had spent a few days with King William of Scotland, renewing their friendship. Then it had been on to Winchester, and a ceremonial crown-wearing in St Swithin's priory, an important reaffirmation of the king's position as ruler of England.

After that the weather had conspired to prevent us from reaching France. We had had reason for concern too; worrying news had come from Normandy. Philippe Capet seemed likely to break the truce agreed at Mantes; his forces were massing near Rouen, east of the River

Seine. Richard had been impatient and fretful, and on the second of May, had ordered the hundred-strong fleet out against his captains' advice. The result had been a delay of ten days. When the conditions improved, it had been none too soon. Verneuil, a castle deep into Normandy that was still loyal to the king, was under attack from the French. John had not presented himself to the royal court either; as far as we knew, he was still in Normandy.

I wondered how long his nerve would hold with the king also here. If previous behaviour were any indication, he would soon be beating a path to Richard's door, I decided.

'We are here now, God be thanked,' Richard said. 'Let us be grateful for that.'

'And let Philippe quake in his shoes when he hears.' There was a wicked, most unladylike gleam in Alienor's eyes.

I hoped John would do the same, the cur.

Unaware of my thoughts, Richard was laughing, the sound that came from deep in his belly, and which signified true happiness.

He and I were alike in that respect, I thought, preferring war, or the prospect of it, to normal life.

Although I burned to make for Verneuil at once, there to deal with Philippe Capet and his army, the king had business that could not wait. Hours after our disembarkation and journey to the nearby town of Caen, a messenger arrived from John d'Alençon, Archdeacon of Lisieux, and a former vice chancellor of England. John had travelled to Outremer with news and messages for the king two years before, and was a trusted ally.

The letter's contents were significant, but not surprising. Richard's wayward brother John – contacted by the worthy archdeacon – wanted to re-enter the fold. If the king came to Lisieux, so would John, to throw himself on Richard's mercy. Alienor had beamed to hear the news, which made me think that she had had a hand in it. Masterful at writing letters, whether to the Pope, state officials or her sons, she was also an adroit politician. Her aim since Richard's return had been quite clear: to reunite her family, and ensure that the throne remained secure. In my mind, Archdeacon John's letter had probably been sent by her command.

The news made the king chuckle, and declare that he had always known John would abandon Philippe once he heard of our arrival in Normandy; now it seemed that he had been preparing to leave him for some time.

And so, after a letter dictated by Richard had been sent to the commander of the garrison at Verneuil, urging him to hold on, we travelled from Caen to Lisieux.

'Imagine if FitzAldelm had taken up with John,' said Rhys. He lowered his voice further; it was early evening, and the pair of us were in a corner of the kitchen in John d'Alençon's house, where we had arrived the day before. 'They would suit each other, eh?'

'Two weasels together,' I agreed. 'It does not bear thinking about. Nor is it likely, thank Christ. The king will forgive his brother, sad to say, but I cannot see him pardoning FitzAldelm after what he has done.'

'Treachery is treachery, and anyone committing it should pay,' said Rhys darkly.

'I agree, but blood flows thicker than water, especially when Richard's only other possible heir is a seven-year-old boy.' This was Arthur of Normandy, son of the king's dead brother Geoffrey. 'Remember too that a mother's love knows no boundaries. Queen Alienor is set on John taking his place by Richard's side, and her influence is not to be underestimated.'

'She is a powerful woman.' Katharina had been listening.

'And more often than not, she gets what she wants,' I said, thinking I was fortunate to retain the queen's favour. It was another reason never to express my dislike of John in public.

'I am familiar with that state of affairs,' said Rhys, managing to wink and neatly avoid Katharina's indignant poke at the same time.

'The cheek of you!' she cried. 'Never am I consulted before you decide to gallivant off, or worse, head into battle.'

'What can I say? 'Tis the life of a liegeman.' Rhys's shrug was eloquent. His eyes went to me. 'I follow my lord, and do his bidding.'

Katharina's disapproving gaze bore down on me. I took the easy way out. 'I am sworn to the king. I obey his commands.'

Momentarily defeated, she waved her wooden spoon at us before stumping back to the pot she had left bubbling over the fire.

'A near escape,' I said, only half joking.

Rhys nodded. 'It will be the floor for me tonight.'

'At least you have someone to share a bed with most of the time,' I countered, thinking of Joanna. Landing in Normandy had rekindled my hopes of seeing her again. Once the campaigning season was over, the king would surely send for Berengaria, and with her would come his sister, my love.

'I thought that was done with.' Rhys was never shy of voicing his opinion, even when it was blunt.

'It is,' I snapped, wishing that Joanna were the fortunate Agnes von Hohenstaufen and I her husband Heinrich of Brunswick, the couple whose love marriage had been allowed to stand.

Rhys gave me a sympathetic look. Darting to a nearby counter upon which sat a stack of fresh-baked pies, he lifted two without being noticed by Katharina and, returning, handed me one. 'Chicken and raisin by the smell,' he said.

Food was no replacement for Joanna, but my belly, stimulated by the pie's delicious odour, reminded me that I had not had any food since dawn. Muttering my thanks, I took a mouthful.

It was but half-eaten when a little girl in a ragged tunic – one of the urchins to be found in every town in the land – came haring in from the courtyard. 'He is here! He is here!'

I grabbed the back of her tunic as she came past. 'Who is here?'

She wriggled, trying to get free, and then looking at me, realised that I was one of the royal party. 'John, sir, King Richard's brother. He has just ridden through the gate. The steward has sent for the archdeacon.'

'Good girl,' I said, and releasing her, proffered the rest of my pie.

I got a grateful look, then she ran on into the kitchen, continuing to announce her news. I noted Katharina's motherly glance.

'Coming?' I asked Rhys.

'I would not miss it,' came the answer.

We followed a passageway that opened beside the stables. Rather than go into the yard – I had no wish to be seen by John, and there was a tiny chance FitzAldelm was with him – I lingered in the corridor.

Everything was noise and commotion outside. The party that had arrived through the darkening air was about a dozen strong, if the number of horses was a guide. My eyes flickered over the men-at-arms and knights, a couple of squires, and an unhappy-looking scribe. It was disappointing but not overly surprising that of FitzAldelm there was no sign. Spying Archdeacon John not fifteen paces away, I peered closer. He was talking animatedly to a slight man with dark red hair: the king's brother John, it had to be. The man turned, revealing his profile.

'There he is, the snake,' I whispered to Rhys.

We could not enter the yard for fear of being seen by John, but God intervened. The archdeacon walked towards us, indicating with a respectful gesture that John should follow. I melted back into the shadows, closing the door so that it was ajar only a hand's breadth. Their footsteps approached, and I held my breath, nervous in case for some odd reason they came into the kitchen passage.

They stopped right outside.

'Are you well, sire?' The archdeacon sounded concerned. 'You must be weary after your journey.' John had come from Évreux, a town granted back to him in February by Philippe Capet.

'I am well enough.' John sounded far from that, nervous, even agitated. 'What kind of mood is my brother in?'

'Do not be concerned, sire –'

'Answer the damned question!' John sounded frantic. Terrified.

I glanced at Rhys, who leered his amusement at John's fear.

'The king is merciful and straightforward, sire. He will be kinder to you than you would be to him.' There could be no mistaking the tone of reproval in the archdeacon's voice.

John took this in silence.

'He is expecting you, sire. Let me take you to him.'

'Aye.' A loud, theatrical sigh. 'The sooner it is done, the better.'

To the king's chamber, I mouthed to Rhys. The instant that the archdeacon and John had gone through into the main part of the house, we stole back to the kitchen. Katharina threw us a look that told Rhys in particular he was not out of trouble, but we did not pause.

I timed our arrival to perfection. The door to Richard's room was still closing, and the archdeacon was waiting outside, near the two on-duty sentries. *Click*. The door shut.

Richard's voice raised in loud greeting. 'Look who it is! My long-lost brother.'

'John.' Alienor's tone was carefully neutral.

Unsurprised that their mother was present, I went to the archdeacon's side. 'Is anyone else in there?'

A shake of his head.

We paused, both unashamed of eavesdropping, as Alienor spoke.

'You are here. That is something at least.' Her tone was still cool.

I could not discern John's reply. He spoke for a second time, and again his words were inaudible. There was no mistaking the meekness of his tone, however. He sounded like a small boy asking forgiveness for bad behaviour.

A moment passed, and then Richard said, 'Get up. Stand up, Johnny.'

He had thrown himself at the king's feet, I thought with disgust. He had no shame, moving seamlessly from staunch ally of Philippe Capet, happy to give away castles and territory, to humble penitent of the king, apologising and begging for mercy. He deserved a kicking, not forgiveness.

'I am sorry, my liege.' Now John sounded as if he were crying.

His hypocrisy was staggering. You would have let your own brother rot in Heinrich's dungeon, I thought. Let him die a captive. I noticed the archdeacon's eyes on me, and realised I had grasped my dagger. Glad the sentries had not noticed, I offered the archdeacon a confident smile, and affected to let my fingers play with my belt buckle, as if avoiding boredom was all I had been doing. His attention moved away, and I breathed again.

John was still apologising. 'What I did was wrong, sire. Unforgivable.'

'The only reason it can be excused is that you are family, and Mama interceded on your behalf.' There was no kindness in Richard's chuckle, just barely veiled contempt. 'Do not be afraid, Johnny. You are a child.'

He is twenty-seven, I thought, yet the king is right. John had acted like a brat. Unhappy with the vast estates and annual income granted him, discontented despite his status as heir to the throne, he had sulked until the perfect opportunity came his way. John had used Richard's imprisonment to try to seize the glittering prize, the throne itself, something that would have been his anyway if the king died childless. With it beyond his reach, here he came crawling back, wanting what had been his beforehand, given freely by Richard, without any treachery or subterfuge.

I could appreciate Alienor's point of view, why it made sense to forgive John, but by Christ, it was hard to stomach. I was glad not to be Richard, because I did not know if I could do what the king was about to.

'You got into bad company, Johnny,' Richard went on, 'and it is those who have led you astray who will be punished, who will feel my wrath.' He did not need to say 'Philippe Capet'.

'I am grateful, my liege,' said John, and he seemed genuine.

Richard clapped his hands. 'It is a long ride from Évreux. You must be hungry.' He sounded like a host addressing a welcome guest. It was as if their initial conversation had not even happened.

'I am famished, brother.' John sounded relieved to move on.

'Come, try this fine salmon that the citizens of Lisieux sent earlier as a gift.' Richard's voice was drawing closer, and I realised the table upon which the fish was displayed must be by the door.

The king spoke again, pitching his tone low so their mother Alienor would not hear, but we, just a few paces away, caught every word.

'I have kissed and made up for Mama's sake, Johnny. Do not think that everything is sweetness and light between us.' Richard's voice was icy, controlled. 'It will take years to regain my trust, *if* you ever manage it. Your titles and lands will not be coming back to you anytime soon either. As for the castles you so freely handed to that Capet dog, forget them. Worthier castellans will be found.'

'I understand, brother,' said John.

'Good.' One word, spoken with hard certainty, and laden with menace. Then, bright and cheerful, the king said, 'Mama, do try the salmon. It is excellent.'

As Alienor joined her sons, I scrambled to marshal my emotions. John had been forgiven; his deceitfulness had been, if not erased, brushed into a dark corner. From this point, liegemen like me would have to offer him the same respect he had commanded prior to his betrayal of Richard.

I felt a hand on my arm; the archdeacon was drawing me away. I walked with him, glad to remove myself from the royal family and their complex relationships.

'You do not approve of the king's response.' The archdeacon saw my shock, and smiled. 'You are an open book, Sir Rufus.'

'Ever has it been so,' I said bitterly, wondering if John would see through me with such ease.

CHAPTER XXIII

I saw John briefly the next day, in the main reception room of the house, but he gave no sign of having recognised me. There were others present, thankfully, and it was clear he was in no mood for pleasant conversation with anyone who knew, even indirectly, what he had said to Richard the day before. He was also in a hurry to be away.

Alienor was the only one who seemed sorry to see him leave. 'Must you go? The good burghers of Évreux will not miss you for another day.'

'I cannot linger, Mama.' John took her hand and kissed it. 'I will see you again soon.'

Richard gave his brother a gruff farewell. 'Do not get too comfortable at Évreux, Johnny. You will be called on before long, to join my campaign to reclaim Normandy.'

Much use he will be, I thought. John's military record had been appalling since his attempt to bring order to Ireland a decade or so before. Everything he turned his hand to, siege or skirmish, had a tendency to end in disaster. The king's comment had been made for appearance's sake, nothing more. It worked too. I saw the approving look Alienor gave Richard, and the smile he gave her in return.

With John departed, the king made immediate plans to make for Verneuil and the relieving of the siege. 'There has been enough delay. The defenders there must be hard-pressed,' he said, adding, 'if they still hold out at all.'

Our most recent news had come courtesy of a messenger to the archdeacon, some days since. Assuming that Richard would soon land at Barfleur, unaware of the storms that had kept us in English waters for ten days, the defenders of Verneuil had rained down insults on Philippe Capet and his army when they arrived.

'It was unwise to open the gates and invite the French king inside, sire,' I said, remembering how Earl Robert had done the same in Rouen. We had got away with angering Philippe, but it could easily have been very different.

'It was, but God's legs, I would have loved to have seen Philippe's face,' said Richard, smiling. 'He would have the warmest of welcomes, the defenders' message said, if only he stepped inside.'

'Philippe must have been enraged by that, sire, and even more so when the gates slammed shut.' This had revealed an extremely unflattering depiction of the French king daubed on the timbers.

'That was also funny.' The king's expression grew serious. 'Let us hope they have weathered the French assault since then.'

'Indeed, sire.' I did not say what I thought, which was that John could have been told to join us at Verneuil, which would have saved us several days.

We set out an hour later. Alienor did not come with us; she had played out her role for the moment, she told the king. She was for Fontevraud, the convent she held in such esteem. 'No, I am not going to become a nun,' she said, smiling at a questioning Richard. 'It is time for me to contemplate, to spend time with God. Send messages there, should you need.'

The king's mood lifted with every mile that we rode from Lisieux. I knew him well enough to decide it was not the leaving of his brother, still less his mother, but the prospect of battle. I was in similar mood, and so was Rhys, even though he had had to endure another ear-bashing from Katharina because she would have to follow us with the half-dozen wagons that had slowly travelled from Barfleur.

We travelled hard and fast, aiming for Tubœuf, a town to the west of Verneuil, on the River Iton. It was there that we would meet the majority of the force of men-at-arms, archers and knights which had sailed with us from England.

I could not wait.

If there was ever a man who deserved to be punished, I had decided, it was Philippe Capet. The motives of others who had done the king wrong were understandable. Leopold took Richard prisoner out of affronted pride. The devious Heinrich had mainly been after money, and ways to improve his chances of taking Sicily.

Philippe had acted out of pure malice.

There was John to consider too, a little devil in my head reminded me, but he was now beyond reproach, unassailable. Nor was his return to favour all bad, perhaps. I was reminded of the saying in Outremer, that it was better to keep an enemy close, the better to anticipate his next move.

We reached Tubœuf on the twenty-first of May, our horses weary, and more than half our party left behind to catch us up. I swear if the French had been outside the town, Richard would have led us to an immediate attack, so eager was he. Instead he had to content himself with a meeting of his captains to discuss strategy. Content is the wrong description, for he paced about the pavilion, irritated that the troops we had left in Barfleur had not yet caught up. They would not be long, perhaps another two to three days, but that was not enough for Richard.

'Philippe will have had word of our coming by now,' he declared. 'The caitiff will press home his attack on Verneuil. We must act fast. I do not want to ride up to its walls to find him ensconced within!'

Rhys entered the partitioned section that formed the meeting area in the king's pavilion. I expected him to come quietly to my side, to report something, but instead he cleared his throat, not a bit self-conscious before so many men far above his station. Men who knew him, like André de Chauvigny – freshly arrived from Poitiers – did not react, but William Marshal looked less than impressed.

Earl Robert of Leicester, who had been interrupted, glared at Rhys.

He gave no indication of caring, instead saying loudly, 'By your leave, sire?'

Richard's attention moved from Earl Robert to me – I shrugged – and then, with evident amusement, to Rhys. 'Speak.'

Rhys took a knee – he did respect the king – and said, 'A knight has ridden into the camp, sire. He is sorely wounded, and he comes from Verneuil.'

Shocked expressions, mutters of concern.

'Have you summoned Ralph Besace?' Richard demanded. This was the king's personal physician who had been to Outremer with us.

'I have, sire, but the knight refused any treatment before he spoke with you. He is here.'

'What? Bring him in!'

'Sire.' Rhys half turned, and beckoned.

In came a figure in a muddied, bloodstained surcoat, supported by a man-at-arms on either side. He was a young man, perhaps twenty-five, but suffering made him look much older. Deep lines of pain were etched on his pale face. 'Sire,' he mumbled, 'forgive me. If I kneel, I fear I will not be able to rise.'

Richard rushed forward. 'A stool – quickly!'

I grabbed one from the pile that had been stacked at the side of the room, out of the way, and came in behind the injured knight as Richard took over from the men-at-arms and, gentle as a mother with a babe, lowered him onto the stool.

'There. Can you sit up?' asked the king, his voice full of concern.

'I can, sire.' The knight tried to smile, then winced.

'Where are you hurt?'

'Here, sire.' He raised a hand towards his right side, where his surcoat was rent and bloodiest. 'When I was riding through the blockade around the town, a Frenchie hit me with his lance. 'Twas a glancing blow, thank God, but it went in nonetheless.'

'A physician should see to you, and at once,' said the king. He glanced over his shoulder. Ralph Besace was hovering just behind him.

'Let me pass on my message, sire,' pleaded the knight. 'I beg you.'

Richard nodded.

'We still hold out, sire, but the town is surrounded, and the Frenchies' catapults have smashed down a goodly part of the walls. It will not be long ere they have a large enough breach to allow an assault.' The knight gratefully took a drink from the cup Richard was holding to his lips, and in a low but determined voice, went on to describe the strength of the French forces and their disposition around Verneuil. This done, he closed his eyes.

Richard urged Ralph Besace forward, and after the knight had been laid on the floor, himself helped to remove the cumbersome hauberk. Ralph cut the man's garments, exposing an oozing hole perhaps an inch and a half in diameter. After a brief examination, he announced to the relief of everyone present that the wound did not seem life-threatening. The lance had pierced the muscles over the hip, but had not entered the abdomen itself.

With the king's blessing, the knight, now semi-conscious, was borne off to the tent that served as an infirmary; Ralph Besace followed.

'We have arrived in the nick of time,' said the king. 'Sweet Jesu, but I wish the rest of our men were here *now*.' He cast a look at Earl Robert. 'Remind me how strong the force already with us is?'

'About fifty knights, sire, six score men-at-arms, and the same number of archers and crossbowmen.'

'And a dozen times that number are coming from Barfleur, more or less?'

'Yes, sire.'

'Half of what we have will be enough for me. You take the other half, Robert, and break through the French cordon. Enter the town. Your numbers should bolster the garrison enough to hold Philippe's troops at bay for another few days.'

'It will be my honour, sire,' said Robert, his face shining with eagerness.

The king saw that I was also keen, and chuckled. 'You are as impatient as I, Rufus. We shall not be long waiting, do not fear.'

'What is your intention, sire?'

'To send another force skirting around the Frenchies to the east; it will cut off their lines of communication. With luck, they will also block Philippe's path should he decide to retreat. Once it is in place, I will lead a column straight to Verneuil, and launch a frontal attack on the French.' Richard grinned, as if the siege were already lifted, and the enemy driven off with heavy losses.

His enthusiasm proved well-founded. Earl Robert sneaked through the French lines under the cover of darkness the following night, and gained the safety of Verneuil without the loss of a single man. Richard sent a force to the east as he had planned; over the next couple of days, it blocked many of the routes back into French territory. The army reached us the day after that, by which point Philippe's one and only attempt to storm the town had failed.

On the twenty-eighth of May, as the king was preparing to make for Verneuil, we had welcome news. Philippe Capet had split his troops in twain, and led half in the direction of Évreux, leaving the rest to continue the siege. It was a foolish decision, but as Richard observed of his French counterpart, not a surprising one. Philippe was a schemer and intriguer par excellence, but his qualities did not generally extend to those of a tactician. It was also possible, I suggested, that Philippe had been scared off by the knowledge that Richard was lurking in the vicinity.

The king grinned with delight, and admitted the same thought had crossed his mind. It made no sense, however, he said, to expect Philippe's depleted forces outside Verneuil to resist a combined attack from him and the town's garrison. Earl Robert would be waiting, and would sally forth when we engaged the enemy.

His opinion proved accurate. The remaining French besiegers fled the day after their king's departure, leaving behind their siege engines. We pursued them for miles, killing any who fought back, taking prisoners and seizing wagons laden down with baggage and equipment. Tiring of the chase, the king brought us back to Verneuil late on the afternoon of the thirtieth of May. Jubilant, Richard led us through the main gate as the garrison chanted his name from the ramparts. The streets were packed with excited, cheering townspeople, come to see their king, who had delivered them from the damnable French.

Richard was in high spirits, happy to receive the adulation; he was also determined to recognise the defenders' bravery and determination. Ordering a parade, he stalked up and down the lines of grinning soldiers, praising them to the skies and giving each one a kiss on the cheek. Every man's name and details were taken, so rich rewards could be paid to them from the royal treasury.

The king would not have admitted it, but I felt these actions stemmed from a sense of guilt. If we had not been delayed from departing England by the weather, if he had not ridden first to Lisieux and the meeting with his weasel brother John, the siege would have been brought to an end at least half a month sooner, saving countless lives inside Verneuil.

We had been savouring the victory for only a few hours when the real reason for Philippe's sudden withdrawal was made clear. Yet another exhausted messenger arrived, and the news he bore shocked us all.

John had made his way to Évreux from Lisieux. Re-entering the town without revealing that he had again switched allegiances, he had massacred the French garrison. Their unwitting commanders were cut down as they sat at table.

The atrocity sent Richard into a thunderous rage. 'Does the whelp think this proves his loyalty?' he raged. Neither I nor Earl Robert had had an answer.

John further showed his true nature a day or two later, abandoning Évreux before the arrival of an incandescent Philippe. The French king, determined to deliver a suitable response to John's barbarity, promptly had the unfortunate inhabitants of Évreux slaughtered: men, women and children. Even babes-in-arms were not spared. The town was sacked, and the churches were burned to the ground.

It was an omen of things to come.

From Évreux, Philippe took his army to the little castle of Fontaine and began a siege. It was as clear a provocation as one could imagine, a mere five miles from Rouen, the capital of Normandy. Richard had already sent Earl Robert there; it was also where John had ignominiously retreated from Évreux. The king hoped that Robert's presence would stiffen his brother's spine, although from his advice before the earl left – there was mention of only allowing John to lead certain-to-succeed missions – Richard did not hold out any real expectation of success even in this simple regard. The earl and John did not have the numbers to go to the aid of Fontaine either.

Nor could we help, because the king had led his army south, travelling a hundred miles to reach the great fortress of Loches by the ninth of June. Surrendered to Philippe under the terms of the Mantes treaty, it was under siege by forces led by Berengaria's giant of a brother Sancho, heir to the throne of Navarre. Honouring the Navarrese alliance with Richard, Sancho had first come to help fight the rebels in Aquitaine and then diverted to attack Loches.

The two men had always got on, so it was no surprise their reunion was emotional. The atmosphere grew strained, however, when Sancho brought up his sister. He was surprised that since his release the king had not sent for her. Sancho told us he had come to Loches via Poitiers, so his stance had clearly been affected by Berengaria. Richard grew a little awkward, which was most unlike him, and declared that he had been at constant war since arriving in Normandy. Wives had no place on campaign, he said, blithely ignoring the fact that Berengaria had been with him almost the entire time we were in Outremer. Sancho was diplomatic enough not to mention this, and seemed content with the king's avowal that he and Berengaria would be reunited once the campaigning season was over.

I was less sure. The king talked of nothing but war, and Philippe Capet, and regaining the territories lost to the French king. He never mentioned Berengaria, and if her name came up in conversation, he expressed no emotion at all. I would not have admitted it to a soul, not even Rhys, but it pleased me that Richard had scant feelings for his wife. That he should have a loving marriage when I, who worshipped his sister, feelings which were reciprocated, could not, was an unfair and heavy burden. If I could not be with Joanna, then, traitorous though the notion was, it seemed fitting that Richard's relationship with his wife was cold.

His lack of interest in her was cause for concern, however. Until he got Berengaria with child, his wretch of a brother remained heir to the throne. That did not impact me at present, but if something happened to Richard, God forbid, John would become king. I did not like to think of my own position if that came to pass.

Calamitous news came for Sancho the afternoon of our arrival. His father the king was dying, and as heir, it was imperative that Sancho return to Navarre at once. He left as the sun was going down, intending to travel day and night, but surrendering the majority of his forces to Richard's keeping. As we found out, wandering their camp that evening, the Navarrese were in bad shape, ill-fed, because supplies had been hard to come by, and downhearted, not just from their leader's departure, but the failure of the siege thus far.

Richard was not discouraged even a fraction. The next morning, after a brutal barrage by our artillery saw two breaches created, one on the south wall and the other on the north, we took Loches by storm. The victory was remarkable, but it was not all down to concentrating the artillery assault on two different positions. As I entered the southern breach, following Richard – he would have it no other way – it was apparent that the garrison was pitifully undermanned. Five knights and two dozen men-at-arms surrendered. He laughed as they lined up in the courtyard, and even as they quailed, thinking his amusement meant a dreadful death, the king announced that they were bravehearts to resist such a large army. He freed the lot forthwith, and allowed the knights to retain their weapons.

'If every castle in Normandy and the Vexin fell this easily, Rufus,' he said to me, 'I would count myself truly blessed.'

I knew why. The contest between him and Philippe Capet would ever be most bitter close to Paris. Here and further south, the French monarch was content to stir up trouble for Richard, but his primary interest always lay in the lands close to his capital, and there the king's losses had been greatest.

'Do you want to ride for Normandy again, sire?'

A good part of our army was not with us; the levies from Anjou and Maine were to the north, attacking the French-held stronghold of Montmirail, and so too was an Anglo-Norman force, which had marched back to besiege the castle of Beaumont-le-Roger. It was probable that neither set of soldiers needed help, but there were any number of other fortresses that needed recapturing.

'Aquitaine needs to be brought to heel first.'

I nodded. The danger there was more pressing. 'You mean Geoffrey de Rançon and Count Adémar Taillefer of Angoulême, sire?'

He snorted an angry laugh. 'Who else?'

Two of Aquitaine's prominent noblemen, they were possibly the king's most troublesome subjects. I knew them of old. Both had risen in rebellion more than once; in recent months, they had been at it again.

'Poitiers is on the way south, sire.'

He gave me a jaundiced look. 'You are thinking about my sister.'

'I would be lying to deny it, sire, but I was also thinking about the queen.' This was a barefaced lie, but for once I delivered it with the naked confidence of a trickster peddling a piece of the True Cross. 'She would be right glad to see you.'

Richard took the bait. He grumbled and muttered, but conceded that it would not delay our progress overmuch to spend a night or two in Poitiers. In truth, I think he had already decided that to avoid seeing Berengaria when we would all but pass her doorstep was a step too far.

That night, I dreamed not of subduing Aquitaine, but of seeing Joanna.

CHAPTER XXIV

Poitiers, June 1194

We clattered into the palace courtyard, and Richard jumped down from Fauvel, acknowledging the greeting of a startled steward. 'Take me to my wife,' he ordered.

'Do you wish to bathe first, sir, or to change?' asked the steward.

'No.'

I clambered off Pommers, unsurprised by the king's behaviour. Part of it, I was sure, was his impatient nature. He was here to see Berengaria, and saw no point in delaying their reunion. There was more to it, though. He was intelligent, calculating, even. Presenting himself to his queen in sweat-ridden, travel-stained clothing delivered a powerful message. He was a king on campaign, and had left his army to come here. I wondered if I was alone in thinking that Richard had another, deeper purpose, to show that he cared more for war than Berengaria.

I hoped Joanna did not think the same of me. Almost two years had passed since we had last seen each other, and my memories of her, of how she *was*, were not as crystal clear as I would have wished. I was unsure of her reaction to my unannounced arrival with the king.

'What are you going to say to her?' asked Rhys, taking Pommers' reins.

The question sounded innocent, but I knew him well enough to feel the jibe. 'I have no damned idea!' Mortifyingly, my colour began to rise as it had when I was a young man.

'Rufus.'

I glared. 'What?'

'Your pardon. I spoke out of turn. I can only imagine how hard it will be to see her and know that what you had in Outremer cannot –' Rhys paused, thinking, and then said, his voice suddenly thick – 'you know what I mean.'

I had no words, so I nodded, grateful that he at least had an inkling of what I was about to endure.

'Rufus?' André de Chauvigny had gone ahead a little; he paused in the doorway to the palace. 'The king is halfway down the corridor. Are you coming?'

'Yes, yes.' I hurried to join him. We entered, and followed Richard.

We walked in silence. My mind was racing.

'Nervous?' asked de Chauvigny.

'As a condemned man on his way to the executioner's block.' I was not lying. My palms were damp and my forehead sweaty, yet my mouth was dry as a bone.

'Unless Joanna is heartless, she will be glad to see you again. And she is not heartless.' After Rhys and Richard, de Chauvigny was the only other person I had told about my love affair. When he had recently joined the king from Poitiers, I had grilled him about her, but gleaned little other than that she was well. She was unaware that he knew of our relationship, so there had been no possibility of her confiding in him.

'In her mind, duty comes before all else,' I said morosely. 'Even if it did not, the king will not allow her to marry for love.'

De Chauvigny's face was a picture. 'He *knows*?'

'I told him when he ordered me to Normandy.'

'God's toes, Rufus! If it were anyone else, I would say it was a miracle they were still breathing. He took it well, then?'

'I feared for my life at first,' I said with a wry smile, 'but he came around to understanding in the end. He was quick to tell me that we could never be wed, however.' I grimaced. 'She is far too valuable as a bride for whichever king, count or earl he deems worthy of her hand.'

De Chauvigny gave me a sympathetic look. 'Always it is so. Political alliances are a vital part of what holds kingdoms together.'

'I know.' I made no attempt to keep the bitterness from my voice.

He gave me a mischievous elbow dunt. 'Joanna is currently unwed. You could arrange a tryst with her while we are here!' Whether he knew it or not, he had put his finger on my secret hope – nay, burning desire.

'I have no idea if she would want the same,' I muttered. 'Nor indeed if it would be a good idea. Some wounds are best left to heal, rather than being ripped open again.'

247

'From the look of you, Rufus, there has been no healing.' His tone was kind. 'A word of advice. School your features before we catch up with the king. It is one thing for him to acknowledge your love for his sister in private, and quite another to see it writ all over your face when others are present.'

His advice was sound, so I slipped on the best mask of pretence I had, and prayed it would be sufficient.

The king had already gone into an inner courtyard, where, a sentry told us, Berengaria and her ladies were to be found.

We increased our pace, entering just in time to hear Richard's greeting, soft and courteous, 'Wife. It is I, your husband.'

Berengaria, who had been talking to two of her ladies, turned in shock. Clad in a sky-blue gown, long black hair in braids, with earrings her only jewellery, she was comely enough, but no beauty.

'R-Richard?' There was joy in her eyes, and pain, and reserve.

He crossed to her in a dozen paces. There was no enfolding her in his arms as he had with Joanna the day both women had left the Holy Land. Instead, he gave her a stiff bow, and taking one of her hands, kissed the back of it. 'You look well, my lady. My heart is glad to see you again.'

'As is mine, husband.' After a heartbeat's delay, she added, 'I had thought you would come sooner.'

It was unusual to see Richard discomfited. He coughed, and said, 'Philippe has taken great chunks of Normandy. He has intentions on half my kingdom, and the rebels in Aquitaine want the rest. Since landing at Barfleur, I have done nothing but ride from siege to siege, rarely sleeping more than two nights in one place.'

The shutters came down. 'I understand, sire,' Berengaria said, her gaze on her fine leather shoes.

Richard stood there, the powerful warleader reduced to silence.

He was saved by his sister. 'Richard!'

Intent on the reunion of the king and his queen, I had not heard Joanna come in. She rushed past without realising, I am sure, who I was. 'Brother! You are here!'

My heart squeezed. She had not changed at all, unless it was to become more beautiful. Elegant, full-figured, with long red-blond hair, she was like a heaven-sent vision. The only woman who had ever had more effect on me was Alienor, one of Richard's sister Mathilda's

248

ladies, and she I had never done more than kiss. Discomfited myself to be thinking of two women at the same time, I shoved the image of Alienor away.

'Lass!' Richard embraced his sister, laughing, and I swear, crying a little. The contrast between his reaction to her and Berengaria could not have been starker.

The queen watched, and although she tried to conceal it, I saw a deep sadness in her.

'Do you not love us, Richard, your wife and your sister?' Joanna had none of Berengaria's reserve. 'Fie on you, brother! Two months it is, almost, since you arrived from England.'

The king offered the same apology as he had given to Berengaria. It sounded no more convincing, but Joanna did not seem interested in pursuing it. 'Tsh, it is of no matter now,' she said, standing back from Richard to stare at him, as if reassuring herself that he was really there. Then, smiling, she kissed his cheek. 'It is wondrous good to see you, but I am overstepping the mark. You are here to see the queen, not me.'

Once more Richard looked nonplussed; his eyes went to Berengaria, who gave him the semblance of a smile. He moved to the queen's side, and spoke quietly to her. They walked away, clearly desiring what privacy could be offered in the enclosed space.

Joanna's gaze moved for the first time to de Chauvigny and me. She was not surprised to see André; he, after all, had been her companion and guardian from Outremer to Poitiers. But me, she had not expected. Her eyes widened. One of her strong, capable hands rose halfway to her mouth. Then her reserve slipped into place. 'Sir Rufus,' she said, light and courteous, her voice still musical.

I knelt. De Chauvigny did the same. 'Madam,' we chorused.

'Rise, both of you. You are safe and well, Sir Rufus, I am glad to see.'

'Yes, madam, thanks be to God.'

'It pleases me that you escaped the rigours of the journey from Outremer unharmed. I know from Richard's letters it was arduous, not to say dangerous.'

'Thank you, madam.' At times, it was thoughts of you that kept me from despair, I wanted to say.

'You did not stay in captivity with my brother.' A trace of annoyance – anger? – was discernible.

I caught her eye. 'I would have stayed with the king, madam, but he sent me away, to Normandy. FitzAldelm was creating mischief there.' I wanted her to know that I had been right; despite my telling her about my enemy's treachery in Outremer, she had forced me to promise not to harm him.

'FitzAldelm?'

'Yes, madam, the very same. Rhys and I almost captured him in Rouen, but he escaped. Later in the summer, we came close again' – obviously, I did not say to murdering him – 'but the rogue got away for a second time. He slew a boy, a lad in my employ.'

Her shock was plain. 'A boy? How old?'

'Perhaps ten, madam.' I could not conceal the tone of accusation in my voice. Jean's pale face as he lay unconscious, dying, was painfully bright in my mind's eye.

'That is terrible,' she said. 'I had no idea FitzAldelm was so black-hearted. If I had, I–'

I nodded, wishing I had taken Rhys's advice, wishing I had convinced Joanna that FitzAldelm was an out-and-out traitor. Most of all, I wished that I had ended his miserable life in Outremer, or in the church in Rouen.

Joanna came closer. 'He was dear to you?'

I glanced about, and was startled to find we were alone – alone in as much as two people can be in a courtyard where others are present. De Chauvigny, the great heart, had affected to walk back to the entrance, where he was in deep conversation with the lead sentry. Richard and Berengaria were at the far end. The other ladies, three of them, were seated on stools a little distance away, and doing a good impression of not watching us.

'The boy, Rufus?'

I brought my gaze round to hers, and my anger melted away. I lost myself in her eyes, just as I always had. 'He was dear to me, yes. Jean was his name.'

'And FitzAldelm?'

'He got away, even though Rhys had stuck him in the leg. I know not where he is now; I assume in the service of Philippe Capet still.' I paused before adding, 'Christ grant that I meet him again ere I die.'

'He will get his just deserts one day. God will see to it.'

It seemed churlish to say that I would rather trust in my dagger, or Rhys's, so I said nothing.

'Let us talk no more about FitzAldelm. It is wonderful to see you, Rufus.' Her tone was genuine.

'It is the same for me,' I said fervently. 'I have thought about this, about seeing you, every day since you left Outremer.'

Our gazes locked.

Joanna felt the same way as I did – it was plain in her eyes.

I wanted to take her in my arms more than anything. Heart pounding, my passion kindled to burning flame, I might have tried, uncaring that Richard and Berengaria and several court ladies would see, but Joanna raised a hand, as if she sensed my purpose.

I froze, spirits falling into the abyss.

'Not here.'

Her words were pitched so low that I wondered if I had misheard. 'Madam?' I whispered, one part of me daring to hope even as another demanded to know what point there was in restarting something that was doomed.

'Meet me here tonight.'

'What time?' I asked without the slightest hesitation.

'Just after matins.'

'Nothing could stop me.'

She was already walking away, back to her ladies. I could have watched her for the rest of the day, but aware that my attention would not go unnoticed, I joined de Chauvigny. He gave me a meaningful look; I gave him a tiny dip of my chin, acknowledgement of his generosity in giving us privacy.

The king and Berengaria were still walking and talking. I tried to get a sense of the atmosphere between them, but the distance made it impossible.

De Chauvigny followed my gaze. 'Let us hope she is pregnant by the time we leave,' he said quietly, so the sentries would not hear.

'Aye,' I said, dark thoughts of John filling my head. 'The sooner the better, for all our sakes.'

'How did Joanna receive you?' This was also in my ear.

'Well,' I murmured.

He gave me an enormous wink, which I affected not to notice.

Behind my reserve, I was already counting down the hours.

Despite my best efforts to keep silent as I dressed, Rhys stirred.

'Is it time?' His voice was muzzy with sleep.

'I think so.' It was hard to judge the passing of the hours, but it was a long while since the bells had rung, and I could not be late for the tryst. I sat up and pulled on my ankle boots.

'Do you want me to stand watch?' He was more awake now.

He would stay far enough away from Joanna and me, but I wanted complete privacy. The increased risk of not having him was worth it. 'No,' I said.

'Be careful. If the king should find out –'

'I know the risks.' I stepped past him – in his usual spot at the foot of my bed – and said quietly, 'Go back to sleep; dream of Katharina.' She was with the troops, following in our wake, and would catch up with us soon.

He chuckled. 'May you find what you seek.'

His words stayed with me as I crept down the passage, past de Chauvigny's door, and down the stairs that led to the great hall. Moonlight shafted in from the glass windows high on the southern wall, shaping the banqueting tables and benches that had earlier seated us during the feast to celebrate Richard's arrival. Not a soul was about, but I stayed close to the wall nonetheless, in the shadows.

A set of double doors gave onto the courtyard from the hall, but I decided they would make an horrendous noise opening and alert any sentries within earshot. I stole through the archway that led towards the kitchens, seeking another way in. My hopes were rewarded; I stopped by the first door on my right, and sliding back the bolt with great care, pulled it towards me a little. I peered out into bright moonlight, delighted. My hunch had been correct. This door also opened into the courtyard.

I could see no one there.

The bells had not yet sounded matins, the time for our meeting, but courtesy dictated I should be there first. Out I went, as nervous as if I were trying to scale the walls of an enemy castle undetected. I kept to the margins of the courtyard, again avoiding the light. No one moved, no challenge was issued. I was alone. Picking a spot midway along the wall opposite the doors into the great hall, I took a deep breath, leaned my back against the cool stone and settled down to wait.

I had no idea how long I would be. Other than marking the moon's position high in the star-glittering sky and waiting for the church bells, it was impossible to judge the hour. I was grateful it was summer; the air was cool and pleasant.

I had not been there long when the matins bells sounded from beyond the building's walls. I grinned, pleased that my judgement had been correct, but very soon after that, my nerves again began to jangle. Joanna had suggested the tryst, yet I was not wholly certain she would come, and even less sure of what I would say to her if she did. The reaction I had hoped for – clear evidence that she continued to care for me – I already had. Was it possible, I wondered, that this depth of feeling, present two long years after seeing one another, might persuade her that love was more important than duty?

I told myself I did not know the answer, ignoring the sneaking, nausea-inducing suspicion that I actually did.

Creak. The sound echoed through the courtyard. My head twisted, searching for the door that was being opened, and instinct took my right hand to my dagger.

A shape emerged to my right, from the same wall I was standing against. My heart leaped; the royal chambers were on the storey above. Wary in case it was a servant on a midnight errand or a patrolling sentry, I stayed put. Not until it was evidently a woman – by the height and shape – did I move.

'Joanna?' I pitched my voice low.

'Rufus!' She hurried forward, but stopped a pace or two before me, as if regaining control of her emotions. 'You are here.'

'Of course, madam.'

She came closer, filling the air between us with her perfume, the same intoxicating one I knew from Outremer. Memories of that time tumbled through my mind. I stared into her eyes, trembling with desire.

'You need not call me madam, you know that.'

I bowed my head. 'Joanna.' It felt wonderful to say her name aloud.

Her fingers caressed my jaw, gently lifted my chin so that we were again looking at each other. 'How I have missed you, Rufus.'

'And I you, Joanna.' My love, I thought.

She leaned in and kissed me. The contact, lips against lips, sent my mind into a complete spin. Her arms wrapped around my waist; mine were suddenly around her shoulders and back. The kiss went on for a long time; it was heavenly. At length, both breathing heavily, we pulled apart a little. We smiled at each other, and my heart skipped a beat.

'We are like two star-crossed lovers.' Her tone was husky. 'I see no need to linger in the courtyard.'

I read her mind, but I wanted to hear her say it. 'Where would we go?'

A languorous look, one that left nothing to the imagination. Then, 'To my bedchamber. I have sent away my servants, and the nearest sentries are outside the king's quarters.'

I wanted to. God, how I wanted to, but I held my passion in check.

She kissed me again, and my resolve began to crumble.

I broke away, before the last of my self-control slipped altogether and blurted, 'How shall things be tomorrow?'

Her perfect lips quirked. 'Tomorrow?'

'Between us.'

A little smile, half nervous, half impatient. 'Rufus, you know the answer to that.'

'Do I, madam?' I pulled away.

Her hands rose in entreaty. 'Rufus, do you not love me?'

'With all my heart,' I said, my voice shaking.

'Come, then.' She beckoned.

'I will, on one condition.'

Uncertainty in her face. 'What is that?'

'In the morning, you will tell Richard you wish to marry me. I will ask his permission for the same.'

Silence descended. My heart bang-banged off my ribs, a despairing beat of pain and loss. It was an unbearable feeling, to have her in front of me, willing, loving, and I about to . . . I was not even sure what.

'Well?' My voice cracked.

'I cannot do that, Rufus.'

'You mean you will not,' I said harshly.

We stared at one another, the emotion between us changed. Gone was love, freshly arrived was its ugly relation, anger, and its siblings, hurt and rejection.

After a moment, she said, 'You are right. I will not.'

'*Why?*' Never had I packed so much emotion into one word.

She did not answer at once; I wanted to shake her, to demand a reply, but I held my peace. This had to come from her, all her.

'Richard will find me a new husband when the time is right.'

'I could be that man!'

A slight shake of the head, as final as the gesture that calls forth the executioner with his axe. 'Worthy and loyal as you are, and brave, Rufus, you do not have the station.'

'That should not matter,' I said from between gritted teeth.

'But it does.'

There was no coming back from this, I knew it in my gut. I made the stiffest of bows. 'Then, madam, I will go.'

Her face worked. There were tears in her eyes. 'Do not let us part on these terms, Rufus.'

'I am not the one who has caused it to be so,' I said, my voice cold as frost. 'By your leave?'

'Go.' She averted her gaze.

There was no farewell, no kiss, not even a goodbye.

I stalked across the courtyard, uncaring who saw me, and slipped through the same door I had entered by. I was raging inside, raging and hurting as badly as if I had been cut by a blade.

I had made the right choice, however. Of that I was certain. Our relationship had been already doomed; Joanna would never have married me. To have spent a night with her and faced the same outcome would have hurt even more. Better to take the cautery iron first, I thought, rather than indulge oneself for a night in the knowledge that it will be waiting in the morning.

I wish I could say that the next day brought a change. It did not. If I was proud, Joanna was even more so. At a meal in the great hall, held early the following afternoon, she acted as if I did not exist. She ignored anything I said in open conversation, and her gaze passed over me as if I were a piece of furniture. The king noticed, although he did not comment. Berengaria did too, and her behind-the-hand comments to Joanna made me wonder if she was aware of our affair.

Not that it mattered if she did, I thought sourly, because it was over. There could be no coming back. My position would not change – on principle – and, I suspected, nor would Joanna's.

The mood in the room remained bright, because Richard was in good humour, and that swept all else before it. He was attentive and courteous to Berengaria, which led me to the conclusion that they had lain together. She was not the effusive type, but her manner towards the king seemed easier, gentler, than the day before. My hope that this would mean our immediate departure – we had Aquitaine to bring to heel, with Philippe Capet still causing mischief in Normandy – was dashed by Richard's announcement that we were to remain for at least another night.

Ploughed furrows need plenty of seed to yield a bountiful crop, I thought. A tender yet exquisitely painful image of Joanna holding a baby – our baby – formed in my head. I shoved it away with brutal force.

'If you are to stay here, sire, might I take some of the troops south?' I asked.

Richard turned from Berengaria, who was laughing at what he had said. His eyes went to Joanna, who had reacted to my question by calling over one of her ladies, and came back to me. 'So hasty, Ferdia? Normally, it is I who is the more impatient.' This was said with a crooked grin.

'True enough, sire, but the Count of Angoulême and Geoffrey de Rançon will not be sitting on their hands while you are in Poitiers. Neither will Bernard de Brosse.' The last noble had recently pledged his allegiance to the French crown.

Richard stared at me. The rebels were not my reason for wanting to leave, and he knew it. So, from Berengaria's look, did she. Joanna's thoughts were unclear; she appeared to be in an animated conversation with the lady she had summoned.

'I see no reason why you should not go on ahead,' he said at last.

'Sire.' I made a grateful bow.

His attention returned to Berengaria.

I could not leave the courtyard fast enough.

CHAPTER XXV

In the event, I had a week sharing the command of the army with de Chauvigny before the king joined us. His fine mood, which we assumed was from a fruitful time spent with his wife, was unaffected by our lack of success. To be fair, we had only been besieging Taillebourg, an impregnable fortress on the River Charente, for three days, but Richard's record, taking it in a third of that time, loomed large in our minds. He was gracious enough not to mention it, but taking charge, he decided on an artillery barrage similar to that which had seen Loches fall. Scarcely had that begun when a messenger arrived.

The letter he carried darkened Richard's mood, and mine also. Even de Chauvigny, who always tried to see the bright side, was quietened by it.

'What was Robert thinking?' thundered the king.

The message included the news that the Earl of Leicester, venturing out of Rouen with only a few companions, had been captured by Philippe Capet. Knowing how important the earl was to Richard, the French king was now proposing a three-year truce. It went unsaid that Robert's release would be contingent to this.

'I assume that if you agree, sire,' I ventured, 'Philippe will keep all the lands and castles he has taken of recent days?'

'That is his intent, precisely. He knows how much I value the earl as a commander.' Richard glowered. 'But I cannot – *I will not* – countenance that French cur retaining so many of my strongholds, even if it means Robert must remain a captive.'

It was a natural decision for the king to make, but I saw my relief not to be in Robert's position mirrored in de Chauvigny's eyes. Philippe's recent actions showed him to be in vindictive mood. Only God knew how long the earl might languish in a French dungeon as a result.

Less than a sennight later, we had more momentous news. Philippe's army was on the march, and making for the town of Vendôme. If his bold move succeeded, he would block the king's approach to Normandy and the Vexin, and the castles there that had to be retaken.

The siege of Taillebourg was abandoned at once; we headed northeast to face the new threat. Despite his intention not to agree to Philippe's proposed truce, Richard sent messengers to the French king, engaging in negotiations in an effort to divert his enemy's attention. Philippe's demands were so outrageous, however, that Richard soon gave up pretending to reach a peace settlement, and his increasingly forceful responses soon saw the exchange of letters dry up. We travelled north, while the French king advanced south.

By the beginning of July, we found ourselves camped below the walls of Vendôme, awaiting the imminent arrival of Philippe's host.

The prospect of a set-piece battle – that most uncommon of things – began to seem possible, even probable. Richard grew more excited as successive scouts brought word of the French army's continuing approach, and it was hard not to be infected by his enthusiasm. The soldiers' morale also soared, because the king wandered the camp all hours of the day, encouraging them, watching their training, and awarding prizes to those who impressed.

'Strike a decisive blow here,' the king told the men over and over, 'and the war could be ended at a single stroke.' It was a prospect that appealed to all. After two months of campaigning, our main gains had only been Loches, Montmirail and Beaumont le Roger.

On the third of July, we had word from several scouts that loud cheering had been heard from the French camp, now only a few miles distant from our position, near Fréteval. Our suspicions about the cause of the celebrations were borne out later, when a French herald brought a letter from Philippe informing Richard that he would attack the following morning.

If I had not seen the message myself, I would not have believed it. During our time in Outremer, Philippe's war making had always been half-hearted. Offering battle to someone of Richard's calibre seemed completely out of character, but there was no denying the herald's presence, nor the royal seal on the letter.

The king was most amused, and pleased with it too.

'I never would have thought it: Philippe has actually grown a pair of balls,' Richard said, chuckling. His gaze travelled around the tent, where we senior knights and commanders had gathered. 'He plans to lead his army against us come the morn!'

We cheered, pleased by the thought of victory over the cursed French. Nothing else entered my mind at least; with the Lionheart in command, defeat was an impossibility.

I did not get much rest that night. Driven from my tent – thanks to the warm, still air, lifting the flaps made no discernible difference to the baking heat within – I tried without success to sleep in the open air. Under normal circumstances, the delight of the glittering sky overhead, and seeing occasional shooting stars, would easily have seen me drift off, but this night, my head was spinning with images of battle and the possibility, however slight, of coming up against FitzAldelm. When I managed to quieten my thoughts, I inevitably pictured Joanna. Anxious to avoid the pain this caused, I would return to the impending clash with the French, which was a poor way to get to sleep.

Exhaustion took me in the end, but I was then woken by the noise of men talking. Furious to have been roused after what seemed a brief period, and long before dawn, I was about to bellow at them to be quiet when I realised it was not just a few individuals. The entire camp was stirring.

I scowled, and throwing off my blanket, sat up.

'You are awake.' Rhys was lying close by, and watching me.

'It seems so,' I snapped. 'Although quite why we need to rise at this ungodly hour I have no idea.'

'The king ordered it.'

I stared at him, aghast. 'When?'

'A short time since. A messenger came, but you did not stir. I told him not to rouse you, that I would pass on the message.'

Annoyed for no real reason – the delay had been short, and no harm had been done – I asked, 'What does the king command?'

'He wants the host ready by dawn.'

This was going against convention – armies took hours to get ready, so battles tended to begin in mid-morning, or even later – but Richard was fond of doing what others did not, and so it made perfect sense.

'He is planning an early advance, to catch the French unprepared.'

'That was my thought.' Rhys was up in one fluid movement. 'Are you hungry?'

'No, but I will eat.' Lining my belly before a fight was something learned of old. I might bring the food up – nerves sometimes did that – but if I did not, it would see me through the next few hours. Go without, and I risked not having sufficient energy to fight.

Rhys went in search of Katharina, with whom he had been reunited when the main body of our troops had caught up with us. I considered trying to don my hauberk, but decided to wait until he got back. I shrugged on my gambeson, and then whetted my sword on an oilstone, the repetitive movement calming my mind. Back and forth, forth and back, until the edge was sharp enough to shave with.

I caught the tantalising smell of fresh-baked bread, and my head turned. Rhys emerged from the gloom, his arms full.

'Where did you get that at this hour?' I asked, incredulous. 'Did you thieve it?'

A mock hurt look. 'Katharina baked it.'

'That woman is a catch.'

Rhys grinned. 'She has an acid tongue by times, but I cannot argue with you.'

Taking the warm loaf he proffered, I discovered that I had an appetite after all.

We advanced at dawn, eager for battle. The king was in the vanguard, as always. I was with him, along with de Chauvigny and the rest of his household knights. Mercadier, his long-serving mercenary captain, a man I intensely disliked, was present too. William Marshal alone had been left behind, his task to command the reserve force. Two hundred and fifty knights we were, the hammer which would smash into the enemy lines when the fight commenced.

The logical ground to meet, a rolling area of meadowland between our position and that of the French, was empty. Peace reigned. Sheep grazed on the dew-glistening grass, birds sang from the hedgerows and trees. None of us were surprised; it was far earlier than normal for an army to manoeuvre into place. Before long, however, our scouts returned, and it became clear that there was more to the bucolic scene than met the eye.

Philippe's army had broken camp, our excited scouts reported, and was in full retreat to the north.

Richard was furious. 'I should have known the rogue was lying! I swear he would avoid a fight with a five-year-old child.'

We laughed.

'You took his challenge at face value, sire, because you would not say one thing and do another,' said de Chauvigny.

'You have the right of it,' said Richard. 'I had been better to remember that truth and the French king are infrequent bedfellows.' He peered into the distance. 'See, there – a dust cloud. Let us go! If we are to be denied battle, we can give chase. Some sport at least shall be ours this day.'

There was no questioning if his decision was wise. By this point we all wanted a fight. Given Philippe's propensity to run, it seemed improbable that he might lay a trap for us, but thinking of FitzAldelm and his wiliness, I pleaded with the king to delay for a short time while the scouts went back out to reconnoitre the land. This also allowed the first body of men-at-arms and crossbowmen to catch up. Richard grumpily agreed that they could be immediately sent on in advance. We would soon overtake them once we rode out, but following our trail at the double, they would be in a position to offer support should we need it.

I need not have worried.

The scouts found no sign of ambush between us and Philippe's encampment. Richard did not seem to care – finding the French camp abandoned, he was intent on riding after the enemy at once – but I ordered the scouts to continue to ride ahead. That way, I told de Chauvigny, we would have some warning if anyone was lying in wait.

I need not have worried in that regard either.

Half a mile we went, and then a mile without a sign of a Frenchman. We were on the right trail, however. The road was littered with items that had fallen off hastily loaded wagons: pots and pans, items of clothing and footwear, a helmet. Two miles further on, we reached a barricade, several carts that had been turned on their sides to block our path. Behind it, we could see men's heads, perhaps two score of them. Off to either side in the trees, I spied more figures. They would be crossbowmen, I was sure of it.

Richard was all for charging straightaway, but he listened to my counsel and that of de Chauvigny. 'One well-aimed quarrel is all it would take, sire,' I said.

'We would lose many horses too, sire,' said de Chauvigny. 'Tarry just a while. When our own crossbowmen arrive, they will soon clear the way.'

Richard did not protest, although he glowered royally.

I went back myself to inform our men that they were needed. Their commander, a florid-faced sergeant I knew of old, responded with alacrity. Word was sweeping through the ranks that the French were close by, and the crossbowmen willingly broke into a ground-covering trot.

I rode alongside, in part so I could harangue Rhys, who, not wanting to be left out of any action, was with them. Could he not run faster, I asked him. Did he want me to carry his shield?

He was not reckless enough to answer back out loud, but whatever imprecations he muttered kept the crossbowmen around him laughing and cheering, which had been my intent from the outset.

The Frenchies' resolve cracked the instant they saw our crossbowmen. Their first volley was ragged and ill-aimed, whereas our men, marshalled well by their sergeants, aimed and shot with cool discipline. Protected by comrades with shields, they advanced in three lines: towards the barricade and into the treeline on either side.

The French loosed a second volley, which was as bad, if not worse, than the first, and then they took flight.

Richard, watching like a falcon stooping over its prey, ordered the charge before our crossbowmen had even reached the wagons.

I had been expecting this. Not allowed by the king to ride in front of him – it was not for me to take a quarrel rather than he, Richard said – I kept pace with him on the right. De Chauvigny, also sensing his purpose, was on his left. The rest of the knights came behind. It was a familiar feeling and, by Christ, it felt good.

As our destriers' hooves drummed the earth, I was reminded of two insane charges I had made with Richard at Joppa in Outremer, when we had put an entire army to flight.

I glanced sideways at the king. Sensing my look, he turned his head. I could not see his face, encased in his helmet, but I knew he was grinning as he saluted me.

'It has been too long, Rufus!' he shouted.

'Indeed, sire!'

A handful of quarrels came our way from the few Frenchies remaining behind the wagons but, by some miracle, none found a target. When the enemy soldiers realised we were going to jump the barricade, the last of their courage seeped away. Dropping their weapons, they ran, making for the relative safety of the trees.

We cleared the wagons and continued along the road. The crossbowmen could chase after the fleeing French.

Richard soon slowed his pace. Exhilarating though it was to gallop, we needed to conserve our destriers' energy. Despite our impatience, there was no particular need to hurry. An army on the retreat does not move fast. As if to prove the point, a pair of scouts came galloping in. The French rearguard was less than a mile ahead. A mixed force of knights and foot soldiers, it was perhaps five hundred strong.

We smashed them with our first charge, as easily as a child breaks kindling for the fire. I will not call it a battle, but a rout. Some of the enemy fought, out of desperation, or perhaps to save their comrades, but their valiant efforts were in vain. Cut down where they stood, or trampled by our destriers, they died by the score. The rest ran and rode for their lives, following the army, or off into the open countryside.

To our delight, the French host was not far beyond their wretched rearguard. Wagons came into sight first, laden down with tents, barrels, broken-down siege engines. Richard left behind several of his household to ensure that the following crossbowmen did not thieve everything of value, and continued the pursuit.

'Ride hard now,' he declared, 'and we might capture Philippe himself.'

We broke into a canter. There was no fighting at all. Cart handlers and camp followers are not fighters, and as we overtook wagon after wagon, they gave themselves up as fast as possible. The soldiers present as protection did the same. If there had been any fight left in them after their king's command to retreat, it was snuffed out entirely by the sudden appearance of the English king and his close companions. Reverential mutters of '*Coeur de Lion*' were audible each time he was seen. Richard, pleased, acknowledged these with a jaunty wave.

Ever the suspicious soul, I kept a constant eye out for an aimed crossbow or a determined knight with a need to prove himself on Richard. Not everyone had his sense of fair play.

The booty we took began to increase in value. Richard checked our progress to make brief evaluations. Three wagons were laden down with padlocked chests full of silver coin. Another cart was full of fine tapestries that must have adorned one of Philippe's castles. Half a dozen wains, axles creaking beneath their loads, held dozens of wine barrels. There were more than a hundred remounts for the French knights, fine-bred destriers each worth a fortune. We also took the contents of the royal chapel, gem-encrusted gold chalices and silver candlesticks, and magnificent silk-embroidered priests' vestments. Seemingly out of place in these wagons were enamelled wooden boxes full of documents marked with the royal seal. After a cursory look, Richard ordered the papers put under special guard until he returned. And the wagons with the wine, he added by way of afterthought. Soldiers, even well-disciplined ones, had a tendency to lose all reason when wine was available in great quantity.

'Anything of significance in the papers, sire?' I asked.

'Nothing much that I could see.' I was about to express my regret when he added in an offhand way, 'One letter had details of my subjects who are willing to switch allegiances and take Philippe as their liege lord.'

'Really?' I asked in astonishment.

'Aye. I shall take a keen interest in reading them later. Truly, God is smiling on me today.'

Spying a church tower in a village a little way off to our left, I toyed with the idea of asking the king if he wanted to give thanks now. It was not in his nature to turn away from a pressing task, however, especially when his quarry was Philippe Capet, so I held my tongue.

How I would regret my decision later.

We continued our pursuit of the Frenchies into the afternoon. Mercadier was on hand to provide Richard with a fresh destrier when his original one tired. Like many of the household, I made use of one of the remounts. Several had caught my eye; with the king's permission, I took charge of a feisty black with a broad white strip down his nose.

Twenty-five miles we must have ridden by the time dusk was falling. I had long since lost count of the wagons taken; our prisoners numbered in the hundreds, if not thousands, although most were ordinary soldiers rather than noblemen or knights.

Philippe had been forced to leave the field twice in forty days, first at Verneuil, where he had lost his artillery, and now at Fréteval, where he had lost his entire baggage train and with it, a large proportion of his treasury as well as large quantities of intelligence documents.

It was a triumph for Richard: an absolute humiliation for the French king.

The victory could only have been improved by Philippe's capture, which made the news we found out a few days later, from late-taken prisoners, bittersweet. The day of Philippe's retreat, weary, wanting divine help, he had stopped to pray in a chapel close to the road north. It was the very one I had considered asking the king to visit. Richard was mightily amused when he heard the news, and laughing, told me there was no way for me to have known. I could not let the matter go. Were there many men with Philippe, I asked a prisoner. Perhaps ten, came the answer. Servants and trusted members of his household. I demanded their names. The prisoner grew frightened, and I told him that he would come to no harm. He quailed before my icy rage. It was of no matter, I said, turning my back.

The prisoner spoke several names that meant nothing to me.

I relaxed, thinking he was done.

Then, 'FitzAldelm, I think one was called, sir.'

I ground my teeth. The knowledge that Richard and I could both have had what we wanted, so simply, was galling beyond belief. Consumed by my old hatred, I did not question whether I would have had the stomach to kill FitzAldelm on sacred ground.

'Let it go, Rufus.' The king's gaze was knowing.

'Sire?'

'It was not to be. God did not want Philippe or Robert to fall into our hands that day.'

'If only we had stopped, sire . . .'

'But we did not.'

'No.' I shook my head grimly.

'There it is. Both of them live to fight another day.' The king chuckled. 'Whatever peace treaty may follow from this will never last.'

I stared at him.

'You and I will have other chances to face our enemies.'

I did my best to accept that.

*

265

I was able to shut FitzAldelm away in the recesses of my mind in the days that followed. In a whirlwind of marches, sieges and skirmishes, we travelled the length and breadth of Aquitaine. Fortress after fortress surrendered, often after our army had been camped outside their walls for as little as a day. No one, it seemed, was willing to face the Lionheart.

Taillebourg, that most impregnable of strongholds, opened its gates. So did Marcillac. The rest of Geoffrey de Rançon's castles were swift to follow. The rebellious lord himself came to beg Richard's forgiveness and renew his oath of loyalty. I was not alone in muttering whether he would have forgotten it by the time he reached home. The king was not taken in by de Rançon's display of fidelity either; as he said to me later, their dance was an old one, and the devil you knew was better than the one you did not.

Count Adémar of Angoulême, de Rançon's friend and ally, was next to feel Richard's wrath. He was wise enough to offer little resistance. We swept through his territory, accepting the capitulation of, among many others, Châteauneuf-sur-Charente, Montignac, Lachaise, and Angoulême itself. I rolled my eyes at Rhys during another ceremony – Count Adémar's – of abject contrition, kingly forgiveness and loud avowals of loyalty.

Posturing and falsity aside, there was no denying the effectiveness of Richard's lightning campaign. Peace had returned to Aquitaine. From Verneuil to the Pyrenees, he was once more the unquestioned ruler.

The same could not be said on the borders of Normandy and in the Vexin, where Philippe's claws had sunk deep, but as July's end saw the agreement of a peace treaty, it was hard to argue with the king's assertion that it was time for his army to rest, and to reinforce the gains that had been made. The titanic struggle between him and Philippe was not over, merely paused. That the treaty would be broken – small castles seized, castellans persuaded to switch sides, town councils won over – went unsaid; the animosity between the two monarchs ran too deep to prevent that. But large-scale hostilities, army against army, would cease. This did not stop Richard from planning and scheming. He was a driven man; he would not countenance a long-term peace until all the castles and territory lost to Philippe had been recovered. He began to discuss new tactics, such as the building of new castles.

One location in particular seemed important to him: on the River Seine at the Rock of Andeli.

We returned to Rouen, where the king was reunited with Berengaria. Joanna, who had accompanied her from Poitiers, also joined the royal court. To my relief, it was easy for me to avoid her company. I had no reason to see her, other than from a distance at the occasional feast. It went without saying that she was as beautiful as ever, but hardening my heart, I thought only of the acrimonious manner of our last meeting. She had made the choice for the way things were between us, not I.

Walling off my emotions made it easier to listen to Richard. Diplomacy had replaced war in his mind, and he sometimes talked at table of finding Joanna a husband, an ally against the French king. The Count of Toulouse's son was one of the names mentioned. Although she was present, Richard did not ask for her opinion on the matter, and Joanna's face never gave away a thing. He did not consult me either; in fact, he acted as if I had never told him about my love affair with his sister. Despite my best efforts, it was bitter medicine to swallow.

I had to move on with my life, I decided. For the first time since my dreams of wedding Joanna, I began to contemplate marriage. I was a good catch: wealthy, with lands in Ireland and England; I was also a close friend of the king. There would be no shortage of candidates; I could think of several sharp-eyed noblewomen over the previous few months who had been eager for me to meet their daughters.

I confided in Rhys, who wasted no time in speaking his mind. I had no real interest in taking a wife just for the sake of it, he told me. 'You would be miserable. I can see your long face already,' he said, so energised that he was wagging an admonishing finger at me. 'For my sake, if not your own, do not even consider it. And Katharina will never let you hear the end of it.'

He was right. I thought of Joanna, whom I could not have, and then of Alienor, the only woman who had affected me similarly. Her I could marry, I thought. If she was still alive and unmarried. If she would have me.

Whether I could find her was another prospect altogether.

PART THREE

PART THREE

CHAPTER XXVI

Chateau Gaillard, on the Seine, late August 1198

The sun was dropping on the western horizon, but it was still hot. Swifts banked and dived, filling the air with their high-pitched skirrs, a reminder that summer was drawing to a close. Voices carried from the new town on the far bank, built at the same time as the castle. I was in a favourite spot on the battlements overlooking the river, able to stand in the shade while a cooling breeze carried up from the water.

Three hundred feet and more above the Seine, I could see little fishing craft, and a larger vessel, a merchantman coming from the coast, or, I thought, perhaps it was carrying Richard's young nephew Otto of Brunswick, one of two recently crowned kings of Germany. After the death of the malevolent Heinrich the previous year, Heinrich's brother Philip had claimed the throne. Unhappy with this, the German princes had also elected Otto. Count Baldwin of Flanders had attended the latter's coronation in June on Richard's behalf. Now Otto was due on another visit, to discuss with his uncle the best way forward against Philippe Capet.

Four and a half years had passed since Richard's release, and I was in relaxed mood. A lot had happened in that time, most of it good. FitzAldelm had vanished, except for the occasional rumour; it seemed he was still in Philippe's service. Resigned to the fact that I would never see my enemy again, I had consigned him to the back of my mind, from where he almost never troubled me.

The king was in rude health, and residing here in his pride and joy, his *bellum castrum de Rupe*, or fair castle of the Rock, as he called it. Two years only it had taken to build; most fortresses took a decade. The cost had been astronomical, twelve thousand pounds, which was substantially more than he had spent on *all* of his other castles since his coronation but, by Christ, Chateau Gaillard was magnificent.

Richard had overseen everything, from the choice of location and the planning to the stone quarrying and construction. Perched on a ridge atop a cliff overlooking the Seine, the imposing castle had three baileys, the outer a pentagon-shape, and the middle enclosing the inner, which also contained the keep. The king's influence and innovations were visible everywhere; he was so proud of Chateau Gaillard that he had been heard to exclaim that he could successfully defend it even if its walls were made of butter.

Not that it was likely ever to be besieged, I thought. In the current climate, Philippe would not dare to lead his army here. Progress against him had been slow but steady since Richard's release. He had humiliated Philippe again outside Issoudun just before Christmas in the year of our Lord 1195, forcing him to flee or risk being taken prisoner. The peace treaty concluded shortly afterwards had made Richard's gains crystal clear. Almost all the castles lost to Philippe had been retaken; those in the Vexin were a notable exception. The French king had also agreed that the rebellious lords of Aquitaine owed their homage not to him, but the Duke of Aquitaine, Richard.

There had been a setback the following campaigning season, it was true – Richard had been wounded in the knee by a crossbow quarrel, and suffered an unheard of defeat at Aumâle – but he had then secured his southern borders, thereby ending more than forty years of hostilities. This had come about by offering Joanna's hand in marriage to the new Count of Toulouse, Raymond VI. The strategic pact had been followed by an alliance with Baldwin, the Count of Flanders, further isolating Philippe Capet.

One of Richard's greatest achievements had nothing to do with disputed castles or land. It was the capture of his enemy the Bishop of Beauvais, the same man who had ensured the king's conditions when imprisoned by Heinrich were as harsh as possible. Taken prisoner in battle by Mercadier the previous year, Beauvais had been languishing in the dungeon of Chateau Gaillard since.

Richard's successes did not extend to his marriage, sadly. His reunion in Poitou with Berengaria four years before had not resulted in a child, nor had their subsequent brief periods together. While the absence of an heir was a very real problem for the king, he sought out his queen less and less. She lived in Poitou, and he at Chateau Gaillard. It was scarcely the joyful union and, as Rhys dryly observed, an unploughed furrow could not yield a crop. Richard did not speak of it to me, or to anyone, as far as I knew, unless he confided in his mother. Nor did he take any lovers. He was, I believe, content to live the life of a warrior king, and did not need a wife and children to complete his life.

Lack of an heir aside, Richard had gained far more than he had lost in the time since his release from captivity. Chateau Gaillard, completed this very summer, was a combative example of this set in stone. With its dominating position over the Seine and close proximity to the Vexin, that most troublesome of areas, its presence made plain the king's intention of taking back from Philippe *everything* that had once been his.

'Rufus? Are you there?' Rhys's voice was coming nearer.

'Aye.' I stepped out from behind the tower I had been using as shade.

Rhys was sweating from the climb. Somewhat thicker around the middle than before – this, thanks to his wife Katharina's cooking – he was now the doting father of a two-year-old boy. I was rather proud that he had been named Rufus, after me.

Fatherhood had not changed Rhys's character. Still eager to go to war whenever needed, still willing to do the dark deeds most men shied away from, he remained my most loyal companion. And friend, I thought. Rhys had been with me since the early days of my incarceration at Striguil, half a lifetime before. In more ways than one, we had grown up together.

'What is it?' I asked, wondering if he had news of an unexpected French attack. Over the years, this had become the norm; we did it to Philippe, and he did it to us. Strike at a hard-to-reach or undermanned castle, and it would often fall within a day or two. Dislodging its new owners often proved trickier, and to have any chance of success required an instant reaction. We had grown used to riding out at a moment's notice.

'Just this.' Rhys brought out a platter from behind his back, and the smell of fresh baking hit my nostrils. 'Honey tarts.'

I reached out with eager hands. 'Katharina made them?'

'Who else? I just ate three in the kitchen. "Take these up for your master," she told me, "before you finish the lot." ' Rhys was well capable; his sweet tooth knew no bounds.

'My thanks to your good wife.' I bit into the first, relishing the crumbling, sweet pastry.

While I was occupied with the delicious tarts, Rhys leaned on the stonework, looking out over the river.

'Otto of Brunswick is here.'

I joined him. The large vessel I had spied was docking below; Otto's family banner had been unfurled at the prow. With two lions on a red background, it was similar to the one used by Henry, the king's father. Of recent years, Richard's standard had three lions, more befitting his status.

I spied a tall, broad-shouldered figure on the deck. 'So he is,' I said.

'Lucky I got the tarts, eh? Katharina will be run off her feet from now on.' Richard was fond of his nephew, and would want a feast befitting Otto's new status.

Grateful not to have to cross Katharina – in business-like mood, she was fearsome – I started a second honey tart.

The banquet that evening was as grand as I had expected. As Richard loudly declared, Katharina and the other cooks had outdone themselves. We ate squabs in wine sauce, mopping up the juices with fresh-baked wheaten bread. There was spiced chicken and saffron stew, a favourite of Richard's, and strong, sweet ice wine to wash it down. In recognition of Otto's recent coronation, we were also served a dish of swan with chaudron sauce. Majestic or not, it turned my stomach; the sauce was made from bird's blood and entrails. It would have been discourteous to refuse a helping, but I managed to pour mine onto the floor unnoticed. It was devoured by a couple of the king's hounds, who were lurking under the table hoping for just such a bounty.

Kingly food for royal dogs, I thought with some amusement.

'What a waste,' an amused voice said in my ear.

Startled and embarrassed, I twisted around. My heart lurched in my chest; my breath caught. A vision stood before me. Older than when I had last seen her, but still blond-haired, blue-eyed, with curves that sent my mind into a spin. 'A-Alienor?'

'Rufus.' A smile that would have melted a block of ice. 'You remember me?'

'Sweet Jesu, how could I not?' My voice was inexplicably hoarse. I made to stand, but she indicated I sit down. My neighbour on one side was de Chauvigny, too diplomatic to eavesdrop, but the other, a household knight, was doing a poor job of trying not to listen in.

I retook my seat. 'You are here with Otto?'

'I still serve the family.' She had been a serving lady to Otto's mother Mathilda, Richard's sister, who was long dead.

Guilt consumed me. My efforts to find Alienor a few years before had ended in abject failure; I had long since given up hope of seeing her again. Incredibly, it had not occurred to me to make enquiries more recently in Otto's household.

'You were not with Otto the last time he was here.'

A shake of her head, a glance down the table. 'I must go.'

'My lady.' Uncaring of what my neighbour thought, I stood and bowed. I watched as she spoke with the pages standing behind Otto, before returning whence she had come, the service passageway that led to the kitchens.

I would have followed at once, but Richard, who had not seen our interaction, called out, 'What think you, Rufus, of my nephew's request?'

I realised that it was not just he who was staring. The youthful Otto was as well. 'Your pardon, sire, I . . .' I flailed for something to say that would not make me out as a complete fool.

De Chauvigny, ever my friend, whispered, 'Otto was asking to join our chevauchée on the Vexin.' This raid was to be made once we had word of Count Baldwin's attack on Artois. The intention was to panic Philippe, assailed on two fronts and, between us, seize as much territory from him as possible.

'You wish to take part, sire?' I asked.

'I do, more than anything!' Otto's face shone with eagerness. 'I have only ever jousted.'

Richard's expression was impossible to read, but I was confident enough of my standing with him to speak the truth. 'Sadly, sire,' I said to Otto, 'I feel it might be wise to refrain.'

'Uncle said that you love to fight! That you are going!'

I looked at the king, whose lips were twitching, and back to Otto. 'He spoke truly, sire. Give me a line of enemies any day rather than a queue of handwringing petitioners. I am but a humble knight, however. My presence on the chevauchée will not draw attention. It would be a different matter for the anointed king of Germany.'

'Philippe is also my enemy!'

I bent my head in acknowledgement. 'He is, sire; I am sure my lord Richard is glad of that. Your supporters, however, might think ill of their fresh-crowned sovereign engaging in an act of war against the French king.'

Otto was not too old to pout, but he was no fool either. 'I suppose you are right,' he muttered.

'You will have your own battles to fight, rest assured, nephew,' said Richard. 'Philip of Swabia will not easily relinquish his claim on the throne.' This was the other crowned king of Germany, one of the von Hohenstaufen family.

Otto scowled. 'If I am to be denied a part in your venture, Uncle, I shall not stay. I am no child, to be left behind while the men go on a chevauchée.'

My heart sank. If Alienor was not to vanish as fast as she had appeared, Otto had to have a reason to remain. 'What if you rode without a surcoat, sire, and without an emblem on your shield?'

'That is a capital idea!' Otto cried. He glanced at Richard. 'If no one knows who I am, Uncle, there is no reason for me not to join you. Say I can come, please!'

The king gave me a curious look; he did not understand my change of heart. I suspected he was also conflicted. His prudent side would have counselled against it, but part of him would have relished the opportunity to take his much-loved nephew to war.

'Uncle?' It was incredible how beseeching one word could be.

'You will obey orders at all times – from me, or Rufus, or any other senior members of my household. You will join the fighting only if we say so. Is that clear?'

'Yes.' Otto was beaming from ear to ear. 'Thank you, Uncle!'

Richard could no longer hide his smile; he too was pleased. Indicating that his page should top up his cup and Otto's, he raised a toast to a successful raid.

I joined in willingly, but my high spirits were because Otto would be staying in the castle until after the incursion into French-held territory. I had a month, probably more, to reacquaint myself with Alienor.

That meant more to me than any chevauchée ever could.

As I cast sidelong looks after Alienor, the table conversation grew even more animated, ranging back and forth about the best course of action against Philippe. The jewel in the crown, the loss that had hurt Richard most, was the mighty fortress of Gisors. As yet the king had refrained from a direct assault; its defences were too well-constructed.

Not until it was isolated completely, Richard declared, something that meant capturing all the nearby French-held castles, would an attempt be worthwhile. Dangu. Sérifontaine. Courcelles. Boury. The list of strongholds went on.

Otto listened, his eyes shining, but I had heard it all before. I had taken part in attacks on some of the castles. After a time, I got up from the table. De Chauvigny's head turned. 'The garderobe calls,' I said, loud enough for my neighbours to hear.

'If you say so,' de Chauvigny said quietly, and he winked.

How perceptive he was. I loved him in that moment.

Alienor was not in the service passageway, so I headed for the kitchens. The first person I saw was Katharina. Face flushed, a smudge of flour on one cheek, she was pointing a long wooden spoon at one of the young lads who worked under her. 'Burn the next pudding, and I swear I will cut your balls off!'

He nodded, terrified out of his wits, and I hid a smile.

'My lord Rufus!' Katharina had seen me. 'This is a surprise. Is all well in the great hall? Is the king unhappy with any of the dishes?' Her tone was concerned.

I made a soothing gesture. 'Worry not. The food is excellent, as always.'

'You are seeking Rhys, then. He was here a moment ago.' Her head turned. 'Rhys!' Her bellow would have woken the dead.

'I am not looking for him.'

Her expression sharpened. 'Why are you here, then?' A heartbeat's pause, and she added a 'sir'.

How was it, I wondered for the thousandth time, that she could get away with the very minimum courtesy required?

'Sir?'

I cleared my throat, uncomfortable that Katharina's interest was about to become all-consuming. 'I am looking for a lady of King Otto's household. She is blonde, and wearing a blue dress.'

Her face lit up. 'You mean Alienor?'

Not trusting my voice, I nodded.

'She went to the cellar with one of the butler's servants, in search of some more good Bordeaux.'

'My thanks.' I hastened past.

'There is no need to go down. She will soon be back.'

I waved a hand, and with Katharina's curious gaze heavy on my back, aimed for the staircase that led to the cellar.

It was cool and dark below, the only light from bracket-held torches every twenty paces or so. The smell of damp and timber filled the air. I followed the sound of voices, finding Alienor and a male servant on the second aisle. She was carrying a jug, he a torch and another jug.

The servant knew me. He did his best to bow, encumbered as he was. 'Sir.'

Alienor's mouth was an 'O' of surprise. It made her even more attractive. 'Rufus,' she said.

I bent at the waist. 'My lady.'

'What are you doing here?'

'Looking for you,' I said simply.

The servant gaped. I could already hear the gossip in the kitchen. 'Give me the torch,' I ordered. 'Take the jug from Lady Alienor, and bring both to the great hall, to King Otto's pages.' He obeyed, and as he passed me, I said in his ear, 'Six silver pennies for your silence.' I got a delighted grin, and then he was gone.

Alienor moved nearer to the passageway and the flickering light of the nearest torch. Even in silhouette, she was mesmerising. 'Rufus, this is hardly the place.'

'My lady, I had to speak with you. It has been so long.'

'Fifteen and a half years.'

My heart thumped. I hoped her exactness meant that she might still care for me. 'Are you married?'

'I was. He died three years since.'

'I am sorry.' Part of me was not; it exulted. 'Have you children?'

There was a pause. Even in the gloom, I saw the sadness rise in her eyes.

'I was pregnant once. The babe did not live to meet the world.'

'That is very sad.'

Her chin came up. 'It was better so. My husband was not a kind man.'

There were so many questions in my head, but before I could ask another, she asked, 'And you – are you married?'

'No.'

'That surprises me. You must have met someone else.'

'I did. She would not wed me.'

'It is my turn to be sorry.'

'No need. If we had married, I would not be standing here.' Before she could react, I blurted, 'I thought of you so often after we parted.'

'Yet you did not write.'

'I am poor with letters. That is a bad excuse. I should have written,' I said. 'You did not send any messages either.'

'That is true. I was heartbroken.'

'I treasured the fillet you gave me. Sadly, the thong came undone one day in Outremer – it had frayed – and I lost it.'

Her expression had softened. 'Rufus, I thought of you also, many times.'

The hammer blow of attraction struck me, just as it had in the courtyard of the castle at Caen, all those years before. 'It gladdens my heart to know that,' I said huskily.

'Enough cozening.' She was all business again. 'If we do not emerge soon, it will not matter how much you offered that servant – tongues will start wagging.'

'You are right,' I said. Every time Alienor looked at me, my knees went to jelly. I would not be the one to suggest ending our meeting.

'I shall go up first. Wait a few moments before you follow.'

I caught her hand as she went to go. She did not pull away. 'May I see you again?'

'I will think about it.'

Before she could object, I stooped and kissed the back of her hand. 'I will live in hope and anticipation, my lady.'

That smile again. 'Farewell, Rufus.'

Giddy as if I had been spun a dozen times in quick succession, I stayed there among the barrels until I judged she had had enough time.

Katharina, eagle-eyed, destroyed my hopes of a discreet re-entry to the kitchen.

'Did you find Alienor, Rufus?' Butter would not have melted in her mouth.

'I did.' By being curt, I hoped to brazen my way through.

Katharina came right up to me, I hoped so no one could hear. 'You were down there for a while.'

My cheeks flamed, as they had when I was young. 'Not a word to a soul, do you hear?'

'Not even Rhys?'

I rolled my eyes. He would hear it from me anyway, I thought. 'Apart from him.'

She placed a finger on her lips to indicate her silence on the matter.

It was not so bad that Katharina knew, I decided, that I might be teased by her and Rhys. I had met Alienor again. The hammer blow had hit me for a second time, and I had not been rebuffed.

I had not felt so happy in years.

CHAPTER XXVII

'You see the towers, there and there, and there?' Richard was pointing.

'Yes, Uncle.' Otto could almost – *almost* – hide his lack of interest.

'Pay attention, boy!' Richard had noticed. 'You might want to build something like this one day.'

I hid my amusement. Consider yourself lucky, I wanted to tell Otto. You have not had to live through the building of this place, and hear Richard extol its virtues from dawn to dusk for months on end.

Nonetheless, my gaze followed Richard's finger, and I listened to his explanation of how the towers studded the walls at intervals to remove blind spots, thereby exposing assailants to constant attack from the garrison. The outwardly built projections along the ramparts were another invention of genius, something Richard had seen in Outremer. They allowed rocks or heated sand to be dropped safely from above.

We walked from the middle bailey to the inner, the king explaining how the gateway's flanking towers meant it could not be approached unseen. Otto nodded and worked harder at feigning interest. Richard next waxed lyrical about the inner bailey's wall. Able to defend much of the castle because of its great height, it had also been built in a rounded fashion, to better absorb damage from siege engines.

'I almost wish Philippe would come and lay siege to the place,' said Richard, 'just so I could stand atop the walls and invite him to do his worst.'

'You could not bear to stay inside the castle, sire,' I said, smiling and picturing the scene. 'A mark of silver says that at the first opportunity, you would marshal your forces and ride out to meet him.'

Richard chuckled. 'You know me too well, Rufus. There is a world of difference between besieging and being besieged. The latter would bore me to death.'

Nonetheless, he began to regale Otto with the details of life during a siege: how important wells were, and stores of food, medicines and equipment. My attention soon began to wander. When I spied Alienor, I was quick to ease myself to the rear of the group. In full flow, Richard did not notice. De Chauvigny did, but he said nothing. Rhys, lurking at the back in case I needed him, cocked his head at me.

'She is over there,' I said.

A corner of Rhys's mouth twitched. 'I saw her.'

He knew who I meant. I had decided the previous evening he should hear it from me first, not Katharina, and so I had told him about Alienor as soon as I had left the kitchen.

'Come over if the king wants me.' Not otherwise, said my stare.

'. . . even if the walls were made of butter.' The king was still in full flow.

Alienor was talking to one of the washerwomen, a hardworking, motherly type by the name of Constance. I walked to within ten paces of the pair, but did not speak.

Alienor saw me, but she continued listening to Constance, who had her back to me. Their conversation was about bed linen, and the washing of it.

I waited courteously, determined not to interrupt as most noblemen would have.

Constance droned on. She would have new sheets in King Otto's bedchamber by sext at the latest. It was not her responsibility, but she would see that the rushes on the floor were changed as well, and the candles.

I raised an eyebrow at Alienor, who, despite her best effort, smiled a little.

Sensing there was someone behind her, Constance turned. 'Sir Rufus, your pardon,' she cried, her face turning red with embarrassment. 'I did not know you were there. Can I be of service?'

'It was the lady Alienor I wished to speak to,' I said.

'O-of course, sir.' Uttering more promises about the bedlinen, Constance retreated. She could not quite conceal her curiosity.

'Rufus.' Alienor dipped her head in greeting.

'How are you?'

'Busy. Working.'

'It is not a good time, then,' I said, concealing my disappointment. 'I shall seek you out again.'

'Walk with me.'

Pleased, I said, 'Thank you.' I cast a look at the king and those around him. Apart from Rhys, no one seemed to have noticed my departure.

We walked towards the guest quarters, which formed part of the buildings within the inner bailey. Reaching the entrance, we went inside, away from inquisitive eyes. Alienor seemed in no hurry to continue with her duties. She asked me about myself, and what had happened in the long years since we had last met. I tried to make my account concise, although it was hard. Never having been one to blow my own trumpet, I mostly mentioned Richard's various quarrels with his brothers and father, and his long-running rivalry with Philippe Capet, and how I had served the king throughout. Alienor was most interested to hear of our campaign in Outremer; I was careful not to mention Joanna, other than in passing. Alienor was riveted by my account of the battle of Arsuf, and after that, the brutal onslaught we had endured at Joppa.

'He charged the entire Saracen army with only twelve men,' I told her, passion making my voice shake. 'And they fled! I have never seen anything like it. Richard was invincible that day. I swear he could have faced ten times the number of enemy and still emerged victorious.'

'You were one of the knights who rode with him, were you not?' I had mentioned this in passing.

Nonplussed, I said, 'Yes, but –'

'Come, Rufus. To fight as you did that day marks you down as someone worthy of standing beside Richard.'

Awkward, but delighted by the respect in her eyes, I muttered something about following where the king led. Then, keen to find more comfortable ground, I changed the subject, relating what had happened on our journey back from Outremer, and how hard it had been to leave Richard in captivity.

'That is long in the past now, thank God,' I said. 'But I have prated on long enough. Tell me about yourself.'

A maidservant came past. I paid no heed; I was beyond caring who saw me with Alienor.

She began. Like mine with Richard, Alienor's tale was entwined with Mathilda, his sister. At the time we had first met, her mistress and her mistress's husband, Heinrich der Löwe, were in enforced exile at

King Henry's court. After residing at Caen, there had been a period at Winchester in England. Mathilda had given birth to a son there, and then, after the emperor Heinrich – the same malevolent ruler who had ransomed Richard – had agreed to an end of their exile, the family had returned to Germany.

As well as attending Mathilda, Alienor had had a lot to do with her children. 'They are a delight, all of them,' she said fondly.

'Otto is the only one I know, and he is a good lad.'

'He can be arrogant – that is something I have warned him about since he was young.'

'It seems to be the natural behaviour of royal children,' I said, thinking not just of Richard, but John. His dead brothers Geoffrey and Hal, the Young King, had been no different. 'You keep your counsel now, I would guess.' I was always careful what I said to Richard. Once a man became king, even his personal friendships changed.

A sniff. 'I rein Otto in when needed. What is he going to do to me, I who wiped his nose and more besides when he was tiny?'

I threw back my head and laughed, my estimation of Alienor rising. She was feistier than I remembered, which attracted me to her all the more. 'You must have been held in some esteem,' I said, 'for your services to have been retained after Mathilda's death.'

Mathilda had passed away in the summer of the year of our Lord 1189, just missing the death of her father, and Richard's accession to the throne soon after.

'I had been with the children for years. I loved them as if they were my own, and they loved me,' said Alienor. 'Richenza and Heinrich, the eldest, had known me since they were little. The younger ones, Otto and William, could not remember a time without me. There was no question but I would stay with the family.'

'You had no thoughts of returning to Chester?' This was where Alienor was from.

A shake of her golden tresses. 'My parents are long dead, and I am not close to my only brother. Nothing remains for me there now.'

It was fortunate, I thought, that she had the security of her employ with Otto's family. 'How old is William now?' I asked. The others were adults, or as close to it as made no difference.

'Five. I wanted to stay behind with him, but Otto would not have it. The boy has nurses enough, he said.' Her expression grew wistful.

'In retrospect, I am glad. Otto is a grown man now; it will not be long before he needs me not at all.'

It was fanciful even to consider a future with Alienor, yet I was. The significant obstacle – assuming that she was interested in me, something I had not yet determined with any certainty – was that she would return to Germany when Otto left, to continue her care of little William. My first priority, I decided, was to see if Alienor and I could rediscover the feelings we had had for each other what felt like half a lifetime before.

'A silver penny for your thoughts.'

'Your pardon,' I said, stalling.

She gave me an enquiring look.

I had always been a poor liar. 'I was thinking about you. Us.'

'Us?' There was no hiding the challenge in her eyes.

I coloured. 'Yes, my lady. I find you more beautiful than ever, and your company is . . .' Praying that my rushed choice was the right word, I added, 'Enchanting.' To my delight, a tinge of pink now marked her face. I hurried on, driven by eagerness. 'I would dearly love to spend more time with you, if that is agreeable.'

Silence.

I battled with instant despair, as a spurned youth might.

'I would like that, Rufus.'

A grin split my face – I could not help it – and I had to stop myself from bending in to kiss her.

It was as if she knew. 'I must away. Duty calls.'

'Can I see you later?'

Her nod fell on me like spring rain on young crops.

September arrived, bringing with it glorious weather. Mornings were dew-laden, with a slight chill, and the days sunny and pleasant. Light remained in the evening sky until almost compline, for which I was grateful. The end of summer was a bittersweet time, knowing that the impending cold, damp and darkness from October onwards would last for nigh on six months.

For now, though, it was a time of warmth and plenty. The last of the crops were being harvested. The hedgerows were heavy with blackberries, and mushrooms flourished in the wheat stubble. Beef cattle and pigs were butchered before the grazing grew scarce. Thanksgiving

Masses were held. The local peasantry feasted and drank. The clash of arms came daily from the tourney field as the knights practised; loud also was the shouting of sergeants, drilling the men-at-arms.

I spent every moment I could with Alienor. She scolded me at first for distracting her from her duties, but it soon became clear that they did not take overlong each day and that, once completed, she enjoyed the diversion. We took walks together, around the castle walls or down into the village. Often I would saddle up a pair of palfreys – she was an accomplished horsewoman – and take her out into the countryside. I knew the area like the back of my hand, having lived there as the castle was built. We rode for miles, always south or west, into Richard's territory, talking endlessly. There were also spots by the River Seine that were perfect for sitting to admire the vista. I went swimming more than once but, to my chagrin, could not tempt Alienor to join me.

I had more success in winning kisses from her, not the first time we went out together, nor even the second. I waited until the third tryst, and to my joy, was met with a passion similar to my own. I wanted nothing more than to take things further, but I did not. A plan was forming in my head. I had no idea if it would come to fruition, but it paid to take one step at a time.

Word came from Artois. True to his word, the young Count Baldwin of Flanders, Richard's ally, had invaded. The town of Aire was taken without a fight, and Saint-Omer besieged. We heard how the citizens had sent frantic messages to Philippe, but as Richard said, laughing, they would be long waiting for his arrival. He had other things on his mind, for Baldwin's incursion was the signal for us to march into the French-controlled part of the Vexin.

Perhaps a week of September remained as we rode out of Chateau Gaillard, three hundred and fifty knights, and five times that number of archers and men-at-arms. My heart was singing. Nestled under my tunic on a leather thong was a little fabric bag. Within was not just a fillet, but a lock of Alienor's golden hair. I had wheedled both from her the previous night, on our last tryst. Now she stood on the front rampart, watching as Richard led the host to war. I blew a kiss to her; she was quick to return the gesture, making me grin.

Rhys, riding just behind, saw. 'Quite the lovebirds, you pair,' he murmured.

'There is no denying it,' I said, grinning like a fool.

Otto, caught up in his own world as the young often are, and thrilled to be setting out on our adventure, was oblivious to my state. That suited for the moment; I had no idea how he might react to Alienor's relationship with me. The king was an altogether sharper blade. Of recent days I had seen his glances as I sidled out of meetings, or arrived late to a council. He had said nothing thus far, and I was content to keep silent. My private life was my own.

As we left Chateau Gaillard behind, however, he chose to comment.

'She is a serving lady to Otto?'

I smiled. As ever with Richard, there was no preamble. 'Yes, sire. I know her of old. Do you remember the first Christmas we spent together at Caen, when your lord father was still alive?'

'Was that the time Johnny slighted you?'

Surprised and pleased that he remembered, I nodded. 'You corrected him, sire. I am still grateful for that.'

'I could have reacted no other way. If Johnny did not know your worth then, he must now.'

I risked, 'Your brother does not like me, sire.'

'Ha! Why do you say that?'

'He did not like you rebuking him that night in Caen, sire. I fear he has held a grudge against me since.' My gut instinct was not wrong. I was too familiar with John's beady, calculating gaze.

'He is the type to harbour ill-feeling, for certes. I shall speak with him.'

'Thank you, sire.' In my mind, it would make scant difference. The malignant John would pay lip service only. I threw up a prayer to Christ and all His saints to prevent a day ever coming when I did not have Richard's protection.

'And you, Rufus? What do you think of my heir?'

His gaze was on me, direct and penetrating. I chose the harder option, because honesty – of a kind at least – was the best policy. 'Sire, I am wary of him. He did not act with honour while we were in Outremer. His dealings with Philippe, what he tried to do . . .' My blood boiled to remember it. 'I would not put it past him to act in the same vein again.'

'He committed treachery, there is no denying. But that is in the past. Johnny is loyal now – the whelp knows his place, and will not risk losing it.'

'As you say, sire.' I could not argue the point. Since being allowed back into the fold, John had been careful to obey Richard. There had been no rumours of dealings with Philippe either. Even so, I did not trust John as far as I could throw him. As for what he thought of me, the less I dwelled on it, the better.

Richard's expression had become contemplative. 'Rufus, you must learn to follow Johnny, even if you do not love him as you do me.'

'I will, sire,' I said, even as my jaw clenched in protest, and I sent up another plea to God that that day never came.

Taking me at my word, Richard changed the subject. 'We had not finished speaking of Otto's serving lady. She is of noble stock?'

'Yes, sire.'

'You seem smitten.'

Relieved to return to topics more pleasant, I said, 'I am, sire.'

'That is well. Years have passed. It is time you found someone.' This was as much reference as the king would make to his sister Joanna.

A pang of guilt cut at me, even though she had ended our love affair, not I. Rumours abounded that Joanna's marriage to Count Raymond VI of Toulouse was an unhappy one, and that the count, who had been wed twice before, was a womaniser of the first order.

'What is her name?'

'Alienor, sire, like your lady mother.'

'A fine name.' Richard thought for a moment, and then said, 'I wish you every joy with her, Rufus, truly.'

'Thank you, sire,' I answered, touched by his sincerity. The ruthless part of me determined that when the time came, if it seemed beneficial, I would use his goodwill to my advantage.

'Enough of women,' Richard declared. He raised his voice, so that Otto, a short distance ahead of us, could hear, 'Let us talk of French-held castles, nephew, and how to take them!'

His face alight with eagerness, Otto reined in.

In the event, Richard's plan had to be put on hold. A dust-covered messenger on a sweat-lathered horse came in soon after with news that changed our priorities on the instant. Emboldened, perhaps by communications with a spy at Chateau Gaillard – it was inevitable there was at least one – and thus word of the king's departure, Philippe had crossed the Seine in force and was travelling west. His intent would be the same as our own: to take whatever strongholds he could.

The message was carried by one of Mercadier's sergeants, who had been out on patrol. He reported Philippe's location to be between the French-held castle at Vernon and Richard's castle at Jumièges, which was close to Rouen as the crow flew, but separated from it by two great sinuous loops of the Seine. Bizarrely – but normal for the Vexin – Jumièges was on the northern bank, but to reach it the French king was marching to the *rear* of Chateau Gaillard, and behind our position.

It was almost too good to be true. We retraced our route, crossing the bridge at Chateau Gaillard as dusk fell, and continuing for two miles beyond before halting. Richard ordered us all to rest while we could, because the army was to break camp in the middle of the night. It was a routine that everyone, knights and squires, men-at-arms, archers and wagoners, had become accustomed to. As the joke went, even the whores and hangers-on who dogged the army's footsteps were used to rising at an ungodly hour.

We had been on the road for a good while by the time the church bells were tolling prime. Mercadier's routiers had been out all night, exploring the countryside. Several returned with news of Philippe's host; it was about ten miles away, not far from Évreux. Despite its larger size – several thousand men more than ours – Richard was not dismayed. Nor were any of us. If anything, our appetite for battle was whetted. Our record versus the French was unparalleled. Against the insignificant defeat at Aumâle two years prior, the king boasted more than a score of victories.

Before long, the enemy camp was only two miles away. There had been no sign of French scouts, and Mercadier's men kept riding in, bringing us up-to-the-moment information. Hard-bitten routiers, they were soulless killers whom I detested, but by Christ they earned their salt that day. The Frenchies were still wrapped up in their blankets, they gleefully reported, and the sentries were drowsing at their posts. We pressed on, orders passing down the column to keep noise to a minimum.

Mercadier met us closer to the French encampment. His face was drawn; I doubt he had had any sleep, but he was full of energy explaining the layout of the terrain to the king. It was wooded, like so much of Normandy, but his trusty routiers had found a track through. It was one probably favoured by local hunters, Mercadier reported.

'Can two men ride abreast?' asked the king.

'No, sire.'

'And are there no other paths?'

'The nearest one is half a mile that way, sire.' Mercadier pointed to the north.

Richard made an impatient gesture with his hands. 'Even if we use that, it will be noon ere the entire army is through.'

I sensed his reaction, and an expectant thrill ran through me.

'It matters not,' said Richard to Mercadier. 'One hundred knights plus your routiers will be enough to panic the Frenchies, eh?'

Mercadier gave him a hideous wolf's grin. 'Yes, sire!'

Otto could not believe his ears. He positively beamed.

The king glanced at me and de Chauvigny, who were closest. 'Well?'

'That is better odds than at Joppa, sire,' I said, getting a chuckle in reply.

'I am with you, sire.' De Chauvigny was never one to back away from a fight.

'Otto, you are to stay by my side when the fighting starts.'

'Yes, Uncle.' Excitement filled his voice.

Richard gave Mercadier a nod. 'Let us to it.'

We moved out at once.

CHAPTER XXVIII

I should have known that the king would not even wait for a hundred of his household to pick their way through the woods. Lurking at the treeline, a mixture of oak, beech, aspen and moonbeam, he stared at the untidy sprawl of French tents filling the open ground a quarter of a mile distant. He all but danced with impatience as knight after knight joined us.

'How many?' he would ask, and not ten heartbeats later, repeat the same demand. Otto had not even climbed down from his mount, so enthusiastic was he. Mercadier hovered close by, his impatience obvious to a blind man. He had sixty-odd routiers, and it was hard to disagree with his assertion that each one was worth four Frenchies.

'How many?' Richard addressed me without taking his gaze from the enemy camp.

'Fifty-two, sire,' I said.

'Fifty-three,' said de Chauvigny, as another knight emerged from the path.

'That is enough.' Richard had donned his helmet and was swinging himself into the saddle. 'Take much longer, and we will be seen by a man come in search of a quiet place to empty his bowels.'

He was not wrong. Trickles of smoke were spiralling up from the tents: cooking fires. Figures shuffled between some of the tents. Next a hacking cough carried through the cool air.

'Form a line,' ordered the king, urging his destrier out of the trees. He couched his lance. 'As wide as possible. Charge when I say, not before. Shout when I do, not an instant sooner. Sow panic in the Frenchies, and our task is done!'

I urged Pommers towards the king, with de Chauvigny close behind. No one tried to take our places; a longstanding, unspoken agreement let us provide Richard's protection and, by extension today, Otto's also.

'Forward!' said Richard, his voice low. 'Pass the word.'

His order went along the line fast as a flame takes hold in kindling. The king was already moving.

I dug my heels into Pommers' sides, and he went from standing to the trot in two paces. I could feel his tension; a veteran of many battles, he knew what was about to happen. Like me, he wanted to charge *now*. I leaned forward over his neck. 'Steady, boy,' I told him. 'Soon.'

Richard led us on, holding back from the full gallop. It was not about reaching the French camp quickly, but about being able to pursue our enemies for miles.

A hundred paces we went, one fourth of the distance, trampling the grass flat.

The king increased our speed to the canter. Still he gave no shout, no war cry.

I glanced to either side, exulting in the sight. Our number was small, but we were a stirring sight. Hauberks that reached to our knees, wearing the new-style great helms, each of us had a couched lance projecting far out over our horses' heads. Further out were the routiers, less well-armoured, but just as lethal.

The element of surprise could not last forever.

A half-asleep Frenchie, yawning as he ambled from between the tents, heard the drumming of our destriers' hooves. He stopped, stared in total disbelief at the line of horsemen thundering towards him. Then, full bladder forgotten, he turned and ran, screaming at the top of his voice.

Richard urged his destrier into a gallop, as did we all.

'*Dex aie!*' the king bellowed.

We answered in full tongue, like a pack of hounds closing on the quarry.

Our line broke up the instant we reached the enemy camp. It was an impossibility to stay together. Richard had skewered a man-at-arms emerging from a tent, and was trying to free his lance. I shot past, my gaze fixed on a crossbowman. More alert than his comrades, he already had his weapon spanned and loaded. I have no idea if he knew who Richard was, but the red crest on the king's helmet marked him out as an important noble. As I closed, coming in from an angle, the crossbowman levelled his weapon. His finger tightened on the trigger, and raw fear consumed me.

Then the point of my lance punched into him. The quarrel shot up into the sky, going nowhere. The crossbowman, pierced through and through, was picked up bodily by Pommers' momentum. His face contorted with agony, but he was beyond speaking, a dead man already. I let go of my lance; it was useless now. Hauling on the reins, fingers clawing for my sword hilt, my eyes searched desperately for the king.

I need not have worried. He came cantering around the nearest tent, and saluted me with his already-reddened blade. 'Let us hunt Frenchies, Rufus!' he shouted.

'Aye, sire!'

That is what we did. Our attack had caught Philippe's soldiers completely off guard. The majority were either asleep or just clambering from their blankets. If there had been more of us, we would have wreaked an almighty slaughter, but six score men cannot annihilate an army. What they *can* do is cause complete and utter panic. Shouting '*Dex aie*', moving at speed between the tents, we gave the impression of a much larger force. Terrified out of their wits by our sudden appearance, few Frenchies put up any resistance.

As I heard later, the second part of Richard's masterplan, for two hundred archers and crossbowmen to follow the initial force of knights, also paid off in royal style. The fastest among them came charging into the enemy camp moments after our attack, loosing volley after deadly volley at the frightened, milling French. Any question of a stand, a decent show of resistance, vanished. Men broke and ran, sprinted for their lives. The injured were abandoned; those who fell in the stampede were trampled underfoot.

What we had not appreciated, what Mercadier's routiers, wary of going too close to the enemy position, had not seen the night before, was that this was not Philippe's main encampment. For reasons that were never made clear, the main portion of the French host was camped a mile and a half further to the west.

Alerted by the shouts and screams, enough of them were able to get up and arm themselves before Richard arrived. Perhaps half the king's force remained – thirty-plus knights and the same number of routiers – the rest were behind our position, pursuing and killing Frenchies in the first camp.

A line of horsemen was waiting for us – it was a ragged formation, full of gaps, and most of the riders were not wearing armour

– but it was a line, nonetheless. Behind them, purple-faced sergeants shouted orders at their crossbowmen, of whom at least thirty were visible.

My heart skipped a beat. I cared nothing for myself, but the king had to be protected from danger. Close in, a quarrel could punch through a hauberk with ease.

Richard was unconcerned – naturally. He slapped his thigh. 'Ready, messires? A quick charge, and these Frenchies will also break!'

'Sire,' I said. 'The risk is too great.' There are only so many times you can trust to luck, I thought.

The king's head twisted. Within the slit of his helmet, his eyes were cold. 'I shall be the judge of that, Rufus.'

'I do not mean the French horsemen, sire. Look at the crossbowmen. More of them are arriving with every moment that passes.'

'They will run too.' Richard's tone was bullish.

'Maybe, sire, but they will loose at least one volley.' De Chauvigny had seen too. He was as unhappy as I.

'God's legs! It is not as if I have never charged crossbowmen,' cried Richard.

'Indeed, sire, but there is no need to attack these Frenchies now,' I urged. 'They will not stand for long; they are only here so that Philippe and the rest of their comrades can retreat.'

The king grumbled and muttered, but the brief pause in the fighting had seen the red mist lift from him. He knew as well as we did – had seen it happen before – the foolhardiness of an unnecessary charge against missile troops.

My hunch proved correct. It was not long before the line of French began to pull back. The crossbowmen came to the fore, allowing the horsemen to turn around and retreat. They then did the same, but walking backwards, their crossbows at the ready. We let them go.

Not all of the enemy host was acting in such a disciplined manner. As we soon discovered, again thanks to Mercadier's routiers, large groups of Frenchies were fleeing pell-mell back towards Vernon. Philippe's livery had been spotted in one such party, and was already several miles away. Richard let out a frustrated laugh to hear it, declaring that the French king ever seemed destined to evade him.

There was no denying the scale of the humiliation to Philippe, however. Mightily encouraged, Richard gave orders that we were to carry the fight to the French again, not pursuing the enemy host, but returning to our original purpose, seizing castles in the Vexin.

On the twenty-seventh of September, we forded the River Epte at Dangu. Bypassing the castle there, Richard led us first to Courcelles, which opened its gates within moments of our arrival, and then nearby Boury, where the overawed defenders did the same. Returning to Dangu, and informing the garrison commander what had happened, the king accepted its immediate capitulation. Our good fortune continued. William de l'Etang, tasked with the capture of Sérifontaine a few miles away, sent word that he had also been successful.

We feasted in the hall at Dangu that evening. Richard was in jubilant mood. 'Four castles in one day! That is a record, for certes.'

'The net is closing around Gisors, sire,' I said.

'At last,' said Richard.

Gisors had been a thorn in his side for years. The powerful bastion had been lost when its castellan, isolated and vulnerable during his captivity, had surrendered to the French crown. Our day's work had seen Sérifontaine, north of Gisors, and Dangu, Courcelles and Boury, south of it, pass into the king's hands.

''Twould be good to appear outside the walls of Gisors with siege engines,' said de Chauvigny. 'I wager that Philippe's response would be to throw his entire army at us.'

'It would – he is too proud to allow Gisors be taken. It means I have to take the slow, patient approach, which has never been my favourite,' said Richard, smiling as we all laughed. 'Cut Gisors off from the surrounding farms, as we will do this autumn and winter, and its garrison will have no food. Philippe will send grain wagons to its aid, but they will be easy prey for our raiding parties.'

'And once he has handed Gisors back, sire?' I asked. Its return would mean the losses suffered while Richard was in captivity had at last been made good.

'Rufus, I thought you would know. Finally, we shall be able to make plans for a return to Outremer. Saladin's sons have been quarrelling since his death. The opportunity to defeat the Saracens has never been greater.' He raised his cup in a toast. 'To the conquest of Jerusalem!'

Voices lifted in loud agreement.

As I lifted my own cup and echoed Richard's words, I was not so sure.

I rose early on the twenty-eighth, still troubled by my feelings of the previous evening. The hall, which had been turned into a dormitory for the household knights, was quiet. Rhys was not in his customary place at my feet; it felt odd, even though it was I who had given him permission to be with Katharina. I dressed quietly, succeeding in my efforts not to wake de Chauvigny, sleeping beside me, and padded to the main entrance.

It was crisp and cold in the courtyard. There was a new, autumn dampness to the air; I did not like it. And yet it was more pleasant than Cairlinn, my family home, which would already be much colder. It had been my heartfelt dream for decades to return there, yet of recent times I questioned whether I could ever do so, and not just because of the climate. I thought of Alienor, and wondered if we had a future together. Meanwhile, I was supposed to find enthusiasm for returning to Outremer. My confusion felt disloyal to the king, which left me even more uneasy.

A figure emerged from the stables, leading a horse I recognised – a fine grey from Lombardy. Rather than a groom, it was Richard. Surprised, I crossed the courtyard. 'You are up with the lark, sire.'

'So are you.' He cast an eye at me. 'Were you dreaming of Alienor?'

My lips twitched. 'I might have been, sire.'

'Maybe it is time you wed. Have you given thought to that?'

'I have, sire, truth be told.'

'You are well past the age most men have taken a wife.'

I have only ever thought of it twice, I wanted to say. It was not the time to mention Joanna, however, who could never have been mine. I shrugged. 'I have not had the time, sire. We have not been exactly idle these past ten years.'

He laughed, that belly sound of genuine amusement. 'True enough, Ferdia.' He tied the reins to a hook set in the wall, and set to brushing the grey's coat. 'It is not quite that simple, though.'

'Sire?'

'Opportunities that present themselves have to be taken, nay, seized, lest they pass us by.'

The king was offering me advice, I was sure of it. He might have said more, but Mercadier appeared, scratching his beard.

He and the king fell into animated conversation about the patrols that would traverse the Epte, seeking out French forces. Philippe had retreated east from Vernon to Mantes, but that did not mean a halt to hostilities. The two kings were engaged in a constant chess match, moving and counter moving in anticipation of the other. Richard had the upper hand, thanks to his recent victories and to Count Baldwin of Flanders, whose siege of St Omer continued.

'It is well that the men should rest in the castle for the day,' said Richard, 'but I cannot sit on my hands. I shall lead one of the patrols.'

Mercadier bowed his head. 'As you wish, sire.'

'Rufus, will you scent out the Frenchies with me, or languish here, thinking of your lady love?' This got a raised eyebrow from Mercadier, who knew nothing of Alienor.

A little stung, but not wishing to be left to my own thoughts either, I said that I would like nothing more.

'Best line your belly with some food,' the king advised. 'It might be a long day.'

'By your leave, sire,' I said, making for the outbuilding where the domestic staff were sleeping. Katharina might not appreciate being woken so early, but Rhys would not want to miss this.

It was mid-morning ere we departed. Richard had failed to evade his clerks, and had spent an ill-tempered two hours listening to letters from his officials and subjects, and dictating responses to a pair of harassed scribes. The communications had come from the locale, but also Brittany and Poitou, London and Winchester, Normandy, Aquitaine and York. There was even a letter from the Archbishop of Dublin. The vast majority were pleas, for Richard to settle quarrels and land disputes, to rule which noble should take what office, to arbitrate over a decision made by a bishop and disagreed with by his flock. Some were more serious, revelations of discontent and even rebellion from various parts of his realm. All required answers.

This duty, drudgery for the main, was an intimate part of being a king, a ruler. Not a day went by without the arrival of messengers with bulging leather satchels. The king was fond of the saying that the wax-sealed parchment rolls they contained were the bane of his life. A private joke between the household knights ran that half Richard's delight in fighting the French derived from the impossibility of dealing with routine paperwork while he was doing so – not that any of us would have volunteered for the onerous duty.

Free at last – telling his unhappy officials, for the mound of letters had not all been dealt with, they could wait until another day – Richard had roared for his squires to arm him. There was no hauberk and great helm; those were reserved for battles, and our need today was for speed. Instead he wore over his tunic and gambeson a surcoat with the three Angevin lions gold-embroidered on a red background. An old-fashioned helm with a nasal guard sat on his head. He had his sword, and a heater shield also displaying the royal insignia.

I was armed and dressed in similar fashion; so was Rhys. What made the king stand out from the hundred-strong patrol was his great size and the three lions that shouted his status to any man with eyes in his head. I asked Richard not to use them, in case we met a stronger French force. It was more for form's sake; I was unsurprised when he laughed in my face. It was in a friendly way, though; he said I could no more ask a leopard to change his spots.

De Chauvigny tried then, because, he averred, he loved his cousin the king. Still laughing, Richard kissed him on the cheek, and repeated what he had said to me.

'In that case, we must stay close by you, sire,' said de Chauvigny.

'Keep up if you can,' challenged the king.

I had always loved Richard's devil-may-care attitude, indeed had acted so myself on innumerable occasions, but the lustre of its attraction was fading. 'How many times can he do this and escape injury or worse?' I asked de Chauvigny under my breath.

'The same goes through my mind every time we ride against the enemy.' De Chauvigny's expression was sombre. 'But it is in Richard's nature to act so, and he is the king, our sworn liege lord. What can we do but follow him?'

I had no answer, and it was in grim mood that I rode out of Dangu at Richard's back. It had been a dry summer, and the Epte was low. I had had to swim my horse across the ford on previous occasions; today the water did not reach our stirrups. We rode to Boury, a distance of two-and-a-half miles, and there spoke with the new castellan, appointed just the day before. Not a Frenchman had been seen, he reported happily, thanking the king again for his new position.

Mercadier was with us. 'When it comes to scouting, sire, I am your good luck,' he had declared in his throaty voice, and smiling, Richard had agreed. Leaving Boury, Mercadier offered to ride out in front, that he might spy any Frenchies before they saw our main force.

The king was in ebullient mood, talking about how Gisors might be best isolated. Otto, whose eagerness meant he took part in every action he was allowed, was offering his opinions. I was barely listening. It did not matter; de Chauvigny and Otto were fully engaged. As I swatted away the last of the year's flies, I felt tired. Tired of not living in one place – spells in this castle and that aside – up and down the land. Poitou. Aquitaine. Normandy. The Vexin. I had lands in England granted to me by the king, and lived off their generous rents, but I had never seen them. I was lord of Cairlinn, yet did not even know if I wanted to return there. I could call nowhere home.

I was also tired of rebellious nobles, who, when brought to heel, rebelled again the first time the chance came their way. I was tired of war, and of killing. Tired of fighting the French. Fatigued beyond measure of the capricious Philippe Capet and, likewise, Richard's rivalry with him, which seemed as if it would never end. I was bone-weary, in fact.

Full of guilt, I glanced at the king, but he was oblivious, locked deep in a back-and-forth argument with de Chauvigny about the best way of dealing with the ever-rebellious nobles of Aquitaine. I had heard it all before. I fell to thinking about more pleasant things: Alienor, and if she would accept a proposal of marriage. This was my heartfelt plan, mentioned to no one. I had no idea if she would agree, but I had high hopes. Otto would be my greatest obstacle, because of his long-held emotional attachment. My best chance of success with him lay with Richard. After his kind words about Alienor, I had decided that the king would probably intervene on my behalf if I asked.

A repetitive, familiar sound caught my attention. Drumming hooves, coming our way. I stared down the track, which led east, and then at the king, Otto and de Chauvigny. None of them had heard. Gut instinct told me it was Mercadier and, sure enough, his squat figure proved to be astride the horse that came galloping into sight.

'Sire!' The routier captain's shout echoed. 'The French! The French are close!'

Richard stopped mid-sentence. We exchanged loaded glances.

Mercadier brought his horse to a skidding halt, throwing up clouds of dust. 'Philippe's army is close, sire!'

'*Mon Dieu*, is he coming for us?' demanded Richard, hope lighting up his face.

Mercadier laughed. 'No, sire, he has no idea we are here. The fool is travelling north-west, towards Courcelles.'

'By these ten fingerbones, he must think it holds out still,' said the king.

'That was my thought also, sire,' answered Mercadier, leering. 'His soldiers are in marching formation, spread out over miles. They are ripe for the plucking.'

'Alas that we number only five score, sire,' said Otto, who did not know the king as well as the rest of us.

'Where are the nearest patrols?' Richard asked Mercadier.

'Not far, sire. I can send men to fetch them.' Six other groups, similar in size to our own, were scattered through the countryside, each advancing eastward like us.

'How long to gather them?' Richard's expression was as fierce as I had ever seen it.

'An hour, sire, maybe two.'

'Make it one. Send word to Dangu also. The entire army is to follow our path, with all speed.'

Mercadier saluted, and whipping his horse into a gallop, went off down the line to find his men.

CHAPTER XXIX

We withdrew into the trees on one side of the road. It was not a good idea to advance for the moment, in case of being seen by French scouts. The king, who had climbed down from his grey, paced about, eager as a ravening lion starved of its food. His restlessness added to our own desire to act. Men were picking fingernails with daggers, talking excitedly to each other, slurping water from their flasks. Others repeated the checks they had made at Dangu: girth leathers, sword belts, buckles and straps. I asked Rhys about Katharina, and he countered by enquiring after Alienor. I decided to bring him in on my plan of asking for her hand.

He let out a half-stifled yelp, and clasped my arm, grinning. 'By my hilt, that is the best news I have heard in many's the month.'

I was touched by his fervour. 'You think she will have me?'

'If she does not . . .' Rhys paused, and I could tell he was moderating his words – 'her wits must be curdled.'

I was pleased, but wise enough to know that the approval of friends did not equate to a woman's consent. Not until I had heard Alienor herself agree would I believe it was truly possible.

I did not want to tempt fate by discussing it further, and Rhys had been with Katharina long enough not to need to prate on about her. A companionable silence fell between us, but there was no peace to be had. Our mounts stamped about, and flicked tails and ears, unhappy with the horseflies. A blackbird shrilled its anger at our presence. From some distance away came the repetitive thud of an axe, a local whose need for timber was great enough to risk breaking the law.

Soon our wait felt like an eternity.

'How long will he delay?' I muttered to John de Préaux. Brother of Peter, with us at Joppa, and William, who had given himself into captivity to save the king, John was also a worthy knight.

'You know how he is. Not long.' John, a lugubrious character who was fond of dice, shrugged. 'We could ride off now, you and I, and see how he reacts.'

'He would not take kindly to that! A hundred silver pennies to see you do it.'

John gave me a look.

I chuckled. We both knew that neither of us would act until Richard said so.

The king lasted until three of the patrols had joined us. Two hundred and ninety-something men, we were, scarcely a force to attack an army. That did not stop Richard. Hugues de Corni, a native of the area, had offered to lead us the last distance towards the enemy. With the king by his side, he took us along a winding path that ran roughly parallel to the road.

I kept close behind, with de Chauvigny.

William Marshal was there too, the old rogue. Nothing kept him from a fight, or a chance to impress Richard. Loyal though he was, and honourable, there was a self-serving aspect to Marshal that had never sat well with me. Yes, he had stayed true to his various masters, the Young King, then the father Henry and now Richard, but by Christ he had done well out of it too. Lord of Striguil, ruler of vast estates he was, and husband to Isabelle, the girl who had befriended me half a lifetime ago. Their marriage was reputed to be a good one, which made me happy. They had five offspring already, or even six.

Good luck to him, I thought. May I be so fortunate.

'By all that is holy,' said Richard.

I stared over the king's shoulder. De Corni had brought us to a vantage point, a rocky outcrop part-sheltered by trees, from which we could see the road to Courcelles. It was packed with soldiers, on foot and on horse. Banners and pennants hung from spears; bursts of song could be heard. Messengers rode up and down the column, relaying orders.

'Mercadier was correct,' I said.

'Yet again he proves his worth.' Richard was delighted.

'If you engage with them today, great honour will be yours, for they will be routed or taken captive,' said de Corni. 'Sire, enhance your reputation this very day.'

'If, Sir Hugues? If?' Richard twisted in the saddle to regard me and de Chauvigny. 'What say you pair?'

'It would be wise to wait for reinforcements, sire,' said de Chauvigny, but his mouth was twitching.

So was mine, because despite the insanity of it, I too was infected by Richard's enthusiasm. 'Let us charge the Frenchies, sire.'

'We shall, we brothers-in-arms.'

I felt that Richard's smile then was for me alone. Gone were my feelings of doubt. All I wanted was to follow him into battle.

'Now we shall see who will be swift on his horse today. God is with us! Let us attack them!' So saying, Richard urged his Lombardy grey forward.

Out from the cover of the trees we came, and spread out in a massive line, one deep. Richard's tactic was deliberate. The more of us the Frenchies thought there were, the better. Formed up swift and eager, he gave the order to charge and we thundered towards their dense-packed ranks, like three hundred avenging angels.

Instant panic broke out. The French assumed, naturally, that the attack was in force. Horses reared, men were unhorsed, soldiers fled into the woods on the opposite side of the road. Captains and sergeants roared in vain. Utter chaos reigned. There would be no coming back from it.

We smashed into the column, lances punching men from their saddles, and right out through the other side. Wheeling, close to the king and Otto, hauling out my sword, I drove at the Frenchies again. A knight in a green surcoat cut at me; I parried the blow, and thrust at him. He took the blow on his shield, but it splintered, and he was rocked back in the saddle. Before he could reply, I cut at his head. My sword rang off his helmet; he must have seen stars, for he slumped down, and a heartbeat later, toppled off his mount. I went after the king, who had already driven back through the French.

We were too few to hurt Philippe's host badly. Even when your opponents are running away, it is impossible to kill thousands of them. Richard's command was that we sow fear by the bushel, and if possible, find the French king. With luck, we might capture him, and if our comrades from Dangu arrived quickly, the quantities of prisoners and booty taken would be vast.

Our first task was already complete. Our unexpected appearance had caused utter terror among the French. The wondrous thing about striking fear into an enemy is the speed with which it spreads. Quicker than a man can run, faster even than a galloping horse, it travels with a life of its own, and with the greed of a fire set in bone-dry summer grass.

I had never had an appetite for slaying men who are fleeing for their lives, and today was no different. I attacked any Frenchies who showed interest in a fight, and killed or injured several, but I made no attempt to cut down their terrified comrades. The king had an even harder time finding foemen, because his fearsome reputation meant that few of the French would stand and face him, let alone cross blades.

Rhys, however, was ever on the lookout for ransom money, and so was continually leaping down from his horse to demand the surrender of any noblemen whose armour or regalia looked worthy of it. I shouted to him that he could find me later, and got a grateful wave of his bollock dagger, before chasing after the king.

He had ascertained, from a defeated French knight, that Philippe was a good way further up the column. 'God's legs, but we shall have him today – I can feel it in my bones! On!'

We rode. Great clouds of dust had been sent up by the enemy host. It was thanks to the long, hot summer, which had dried out every road in Normandy and the Vexin. Instead of mud, often the bane of our existence as we travelled, endless dust cursed us now. Powdery and choking, it caught at the back of my throat, and stung my eyes. It stained my sweat-dampened surcoat red-brown. I could even feel it working its way through my socks.

The king reined in at one point to drink some water. 'Does it remind you of Outremer?'

I tried to speak and managed only to cough. Then I spluttered a 'Yes, sire.'

'Would that I had been with you then!' Despite this regret, Otto looked to be having the time of his young life.

'God willing, you might accompany us when we return,' said Richard.

Otto, also wearing a simple helm with nasal guard, beamed from ear to ear. 'Thank you, Uncle. We shall fight the Saracens together!'

Animated, lost in a dream of taking Jerusalem, he did not see two French men-at-arms climb to their feet from among the corpses. One had a crossbow, the other a spear. Down came the crossbow, aiming. Back went the spear for a thrust.

Instinct took over. Leaning so far forward that I was almost unseated, I used the flat of my blade to slap Richard's horse on the rump. Trained though it was, the grey took fright and galloped away, with the furious king doing his best to drag it to a halt.

Deprived of Richard, his intended target, the crossbowman turned on me. Otto was a stripling youth whom he did not recognise, whereas I, a prominent knight, had prevented him killing the English king.

I threw up my shield, hoping he would aim at me, but the Frenchie knew better. On foot, against a horseman, take the easy target. *Click* went his crossbow, and my faithful mount staggered. I was already kicking my boots out of the stirrups, so when it went down a moment later, I managed to jump clear.

I would have tackled the crossbowman first, to prevent him doing me serious injury with his next shot, but Otto was in trouble. The second man-at-arms had stabbed his horse in the chest, and was doing his best to bury his spear next in the young king.

I shouted, hoping to distract the man-at-arms. His eyes flickered to me, and went back to his target. Another lunge, and this time he did not miss. The spear entered Otto's thigh, sliding deep into the meat. Otto screamed; the man-at-arms bared his teeth in satisfaction.

He was still grinning when my blade came in sideways and took his head from his shoulders. Crimson sprayed. His grip on the spear slackened. Otto roared again.

I was turning. Turning, twisting desperately to try to prevent what I knew I could not. Too late. Another soft *click*. There was time to think how much I hated that innocuous, ball-clenchingly awful sound, and then a smith's hammer struck me in the right hip.

I stumbled, but managed not to fall. The crossbowman was ten paces away, torn between looking at me and his weapon, which he was frantically trying to reload. The pain hit, an immense explosion that burst upward from my hip and all but overwhelmed me. Knowing I was badly hurt, I made for the Frenchie, praying for the strength and the speed to reach him before the next quarrel finished what the last one had started.

Five paces I went, lurching like Rhys after a night on the wine. My enemy had the weapon spanned, and was reaching for a bolt. Agony consumed me. My strength was going fast. Seven paces, and he had the crossbow loaded. Eight. He aimed it straight at my chest, covered only by a gambeson and tunic. I was staring Death in the face. I ducked below my heater shield, which was not thick enough to stop a crossbow bolt. I took the ninth step.

Click. Punch. The quarrel drove straight through the shield. Again the smith's hammer struck me, below the ribs, but it had been robbed of some of its force. Again I staggered, but I took a tenth step and closed with the Frenchie, now holding a useless crossbow. His eyes widened. Marshalling the last of my energy, I stuck him in the guts. It was a pathetic thrust by my normal standards, but you do not have to sink a blade deep into a man to reduce him to a shrieking, bleeding child. In it went, perhaps three fingers' depth, and he screamed. I tugged it free, hoping to stab again, for I had not caused enough injury to stop him reloading for a fourth time. Before I had the chance to – to my dying day, I will never know if I would have succeeded – my ears filled with a cry of '*Dex aie!*' Hooves pounded a familiar beat.

Vision blurring, I made out the Frenchie's gaze travelling over my shoulder, and his expression becoming one of terror. He whirled about, eager only to run.

And then, with sickening speed, the ground came up to meet me.

The first thing I was aware of was pain. Pain in my chest. Pain in my right hip. Everywhere hurt, in fact. Unsure if that meant I was alive or dead, I opened my eyes. To my surprise, I could see. Above was a stone ceiling. Peeling a dry tongue off the roof of my mouth, I licked my lips. Christ Jesus, but the pain was bad.

'He moved!' A man's voice, one I did not recognise.

A face appeared over me, a kindly, middle-aged one. He had a tonsure.

'You are a monk,' I croaked.

'Indeed I am, Sir Rufus.'

'I cannot be in Hell then. Is this Heaven, or Purgatory?'

He smiled. 'You are in Dangu castle, Sir Rufus, where you have lain these two days and nights, unconscious.' He lifted a cup to my mouth. 'Drink.'

The watered-down wine tasted like nectar. I would have kept swallowing, but he soon took it away. 'More soon. You must rest first.'

'Rest?' I tried to sit up, but managed to lift one shoulder a few inches from the mattress before, dizzy headed and in exquisite amounts of pain, I had to lie back down.

Hinges creaked.

'Sire,' said the monk.

Richard came into view, bending over me, his face full of concern. 'Ferdia!'

'Sire.' Again I tried to sit up, but I was weak as a kitten, and could not stop him pushing me back, gently.

'I am glad to see you in the land of the living again. Too many hours I have spent here, not knowing if you would wake.'

I gave him a weak smile. 'Being hit by one quarrel might count as bad luck, sire, but two is plain stupid.'

'I will not chide you now about striking your king's horse so that it fled the field.' His voice was mock stern. 'Had you not done that, you would not be lying here.'

'You might be sleeping the long sleep instead, sire.'

'I know it, Ferdia, and I will not forget.'

Our eyes met. We said nothing for several moments.

'Otto, sire, is he well?'

'He will live, thanks to you, although he will travel back to Germany in a litter.'

'And the French?'

A broad smile. 'We chased them all the way to Gisors. Had it not been for the dust, the whole host would have been captured. As it was, the press of Frenchies on the bridge over the Epte was so great that it collapsed. Twenty knights drowned, maybe more. Philippe would have also, had he not been pulled from the water by some priests.' A rueful chuckle. 'The paltoner escaped me again.'

'It was a great victory nonetheless, sire.' Pain hit again, and I closed my eyes.

'Here I am, prating on, and you are unwell. Forgive me, Rufus.'

'No matter, sire.' I dreaded his answer, but I wanted to know. I found his gaze with my own. 'My injuries, are they . . .?'

'You were lucky. Brother Peter can explain better.'

A shuffle of shoe leather, and the monk reappeared beside Richard. He bent his head towards the king. 'God was holding his hand over you, Sir Rufus, truly he was. I understand from King Otto that the crossbowman was close to you.' I nodded, and he continued, 'The first quarrel glanced off your hipbone rather than breaking it, and the point came out the other side. The removal was simple. As long as the wound stays clean, you should make a good recovery.'

The excruciating throbbing at the base of my ribs framed my next question. 'And the second?'

Brother Peter made a face. 'That is of more concern, although by some miracle, the quarrel did not damage your lungs. I do not think it pierced any of your vital organs either, but we shall not know that for a while. You must have some onion soup soon.'

Dread snaked up my spine. Peter would check the injury to my belly regularly afterwards, and if the powerful odour of onions became discernible, my guts had been sliced, and I was a dead man. 'Do not let me have a soup wound,' I said, voice shaking.

'You do not.' Richard's grip on my shoulder was firm. 'God would not give my best knight such a miserable fate.'

His words filled me with pride. 'If I live, sire –'

He interrupted, fiercely. 'You will, I know it!'

I smiled, grateful for his confidence.

'Speak.'

'I have a boon to ask, sire.'

'If I can grant it, Ferdia, I will.' He looked down at me, intrigued.

'Speak to Otto on my behalf, sire.' I hesitated, and then spoke my heart's desire out loud. 'To grant his approval that I wed the lady Alienor.'

He laughed, then saw my upset. 'Peace, my friend. I am not making fun. I thought you were going to ask me for something grand. Lands, or a title, or I know not what!'

'That is all I want, sire.'

'It will be my honour to ask him.'

'Thank you, sire.' I lay back on the pillow, pleased, but suddenly weary beyond measure. I was asleep before Richard left the room.

A week later, Otto and I were taken back to Chateau Gaillard in a litter. It was either that indignity, said the king, or stay there to recuperate when he and the rest of the army left. There was no question of riding; it would be a month at least before I was fit enough for that. I cannot say I enjoyed the experience. Even with the poppy juice prescribed by Brother Peter, I felt every jolt of the journey.

My discomfort was added to by Otto's presence. Confined to the infirmary, while he recuperated in the king's quarters, I had not yet had the opportunity even to think of asking him my heartfelt desire. Now was not the best time, I concluded. Otto's drawn face showed that the litter's unpredictable motion was also causing him considerable discomfort.

If I had thought that not mentioning Alienor would avoid uncomfortable topics of conversation, I was mistaken. The young king insisted on thanking me over and again for saving his life. It had been a novice's mistake, Otto said, not to have seen the French men-at-arms playing dead. I protested, saying that I had not noticed them either, but he would not have it.

'But for you, Sir Rufus, I would have died.'

'It was nothing, sire,' I said, reddening. If only I had seen them sooner, I thought, then my grievous wounds might have been avoided. The dark mood which had been hovering wrapped itself a little closer. I tried to shake it off, telling myself that it was remarkable that I had escaped serious hurt in Richard's service until now. This truth did not make it any easier to accept the prospect of several months' recovery.

'If there is anything within my power to grant, you need but ask.'

That took me from my brooding. 'Your pardon, sire?'

Otto repeated what he had said.

Here it was, I thought, the opportunity I had longed for, handed to me on a plate. Only a fool would pass it up.

'You are most gracious, sire. Funnily, there is something I would beg of you . . .'

Weeks passed. My strength steadily returned, helped by the excellent care I received from Ralph Besace, the king's physician who had been with us at Outremer. Although I burned to return to weapons training and riding, I took his advice to crawl before I walked, and to walk before I ran. Not literally, of course. I paced my room, back and forth, the moment I could, and when strong enough, moved to the nearest staircase. Up and down I went, so many times that every brick and piece of mortar became familiar.

Rhys looked after me as if I were his own child, and Katharina, bless her, cooked day and night to ensure that I had every delicacy I desired. To my delight, Alienor visited me every day. That spoke volumes. We got on famously, thank Christ, but I was not in much state to win her heart completely, at least at first. I contented myself with trying to make her laugh, and learning everything I could about her.

She was a remarkable, strong-willed woman, who knew her own mind, and who railed against the constraints placed on her by society. 'It would have been better to have been born a man,' she sometimes said. I was never able to stop myself protesting at this. She asked why the first time, and I blushed and said because I would not have been able to lose my heart to her. Colour rose in her cheeks then, and she changed the subject. I felt encouraged, and resolved to work even harder at winning her affections.

The king came to visit every day that he was not out campaigning against Philippe. Activities in that regard would soon quieten; as Richard revealed, neither he nor the French king had infinite resources. It cost a fortune to keep an army in the field for months on end. When the garrisons of the dozens of castles were taken into account, the financial cost escalated to eyewatering levels. Philippe was at a real disadvantage here. He also had to maintain numerous castles; in addition, he was fighting a war on two fronts, in the Vexin and in Artois, against Baldwin of Flanders.

Money was not the only reason Richard wanted to close hostilities for the year. Inflamed by the huge humiliation at Gisors – twenty knights drowned, more than a hundred taken prisoner, Philippe dragged from the River Epte in the nick of time – the French had resorted to *guerre à outrance*, with no quarter asked or given. Atrocity followed atrocity, with blinding and amputating hands the new norm. Richard had rarely been one for such brutality, but pressured by his outraged captains, he had sent Mercadier and the worst of his routiers to a trade fair at Abbeville, where they slaughtered and plundered with abandon.

This was not a road that the king wished to continue on, but nor did he want to be seen to back down first, especially as he had the upper hand. It was welcome news, therefore, when in October Philippe sued for peace. He offered to return every stronghold taken from Richard in Normandy, except for Gisors. Its future would be determined by a panel of twelve local barons, half appointed by Philippe and half by Richard.

Sensing weakness, the king demanded that Baldwin and his other allies were included in the treaty. An angry Philippe refused, so Richard sat back and waited. His tactic paid off. A sennight later, with supplies, food and money running short, Philippe agreed to the terms, but only until the thirteenth of January in the new year, that of our Lord 1199.

For the moment, said Richard, this concession was enough.

CHAPTER XXX

Chateau Gaillard, January 1199

I t was dark by the time the galley reached the dock at Les Andelys, below the castle. Stars glittered in the cloudless sky, and my breath smoked before my face as I followed the king down the gangplank. Servants were waiting, holding up torches to light our path. Frost glittered on the jetty. My hip ached, as it tended to since the cold weather began. The sooner we gained the warmth of the great hall, I thought, the better.

We were returning from a meeting with Philippe, which had taken place halfway between Chateau Gaillard and Vernon. The meeting had seethed with tension throughout. First Richard refused to step ashore; in turn, the French king declined an invitation to board the English royal ship.

'What a waste of an afternoon,' said the king. 'We could have been out hawking.'

'You agreed on something at least, sire,' I said.

'A five-year truce sounds good, aye,' he growled. 'But we did not settle any of the fine detail. That bodes ill for the treaty lasting more than a few weeks.'

I exchanged a glance with de Chauvigny and Rhys. It was hard to argue with the king's logic, and even harder to know what to say.

Richard's boots crunched on the frosty planking; he strode on without speaking. Now and again, he muttered under his breath, which was never a good sign.

Into this simmering atmosphere came hurrying Pietro di Capua, the papal legate who had arrived a month prior. Smug and supercilious with everyone bar those of the highest rank – to these, he was both unctuous and obsequious – Pietro had been sent by Pope Innocent III to help Philippe and Richard reach agreement. It did not help Pietro's cause that from the outset, he showed a markedly pro-French attitude, nor that it was said of him that he was an expert in standing every argument on its head. Now clad in a fur-trimmed robe, skull cap and red calfskin shoes, he was every inch the church plenipotentiary. Most men would have been awestruck, but Richard barely gave the legate a second glance.

'Sire!' Pietro called. His high-pitched voice was at odds with his portly stature, and another reason that made it easy to dislike him. 'Welcome back, sire.'

De Chauvigny said in a low voice, 'I have no wish to stop him venturing into the lion's den. Have you?'

I shook my head. The bigger the man, the harder the fall, I thought.

'Not now,' Richard said, drawing near to Pietro.

The legate did not listen. 'How was the meeting with King Philippe, sire? Did you reach agreement?'

'Of a kind.'

Pietro clapped his hands. 'That is good news, sire, no?'

'It will not last.' Richard passed by Pietro without pause. A little surprised, the legate hurried after the king.

'It can be a start, surely, to something more, sire? Great trees from small seeds grow, as the saying goes.'

'Mayhap.' Richard's tone was growing impatient.

Pietro seemed deaf to it. 'Perhaps I could be present at the next meeting with Philippe, sire? I would be more than happy to draft the treaty between you.'

'We agreed no terms.'

Pietro looked startled. 'No terms, sire? What was agreed, then?'

'A five-year peace. That is all.'

'And when will you meet again, sire?'

'Philippe seemed unprepared to return all my possessions in Normandy, therefore I saw no merit in further negotiation.'

If Pietro did not now realise that this was an inopportune time, I thought, he was a lackwit of the first order. As I later decided, he was not stupid, just too wrapped up in his own self-importance to see what was in front of his face.

'Oh, sire, it is such a shame and such a wrong that there is such great hostility between the two of you; if things go on as they are, the holy land of Jerusalem will be lost in its entirety. For the sake of God, think of a way in which it might be returned, lest Christianity be lost.'

'I seek nothing less than I am entitled to,' said Richard. 'If a truce were possible under the terms of which I suffered no loss, or saw my estate diminished, I would be very keen on it, and agree to it on a permanent basis. Tell me the form it will take; I shall hear it and put the wrong interpretation on the terms you cite, if only it can come about; indeed, I shall be most happy to abide by them.'

'Sire, in truth, no man can have all he would like to have.' Incredibly, Pietro's tone was reprimanding. 'Things do not happen like that; rather, let each hold what he has, and let the truce be sworn on those terms.'

'May such a truce never endure! What is this you are saying? It seems to me that you have gone back on everything you said before.' Pietro had agreed to Richard's insistence on retrieving all the castles lost to Philippe. 'It is a shameful matter when a worthy man contradicts himself, when he lies and cheats. Are you trying to pull the wool over my eyes? Philippe has my castles and land, and here you come asking me to let him have free possession of them!'

'Please! For the sake of God, please, fair lord. You really ought to bear in mind the plight of the Christians in Outremer. They suffer daily indignities at the hands of the accursed race, the Saracens, while you think only of a petty quarrel with Philippe. What are a few castles in Normandy beside Jerusalem, the holiest shrine in Christendom?'

Without knowing, Pietro had placed a lit taper in a ready-to-burn bonfire. Stopping dead, so that we had to also, Richard erupted. 'You forget yourself! Philippe left me in the Holy Land, to shoulder the whole burden of the fight against Saladin, and this while he skulked back to plot and scheme, and to steal my lands and castles. But for him, I would have retaken Jerusalem long ago!'

Pietro's yellow face had drained of colour. 'Sire, I –'

'Silence! I am not finished! When I came back from Outremer, what protection did the Church offer me then?'

Pietro shook his head in mute acceptance, and I thought he had learned his lesson.

Richard stalked on, and the legate hurried after him.

De Chauvigny, Rhys and I followed.

'You have made your opinion on the war against the Saracens clear, sire, but there is another matter of concern,' said Pietro.

'He is determined, I will give him that,' whispered Rhys, the corners of his mouth twitching. He knew as well as I how the king would react if provoked further.

'Oh yes,' said Richard, his tone clipped and curt, 'and what is that?'

'The Bishop of Beauvais, sire, whom I believe languishes even now – quite wrongly and unjustly – in a dungeon below this very castle.'

'God's legs!' roared the king. 'The sun will rise in the west ere I release that treacherous robber!'

'He is an anointed bishop –'

'Upon my soul, he is not! He has been deconsecrated, and is a false Christian. It was not as a bishop he was taken captive but as a knight of great reputation, fully armed and with his helmet laced. I can tell you, Sir Hypocrite, that were it not for your role as envoy, Rome would not prevent me from giving you such a hiding to take back to the Pope as would engrave my deeds on his mind.'

'Sire, I –' Pietro's voice was shaking.

His rage now out of control, Richard shouted, 'And as for the Pope! Did he raise a finger to help me when I was in prison? And now he asks me to free a robber and arsonist who has never done me anything but harm! Get out of here, traitor, liar, and bought-and-paid-for so-called churchman! Take care that I never see you before me on field or on the open road!'

Pietro turned and fled, so anxious to get away from the king's wrath that he left a calfskin shoe behind on the jetty.

Having kicked the shoe into the river, Richard stormed on towards the castle.

None of us dared to go near him. As Rhys said, it would have been less dangerous to approach a wild boar wounded by the huntsman. There was no need either, I decided. Pietro was gone, and the king's temper would blow over. It always did.

When William Marshal heard what had happened, he declared he would speak with Richard, who had stormed off to his bedroom.

'On your own head be it,' I warned Marshal.

Afterwards, I wondered if I should have tried, because incredibly, Marshal managed to talk to the king. He even persuaded Richard to accept Philippe's terms, those advised by Pietro, that he accept the loss of his castles in Normandy. It was not that simple, of course. Invest the castles closely, as Richard had previously talked about, and they would soon become mill weights around Philippe's neck. They would surrender one by one, Marshal advised, giving the king what was his by another route. Richard saw the wisdom in that; perhaps he always had. It was not impossible that his rage had been part act, part real, and that agreeing to Philippe's terms was what he would have done anyway.

At the time, though, I had more on my mind. Relations with Alienor had been steadily improving. We spent every possible hour in each other's company, walking, talking, laughing. In privacy, we kissed, often, and caressed as much. We had professed our love for one another more than once, and on several occasions, taken physical matters further, although we had not lain together. I do not know if she would have, but I did not push for it. Keep the best until last, went the saying.

More than once, curious, Otto had asked if I had put the question to Alienor. I had answered him honestly, no, because I was not sure if she would say yes. If I did not ask, I would never know, the youthful king had teased me. Ah, but it was easy for him, I thought, who had never known love and lost it, as I had. Truth be told, I was wary of rejection. The hurt from my love affair with Joanna not long healed, and recently recovered from serious physical injury, I could not bear the thought of fresh agony.

Now, though, I had to act, if I was not to lose Alienor forever. Otto had stayed at Chateau Gaillard for the Christmas festivities, and then to see how Richard's meeting with Philippe would unfold. With his injury healed, he could no longer delay returning to his kingdom, from which messengers came more and more often. He was due to depart two days hence. Alienor would leave with him, and the prospects of seeing each other again after that were slim indeed.

Making my excuses, I left de Chauvigny in the great hall. Then, without even taking off my cloak, I went in search of her. Guessing that she would be with the other ladies who resided in the castle, I was crossing the courtyard when by happy chance I saw her coming towards me. As ever, her beauty struck me like a blow. I never tired of the feeling.

'My lady,' I called.

'I thought it was you, Ferdia. You are back.'

'Aye, just now.' I grimaced.

'It did not go well, then?' Like everyone in the castle, she knew that the king had gone to meet Philippe.

I told her the sorry tale, including Pietro's intervention, and how it had been received. She pealed with laughter at that. 'I wish I had been there!'

'It was worth seeing,' I said, chuckling.

'And the king really kicked Pietro's shoe into the river?'

'Aye.'

'Is that what you came hotfoot to tell me?' As ever, she had put her finger on the pulse.

'It is not,' I said.

'You were chilled, and needed to warm up, is that it?'

'No,' I said. 'Walk with me, if you would.' I took her hand, and unresisting, without demanding to know why, she let me guide her up onto the battlements. I found shelter from the bitter cold in the lee of a guard tower, which was fortunately unoccupied. I had no wish to be eavesdropped upon.

I wrapped my arms around her, and she leaned into my embrace. Sweet Jesu, but it felt good. After a moment, she leaned back a little, and stared up into my face. 'You did not ask me up here for privacy, Ferdia, for we might have that in your chamber, or for warmth, because despite your cloak and mine, it will not be long before we freeze.'

I bent and kissed her.

She pulled back, but not quickly. 'That is not why we are here either.' She poked me in the chest with a finger. 'What is it?'

'Alienor, I love you. I do not want you to leave.'

Her gaze met mine. 'My heart is also sore at the thought. I serve King Otto, however. When he goes, so must I.'

'Not if . . .' I hesitated, and then pulling away from the embrace, got down on one knee, uncaring of the freezing cold stone. 'Not if you will have me as your husband.'

For once, words failed her.

'Alienor, will you marry me?'

She did not immediately reply, and my heart stopped.

Smiling, she gave me a gentle cuff round the head. 'I thought you would never ask.'

'So you will?'

'Yes. Yes. Of course!'

I thought I would explode with joy.

CHAPTER XXXI

Châlus-Chabrol, near Limoges, Aquitaine, late March 1199

The afternoon was failing, and I was standing outside my tent in Richard's camp, which lay several hundred paces from the small castle. Like everywhere in Aquitaine, there was woodland close by. At this distance, the trees seemed bare still, a sad shade of brown, but I had ridden through them earlier in the day, and seen enough tiny green buds to take heart. Winter was long, but it was retreating before the imminent arrival of spring. As if to prove it, the temperature was a great deal more pleasant than in Normandy, far to the north.

If fortune favoured us, I would be back in Chateau Gaillard to enjoy the April sunshine with Alienor, my wife. The thought of her warmed my heart. We had wed after my night-time proposal. As I had said, after so long, there was no reason not to act straightaway, and laughing, Alienor had agreed. Watched by the king, Rhys and Katharina, and my close companions of the household, we were married two days later by a priest in the castle's chapel.

It was, and would remain, in my opinion, the happiest day of my life.

A month of wedded bliss had followed. Although there were breaches of the truce between Richard and Philippe in February, none were serious enough to merit the king riding forth from Chateau Gaillard.

It was not to last.

In late February, the ever-troublesome Count of Angoulême and the Viscount of Limoges had again raised the flag of rebellion in Aquitaine. Mercadier was sent south to deal with them, and on the way fell afoul of a band of renegade routiers. It seemed too much of a coincidence that the ambush had nothing to do with Philippe, although he denied it, and the aggression weakened the already fragile peace.

By the beginning of March, Richard had decided to travel south and join Mercadier. He could not help himself. Naturally, I went with him;

Rhys did too. Had it not been for their two-year-old son, Katharina would have accompanied us too. We had not been three days on the road when a messenger brought word that Philippe was up to new tricks. Aware that the king had left, he had ordered the construction of a new castle on the Seine between Gaillon and Les Andelys. At just eight miles from Chateau Gaillard, it was a direct challenge to Richard. A slap in the face, the king called it.

In response, he sent an official letter straight to Philippe. Any work completed was to be demolished at once. Fail to do so, the message baldly stated, and the truce was at an end. The tactic worked. By the time we reached Chinon, the same messenger – gaunt-faced with exhaustion – had returned with the French king's sulky reply. Philippe could not help stirring the pot, however. Even as he agreed to cease castle-building, his letter accused Richard's brother John of again switching sides, and re-joining the French camp. He had even sent accompanying documents that purported to confirm John's treachery. Although they had been less than convincing, it had reawakened old, perhaps-never-quite-healed distrust.

'Ho, Rufus! A penny for your thoughts.' It was the king.

'Sire, I . . .' Caught on the spot, unwilling to admit my dark thoughts about John, I struggled for a reply.

'You were thinking about your beautiful wife, or I am no judge.' Richard was clad in a dark-blue tunic with matching hose. His golden curls were covered by a simple helm. He had a heavyweight crossbow and quarrels with him. It was his afternoon ritual to wander around the perimeter of our blockade, taking pot-shots at the defenders. I often accompanied him, making sure that he stayed out of harm's way. It was not his habit to wear armour, nor to take kindly to my suggestions that he do so.

'You are shrewd, sire.' I smiled.

'It will not be long ere you are reunited. This place' – he gestured at the walls of Châlus – 'will soon fall. Nontron will be next.'

My eyes were drawn to our objective. By common agreement, the garrison numbered in the region of fifty, and in all likelihood, was fewer than that. We, on the other hand, had almost two thousand knights, men-at-arms and archers. Despite this overwhelming numerical advantage, and the diminutive size of Châlus, the castle was proving difficult to take. The defenders were resolute, and the fortifications well-built and thick. Travelling fast and light meant that we had no wall-breaking catapults, so Richard had had to order his sappers to undermine the defences. The process had thus far taken two days, and achieved limited success. Part of the walls had tumbled into the ditch, but not enough to allow our men to venture an assault. We could have starved the garrison into submission, of course, but the impatient king refused to wait. Besiege every rebel-held stronghold, he declared, and we would still be in Aquitaine at Christmas.

'What think you, Rufus?'

I coughed, unwilling to admit that I would rather have been with Alienor, the love of my life. Strange and wondrous though it was, she had filled my heart even more than Joanna. 'The campaign will take as long as it takes, sire,' I said eventually.

'It will be short! The rest of Adémar's strongholds will surrender when the defenders here capitulate. Or maybe it will be after Nontron falls.' He thumped my arm. 'After that, we can return to Chateau Gaillard.'

'Am I that easy to see through, sire?' Chuckling, he gestured that I should walk with him. Snatching up a rectangular shield, I obeyed.

'You are better than you were, Rufus, but I have known you long enough. I saw your face in the church when you were looking at Alienor. She is your world, I see that.' I went to protest, but he clouted me, one of his marks of affection. 'Peace. It is a good thing. Some critics would say that I should show the same love for Berengaria, that if I did, I might have had a son long since.'

It was unlike Richard to be so frank, I thought, wondering what had him in such ruminative mood. I felt his eyes on me, and said, 'That is not my business, sire.'

'Nor is it, Rufus, but I need an heir. Johnny, it seems, is ever to be the traitor.'

That was what was on his mind, I decided. It was more than possible that Philippe's accusation was false, but his allegation had fallen as rain on seedlings. Richard's response had been instantaneous; all of John's property had been seized.

'At least he has not fled to Paris, sire,' I said, not even understanding why I was mounting a defence of John, whom I intensely disliked.

'That is true. His denial of the allegations was also robust.' Richard looked troubled. 'Mayhap he is loyal after all.'

'Time will tell, sire.'

'Indeed it will, and in the meantime, the task of finding another heir –' there was a tiny pause before he added – 'or begetting one of my own, should not be forgotten.'

'There is Arthur, sire.' He was the son of Richard's dead brother Geoffrey.

'Aye, but can his mother be trusted?' Geoffrey's wife Constance had made overtures to Philippe in the past.

'Who knows, sire?' Even after this long, I was wary of voicing an opinion against someone who was part of the extended royal household, and in truth, I had no idea about Constance's loyalty or disloyalty.

'I do not, and that is for certes.' Richard shook his head, as if clearing it. 'I should make things right with Berengaria. She is not yet too old to bear a child.'

I said nothing, instead letting my gaze wander along the ramparts. Not a defender was to be seen, which did not surprise me. By the king's order, crossbowmen and archers were on duty from dawn to dusk. Anyone foolish enough to show themselves was subjected to relentless volleys of quarrels and arrows. The defenders appeared from time to time when our sappers were at work, some protecting the rest as they lobbed rocks down on our men, but with darkness looming, our efforts for the day had ceased, and so had theirs. Like as not, I thought, they were doing the same as our soldiers: sitting around their fires, drinking and hungrily eyeing pots of simmering stew.

'Can you spy anyone, Rufus?'

'Not a soul, sire.' Nonetheless, I had the shield ready to throw up in front of the king. For the thousandth time, I wished he would wear his armour. He had taken us to within fifty paces of the walls, easily within the killing range of a crossbow.

We continued our circumnavigation of the walls, Richard taking the salutes and grins of our soldiers with an easy grace. He called out several names, congratulating men-at-arms on their efforts, and agreeing with their declarations that the castle would fall the following day. I was well-used to the king's skill, but it never failed to impress. Each man he spoke with was visibly delighted; he would tell his comrades, who, encouraged, would make greater efforts to win their lord's approval.

Before long, we had come back to our starting position.

'There will be no sport tonight.' Richard sounded disappointed.

'No, sire.' I was relieved.

The king threw a last glance over his shoulder. 'Ha!'

At his cry, I turned, spotting a familiar figure.

'It is Sir Frying Pan!'

Our men had given the affectionate if sarcastic title to the soldier, who bore a frying pan in place of a shield, and used a crossbow to poor effect. As we watched, one of our soldiers shot a bolt at him, which he neatly deflected with his pan.

Richard applauded.

Sir Frying Pan's head turned.

'He sees us,' said the king, spanning his weapon.

'There is a comrade with him, sire,' I said, thinking that two crossbowmen were far more dangerous than one. I stepped in front of Richard, shield at the ready. 'It is poor light for shooting, sire. Can you not try again tomorrow?'

'You are no sport, Rufus! There is time for one essay at least.' The king waited as Sir Frying Pan and his companion paced along the rampart.

Uncomfortable with the situation – we had now strayed to within forty paces of the wall – I glanced back and forth, towards our enemies and then at the king, trying to make sure I was presenting the biggest target possible.

'Sir Frying Pan!' Richard's shout carried through the darkening air.

The first figure lifted his crossbow in reply, and came to a stop opposite us. He set down his frying pan. The second man was already loading a quarrel. Something about him was familiar, but I was so concerned about the king that I had no time to dwell on it.

Tense, making sure I was in front of Richard, and acutely aware that I had no helmet, I dropped down behind my shield so that only my eyes showed. It would take a miracle for either of the pair to hit me, I told myself. My gaze went from Sir Frying Pan to the second man, who had a block for a head. Old memories stirred. I squinted.

'God's legs, what I would give for more light!'

I shot a look at Richard. He was two steps behind me. The crossbow was up and ready, and he was peering down the quarrel, almost over my shoulder. He had enough protection, I decided.

Click. One of the Frenchies had taken a shot.

The sound made my skin crawl, as always. Air moved. A bolt went past on my left. It was difficult to know how close it had been. *Click*. The second bolt thunked into the ground three feet to my right.

'Curse it, I cannot make them out well enough,' said the king.

To my alarm, he walked around me, several paces closer to the walls. 'No, sire, please!' I hissed, terrified in case our enemies heard and realised who they were aiming at, and also because Richard was now out in the open.

Click. The king shot.

No sound of contact with stone, metal or flesh reached us. An instant later, we heard a skittering noise as the quarrel landed somewhere within the castle.

Quickly, I moved in front of Richard again. 'Stay behind me, sire, *please*,' I whispered.

'I cannot see with you in my way, Rufus.'

'It is too dark to shoot, sire. Do not waste your bolts.'

He snorted, and before I could react, stepped out from the protection of my shield. He had the crossbow already raised to his shoulder.

Click.

Click.

Click.

The sound of the three triggers came within a single heartbeat.

I did not hear where Richard's quarrel went this time, because my ears filled with his bitten-back gasp of pain. My head turned; he was staggering sideways.

Clawing back panic, I raced to put myself before him again, lest the cursed pair on the ramparts loose more bolts. 'Are you hit, sire?' I hissed.

'Aye.' Richard's voice was strained, but he had regained his balance. 'We had best get back to my tent. I can walk – do not try to help. The men must not see.'

'Sire.' Facing the castle, my shield high, I followed him. It was not difficult; he was moving like an arthritic greybeard. Oddly, as if they were satisfied with one hit, the crossbowmen did not shoot again, and so at four score paces out, I risked a look at the king.

Cold, sickening fear swelled in my chest. The quarrel had struck Richard in the angle between neck and left shoulder. Short of a direct hit in the chest or belly, I could think of few worse places. I threw up fervent prayers, offering God daily Masses for the rest of my life, all my riches, anything that would see the king's injury as mild. Beneath my passion, however, I was fighting pure panic.

Richard's breath was hissing between his teeth; now and again, he paused for a moment, to regain his strength. When I dropped the shield and tried to take his arm over my shoulders, he shoved me away with his good hand. 'Pick it up! No one must see that I am hurt.'

I obeyed. It was bitter medicine to walk behind the man I had served for half my life, unable to help him, as his pace grew slower and slower.

It was small solace that no one came close as we wove our way into the camp. No one, that is, save Rhys, who had been waiting for me to return. Looming out of the dusk, he took in what had happened at one glance. Richard barely noticed him. Rhys darted to my side.

'Find Mercadier's surgeon, quickly,' I muttered, wishing instead for Ralph Besace. He was far away, though, in Chateau Gaillard.

The sentries outside the king's tent were shocked by the king's appearance, but they understood my savagely gestured finger to my lips. So did Richard's squire, a sturdy lad by the name of Henry. Dropping the shield, I helped the king over the threshold. He did not protest. Indeed, it was my strength that brought us to the stool he favoured when we sat around the campfire.

He sagged down on it with a loud sigh of relief. 'God's legs, but it hurts.' His hand came up to the bolt.

'Sire, leave it,' I urged. 'The surgeon will be here soon.'

'Fetch my dagger, Henry.' A weak wave at the chest which held his weapons. 'And clean it in some wine.'

The squire scurried to obey.

'Fetch me light, Rufus,' Richard commanded.

The surgeon would need them to work, I told myself, lighting several bowl oil lamps. 'And bandaging, Henry,' I directed.

'Cut away my tunic and shirt, Rufus,' said the king.

I did it, using my own knife. My stomach turned over as the blood-sodden fabric came away. The injury was even worse than I had thought. The quarrel had driven in at least four inches, perhaps more. I said nothing to the king.

'And my mirror.'

I handed him the polished disc of silver. He held it up with his right hand, wincing. 'Light. I need light.'

I took up two oil lamps and brought them close to the mirror. My eyes went from the king's face, which was almost entirely shorn of colour, to the bolt.

'Well?' Richard was no longer staring at the mirror, but me.

'It is bad, sire.' I could not say any more.

The king tugged on the shaft, which made him grind his teeth in agony, and shifted it not at all.

Now my spirits plummeted. The quarrel had a barbed head.

'The dagger, sire.' Henry's voice was cracking; he had seen too.

Richard exchanged the mirror for the blade. 'Hold it up, Henry.'

'Sire, please wait for the surgeon,' I said. 'You cannot see well enough to remove it yourself.'

'You can. Will you do it?' The dagger was thrust in my face.

'I am no surgeon, sire. Mercadier's man is. If you will just –'

'If you will not do it, curse you, hold the lamps!'

Gritting my teeth, I held them as close to the mirror as I could. The king did not hesitate. Somehow grasping the end of the quarrel with his left hand – which made him cry out – he mastered his pain and brought the tip of the dagger down towards the point where wooden shaft met flesh.

'There?'

I stared. Prayed. 'Yes, sire.'

He eased the point in, unable now to stop himself gasping, and worked the steel from side to side. Blood flowed. The quarrel moved, but did not come away. Richard's arm dropped. Sweat was running down his face; he was breathing fast, like a trapped wild beast. The dagger dropped to the floor.

'Well?' he demanded, panting.

I made a pretence of inspecting the wound. 'It has not moved, sire. The head is buried quite deeply. Perhaps it is caught under your collarbone.'

His lips peeled back in a snarl of fury, and before I could stop him, he reached up towards his shoulder. With a convulsive tug, he wrenched at the shaft. There was a cracking, splintering sound. He gasped in pain. His hand came away.

'I have it!' Richard sounded weak, but triumphant.

My gaze moved from the length of iron that jutted from the ghastly wound to Henry, whose face, I judged, was even more horrified than my own.

'Well?' The king's eyes were closed.

I searched for my voice; it came out as a dry croak. 'The shaft broke, sire.'

His right hand, covered in blood, came up to chest level, but he did not have the strength to take it any higher. It fell back by his side. Richard's eyes, which had opened, closed again.

'Sir!' Henry hissed. He was pointing at the king's wound.

Horror filled me. Richard's efforts had started fresh bleeding. Small vessels sprayed crimson everywhere: down the king's chest and arm, onto my hose, on the floor. 'Give me those bandages!' Taking a wad from Henry, I laid them around the quarrel as gently as I could, and then pressed down.

A deep, animal sound came from Richard.

'I am sorry, sire,' I said.

He did not respond.

Commanding Henry to also go in search of Mercadier's surgeon, I kept pressure on the wound and did my best to remain calm. The king would come through this, I told myself. He had been ill so many times before, with quartan fever and battle wounds. He was as strong as a lion. It would take more than a crossbow bolt to kill Richard.

Henry returned almost at once, with a grim-faced surgeon and Rhys close behind. I had no idea of the man's ability, but Mercadier was not one to suffer fools lightly. I stood aside and let him do what he could.

The surgeon's examination caused Richard to lapse into complete unconsciousness. It was better so, said the surgeon, and I agreed. We laid out the king on his bed, and arrayed a dozen oil lamps close by.

A lot of blood flowed as the surgeon worked with probes and a thin, razor-sharp knife. He swore profusely and exquisitely under his breath, a long litany of blasphemies I will not repeat, but he succeeded. The quarrel's head came out in a torrent of blood, which I hurried to stem with fresh bandages. It seemed an eternity before the surgeon declared the haemorrhaging to have stopped. He mixed up a thick paste, using betony, comfrey and woundwort, and applied it to the ruin that had been Richard's shoulder, before, with my help, strapping up the whole area.

I stepped away from the king, drained as if I had run ten miles in my hauberk.

'Well?' I demanded.

The surgeon used the back of his arm to wipe his forehead clear of sweat. In its place, he left a long red trail of blood. 'I have done my best.'

I was by his side in a heartbeat. 'Will he live?' I said into his ear.

The up-down of his shoulders was like the knell of doom, and his words, 'It is in God's hands now', afforded no ease either.

So fearful was I for the king's life, I almost threatened the surgeon with gelding, but I held my peace. It was not his fault that Richard had made his job twice as hard by breaking the shaft of the quarrel, and besides, the killer Mercadier was his master. And so I slumped to the floor by the king's bed, uncaring that my arms and hands were crusty with dried blood, and prayed like I had never done in my life.

I had no idea if my pleas would help – I had scant evidence in my life that such appeals made any difference – but I had to ask. Almighty God had the power to do whatever He wished. There were few people in the world as important as the king of England, I thought. Surely God will see that.

My prayers uttered, with the king mercifully still asleep, I found my mind casting back to the figure who had been with Sir Frying Pan. Few men had such a square, block head. Could it be my old enemy, FitzAldelm?

In the years since he had given me and Rhys the slip in Rouen, I had heard nothing of him but vague rumours. It was said that he appeared now and again in Normandy, making overtures on behalf of Philippe Capet to nobles whose loyalty to Richard was in question. There had also been tales of him at the court of the Holy Roman Emperor, and reports once that he had met with the Count of Toulouse. It was far from clear if any of the stories were reliable, but as I had said to Rhys more than once, their nature suggested that FitzAldelm worked for the French king as a spy or an envoy, or both.

My mind raced on. It was possible that FitzAldelm had been sent to engage with Adémar of Angoulême. The figure I had seen might be him, but I had no idea what he was doing at Châlus. The next thought hit with the force of a winter storm. Had FitzAldelm's quarrel hit the king?

Like a furnace stoked to fresh flame by a bellows, my hatred for him came flooding back. I climbed to my feet and checked on Richard. To my relief, he was sleeping peacefully. I touched his hand, and told Henry, sitting close by like a faithful hound, that I would be back soon.

I went in search of Rhys. He needed to know.

CHAPTER XXXII

By the following morning, Richard had rallied somewhat, enough to have me and de Chauvigny give him an account of our men's positions, and the state of the castle's defences. He gave orders for our force to be split up, and men sent to invest the nearby stronghold of Nontron. The campaign to subdue Adémar had to continue, he said. Richard would have risen from his bed to command the assault had not I and de Chauvigny insisted he remain in his tent. When the surgeon came and we told him, he also beseeched the king to rest. 'You must, sire, if you are to get better.'

Richard had grimaced then and, when the surgeon had gone, ordered that his mother be summoned from Fontevrault. Catching my look at de Chauvigny, he had muttered, 'Just in case, you understand.'

I gave de Chauvigny another look. He was as worried by the king's condition as I, but we did not speak about it. Voicing our concern would make it real, and if we kept silent, it might go away. So went my scrambled thinking.

I did not mention FitzAldelm to the king. He was too ill to be burdened with extra worries, I decided, and I was still not certain that my enemy was inside Châlus. I had set Rhys to watching the defenders; I might find out that way. If not, when the castle fell, as fall it would, and FitzAldelm was among the prisoners taken, I could drag him in front of Richard. That was, I thought darkly, if I could prevent myself from slitting the cur's throat on the spot. My white-hot desire for revenge came not so much from our old feud, but because his quarrel might have been the one to mortally wound the king.

A rope snapped on our best catapult that day, reducing our artillerymen's ability to damage the walls. The sappers did better, working with a ferocious energy. I had no doubt that their efforts were a direct response to the king's injury. Even though we had made no announcement, and sworn Richard's sentries to secrecy, trying to prevent the grave news from spreading was akin to preventing water leaking from a sieve. There were worried faces everywhere in the camp, and men had taken to lingering near the royal tent, hopeful for news.

Châlus had not fallen by the day's end, and Richard remained stable. The surgeon examined his wound, and pronounced that he could see no signs of putrefaction. Watching over his shoulder, my nerves in shreds, I was pathetically grateful to see none of the tell-tale signs either. We summoned the local priest and ordered him to have Masses said for the king.

I slept little, plagued by dark dreams of Richard dying, John triumphant and FitzAldelm escaping yet again. Unsettlingly, of Alienor there was no sign. I bottled up my foul temper, and went to see the king. I had spent the first night on the floor by his bed, but he had commanded me to my own tent after that, telling me he was not a child in need of cosseting.

Richard's face was gaunt, and a sheen of sweat marked his forehead, but he was alert. He listened to Mercadier and me setting out our plans to seize the castle, and ordered us to get the task done. And so that day went, and the next. I worked with the sappers, as if by placing myself into danger and working until every sinew groaned, I could forget the king's condition. Dust-covered and sweat-drenched by nightfall, I would go and report to Richard.

I came to dread seeing him, and lacerated myself with guilt for feeling this way. I felt even greater shame that I did not wish myself in the king's place, as I once would have done. The thought of life with Alienor was too precious.

Each day, the king sank further. He slept most of the time. The wound in his shoulder had putrefied, and the flesh around it was a furious deep red. A smell of decay permeated his tent, a stench that was all too familiar. If anyone spoke the word 'gangrene', however, it was whispered.

The surgeon dosed Richard with tinctures of this and solutions of that, and checked his urine twice daily. He was going through the motions. Mercadier had to be stopped from torturing the poor man in an effort to achieve what was to all intents and purposes a miracle cure.

On the fourth evening since he had been shot, Richard awoke as I entered. His lips curved upward. 'Rufus.' His tone was tremulous, a husk of what it usually was.

'Sire.' My own voice cracked, traitor that it was.

'Sit by me.' His right hand patted the coverlet, an indication to approach.

I obeyed, trying not to smell the foul odour that increased as I drew near. His eyeballs were deep-sunken, and his skin had a new, greyish tinge. It was the pallor of a corpse. I had seen it on countless men before, and not a single one had survived. Miserable, I perched on a stool, and gazed into Richard's eyes. This was the man I had followed and served for seventeen years, whom I loved as a brother. Who was dying in the worst possible manner imaginable.

'I am here, sire,' I said.

'Rufus. Ferdia.'

Tears welled. I could no more stop them than fly to the moon. I nodded.

'Do not weep. I am not done yet.'

I wiped the arm of my tunic across my face, and pulled my lips upward. 'Yes, sire.'

'How goes the siege? I have heard no sounds of battle, nor cheering.'

'The castle stills hold out, sire, but we will have a breach by the morning. The sappers are sure of it.'

He smiled, but his eyes were closed. 'I would meet the man who killed a king. Sir . . . Frying Pan.'

'It might not have been him, sire. There was another crossbowman, remember?'

No answer.

I had to say it. 'I think the second man was FitzAldelm, sire.'

This made Richard stir. There was a spark now in his previously dull eyes. 'Robert FitzAldelm?'

I quietly laid out my theory. Finishing, I had almost convinced myself that a fever had taken hold of me, as it had the king. 'I was probably imagining it, sire.'

His hand seized mine. It had more strength than before. 'I do not think so. When Châlus falls, bring him to me.'

'I will, sire, on my soul.'

'Good. Now, have my scribe come hither. Letters must be written. To Johnny, to William Marshal, to the various archbishops. My seneschals will need instruction as well.'

'Sire, is it wise to spread the news of your –' I flailed for the word – 'illness,' I finished.

A little chuckle. 'I did not come down with the last rain shower, Rufus. I will send orders only. No one outside this camp can know my fate, until Johnny at least is safely out of Brittany. I would not have my mother lose two sons in quick succession.'

His words made clear that his reasoning remained sound – if the unhappy nobles in Brittany heard of Richard's demise, they might capture or kill John, in order to curry favour with Philippe Capet.

'Go to, Rufus.'

I obeyed, dumbfounded by Richard's ease, his unconcerned manner. I was doubtful that I could act so, lying on my deathbed.

Rhys was waiting outside the tent. I saw by his face that he had news. We walked away, lest the sentries overhear.

'How is the king?' he asked.

'Still alive, somehow.'

Rhys had always been blunt. 'How long?'

'I have no idea. I pray that his lady mother arrives before –' I could not say the words. I cleared my throat. 'Have you something to tell me?'

'Aye. I saw FitzAldelm not long since, on the battlements with Sir Frying Pan.'

I pinned him with my gaze. 'You are sure?'

'I could not be more certain.'

'He is mine to kill, remember?'

Rhys grimaced. 'I would say the king takes precedence.'

My lips quirked at his riposte. 'That is true. Neither of us have need for concern then. I cannot see Richard granting clemency.'

We were able to take some comfort in that.

Rhys and I stood poised, eager as leashed hounds with the scent of the prey fresh in our nostrils. It was mid-morning on the first of April, and a section of the walls had just collapsed, the sound thundering in the chill spring air. The great cloud of dust sent up was gradually settling, revealing the damage.

'The breach – look, it is large enough!' I pointed.

Men were cheering, clapping each other on the back.

'They have to surrender now,' said Rhys.

'Aye,' I growled, imagining FitzAldelm's surprise when he saw me.

A short time afterwards, as our knights and men-at-arms were massing for an assault on the gaping hole in the walls, the front gate was opened. Out walked a man-at-arms bearing a white staff and standard. Although these marked him out as a herald, his face was as pasty as week-old whey when he was brought in front of me and Mercadier.

Châlus was ours, he said, his voice shaking.

'As it was before we arrived, you dog!' Mercadier had a white-knuckled grip on his bollock dagger.

The herald blanched further.

I laid a hand on Mercadier's arm, and he subsided a fraction. I said to the herald, 'The garrison will march outside immediately, without their weapons. Go!'

Eager to be away from Mercadier, he went as fast as his feet could carry him.

The defenders began to emerge almost at once. They must have realised, I muttered to Rhys, that delaying any further risked cutting the fragile thread from which their fates hung.

Rhys counted them one by one. 'Thirty-six men and three women,' he said in disgust as the raggletaggle group neared us. 'The king is going to die because of thirty-nine fools.'

'We should crucify them all.' Mercadier's tone was matter-of-fact.

He would do it too, I thought. 'The king has given no such order,' I said, returning Mercadier's hard stare.

'What do you care for these Aquitanian scum, and whether they die on a cross or swing from a rope?' he retorted.

'Two men only I want to see held responsible for their actions: Sir Frying Pan and the man who was with him,' I said. 'The others were following orders, no more. It is not their fault that Richard lies dying.'

Mercadier did not like it, but pre-empting his ruthless tendencies, I had made sure that more of the king's men-at-arms were present than his routiers. There was little he could do.

The garrison came to a halt before us. There were perhaps twenty men-at-arms and almost that number of stable hands, cooks and lowly castle staff. Three men had surcoats, marking them as knights. One was FitzAldelm. When he saw me, his jaw fell open. I did not acknowledge him in any way – I would not give him the satisfaction – but by my side, Rhys was bristling like a mastiff in the fighting pit.

A short, balding man in a well-cut tunic stepped forward. 'I am Bertrand de Gurdon, the seneschal of Châlus. I throw myself and the lives of my men upon the mercy of King Richard.' He looked at me and Mercadier, clearly unsure who had precedence.

'Is this everyone?' snarled Mercadier.

A wary nod. 'Every last soul.'

'Where is Sir Frying Pan?' I demanded, and when de Gurdon gave me a blank look, I added, 'The man who uses a frying pan for a shield.'

'Pierre,' called de Gurdon over his shoulder.

The individual who came forward was unremarkable in every way. Of average height, with short-cropped brown hair, and wearing a sweat-stained gambeson, he could have been any one of the thousands of men-at-arms I had seen over the years. He glanced at me warily, and then stared at his muddied boots. 'I am Pierre Basile,' he mumbled.

'The man with the frying pan?' Mercadier spoke through clenched teeth.

He did not look up. 'Yes.'

'Who was with you on the walls four nights ago?' Mercadier's voice was sibilant, and laden with menace. 'You were both shooting crossbows.'

Basile gave us a confused look. 'Several men have been with me.'

'This one has a block-shaped head,' I said, staring at FitzAldelm.

Basile twisted around to look at my enemy, who was already coming forward.

'I was with him on the night in question,' said FitzAldelm, adding with a sneer, 'It has been a long time, Rufus.'

My temper threatening to burst its banks, I cried, 'Seize them!'

De Gurdon looked on, not understanding, as Rhys and half a dozen men-at-arms swarmed forward. I said nothing to prevent the initial punches and kicks that rained in. Only when FitzAldelm and Basile crumpled to the ground beneath the hail of blows did I intervene. 'Harm them no more,' I ordered. 'Let us to the king.'

I led the way with Mercadier. Then came FitzAldelm, and Basile, their arms held tight by men-at-arms. Rhys was right behind the former, and, I thought, probably with a dagger pressed into the small of FitzAldelm's back. It would be quite the trial for him not to slide it home before we reached our destination.

There had not been time for word of the two captives to spread, but men quickly guessed who we were hurrying to the royal tent. Before long, a furious mob hemmed us in on either side, and then blocked our way. Curses were hurled by the dozen, and requests made for God to strike them down. A grizzled archer stepped in front of Basile, and with exquisite precision, hawked a great gob of phlegm into his face. When another did the same to FitzAldelm, he got back a look that would have killed. The soldier just laughed. He did back away, however, when I roared at him.

'Harm these men, and you will suffer the king's justice,' I announced in a loud voice. A path opened; resentful faces stared at us from close range as we pushed by.

'You will pay for what you have done!' shouted a man-at-arms who had served Richard for more than a decade. 'Murderers!'

If they had not suspected their plight before, or who they had injured, Basile and FitzAldelm did now – real fear crept over both their faces.

My mind was racing. After so long, FitzAldelm was in my grasp, and yet he was not. He was the king's prisoner, not mine. Richard alone would decide his fate. I decided that he would not grant FitzAldelm and Basile a death-bed clemency, a sop to ease his path into Heaven. No, FitzAldelm would get the fate he deserved. Little Jean would be avenged at last.

Into Richard's tent Mercadier and I went, leaving the prisoners outside. Incense burned in a brazier, but it could not mask the cloying stench. It took real effort not to constantly gag. The squire Henry, who had barely left the king's side, gave me a pathetic, grateful nod. I gave him a warm smile. Perhaps I would take him under my wing after . . . I shoved away the thought.

Abbot Milo, who had arrived from Poitiers that morning, was on his knees by the king's bed, praying. A kindly type, he nonetheless frowned at the abrupt manner of our entry. 'Sir Rufus, I –'

'Your pardon, Father Abbot,' I said. 'I am here by the king's order.'

Rising with a wince – he was old – Milo bowed and moved aside. Mercadier let me approach Richard first, a tacit acknowledgement that I was closer to the king than he.

A fist of grief clenched my heart as I reached the royal bed. The blankets covered not the giant I had served, but a skeletal figure. Richard's red-gold hair was lank and matted, and except for pinpricks at his cheeks, his face was devoid of colour. His eyes were closed, and I had to moisten a finger and place it at his nostrils to be sure he was still breathing. I shot a look at Abbot Milo. 'Has he been conscious?'

A sad shake of his head. 'Are you sure this is the time . . .?'

'Yes, Father Abbot.' I stooped and placed my lips close to Richard's ear. The smell of rotting flesh was unbearable. 'Sire,' I whispered.

There was no response.

CHAPTER XXXIII

'S ire,' I said, louder. 'I have Sir Frying Pan here, and Robert FitzAldelm.'

The king's eyelids flickered. He woke. His eyes slowly focused. 'Rufus.'

'Châlus has fallen, sire. Sir Frying Pan and FitzAldelm are prisoners. Shall I bring them in?'

A tiny nod.

'One moment, sire.' I glanced at Mercadier, who hurried to the entrance, and then with the king's permission, I eased a pillow under him, so he could better see.

In came the prisoners, roughly urged by four men-at-arms, two to each. Rhys had been left outside. Basile saw who was in the bed, and began to tremble. FitzAldelm, give him his credit, remained more composed, but even he could not hide his fear.

Richard ignored FitzAldelm. 'You are Sir Frying Pan?' he asked Basile.

Basile fell to his knees. 'Yes, sire.'

'One of you hit me with a bolt. Was it you, or your ill-favoured companion?'

'I-I do not know, sire. We shot at the same time.'

I was unsurprised, and did not think he was lying. The light had been so poor I had no idea either whose quarrel had done the damage. I expected Basile to beg for his life, but he did not, even with Richard's still-intense gaze bearing down on him.

The king's attention moved to FitzAldelm. 'Once, Robert, I considered you a trusted member of my household. Now you stand before me, an agent of Philippe's these past years, and a regicide, or accomplice to regicide. You are also a murderer of children. How is it that you have sunk so low?' Weak though it was, the king's voice carried heartfelt contempt.

FitzAldelm drew himself up, somehow managing to look haughty. 'My conscience is clear. I have nothing further to say, sire.'

'That is fitting.' The vein that signified Richard's purest rage began to pulse. 'Mercadier, take this losenger outside and flay his skin from his body.'

The routier captain leered.

Basile's voice cut into the momentary silence. 'Am I to receive the same fate, sire?'

'I set you free,' said the king. 'You were merely doing your duty. Robert here is a different creature altogether.'

Basile began to weep with relief. It was not for me to decide his fate, I thought, fighting back rage. Mercadier looked even more unhappy than I felt.

'He is a lowly soldier, and I am a belted knight!' shouted FitzAldelm. 'I do not deserve this!'

Mercadier moved as fast as a striking snake.

The back of the hand blow sent FitzAldelm flying. But for the grasp of the men-at-arms who held him, he would have fallen.

'How dare you speak to your liege lord the king in that manner?' Mercadier was incandescent.

FitzAldelm said nothing; indeed, he was lolling between the men-at-arms like a child's plaything.

Mercadier smiled, the kind of smile that only someone who has sliced off a man's skin before could give. He gestured at the men-at-arms. 'Outside.'

Much as I hated FitzAldelm and was happy that he should die, I had no wish to see him reduced to a screaming, bloody ruin. I turned my attention back to Basile.

I often wondered afterwards how what happened came to pass. The men-at-arms swore blind that they had kept a tight hold of FitzAldelm, but I think they must have relaxed their grasp after Mercadier's blow had apparently stunned him. Whatever the reason, FitzAldelm slipped free, first one arm and then the other. Cries of alarm came from the men-at-arms. I spun, only ten paces away, but too far to prevent Fitz-Aldelm leaping forward to snatch Henry, who was crossing the tent towards the king. Another blink of an eye, and he had Henry's dagger snugged under his chin.

Henry's eyes bulged with terror.

Time stopped.

I took a step towards FitzAldelm. The men-at-arms who had been holding him drew their knives. So did Mercadier.

'Let anyone come closer, and I will slit this rat's throat,' said Fitz-Aldelm. His wrist twitched. A line of blood sprang forth on Henry's neck, and he whimpered.

'You will not get out of here alive, Robert,' murmured the king.

'Maybe not, but I will take your squire with me, and I will avoid being flayed.'

'The boy has done nothing to you,' I said. 'Let him go.'

FitzAldelm curled his lip at me, and tightened his grip on Henry.

The king said nothing. It was a mark of the severity of his condition that he did not act, or shout orders as he would normally have done. Mercadier also seemed paralysed by indecision. The men-at-arms would not act unless told to do so, and Abbot Milo would not have said boo to a goose. Rhys would have stuck FitzAldelm good and proper, but he was outside.

'Fight me,' I challenged.

FitzAldelm stared.

'Fight me,' I said again. 'One to one. If you kill me, I beg the king to set you free.'

'You are in a hauberk! I would have no chance.'

'I will take it off.'

Mercadier protested, but hope rose in FitzAldelm's dark eyes. He glanced towards Richard, as did I.

'So be it,' said the king. 'Go to, Rufus.'

'I will not let you down, sire,' I said, feeling a fierce joy. My long-held heart's desire, which had so often seemed impossible, had fallen into my lap.

FitzAldelm seemed no less pleased. With the dagger tight under Henry's chin, he made his way outside. I followed.

Shocked cries rose from the throng of soldiers outside.

Rhys was the first person I saw. He was staring at FitzAldelm with an expression of utter hatred. Next he gave me a 'What in Christ's name happened?' look. There was no time to explain. Loudly, I announced that FitzAldelm and I were to fight to the death, and if he won, he was to go free. 'This, by the king's own order,' I shouted.

340

'I do not trust them.' FitzAldelm's eyes were roving over the angry faces around us. 'Mercadier, swear that you will honour the king's command, and keep these beasts from tearing me apart,' he said.

It was a shrewd move. Few men would go up against the merciless routier captain.

With evident reluctance, Mercadier obeyed.

'A sword and shield for FitzAldelm,' I said.

A man-at-arms offered his blade to FitzAldelm, who took it with great suspicion. After a moment of hefting it, and swinging it up and down, however, he appeared more satisfied. The man-at-arms waited, ready to hand over his plain heater shield.

'Help me, Rhys,' I said, taking off my mailed gloves and undoing my belt. With his assistance, I shed my hauberk, and then my mail stockings. The removal of the huge weight was a joy; my body rose a little, as it always did.

'Are you ready?' said Rhys in my ear.

Our gazes met. In his I saw complete trust. 'I am,' I said.

His hand tightened on my shoulder. 'Do it for Jean.'

An image of that little boy, dying, filled my mind. Husky-voiced, I said, 'I will.'

I turned to regard FitzAldelm, who still had hold of Henry. Taking my sword from Rhys, I drew it and tossed aside the scabbard. He gave me a heater shield, which I noted had Richard's three lions emblazoned on its front. I was glad. 'Are you ready, FitzAldelm?' I asked.

His eyes went to Mercadier. 'You will honour the king's command if I win?'

'I will,' said the routier captain. As FitzAldelm nodded, he added, '*If* you win.'

FitzAldelm sneered, and with a curse, released his grip on Henry. Not expecting this, the squire staggered forward. Men-at-arms leaped in to help him out of the way. 'Good lad,' I cried. 'You did well.'

A circle formed, perhaps twenty-five paces across.

FitzAldelm took his shield, and we walked towards one another.

Men began to shout my name, and Richard's. I could hear Henry's piping tone, and Rhys's Welsh-accented French. No one was calling for FitzAldelm.

Oddly, comfortingly, it seemed as if I had always been destined to come down to this, going blade to blade with the man I hated most in the world. My awareness shrank. I forgot the dying king, his malevolent brother John, Alienor. I saw none of the crowd, just FitzAldelm. Even the onlookers' cries died away.

We closed to within ten paces, and halted. Neither of us had armour, which meant that the first blow to connect properly could end the fight. Sweat pricked my eyes; I blinked it away. I remembered Jean, his impudence, and his cheeky smile. I remembered how FitzAldelm had gutted him, just so he could escape from me and Rhys.

The red mist came down. I tensed, about to hurl myself on my enemy and batter him groundward with the sheer force of my attack.

'Do you remember how your brat – Jean, was he? – mewled when I stabbed him?'

FitzAldelm's words landed with the shock of an upended bucket of icy water. Cold reason returned. He wants me to lose control, I thought, so I must not.

Instead of answering, I slid forward, shield in front of my face, and thrust hard with my sword. I caught him off guard, and its tip drove into his shield. He was pushed back, and I easily ducked below his wild return swing. I thumped my shield into his, one, two, and as he staggered, I cut down from waist level with my blade. There was little force in it because of the tricky angle, and sensing my intention, FitzAldelm threw himself to the side. My sword missed him, thwacking into the dirt instead.

I threw up my shield just as his blade came blurring down from above.

By some miracle, it hit the shield's rim, not the top of my skull. Wood splintered, my arm jarred with the force of it, but I had not been hurt. I probed at him with my sword, giving me the time to shuffle backwards, out of reach.

There was a four-inch deep cut in my shield. Another strike of similar force, and it would split apart, leaving me defenceless. The first trace of fear reared its ugly head inside me. I thought of Jean, but kindly, and set aside my anxiety. Avenging him was all that mattered. I was not going to die here. I was not going to die at FitzAldelm's hands.

He came forward again, hard and fast.

We traded blows. Iron screeched off iron. Sparks fell. Back and forth we hammered at each other, our strength roughly equal. He dropped low beneath my next swing and, emulating my first move, thrust straight at me.

Anticipating this, I twisted and leaned backward, letting the force of his drive carry him bodily forward. I managed to catch his left wrist with my sword point as he was carried past. He yelped, and then stumbled over my locked-knee leg, which I had shoved awkwardly into his path.

Down he went, sprawling onto his face.

I was aware of loud cheering as I booted him. 'I will not stab you in the back. On your feet.'

Confident, I was standing too close. He kicked sideways, catching me painfully in the ankle. It was my turn to be unbalanced. Rather than try to get up, FitzAldelm rolled towards me, and there was a dagger in his hand.

The pain as he stabbed it into my boot-clad, mail-less right foot was exquisite. It went in deep; I felt it grate off bone. Even as I screamed, I did not pull away. Instead I thrust with my sword, which was by my side, and pointed at the ground. The steel ran clean through one of his calves, and it was his turn to roar. I freed my blade before he tugged out his dagger, and stabbed downward again. It was a poor effort, but by happy chance, I sliced open his *other* leg.

He lunged at me with his dagger, but weak with pain, it was half-hearted. I shuffled away beyond his reach, biting my cheek against the agony radiating from my foot.

We glared at each other. He grabbed for his sword, but it was out of reach.

The roaring of the onlookers was deafening now. 'Ru-fus!' they bellowed. 'Ru-fus!'

I cared not a whit. 'Go on,' I said to FitzAldelm. 'Pick it up.'

He needed no second telling. Scrabbling on hands and knees, he seized the blade and with it as a staff, managed to stand. The hose below both his knees was soaked and red; he was lamed, and bleeding badly.

I hobbled towards him with grim purpose.

'You have a shield and I do not,' he said.

'Correct,' I said, closing in.

'We are knights. This should be an equal contest.'

'Was it equal when you, an adult man, slew Jean – a small boy?' I demanded. I thrust at him, and he leaned away from the blow, just. He countered with a hack that I took on my damaged shield, and paid the price for that as I cut in on the return, opening the meat of his thigh. He yowled, and lurched backwards, barely staying upright.

I aimed for his head with a swingeing sideways cut. He met my blade with his, but his strength was gone, and my sword caught him a glancing blow just above the ear. His eyes rolled upward. Knees buckling, weapon dropping from nerveless fingers, he toppled.

Wary, with my sword poised, for he had sprung so many surprises over the years, I stared at him. He was pathetic, and did not resemble the monster who had foully slain Jean, who had tried to murder me twice. My pity was short-lived. This opportunity could not be let slip. It was time to end our feud.

A tense silence had fallen.

I poked FitzAldelm with my sword tip, cutting through his tunic and shirt to the flesh. He groaned. 'Get up,' I ordered.

'I cannot.' Finally, there was fear in his voice.

'Up,' I hissed, 'or by Christ, I swear I will let Mercadier at you with his knife.'

He stirred, and forced himself onto his knees. He met my gaze, and as he had so often done, sneered. He opened his mouth to speak.

And I rammed my sword into it. Teeth shattered, blood flowed, and his shocked eyes met mine. The point of my blade burst out the back of his neck. I slid it home to the hilt, and leaning in, I said into FitzAldelm's ear, 'That is for Jean, you bastard. Know also that it *was* I who slew your mongrel of a brother.'

FitzAldelm was dying, but he heard me, I know it, because he tried to say something. Fittingly, he was prevented by his own blood, filling the back of his throat. I let go of my sword, and he fell.

I did not stay to see him exit this life. I had done what I needed to.

Uproarious cheering rose to the skies.

As I made to walk away, the pain of my wound hit me with its full force. If Rhys had not been there with little Henry to support me, I would have landed on top of FitzAldelm.

'You need the surgeon,' said Rhys, tender as a mother with her babe.

'No. I must speak with the king first.'

He did not argue.

We found Richard conscious, his eyes brighter than they had been for days. 'You are wounded, Rufus,' he whispered.

'It is small hurt, sire, compared to yours.' I hung my head, and tears flowed again. I had slain my enemy, but that had not cured the king.

'FitzAldelm?' Richard asked.

'Gone to Hell, sire.'

'Mayhap I shall see him there.'

Hearing the king's weak chuckle, the protest died on my lips. That he was capable of such gallows humour was awe-inspiring.

Richard ordered that I was to be taken to the surgeon, and closed his eyes.

'God keep His hand over you, sire,' I said, and let Rhys and Henry help me away.

There is nothing that can be said of the end that does not break my heart. Nothing. Thanks to illness, I was robbed of the time I might have spent with the king. Almost a week I lay in my blankets, nursed by Rhys. It was not the wound caused by FitzAldelm's sword that laid me low, praise the saints. That would have given me an end like Richard, or Duke Leopold, who had died years since from a gangrenous foot.

By sheer good fortune, FitzAldelm's blade had run between two of the long foot bones, without breaking them. The injury would heal in time. What struck me down was dysentery, the enemy of soldiers in camp since the dawn of time. Gripped by agonising stomach cramps, and suffering frequent bouts of bloody diarrhoea, I was confined to my tent. Much as I wanted to see the king, the surgeon had forbidden me in case Richard also contracted dysentery. Incredibly, he was still clinging to life, but as the surgeon said, that would have pushed him over the edge.

Miserable, I had to content myself with news brought to me some-times by Rhys, but more often than not, Henry. The little squire had taken to me, much as I had to him. There was no doubt that the poor soul needed respite from the fetid, death-bound atmosphere of Richard's tent.

I did not question him overmuch, for there was not much to tell, apart from two things. The first was that, perhaps unsurprisingly, Mercadier had disobeyed the king's orders, and flayed Basile alive. The second, more cheering, was that Queen Alienor had arrived. Richard spent his periods of lucidity with her, and dictating letters to officials throughout his realm. He sent no word to Berengaria. No mention was made in the royal messages of his illness either, Henry reported, but the king's commands would see his wishes carried out for months into the future. By then, I guessed, he hoped that John would have a firm grip on the reins of power.

What that meant for me, I dreaded to think, but with hours upon hours to brood, I had opportunity aplenty to ponder my relationship with the king's scheming brother. Perhaps I could repair things with him, or more likely, he would spurn me. One thing only was certain. My future was clouded, as it had not been for years. John could do what he wished once he took the throne. The lands granted to me by the king in England, and in Ireland, Cairlinn, might be confiscated. I could lose my position at court – not that I particularly wanted to be part of it once Richard was gone. I had been part of the royal household only because of my loyalty to the king.

That it might all end in so abrupt a manner was a bitter realisation. I was quick to remind myself, thinking of the king, that there would soon be time enough to address my own affairs. For now, and as it had been for years, my priority was Richard.

On the afternoon of the sixth of April, Henry came with calamitous news. The king was not long for this world, he said, his voice shaking. Abbot Milo had heard Richard's final confession and given him Extreme Unction.

Although I had been expecting this news, its finality had the same impact as a charging knight. Limbs trembling, sweating, my heart pounding, I rose from my bed, and had Rhys help me get dressed in my finest clothes. It mattered not to Richard now that I had dysentery, I said.

'Even now, it does not seem real that he is dying,' Rhys muttered.

'It sounds stupid, but I thought he would live forever,' I said.

We sorrowfully made our way to the royal tent. The sentries were sombre-faced, but confirmed that the king yet lived. His lady mother was with him, and Abbot Milo, no one else.

I did not know if Queen Alienor would protest at my entering, but I did not much care. I had to see Richard before the end. I raised my eyebrows at Rhys, but he shook his head, no. 'I wish to remember him as he was. Wish him Godspeed.'

Henry led me inside. We made not a sound. It was gloomy within; a few oil lamps were the only light. The stench of decay had been muted by incense, not just in burners as before, but also in the glowing brazier that warmed the tent.

Alienor was perched on a stool on Richard's good side, and Milo was on the other. They looked up as we approached. The king did not move, and but for his embroidered coverlet, resembled a corpse laid out on the catafalque.

Alienor had aged terribly; deep lines of grief were etched in her already-lined face. She gave no indication of recognising me.

I bent my knee, and said, 'I am Sir Rufus, madam. One of his companions.'

'Of course. I remember. You have come to say goodbye.'

Again the finality sank in with the agony of a blade. 'Yes, madam.'

Alienor glanced at her son. 'He has not been conscious since Abbot Milo heard his last confession.'

I absorbed this cruel blow. 'At least he suffers no more, madam.'

A sad nod. 'Indeed. Come. Make your farewell – that is what Richard would want.' She signalled to Abbot Milo, who moved aside so that I could approach.

I sat on the stool, and after a moment to steel my nerves, looked at Richard. There was a pale, waxen sheen to his skin, and his eyes were sunk deep into his skull. His breathing was shallow, and hard to discern. He barely resembled the confident, battle-loving giant I had served for so long.

'I am here, sire,' I said, hating how my voice – wobbling – could play me false with four simple words.

The king did not stir.

'Tell him who you are,' Alienor whispered.

'It is Rufus, sire. Ferdia.'

No reaction.

I stared at the floor, tears pouring down my cheeks.

A rattling gasp.

I looked up. Richard's eyelids had opened, and his gaze was on me. His lips framed my name, Rufus.

'I am here, sire,' I said, holding back my grief through sheer effort.

'Most . . . loyal . . .'

'I am your man, sire, always, as is my squire Rhys. He bids you Godspeed.'

The corners of his mouth curved upward, just a little.

'Fauvel . . .'

I leaned closer, listening hard. 'Fauvel, sire?'

'Take him . . . better you than . . . Johnny.'

'My thanks, sire.' I had to bite back a chuckle. John was no horseman; Fauvel, most magnificent of horses, would be wasted on him. Thoughts of John made me think of my future. 'I wondered, sire, if I might return to Ireland, to Cairlinn, after . . .' I could not finish the sentence.

'After I am . . . dead.'

'Yes, sire.'

'You . . . and Johnny . . . never got on . . .'

I waited, with bated breath. The last time we had talked of this, Richard had wanted me to serve his brother.

'Go . . . with my blessing.'

I shot a look at Henry, who was hovering close by with a cloth to wipe the king's forehead, and said quietly, 'Your squire, sire–'

'Henry?'

'Yes, sire. Would you like me to care for him?'

A pause, then, 'That is . . . kind. His mother . . . dead . . . father . . . infirm.'

'It is the least I can do, sire.'

I could feel Alienor's stare. Aware that I must not take up too much of what little time remained to the king, I stood and bowed. 'Farewell, sire.'

Richard looked at me one more time, and smiled. His eyes closed then, and I knew I would never see him again in this life. Fresh, hot tears ran. My heart ached. I bowed to Queen Alienor, gave a nod to Abbot Milo, and told Henry to find me later. Then I left before my grief took control.

'You are still weak.' Rhys took me by the arm as I emerged. Grateful, I made no protest. We both knew that his grip was for more than physical support. 'Is he gone?' Rhys asked.

'Almost. His mother will see him from this world.'

Hard burden though that was, it seemed fitting.

As we walked away from the royal tent, the bells in the nearby church began to toll vespers.

'What will you do now?' Rhys asked, quiet enough that no one else could hear.

'Once I have attended the king's funeral at Fontevraud, I am for Chateau Gaillard, and Alienor.' My heart warmed at the thought of her.

'And then?' Rhys added in a whisper, 'You do not need me to say that John is not to be trusted.'

'I do not,' I said, amused that he had said it anyway. 'I shall return to Cairlinn, and show young Henry where I grew up. Will you come?'

He gave me a dig. 'If you think I will be left behind after this long, you are mistaken.'

I grinned. 'What will Katharina say?'

'Neither you nor I will be able to stop her!'

That made me laugh, and forget my grief, if but for a moment.

I was going home.

To Cairlinn.

AUTHOR'S NOTE

I t's something of a miracle that I actually finished this novel. The year 2021 wasn't just about COVID-19 for me, it was also about divorce. This is not the place to go into details; suffice it to say that I have been to Hell and back, several times. As I write this in December 2021, an end is finally in sight, and seems achievable. Roll on 2022, I say.

The third book in a trilogy is always fun to write. This novel was different, because the ending involved Richard's unnecessary death during an inconsequential siege. I was dreading it from about halfway through. Arrogant and headstrong though he was, I had developed a soft spot for the Lionheart. I hope I did him justice at the end. Plenty of tears were shed, I can tell you, which usually means I conveyed the emotion.

The frustrating nature of the texts that survive mean that we know many of the details of Richard's journey from Outremer to coastal Italy, of how he fell into Duke Leopold's hands, and the bargaining that took place during his captivity. After he was freed, there is a reasonable amount of information about his lightning quick visit to England, and the campaign immediately afterwards against his archenemy Philippe Capet. From the summer of 1194, however, the mists descend again. For several years we have only scant, tantalising, infuriating snippet about Richard's on-off war with the French king. Simply put, his fig with Philippe never really ended. The numerous peace treaties nothing more than badly applied sticking plasters that would last. It's likely that both parties knew this; perhaps the treatie agreed simply to allow both sides to draw breath and sourc funding for their war chests.

Because of this gap in the historical detail, and to avoid th becoming Lord of the Rings-like in length, I decided to dra over the four years to 1198.

Readers familiar with my books will know that I make every effort to represent historical events as best as possible, using accounts of the time and textbooks on every subject under the sun. The major events involving Richard in this book are all real, even down to some of the dialogue. While writing *King* I consulted contemporary or near contemporary medieval accounts by Roger of Howden, Gerald of Wales and Ralph of Diss.

An incomplete list of texts that I also used includes *Richard the Lionheart: The Crusader King of England* by W. B. Bartlett, *Richard the Lionheart* by Antony Bridge, *The Canterbury Tales* by Geoffrey Chaucer, *William Marshal* by David Crouch, *Life in a Medieval City*, *Life in a Medieval Village* and *Life in a Medieval Castle* by J. and F. Gies, *Richard the Lionheart* by John Gillingham, *The Normans* by Gravett and Nicolle, *Food and Feast in Medieval England* by P. W. Hammond, *Knight* by R. Jones, *The Medieval Kitchen* by H. Klemettilä, *Medieval Warfare* by H. W. Koch, *Lionheart and Lackland* by Frank McLynn, *The Annals of Roger de Hoveden*, trans. Henry T. Riley, *Henry II* and *King John*, both by W. L. Warren, *Eleanor of Aquitaine: Lord and Lady*, ed. Bonnie Wheeler and John C. Parsons, numerous Osprey texts and articles in *Medieval Warfare* magazine.

Once again I am indebted to Dr Michael Staunton of the School of History in University College Dublin, Ireland, for his generosity and time. A specialist in the twelfth century and the House of Angevin, he cast his eagle eye over the book, checking for errors. *Go raibh míle maith agat, a Mhícheál.*

I do not just write novels. Seek out my Kickstarter-funded digital novellas *The March* (which follows on from *The Forgotten Legion* and reveals what happened to Brennus), and also *Eagle in the Wilderness* and *Eagles in the East* (both featuring Centurion Tullus of the *Eagles of Rome* trilogy). Don't own an e-reader? Simply download the free Kindle app from Amazon and read the stories on a phone, tablet or computer. (If you cannot be persuaded to use an e-reader, these stories are now available in print and as an audiobook! Order *Sands of the Arena* in your local bookshop or online.)

Interested in seeing Pompeii and Herculaneum with me as your guide? Google Andante Tours (tinyurl.com/yc4uze85). Enjoy cycling with an historical twist? Take a look at Bike Odyssey (bikeodyssey.cc);

this company runs epic cycling trips (Hannibal, Lionheart, Venetians, Othello) that I am involved with as an historical guide.

I am a passionate supporter of the charities Combat Stress, which helps British veterans with PTSD, and Médecins Sans Frontières (MSF), responsible for sending medical staff into disaster and war zones worldwide. To raise money for these worthy causes I have walked Hadrian's Wall in full Roman armour – twice. In 2014 I marched with two author friends all the way to the Colosseum in Rome. The documentary about it is narrated by Sir Ian McKellen – Gandalf! The 'Romani Walk' is on YouTube: tinyurl.com/h4n8h6g – if you enjoy it, please spread the word.

I also fundraise for Park in the Past, a community-interest company which is building a Roman marching fort near Chester in north-west England. By summer 2022, the footprint of the fort should be open to the public! Its website is: parkinthepast.org.uk

Thanks to everyone who has contributed to the various causes over the years. To raise money, I auction minor characters in my books. (If you are interested in this for 1812, my novel which will come out in 2023, please email me; contact details below.) The character 'acquired' in *King* in this manner is Katharina, based on my loyal reader and fan Krystal Holmgren, who has also starred in two of my novella length Kickstarter novellas. Thanks, Krystal!

Big thanks, as ever, to my amazing editor, Francesca Pathak – always there, always the voice of reason. Thanks also to the whole team at Orion – it's been a tough two years, but you come up trumps every time! I am grateful to Aranzazu Sumalla and all at Ediciones B in Spain, and Magdalena Madej-Reputakowska and the Znak team in Poland. Cheers too to Charlie Viney, my agent.

I have to mention you, my amazing readers. I have been a full-time author for thirteen years now, thanks to you! Your emails, and comments/messages on Facebook, Twitter and Instagram are an important part of my life. Thank you, Bruce Phillips, Taff James, Tony Fowler, Andy Bull, Milca and Andy Wilson, Adrian Tyte, Charlene Robertson, Jon Charles, Steve Healy, Michael Hurley and many more for the conversations we have had online. Look out for the signed books and goodies I give away and auction for charity via these media. Leaving a short review of this book (on Amazon, Goodreads, Waterstones.com or iTunes!) would be a real help. Historical fiction is currently a shrinking market, and times are far tougher than they were, so a few minutes of your time would help a great deal. Thank you in advance.

Late 2020 and most of 2021 would have been close to unbearable but for the presence in my life of so many wonderful people. These are my mother and father, brother Stephen, Killian, Shane, Colm, Camilla, Euan and Karen, Matt, Sophie and Nick, Jamie and Jo, Philip and Anna, Will and Kelly, Andrew and Jane, Carol, Arthur, Francesca (again!), Dermod and June, Russ, Rob, Simon, Paul Harston and Linda of Linda's Loaf. Thanks also to Simon Walker. You are all amazing, and the best of the best. Thank you from the bottom of my heart. I am also greatly indebted to Sam Harris, and his Waking Up meditation app. It has been an incredible resource, and given freely in a time of need. If you haven't heard of Waking Up, find it in the Google Play Store – it's amazing, and transformational, and I write this as someone who would have been deeply sceptical.

Lastly, I want to thank my inspirational children Ferdia and Pippa, whom I love to the moon and back. I am truly blessed to have you both in my life.

Ways to get in touch:
Email: ben@benkane.net
Facebook: facebook.com/benkanebooks
Twitter: @BenKaneAuthor
Instagram: benkanewrites
Soundcloud (podcasts): soundcloud.com/user-803260618
Also, my website: benkane.net
YouTube (short documentary-style videos): tinyurl.com/y7chqhgo

CREDITS

Orion Fiction would like to thank everyone at Orion who worked on the publication of *King* in the UK. And so would Ben!

Editorial
Francesca Pathak
Lucy Brem

Copy editor
Marian Reid

Proofreader
Linda Joyce

Audio
Paul Stark
Jake Alderson

Contracts
Anne Goddard
Humayra Ahmed
Ellie Bowker

Design
Charlotte Abrams-Simpson
Joanna Ridley
Nick May

Editorial Management
Charlie Panayiotou
Jane Hughes
Bartley Shaw
Tamara Morriss

Rights
Susan Howe
Krystyna Kujawinska
Jessica Purdue
Louise Henderson

Finance
Jasdip Nandra
Afeera Ahmed
Elizabeth Beaumont
Sue Baker

Production
Ruth Sharvell

Publicity
Virginia Woolstencroft

Marketing
Lucy Cameron

Operations
Jo Jacobs
Sharon Willis

Sales
Jen Wilson
Esther Waters
Victoria Laws
Rachael Hum
Anna Egelstaff
Frances Doyle
Georgina Cutler

1812

NAPOLEON: EMPEROR OF FRANCE, MASTER OF EUROPE.

1812. On the eve of the invasion of Russia, half-French, half-English, Matthieu Carrey finds himself in the ranks of Napoleon's five hundred thousand strong army. With Tsar Alexander seemingly ill-prepared, a French victory seems certain. The Grande Armée will obliterate everything in its path.

Carrey's purpose is less clear. Penniless, heartbroken, and naïve to the brutalities of war, his wish is not for conquest, but to settle his debts and find the woman he loves. A French actress, she has gone to star in the Moscow theatre.

From the first week of the invasion, Carrey's situation is balanced on a knife edge. Cold winds and heavy rain sweep the land. Food and fodder are scarce. The countryside teems with Cossacks, Russia's fearsome light cavalry, forcing imperial messenger Carrey to run a lethal daily gauntlet. Closer to home, he receives endless challenges to a duel from his main debtor, a dashing cavalry officer.

Things can only get worse. At Borodino, Carrey undergoes a baptism of fire. Caught up in the maelstrom of battle, threatened by Russian cannon and musket fire, he is thrown into the midst of the bitter hand-to-hand fighting that sees tens of thousands of men slain by the day's end.

Days later, the army reaches Moscow. Carrey and his comrades feast and make merry in the abandoned city. He embarks on a frantic search for his actress, but after a month, the order to withdraw is finally given. Temperatures are plummeting, and the Russians circling like hungry wolves.

Hundreds of miles lie between Carrey and the French border.

To reach it seems utterly impossible.

Coming 2023

LIONHEART

The first instalment in the epic Lionheart trilogy …

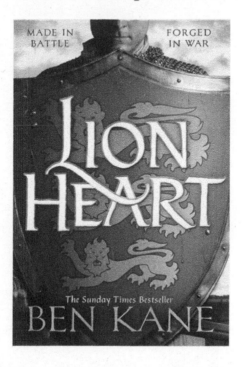

MADE IN BATTLE. FORGED IN WAR.

1179. Henry II is King and the House of Plantagenet reigns supreme.
But there is unrest in Henry's house. Not for the first time,
his family talks of rebellion.

Ferdia – an Irish nobleman taken captive – saves the life of Richard,
the king's son. In reward for his bravery, he is made squire to Richard.
Crossing the English Channel, the two are plunged into a campaign to
crush rebels in Aquitaine. The bloody battles which followed would
earn Richard the legendary name of Lionheart.

But Richard's older brother, Henry, is infuriated by his sibling's
newfound fame. Soon it becomes clear that the biggest threat to
Richard's life may not be rebel or French armies, but his own family . . .

Available to buy now

CRUSADER

The second thrilling chapter in the Lionheart series ...

BATTLE IS INEVITABLE. VICTORY IS NOT.

1189. Richard the Lionheart, finally crowned King of England,
prepares to embark on a gruelling crusade to reclaim Jerusalem.

With him every step of the journey is Ferdia, his loyal Irish follower.
Finally poised to sail to the Holy Land, Richard finds a bitter two-year-long
siege awaiting him. And with it, the iconic Saracen leader responsible for
the loss of Jerusalem, Saladin.

No one can agree who should fill the empty throne of the Kingdom of
Jerusalem and Saladin's huge army shadows Richard's every move.
Conditions are brutal, the temperatures boiling, and on the dusty
field of Arsuf, the Lionheart and his soldiers face their ultimate test . . .

Available to buy now

THE
CLASH OF EMPIRES
SERIES

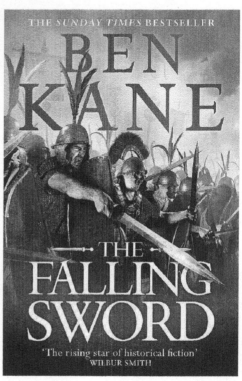

Can Greece resist the might of Rome?

The final showdown between two great civilisations begins . . .

'A triumph!'
Harry Sidebottom

'Fans of battle-heavy historical fiction will, justly, adore Clash of Empires'
The Times

SANDS
of the
ARENA
And Other Stories

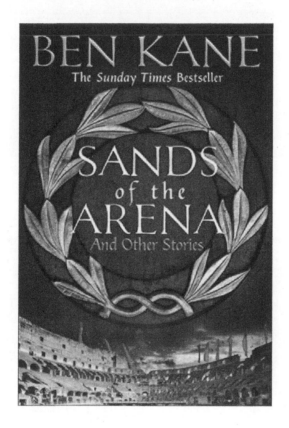

THE EPIC SHORT STORY COLLECTION

Available to buy now